Masterpieces of Victorian Erotica

Edited by
Major LaCaritilie

First Magic Carpet Books, Inc. edition May 2007

Published in 2007

Manufactured in the United States of America
Published by Magic Carpet Books, Inc.

Magic Carpet Books, Inc.
PO Box 473
New Milford, CT 06776

Library of Congress Cataloging in Publication Date

The Masterpieces of Victorian Erotica

Edited By Major LaCaritilie
$17.95 /Canada $24.95

ISBN# 0977431169

Book Design: P. Ruggieri

Contents

Introduction

There is no shortage of great works to compete for the title "masterpiece of Victorian erotica." Indeed, as readers familiar with Dickens or Trollope can attest, the Victorians were nothing if not prolific. Yet to be a masterpiece, a work has to distinguish itself from all others. Maybe it's without equal in its subgenre or the apotheosis of its tradition. Maybe it offers a deeper insight, a more vivid image, or a more surprising turn. Or maybe it is absolutely singular, truly peerless in its style, plot or execution.

Having distinguished themselves in these ways, the works in this volume represent the very best of the Victorian erotic imagination. There is poetry and prose, narrative and instructional guide; there is fetish, queer, s-m, and vanilla; and there is bawdy, tender and daring. For the newcomer to the Victorian erotic universe, these stories are the place to start. For the connoisseur, this collection offers undiscovered delicacies. For everyone, these stories cannot fail to arouse, stimulate and amaze with their delightful sexiness and bold originality.

Moreover, having identified and collected these masterpieces in one place puts us in a unique position to understand just what it was about the Victorians that made their erotica so special. After feasting on these sensual delicacies, the reader will no doubt conclude that sex was written about very differently in the Victorian era. Their descriptions were vivid and explicitly genital—no mincing words here!—their interests were wide-ranging and varied, allowing room for each author to explore his or her special enthusiasms; and their genres were flexible and free-flowing, with dramatic dialogue interspersed with expository prose and occasionally interrupted with didactic passages or political editorials. Yet rarely did they stray but a few sentences from one sexual act or another. As Jane Austin was always writing about marriage, so these writers were always writing about sex. It could even be said that these works are Austin unleashed, where marriage has become the sexual wonderland we would wish for Austin's pure heroines.

With all this to offer, one might wonder why the popularity of Victorian erotica has waned and what contemporary erotica offers that is in any way superior. Perhaps, though, this is the wrong way to look at it. Perhaps it is not so much a matter of contemporary erotica progressing beyond its Victorian predecessors as it is a matter of the modern reader having regressed, preferring the artless prose of men's magazine confessions to the artistry of the Victorian author. Victorians were master storytellers, offering brilliant descriptions, memorable characters, and rip-roaring plots. What more could one want in erotica? Novels were the movies of the Victorian era and Victorian erotica offers every bit of the vivid, imaginative sexuality that our erotic film industry does. If we are spoiled by the moving image and no longer enjoy the written word, we have no one to blame but ourselves.

Indeed, reading many of these works makes me wish they were adapted to film in place of the flimsy, farcical plots that are currently served up by the erotic film industry. What a pleasure it would be to take the costume drama genre back from the Masterpiece Theatre set! What a pleasure to have the bawdy sexual cravings and naughty exploits contained in these works replace the tired conceits of strapping repairmen and lonely housewives!

But I get ahead of myself. There's much about Victorian erotic literature that transcends its time, but there is also much that is of its time and place. Yet many of these Victorian concerns still haunt us:

issues of class, race and national identity all come into play in Victorian sexual imagination as they do in ours. We have no more surpassed the struggle between repression and libertinism than we have rid ourselves of the scourge of poverty or prejudice. Freud's theories of psycho-sexual development, fetish, fixation, and desire are, like these works, over a hundred years old, yet they still speak to us today. Indeed, Freud himself was a cultural and intellectual brother to Victorian erotica writers like Arthur Schnitzler, author of the novel that has recently been adapted to film in *Eyes Wide Shut*, and Viennese erotic artists like Egon Schiele. *Fin de Siecle* Vienna, like London, Paris and Berlin, was a moment when high and low culture touched. These stories may read like penny-dreadfuls, but unlike the thousands of novels that were so quickly forgotten, these ground-breaking erotic works cast their influence over the greatest thinkers and writers of the generation. Oscar Wilde, Guillaume Apollinaire, Pablo Picasso, George Bataille, D.H. Lawrence and Henry Miller were but a few of the modernist giants whose first erotic imaginings were just as surely inspired by works like these.

So, read and enjoy, and be aware that as these stories offer an embarrassment of sexual riches as well as offering a key to our current erotic realities. Some aspects of these stories may feel strange and unfamiliar, but more of them will feel like they were ripped from your last erotic reverie or from the pages of today's best erotic writings.

Marie and Nicole, or, the Kitchen Maid's New Quarters

One day a lady decided that all the maids would henceforth sleep on the top story of the chateau, right under the eaves. They began moving their goods and chattels upstairs, and were to start sleeping there the same evening

I watched them move. As one of them, her mattress under her arm, was climbing the last flight of stairs, I sneaked up behind her and lifted her petticoats.

The first thing I grabbed was a pair of firm buttock cheeks, which I drew back against me, at the same time thrusting my thumb into her moist cunt. She raised no cry, but turning round and recognizing me, smiled as if flattered by my gallantry.

It was Marie, the brunette. I led her up to the top floor and embraced her.

She reacted favorably to the first kiss, and responded actively to the second. Whereupon I seized her blouse at the bosom, and had soon succeeded in slipping inside to caress the firm, brown-tipped hemispheres. A swift movement of the left hand beneath her short dress, and the well-grassed mound was mine.

She squeezed her thighs together and bent slightly forward. I took a nipple in my mouth and sucked it gently, while my finger played with her excited clitoris. Soon I had managed to slip my hand between her thighs, until one, two, three fingers had penetrated her cunt.

She tried to get away, but I pushed her against the wall. I felt her whole body trembling beneath her flimsy clothing. I deftly extracted my John Thomas and thrust it into her box. The position was awkward, the girl was tall and strong, and I would never have been able to screw her unless she had done her share of the work.

So I fucked her standing up. She must have been as hot as an oven, for she quickly reached the climax. I too was on the point of coming, due to the fatiguing position we were in, but just then we heard a noise in one of the adjoining rooms, and Marie broke away. But the sound soon died away. I showed her my dark, red prick, dripping wet from her discharge. She looked at it, and was moved because, as she said, *it was the first time she'd ever seen a city fellow's prick.*

"All right now, tit for tat," I said. "Let's see yours."

She responded modestly. I raised her skirt, laid bare a pair of lovely legs and, between her thighs, an impressive mop of black hair. Thanks be to God she was not wearing panties, as the city-bred girls do, who put on all sorts of airs when you meddle with their roots, despite the fact that they really like it as much, if not more than the peasant girls.

Then I stuck my nose into her Lady Jane; it gave off the odor of raw egg —due to her recent discharge —and of piss. When I began to tongue her clitoris she laughed and let her skirt fall back into place. But I held on tight and, squatting beneath the folds of her dress, let my tongue wander at random across the length and breadth of her body, as a result of which I got an even more impressive hard on. But the sounds began anew, and Marie broke away again, this time for good.

I was obliged to leave, but as Marie turned to go I lifted her skirts one last time from behind, revealing a pair of really splendid, extraordinarily firm buttocks.

"Just a wee bit more, Marie." I said, retaining her by her blouse.

I kissed the cheeks of her rump, manipulated them, opened them to smell her arse-hole, which gave off no odor of shit, but only of piss. But finally she broke away, remarking that it was beyond her powers of comprehension how a fellow like myself could get any pleasure from sniffing a poor peasant girl's stinking parts.

That evening, though, when the covers of my bed were already turned down and I undressed, she returned to me. I was stretching out on my belly, spread a handkerchief beneath me, hugged my pillow and, thinking of all the cunts and buttocks with which I'd ever come in contact, I softly began to stroke alone. Then I rested awhile before starting the procedure all over again. Just as I felt my sperm coming, I heard a voice from behind the door say: "Are you already asleep, Master Philip? I've brought you your water."

I rose, slipped on a dressing gown, and opened the door. It was the same Marie as I had fondled that morning. As soon as she was inside, I locked the door. So great was my desire that my prick was throbbing like a pendulum.

I grabbed the lovely, prettily dressed peasant girl's sturdy buttocks and as I fondled her breasts, planted a pair of savory kisses full on her mouth.

She took it in the right spirit, but when I reached her love lips she said, blushing: "It's my period. It came today." Just my luck! I was as erect as a bare-footed friar, and she was looking at my prick good-naturedly. She played with it prettily. At least I could amuse myself with her hanging gardens. I opened her jacket and her breasts slipped into my waiting hands. Like the girl herself, they were freckled, but aside from that I saw nothing to reproach them for.

I didn't stop pestering her till she let me see, although against her will, her buttocks and Lady Jane, to whose crinkly, reddish hair blood was sticking. I pushed her onto a chair and let her place my dick between her breasts. A most practical method: it disappeared among the fleshy folds of her delectable hillocks. But it would have been better with a bit of lubrication. I told her so. She spat on my prick and squeezed it tightly between her boobies. On top the glans peeked out, and at the bottom my balls were hanging down.

I began to rock back and forth, whispering sweet words to her and at the same time caressing her face or playing with the wisps of curls along her neck. A powerful discharge followed, which she watched attentively, for the position was as novel for her as it was for me.

Having had my fill, I made her a gift of a silk scarf, which she gratefully accepted, once again excusing herself for her condition. She added that the girls who worked with her in the kitchen were late in going to bed, but that they slept much later in the morning than the others who rose early to go milking. Should I venture up there some morning, I'd find more than enough to keep me happy.

L ater that week, I gave Marie a pretty shawl, for it had not been her fault that I hadn't been able to fuck her completely. The other girls noticed it, and without exception became extremely nice to me, for they were no dummies, and were quick to realize how pleasant it must be both to be fucked and to receive a present to boot.

At least that's what one of them told me one morning early, when the profound silence was broken only by the distant rumor of goings and comings in the stables.

I had gone upstairs and discovered an unlocked door which led into two of the maids' bedroom.

The room's atmosphere was one of the mixed odors emanating from the girls' bodies. Their clothes were hanging in disarray from wooden pegs, or were draped across the foot of the bed. At first these odors were disagreeable, but as soon as one got used to them they became exciting rather than suffocating: the veritable *odor di femin* —the perfume which gives an erection.

The beds, made in the ancient style, were double. They were all empty except one, in which a lass lay snoring deeply.

She was lying on her side, turned toward the wall. One of her feet was on the wooden bedstead, and her buttocks were nicely exposed, since she was sleeping in the nude.

Her coarse nightdress was draped over a wooden chair, on which the rest of her clothes were also strewn. The sleeping beauty, whose name was Nicole, had not the faintest notion that she was being scrutinized from head to toe. Her skin could have been softer, but her frame, though rough-hewn, was not skinny.

I brought my head close to her buttocks and inhaled the penetrating odor of sweat. Her arse-hole showed a few traces of her last shitting. Below it her well-formed slit, crowned by chestnut hair, was clearly visible.

I softly tickled her buttocks' cheeks and cunt. As soon as I had inserted my finger she gave a start and turned round, and I could contemplate her from in front. Her fleece was crinkly and smelled strongly of urine, which fact I remarked when I stuck my nose against it.

I might add that the maids washed their cunts only on Sundays. As a matter of fact, there are many fine ladies who seldom have the time to wash themselves. But coming back to that odor, it had aroused me, and I was already hard.

I bolted the door and stripped. Then I spread her thighs apart. She half-opened her eyes. "Nicole," I said, thrusting three fingers into her box, "you're my little sweetheart. Look what an erection I've got!"

She stirred, pointed toward the other room, and said: "Marie's in there too."

"No matter. We've got time to have a go before she wakes up. Look what I've brought you."

And I handed her a little imitation jewel ring that I'd bought from a passing peddler. Then without another word I kneeled between her thighs, which she willingly spread. I let her play with my tool and balls awhile, and reciprocated by tickling her cunt. When she was well oiled, I drove it in up to the balls, took her under the buttocks and tickled her arse-hole. She clasped me about the neck and we plunged into a frenzy of voluptuousness which, after a brief bout, ended in a violent discharge on both sides.

During the act she had perspired profusely, and her healthy peasant odor made me hope that we could start all over again. But she was afraid of becoming pregnant. Besides, it was high time for her to be up, for it was Marie's day to sleep late. I had completely forgotten that Marie was there, and Nicole laughed heartily when I said that I'd certainly like to wake her up.

While Nicole was wiping her private parts with her nightdress, I entered the other room. Marie was lost in a deep sleep.

She was also lying in the nude, but had the blankets pulled up to her bosom. She was sleeping on her back, with her arms cocked behind her head so that the thick black bushes of her armpits were in full view.

Her pretty breasts were thrown into fuller relief by the position of her arms, on either side of which her long rich locks tumbled gracefully down. The whole picture was charming to behold. What a pity she was a mere peasant! I have never understood how a man could prefer a lady's affected charms to the natural beauty of a peasant girl.

Her impeccably clean nightdress was lying beside her. I sniffed it and was astonished by the healthy odor with which it was impregnated.

Softly, softly, I drew the blankets back and stood there admiring her naked form. I remained motionless an instant, amazed by the beauty of her well-proportioned legs, her grassy Venus mound, whose heavy hair extended from her love lips to her thighs. She awoke when I began to caress her breasts. At first startled, she hastily drew the covers over her. Then she recognized me and gave me a broad smile.

Just then Nicole stuck her head inside and said: "Stay in bed, Marie, I'll take care of your work for you." And with that she left.

I covered Marie with kisses until she was hot. I asked her to get up and had her walk about the room while I examined her lovely body from head to foot and from all sides, marveling at her beauty.

Then I took her in my arms, and for a long time we stood there in a close embrace.

I placed my hands on the cheeks of her behind and pulled her belly close against mine. She could feel the full stiffness of my prick, her love hair tickled my balls.

She enjoyed the sport. She put her arms around my neck, hugged me to her. I plucked some hairs from her armpits. She was completely beside herself with desire. I put my hand into her cunt, which was moist and distended. Her clitoris was very hard.

We got into bed. I made her rise to her knees and hold her buttocks high. I experimented feverishly with her pothole. Her cunt, crowned by jet black hair, was half-opened, and after reveling in the sight of the red interior, I rubbed my glans against her lips.

She enjoyed the stroking and seconded my movements. Softly I pushed it till it was all the way in, then drew it out again, back and forth, until felt myself on the point of coming.

She acted like one possessed. Her cunt, completely distended, gripped my member tightly. I thrust it in up to the hilt, hugged her buttocks, seized her hanging beauties, and rocked like a maniac, completely gone. She sighed deeply at every stroke. With one hand I pressed her boobies, with the other I tickled her clitoris. We came simultaneously. I heard my prick slapping inside her wet cunt. We lay there as though dead.

When I withdrew I still had a hard on. Marie was ashamed, because she had never done it that way.

What she'd most enjoyed had been the slapping of my balls against the lower part of her cunt. I had not yet had my fill, and would gladly have stayed a while longer with that lovely, blooming lass. Had it been possible, I would have married her.

She told me that she had to get downstairs. She slipped on her blouse and I helped her to dress. She smiled at me amicably. I examined her from all sides once more before leaving. I promised to buy her a fine souvenir, and she agreed to come and spend the night with me sometime soon.

A Country Party

Elaine, Lord William's young wife, and I affected no gaiety upon our departure at eight of the evening of our first country party, for it was to be seen by the Governess that we were upon solemn business. By good fortune she was a rather vague lady and would no doubt have forgotten by the morrow what the purpose of our outing had been. Elaine hadn't been keen on going but had agreed on the condition that she and her husband not speak of the goings on there.

The house of the Rt. Hon. Edward Eastwood and his family was one of the grandest in the neighborhood. It was said often enough in joke that all looked up to them, for their mansion stood upon a slow rise among many rolling acres. The jogging of the carriage as we made our way there did nothing but encourage my now passionate temperament, for my bottom bounced up and down all the while as did Elaine's. It being dusk already we could see little enough of her husband who accommodated himself on the seat opposite, but I did not doubt that his thoughts of the advancing night were as much as mine.

The house was well lit as our carriage at last approached the entrance. But a single aged servant appeared to be about the place, though the reason for this soon struck me. All others had been dismissed for the night, perhaps locked in their rooms with their supper or packed off to an inn. Thus there were to be no witnesses as to what followed other than the assembled gentry.

As Elaine and I had already surmised, they were not many. I counted as many ladies as gentlemen and found the score not greater than fourteen. Among the former were several beauties of local distinction. By good fortune I knew none of them. All were perfectly polite and utterly discreet, as I discovered. Mrs. Eastwood was a lady of remarkable charm, approaching then her fortieth year, who herself met us in the hall and took our cloaks without the faintest hint of embarrassment.

"You have come well provided for," she said with a laugh to Lord William while gazing both Elaine and I up and down most approvingly. "You have advised them well, William, I trust, for there are to be no understandings."

Such boldness took me as equally by surprise as it did my cousin. We exchanged the most furtive glances. A purplish hue spread meanwhile over Lord William's features. The doors to the drawing room being closed, we all stood alone.

"Ah, as to that, perhaps we might converse privately," he said. His voice sounded exceedingly strained. I stared at my feet as did Elaine.

Mrs. Eastwood shrugged in a languid manner. "If you wish." she declared and led him into a small side room, though leaving the door ajar of a purpose, as I surmised. A muttering came to our ears and then a faint laugh from our hostess.

"My dear William, discretion is all here. You above all should know that. I make no demur myself about the presence of Elaine and nor will anyone else. What? I cannot hear what you say, and really I cannot keep the others waiting. She must be put up to the gentlemen as needs be, as we all are. That is the sport of it. You had no need to bring her, my pet. Let me speak with her for I do not wish her to enter upon the proceedings in total innocence, though should she wish to make play upon struggling a little that will be all the more fun. As to the other very pretty young lady who accompanies you, I will have her no more in the dark than Elaine."

"Oh, I say! But Mavis..."

All was lost, or all was gained, depending upon one's philosophy, for Lord William's interruption was itself interrupted by the emergence of our hostess who clearly was determined to have no break in her evidently smooth affairs.

"Elaine, my dear, there will be much pleasantry tonight for which you must forgive us, as I am sure that—Eleanor, is it not?—will also. Within half an hour or so when all have been well warmed with wine we shall call upon the ladies to present themselves, by which I mean you will doff as gracefully as possible such outer attire as you have, including of course your drawers."

A gurgling sound came from behind her as these words were spoken. My Lord William stood in the doorway of the side room as might have Hamlet or Macbeth. No sooner had this sound struck softly upon us than Mrs. Eastwood, persuading herself between us, took us both by the elbows and steered us towards the drawing room, talking as merrily meanwhile as if we had been attending a fete.

Within was such a bubbling of voices and laughter as immediately warms the senses. Though the hall had been well lit, the drawing room was otherwise. A single chandelier had been lit in the centre of the ceiling, the gas mantles being dimmed so that while the middle of the room was sufficiently illumined, pools of shadow lay all about around the sides which gave a cozy atmosphere. The room was naturally commodious, there being some five large sofas and divans placed about the walls for such comfort as would be required. A huge sideboard accommodated piles of tiny sandwiches and canapés together with an impressive number of bottles and glasses.

"You, my dear, are one out, for we have an equal number of ladies and gentlemen, but as such you make a piquant addition to our party. You will not be put out if you are attended to simultaneously by a lady and gentleman? Of course, you will not, for there are many couples here who like to dally with a young woman together before disporting themselves," our hostess said calmly enough to Elaine.

Before Elaine could gather herself to reply—though I know not what she would have said—we were surrounded by admirers of both sexes and drinks placed in our hands.

"All are known by names other than their own, of course, so you may use any pseudonym that you wish," remarked Mrs. Eastwood helpfully and then disappeared to the other side of the room the while that my Lord William made his hesitant entrance and stood regarding me. I moved towards him upon instinct and stood by his side. Elaine, throwing me a somewhat frantic glance, found herself sandwiched between a gentleman of some forty years and a young woman scarce older than herself. Even as we watched I heard the girl declare, "Let me kiss you, for you have such lovely lips."

At that, and while others watched the trio as fondly as might parents observing their children at play, Elaine was embraced by the looping of the girl's arms about her neck. I believe she might have started back, but all happened so quickly that there was naught for her to do but surrender to the moment. As if to encourage them a beautifully attired couple standing by merged to one another as if they had waited long for this moment and exchanged the most lascivious kisses which all then fell to partaking of save for my Lord William and I who stood apart as two who enter a room and see no one but strangers before them.

As may be thought, this state of immobility lasted not long. Moving swiftly behind Elaine, the gentleman whose female partner was impressing ever more passionate kisses upon her lips, raised her skirt so quickly that she had not time to retreat—nor any space to do it in—before her shapely legs were fully bared and her proudly-filled drawers were displayed to all. Giving her no time to wriggle from between them, he then fumbled his trousers and thrust his erect penis between her thighs just above her stocking tops.

"Down with their drawers!" a voice cried, whereat several of the ladies made great play of shrieking and endeavouring to run all about, though not with such energy that they were not quickly made as captive as my cousin who could be seen moving her face agitatedly from side to side while the gentleman into whose stomach her bottom was pressed, held her waist tightly and so allowed his companion to further her endeavours by unfastening Elaine's corsage. Isolated in a corner as I seemed to be with my Lord William, I could but watch dry-mouthed as my cousin's lustrous firm titties were brought into view while the gentleman's sturdy penis moved to and fro between the backs of her bared thighs.

All was now as a scene painted in one's own erotic dreams. All about were to be seen suspended stockings, corsets, arid emerging breasts and bottoms as the females everywhere were being disrobed. Some fumbled for their partner's cocks at the same time while others pretended a ridiculous coyness which however did not abate the strip-pings. A cry from Elaine announced that her own drawers were being descended. Quite without thinking I sank down upon a sofa in company with my Lord William whose arm stole about my shoulders. I turned my flushed face to his. Our mouths met in the wildest of kisses. Scarce knowing what I was at, I felt for his prick which stood as a bar of iron under the fine dark cloth of his breeches.

Moans, cries, laughter, squeals, came to our ears while blindly our tongues met and whirled. Feverishly he fondled my breasts and then, dipping one hand into my corsage, sleeked his palm over the silky swollen surfaces to taunt my stiffening nipples. I fell back, encouraged by the seeking of our hands, unbuttoning him as I did so. The long thick prong of his penis came into my hand. I was as one possessed. Forgetful that he thought of me as naught but a novice, I rubbed the great shaft fervently. His hands sought my gown and threw it up, tearing at the waistband of my drawers.

"Let me kiss her. How pretty she is!" a voice sounded dimly from above. My Lord William moved from me, allowing me to see who had spoken. Above us, legs astride and with a well-puffed mount displayed, stood a beautiful woman of about thirty whose attire consisted solely of a fetching black waist corset, stockings and shoes. Lying half beneath my Lord William as I was, I had not time to stir nor rise before she lay down alongside me and captured my lips in a breathless kiss. Therewith my Lord William stirred and must have slid to his knees so that he knelt beside the sofa and, pressing back my legs, applied his mouth to the succulent haven of my cunny.

"What is your name?" she asked amid fervent tonguings.

"Rose," I gasped for want of anything else to reply, while her hand dipped as freely in my gown as my Lord William's had. My bottom being cupped and slightly lifted now on his broad hands, I wriggled madly at the invasion of his tongue between my lovelips.

"William, let us have her things off," the unknown murmured, causing me to feel somewhat like a piece of property, though all was such and I so feverish by now in my responses that I made no demur as I was drawn up between them and quickly bereft of all save my shoes and stockings. My titties, bottom, thighs and cunny all being caressed the while, I was in a perfect fever to be fucked as was evident in the way I rejoined our triple embrace once more upon the sofa. Even so, I had not failed to glimpse Elaine and neither, from the rubicond hue on his face had my Lord William. Having surrendered to the opportunities of the moment as quickly as I, she was upon her hands and knees on the floor receiving a sturdy penis from the rear. All about us indeed were such scenes of libertine delights, the gentlemen being by then in as great a state of nudity as the ladies and all cocks rampant.

"I adore kissing young girls while they are being fucked," my female companion declared, and so it seemed, for while we pecked amourously at each other's lips and caressed each other's breasts, my Lord William made ready so swiftly that his bulky, naked form pressed against my quite tingling nipples, Davina—as she appeared to be called—breathed teasing words into my mouth even as the lusty shaft drove up into my cunny.

"Is he your first, or have you been a truly naughty girl?"

"My f… f…first," I stammered. All my senses reeled. The selfsame cock that I had but once enjoyed now plugged me again to the full. I felt the brushing of our pubic hairs together. Our three tongues joined. My legs being drawn up, I wrapped them about his waist. We jogged, we writhed. His prick sluiced in and out, causing me the most exquisite raptures which were all the more enlivened by the caresses that Davina and I lavished upon one another. The triple kisses in the very midst of being so manfully pleasured added to our bliss.

"She is coming," breathed Davina who with seeking fingers could feel the rippling in my belly. Her tongue plunged into my mouth anew. My Lord William's fingers sought her bottom, causing her to churn her hips, bending as she was then with one knee on the edge of the seat. I came, I sprinkled, I melted, I urged his thrusts with sensuous movements of my bottom. Our moans resounded, mingling with those all about us, though in my lowly posture I could see naught.

Frothing then all within me and labouring like a shire horse, my Lord William offered me in turn his libation which pulsed jet upon jet within me while Davina announced her own delirious pleasure by tonguing our mouths in turn. Febrile quivers shook us. My tight cunny seemed to suck upon his embedded penis, imploring every spurt and drop until, in withdrawing at last, his well-soaked knob smeared my thighs with our mingled juices. I floated. Warmth and satisfaction spread in easy waves throughout my uttered charms. With a soft gurgle, Davina eased herself off of my Lord William's probing finger and sat up languidly to look all about.

"Ah, Elaine is having her dosage," she declared to my full surprise at having so casually uttered my cousin's name. With something of a satisfied grunt my Lord William removed his heavy weight from my body. I drew up my knees and swivelled on to one hip, leaning into a corner of the sofa. My Lord William's thick pendant cock oozed its last pearl. His eyes were transfixed as were my own for a moment on Elaine who now lay with her head and shoulders beneath a large oak table, couched beneath a second stallion whose balls swung under her bottom, her ankles crossed about his waist.

"How well she takes him," Davina murmured, having seated herself on the other side of my Lord William so that he was between us. Her hand stroked his trunk-like thigh. His eyes appeared glazed. Kneeling beside Elaine was the young woman who had first kissed her and who was now entertaining a rigid penis in her bottom. But a few feet away— and all at the centre of other heaving couples—our hostess was being steadily fucked.

The scene blurred, came clear, and then blurred again before my eyes. Stealing my right hand sideways I mischievously stroked my Lord William's prick the while that Davina dandled his huge balls. His cock stirred almost immediately, thickening to my touch.

"See how she wriggles her bottom," Davina said of Elaine who, while she could not possibly have heard and indeed must have been utterly lost in her sensations, appeared at that moment to twist her lovely face all about and gaze directly at us across the carpet. At that my Lord William's jaw literally gaped for he sensed that their eyes were locked even though I felt certain Elaine would have seen nothing but a swirling of bodies and faces. Rock-hard as it now became, his re-erected penis stuck up in the half encirclement of my fingers. Elaine opened her legs wider by letting her feet slip to the floor. A species of snorting moan escaped my Lord William. The man's cock was clearly to be seen pistoning in and out between the lips of her love dell whose well-furred fringe looked utterly enticing.

"Oh pray, Lord William, dear Elaine will be much confounded at your seeing her," I uttered. The words seemed to bring him to himself.

"Shush, Rose, for we may all do as we wish—do not spoil the sport," enjoined Davina who obviously knew clearly enough my cousin's identity yet batted not an eyelid about the matter while all about us bodies slapped together, tongues writhed, and pricks worked steadily in such orifices as were freely offered to them.

"No, no—oh, do not look!" I burst, for while I knew the situation to be truly bizarre yet I feared lest Elaine might think I had turned traitor to her. Rising and throwing myself against him between his legs so that the crest of his tool rubbed against my bush, I pretended even greater alarm than I felt and urged that he must carry me out. Momentarily embarrassed perhaps at all that was about—though I confess to knowing less about human nature than I do now—I was borne in a moment from the room into a smaller reception room where with scarcely a word I was fucked again upon the floor as lustily mayhap as I have ever been.

"The naughty girl, ah the naughty girl!" he groaned with every stroke, yet I will pass over now the fevers of the rest of that night which in many senses were but a preamble to all that followed. Others entered upon us once we had spilled our liquid pleasures. My Lord William took himself upon Davina while I, mounted successively by two gentlemen, could do naught but swim in lost passions until my cunny literally bubbled with sperm.

By midnight all were as exhausted as could be. A strange quiet fell as various assortments of clothing were recovered and the ladies made haste to dress even before the gentlemen. A little simpering, some final kisses, and all was concluded. I, entering not upon the main scene until caution apprised me of the right moment, found Elaine huddled in a corner, fully dressed.

"Oh, I cannot face my husband!" she entreated as quietly as possible.

"What nonsense, he has seen nothing, we were in the other room," I said.

Her relief was evident, asking me again and again if it were true. Most tactfully he was nowhere to be seen. With furtive mien and not a little blushing she made her way out with me into the hall where my Lord William was bidding adieu to our hostess. Impeccable and unsullied as she again looked, we might well have been leaving the most sedate of gatherings.

"You will come again? I trust you will for it has been most pleasant," she murmured as though to all three of us at once. Seeing that neither Elaine nor her husband appeared ready to answer, I gave a polite nod of my head. Despite my relative youth and the positive whirlwind I had been through, I found to my pleasure that I was perfectly in control of myself—admiring also as I did the exquisitely civilised manner of our hostess.

"I doubt it not," I replied and shook her hand. From the expression in her eyes I gathered that her interest in me had increased threefold. A few more polite murmurs and we went out upon the dark drive to the carriage where my Lord William had to shake the coachman to awaken him, poor fellow. Then within did we settle ourselves. In a way, all had been briefer than I thought it might. Had it not been for the presence of Elaine, we might have greeted the dawn there.

The Education of Emma

When I had passed my eighteenth year at our ancestral home, I was sent to Miss Birchbottom's academy to finish out my education. Her house was situated at Edmonton, so famous for Johnny Gilpin's ride. It was a large spacious mansion, formerly belonging to some nobleman, and stood in its own grounds. What were called the private gardens, next the house, were all enclosed in high walls, to prevent the possibility of any elopements.

Beyond these, in a ring fence, there were several paddocks for grazing purposes, in which Miss Birchbottom kept her cows and turned the carriage horses, when not in use (which was all the week), for we only took coach, carriage, or whatever the conveyance might be, on Sundays, when we were twice regularly driven to the village church, nearly one-and-a-half miles distant, for Miss Birchbottom's ladies could not be permitted, upon even the finest days, to walk there. We always called the vehicles coaches, although they were a kind of nondescript vehicle, and having nearly three dozen young ladies in the establishment, we filled three of them, and formed quite a grand procession as we drove up to the church door, and there was generally quite a little crowd to see us alight or take our departure, and, as the eldest girls assured us, it was only to see if we showed our legs, or displayed rather more ankle than usual. We were very particular as to silk stockings, and the finest and most fashionable boots we could get to set off our limbs to greatest advantage, and, in wet weather, when we were obliged to hold up our dresses rather more, I often observed quite a titter of admiration amongst the spectators, who curiously, as it seemed to us, were mostly the eldest gentlemen of the place, who evidently were as anxious to keep their sons away from the sight of our blandishments as Miss

Birchbottom could possibly wish; at any rate, it seemed to be understood to be highly improper for any young gentleman ever to present himself at what we called our Sunday levee.

We were never allowed to walk in the country roads, but on half-holidays or any special occasions, in fine weather, our governess would escort us into paddocks, and a little wood of three or four acres, which was included within the ring fence, where we indulged in a variety of games free from observation.

The school was very select, none but the daughters of the aristocracy or officers of the army or navy being admitted to the establishment; even the professions were barred by Miss Birchbottom, who was a middle-aged maiden lady, and a very strict martinet.

Before I went to this school, I always thought such places were conducted with the greatest possible propriety as to morals, etc., but soon found that it was only an outward show of decorum, whereas the private arrangements admitted of a variety of very questionable doings, not at all conducive to the future morality of the pupils, and if other fashionable schools are all conducted upon the same principles, it easily accounts for that aristocratic indifference to virtue so prevalent in my early days.

The very first night I was in the house (we slept, half-a-dozen of us, in a fine large room), I had not been settled in bed with my partner more than an hour before quite a dozen girls invaded the room, and pulled me out of bed, to be made free of the establishment, as they call it.

They laid me across one of the beds, stuffed a handkerchief in my mouth to prevent my cries, and every one of them slapped my naked bottom three times and some of them did it very spitefully, so that my poor rump tingled and smarted as if I had had a good birching. Sarah White, my bedfellow, who was a very nice kind-hearted girl of nineteen, comforted and assured me all the girls had to go through the same ordeal as soon as they came to the school. I asked her if the birch was ever used in the establishment.

"Bless you, yes," she replied; "you are a dear love of a girl, and I shall be sorry to see you catch it," kissing me and rubbing my smarting bottom.

"How hot it is, let's throw off the bedclothes and cool it," she added.

"Let's look at her poor bottom," said Miss Laura Van Tromp, a fine fair Dutch girl; "shall we have a game of slaps before Mdlle. Fosse (the French Governess) comes to bed?"

"Yes, come, Emma dear, you'll like that, it will make you forget your own smarts; get up Cecile and Clara for a romp," addressing the Hon. Miss Cecile Deben and Lady Clara Wavering, who with the French Governess made up the six occupants of our room. "You know Mdlle. won't say anything if she does catch us."

We were soon out of bed, with our nightdresses thrown off, and all quite naked: Sarah, a thin, fair girl with soft large blue eyes, always such a sure indication of an amorous disposition; Cecile, about eighteen, a nice plump little dear with chestnut hair and blue eyes. Lady Clara, who was just upon twenty, was dark, rather above the middle height, well-proportioned, with languid, pensive hazel eyes, whilst Laura Van Tromp was a fat Dutch girl of nineteen, with grey eyes and splendidly developed figure.

It was a beautiful sight, for they were all pretty, and none of them showed any shamefacedness over it, evidently being quite used to the game; they all gathered round me, and patted and kissed my bottom, Cecile saying, "Rosie, I'm so glad you've so little hair on your pussey yet, you will keep me in countenance; these other girls think so much of their hairiness, as if they were old women; what's the use of it, Sarah, now you have got it," playing with the soft fair down of Miss White's pussey.

SARAH. – "You silly thing, don't tickle so, you'll be proud enough when you get it."

LADY CLARA. – "Cecile, dear, you've only to rub your belly on mine a little more than you do, that's how Sarah got hers."

LAURA – "Rosie, you shall rub your belly on mine; Clara is too fond of Cecile. I can make yours grow for you, my dear," kissing me and feeling my mount in a very loving way.

SARAH. – "Listen to Grey Eyes Greedy Guts, you'd think none of us ever played with the Van Tromp. Rosie, you belong to me."

We now commenced the game of slaps, which in reality was similar to a common children's sport called "touch." Ours was a very large room, the three beds, dressing tables, washstands, &c., all arranged round the sides, leaving a good clear space in the centre.

LADY CLARA. – "I'll be 'Slappee' to begin," taking her station in the middle of the room.

Each girl now placed herself with one hand touching a bedstead or some article of furniture, and as Clara turned her back to any of us we would slip slyly up behind and give a fine spanking slap on her bottom, making it assume a rosy flush all over; but if she could succeed in returning the slap to anyone before they regained their touch, the one that was caught had to take her place as "Slappee."

We all joined heartily in the game, keeping up a constant sound of slaps, advancing and retreating, or slipping up now and then to vary the amusement, in which case the unfortunate one got a general slapping from all the players before she could recover herself, making great fun and laughter. You would think such games would soon be checked by the governess, but the rule was never to interfere with any games amongst the pupils in their bedrooms. Just as our sport was at its height the door opened, and Mdlle. Fosse entered, exclaiming, "Ma foi, you rude girls, all out of bed slapping one another, and the lamp never put out, how indelicate, young ladies, to expose yourselves so; but Mdlle. Birchbottom does not like to check you out of school, so it's no business of mine, but you want slapping, do you? How would you like to be cut with this, Mdlle. Kootch?" showing me a very pretty little birch rod of long thin twigs, tied up with blue velvet and ribbons. "It would tickle very differently to hand slapping."

"Ah! Mademoiselle, I've felt much worse than that three times the size and weight. My poor old grandfather, the General, was a dreadful flogger," I replied.

MADEMOISELLE. – "I thought girls were only whipped at school. You must tell me all about it, Miss Emma."

"With great pleasure. I don't suppose any of you have seen such punishment inflicted as I could tell you of," I replied.

The young French lady had been rapidly undressing herself as this conversation was going on. She was very dark, black hair over a rather low forehead, with a most pleasing expression of face, and fine sparkling eyes, hid under what struck me as uncommonly bushy eyebrows. She unlaced her corset, fully exposing a beautiful snowy bosom, ornamented with a pair of lovely round globes, with dark nipples, and her skin, although so white, had a remarkable contrast to our fairer flesh. There seemed to be a tinge of black somewhere, whereas our white complexion must have been from an original pink source, infinitely diluted.

MADEMOISELLE. – "Ah! You Van Tromp, ou est ma robe de chambre? Have you hidden it?"

LAURA. – "Oh! Pray strip and have a game with us. You shan't have the nightdress yet."

MADEMOISELLE. – "You shall catch it if you make me play; your bottom shall smart for it."

We all gathered round her, and although she playfully resisted, she was soon denuded of every rag of clothing. We pulled off her boots and stockings; but what a beautiful sight she was, apparently about twenty-six, with nicely rounded limbs, but such a glorious profusion of hair, that from her head, now let loose, hung down her back in a dense mass, and quite covered her bottom, so that she might have sat on the end of it, whereas her belly, it is almost impossible to describe it, except by calling it a veritable "Foret Noire." The glossy black curling hair, extending all over her mount, up to her navel, and hanging several inches down between her thighs.

"There, Mdlle. Emma," she exclaimed, sitting on the edge of her bed, "did you ever see anyone so hairy as I am? It's a sign of a loving nature, my dear," nipping my bottom and kissing me as she hugged my naked figure to hers. "How I love to caress the little featherless birdies like you. You shall sleep with me sometimes. The Van Tromp will be glad to change me for Sarah."

"We cannot allow that," cried two or three of the others together.

"Now you shall be 'Slappee' with your birch, Mdlle."

"Very well," said the lively French lady. "You'll get well touched up if I do catch any of you."

Then we commenced our game again, and she switched us finely, leaving long red marks on our bottoms when she succeeded in making a hit. Her own bottom must have smarted from our smacks, but she seemed quite excited and delighted with the amusement, till at last she said: "Oh! I must be birched myself, who will be the schoolmistress?"

SARAH. – "Oh! Let Emma! She will lecture you as if you were a culprit, and give us an idea of good earnest punishment. Will you, Emma? it will amuse us all. Just try if you can't make Mademoiselle ask your pardon for taking liberties with you, do, there's a dear girl."

"Yes! yes! that will be fine," cried the others, especially Lady Clara, who was already seated on her bed with Cecile as her partner.

LAURA. – "Mdlle. wants Emma for her bedfellow to-night, so let her tickle her up with the birch; don't spare her, Rosie, she's so hard to hurt; come Sarah, let us enjoy the night together."

Thus urged I took up the rod and, flourishing it lightly in the air, said, laughing, "I know how to use it properly, especially on naughty bottoms, which have the impudence to challenge me; now, Mdlle., present your bottom on the edge of the bed, with your legs well apart, just touching the floor, but I must have two of them to hold you down; come, Sarah and Laura, each of you hold one arm, and keep her body well down on the bed, there, that will do just so, hold her securely, don't let her get up till I've fairly done."

EMMA. – "Mdlle. Fosse, you are a very wicked young lady to behave so rudely to me as you have done; will you beg my pardon, and promise never to do so any more; do you feel that and that?" giving a couple of stinging little switches across her loins.

MADEMOISELLE. – "Oh! no! I won't apologize, I do love little featherless chits like you!"

EMMA. – "You call me a chit, do you? I'll teach you a little more respect for your schoolmistress; is that too hard, or perhaps you like that better," giving a couple of slashing cuts on her rounded buttocks, which leave long red marks, and make her wriggle with pain.

MADEMOISELLE. – "Ah! Ah! Ah-r-r-re, that's too hard. Oh! Oh! you do cut, you little devil," as I go on sharper and sharper at every stroke, making her writhe and wriggle under the tingling switches which mark her bottom in every direction.

EMMA. – "Little devil, indeed, you shall beg my pardon for that too, you insulting young lady, how dare you express yourself so to your governess, your bottom must be cut to pieces, if I can't subdue such a proud spirit. There – there – there!" cutting away, each stroke going in on the tender parts of her inner thighs. "Will you be rude again? will you insult me again, eh? I hope I don't hurt you too much, pray tell me if I do. Ha! Hal! Ha!!! you don't seem quite to approve of it by the motions of your impudent bottom," cutting away all the while I was speaking, each stroke with deliberation on some unexpected place, till her bum was rosy all over, and marked with a profusion of deep red weals.

Mademoiselle makes desperate efforts to release herself, but Lady Clara and Cecile also help to keep her down, all apparently highly excited by the sight of her excoriated blushing bottom, adding their remarks, such as, "Bravo, Bravo, Rosie, you didn't think she would catch it so, how delightful to see her writhe and plunge in pain, to hear her scream, and help to keep her down," till at last the surprised victim begs and prays for pardon, crying to be let off, with tears in her eyes. This is the end of the night's amusements, for all now resume their night chemises and retire, Mdlle. taking me to sleep with her. "Ah! *Ma cherie*," she exclaimed, as the lamp was put out and I found myself in her arms, "how cruelly you have warmed my poor bottom, and have you really seen worse than that, Rosie?"

"Oh! far, far worse, Mdlle., I've seen the blood flow freely from cut up bottoms," I replied, at the same time repaying her caresses and running my hand through the thick curly, hair of her mount, as she was feeling and tickling my pussey. "There, there," she whispered; "nip me, squeeze that little bit of flesh," as my hand wandered to the lips of her hairy retreat, "tickle me as I do you," putting me in great confusion by her touches, for I had never experienced anything like it before, except the melting, burning sensations of the same parts at the conclusion of my previous flagellations.

This dalliance continued between us for some months, and I soon became an apt pupil in her sensual amusements, being emboldened by her freedoms, and heated by a most curious desire to explore with my fingers everything about that hairy paradise. Meanwhile she tickled and rubbed the entrance of my slit in a most exciting manner, and suddenly she clasped me close to her naked body (our chemises were turned up so we might feel each other's naked flesh), and kissed my lips in such a rapturous, luscious manner as to send a thrill of ecstasy through my whole quivering frame, her fingers worked nervously in my crack, and I felt quite a sudden gush of something from me, wetting her fingers and all my secret parts, whilst she pressed me more and more, wriggling and sighing, "Oh! oh! Emma, go on, rub, rub"; then suddenly she stiffened herself out straight and seemed almost rigid as I felt my hand deluged with a profusion of warm, thick, sticky stuff.

After a few moments' rest she recovered herself, and said to me: "Listen! listen! The others are all doing the same. Can't you hear their sighs? Oh! Isn't it nice, Emma dear?"

"Yes! Yes!" I whispered, in a shamefaced manner, for I seemed to know we had indulged in some very improper proceeding. "Oh! Mademoiselle, do they all do it? It's so nice of you to play with me so."

MADEMOISELLE. – "Of course they do. It's the only pleasure we can have in school. Ah! You should be with Lady Clara or the Van Tromp, how they spend and go on in their ecstasy."

"What is spending?" I whispered. "Is that the wet I felt on my fingers when you stiffened yourself out?"

MADEMOISELLE. – "Yes, and you spent too, little bashful. Didn't the birching make you feel funny?"

EMMA (in a whisper). – "Even when I have been cut so that the blood flowed down my legs, at last I suddenly got dulled to the pain, and came an over with a delicious hot burning melting feeling which drowned every other sensation."

MADEMOISELLE. – "Emma, you're a little darling. Would you like to feel it over again? I know another way, if you only do to me exactly as I do to you, will you?"

I willingly assented to the lovely Francaise, who, reversing our positions, laid on her back, and made me lay my body on hers, head downwards. Our chemises were turned up close under our arms, so as fully to enjoy the contact of our naked bodies, and I found my face buried in the beautiful mossy forest on her mount, and felt Mademoiselle, with her face between my thighs, tickling my little slit with something soft and warm, which I soon found out was her tongue. She passed it lovingly along the crack and inside as far as it would reach, whilst one of her fingers invaded my bottom-hole, and worked in and out in a most exciting way.

Not to be behind hand, I imitated all her movements, and burying my face between her thighs, revelled with my tongue and fingers in every secret place. She wriggled and tossed her bottom up and down, especially after I had succeeded in forcing a finger well up the little hole and worked it about, as she was doing to me. Although it was all so new to me, there was something so exciting and luscious in it all; to handle, feel, and revel in such a luxuriously covered pussey and bottom excited me more and more every moment; then the fiery touches of her tongue on my own burning orifices so worked me up that I spent allover her mouth, pressing my slit down upon her in the most lascivious manner, just as her own affair rewarded me in the same manner. After a little time we composed ourselves to sleep, and with many loving expressions and promises of future enjoyment.

This was my experience the first night of my school life, and I need not weary you with repetitions of the same kind of scene, but simply tell you that it was enacted almost every night, ´and that we constantly changed our partners, so that was the cause of my acquiring such a penchant for female bedfellows, especially when they have been previously well warmed by a little preparatory flagellation.

Miss Birchbottom was a stern disciplinarian in her school, and we often came under her hands, when she wielded the birch with great effect, generally having the culprit horsed on the back of a strong maid servant, who evidently delighted in her occupation.

I must be drawing this story to a close, but will give you one illustration of how we were punished in my time.

I cannot exactly remember what my offense was, but it was probably for being impertinent to Miss Herbert, the English governess, a strict maiden lady of thirty, who never overlooked the slightest mark of disrespect to herself.

Miss Birchbottom would seat herself in state upon a kind of raised dais, where she usually sat when she was in the school-room. Miss Herbert would introduce the culprit to her thus:

MISS HERBERT – "Madame, this is Miss Kootch, she has been disrespectful to me, and said I was an old frump."

MISS BIRCHBOTTOM. – "That is a most improper word to be used by young ladies, you have only to take away the *f*, and what remains, but a word I would never pronounce with my lips, it's too vulgar. Miss Emma Belinda Kootch (she always addressed culprits by their full name), I shall chastise you with the rod; call Maria to prepare her for punishment."

The stout and strong Maria immediately appears and conducts me into a kind of small vestry sacred to the goddess of flagellation, if there is such a deity; there she strips off all my clothes, except chemise and drawers, and makes me put on a kind of penitential dress, consisting of a white mobcap and a long white garment, something like a nightdress; it fitted close up round the throat with a little plain frill round the neck and down the front, being fastened by a band round the waist,

Maria now ushers me again into the presence of Miss Birchbottom, all blushing as I am at the degrading costume, and ridiculous figure I must look to my schoolfellows, who are all in a titter.

Maria lays a fine bunch of fresh birch twigs (especially tied up with ribbons) at my feet, I have to pick it up and kiss it in a most respectful manner, and ask my schoolmistress to chastise me properly with it. All this was frightfully humiliating, especially the first time, for however free we might have been with one another in our bedrooms there was such a sense of mortifying shame, sure to be felt all through the proceedings.

Miss Birchbottom, rising with great dignity from her seat, motions with her hand, and Miss Herbert assisted by the German governess, Frau Bildaur, at once mounted me on Maria's broad back, and pinned up the dress above my waist, then the English governess with evident pleasure opened my drawers behind so as to expose my bare bottom, whilst the soft-hearted young German showed her sympathy by eyes brimming with tears.

MISS BIRCHBOTTOM. – "I shall administer a dozen sharp cuts, and then insist upon your begging Miss Herbert's pardon," commencing to count the strokes one by one, as she whisks steadily, but with great force, every blow falling with a loud "whack," and making my bottom smart and tingle with pain, and giving assurance of a plentiful crop of weals. My red blushing bottom must have been a most edifying sight to the pupils, and a regular caution to timid offenders, two or three more of whom might expect their turn in a day or two; although I screamed and cried out in apparent anguish it was nothing to what I had suffered at the hands of Sir Eyre or Mrs. Mansell; the worst part of the punishment was in the degrading ceremony and charity girl costume the victim had to assume.

The dozen duly inflicted, I had first to beg Miss Herbert's pardon, and then having again kissed the rod, and thanked Miss Birchbottom for what she called her loving correction, I was allowed to retire and resume my own apparel. I could tell you about many punishment scenes, but in my next shall have the grand finale to my school life, and how we paid off Miss Birchbottom and the English governess before leaving.

Louise, Kate and Me

To the Reader,

Very little apology will be needed for putting in print the following highly erotic and racy narrative of a young patrician lady, whose adventures I feel assured every genuine lover of voluptuous reading will derive as much or more pleasure afforded your humble servant. The subject of these memoirs was one of the brightest and most charming of her sex, endued with such exquisite nervous sensitiveness, in addition to an unusual warmth of constitution that she was quite unable to resist the seductive influences of God's finest creation; for God made man in his own image, male and female, created he them; and this was the first commandment, "Be faithful and multiply, and replenish the earth" – see Genesis, chap. I. The natural instinct of the ancients instilled in their minds the idea that copulation was the direct and most acceptable form of worship they could offer to their deities, and I know that those of my readers who are not bigoted Christians will agree with me, that there cannot be any great sin in giving way to natural desires, and enjoying, to the utmost, all those delicious sensations for which a beneficent Creator has so amply fitted us.

Poor girl, she did not live long, and in thoroughly enjoying her few briefs years of butterfly life, who can think her wicked! The scraps from which my narrative is compiled were found in a packet she had entrusted to a devoted servitor, who, after her sudden and premature death at the early age of twenty-three, entered my service. We join our heroine as she is boarding with Louise—and two happier practitioners of tribadism there have never been. She awaits her reunion with Bertram, for purposes that shall become abundantly clear. You, dear reader, shall join the story in medias res, but I trust it shan't result in undue confusion.

So, without further ado, her story:

I had to wait till the Christmas vacation before I could be introduced to Bertram, who, between ourselves, Louise and I had already devoted to the task of taking my virginity, which we did not think would prove a very difficult operation, as with so much finger frigging, and also the use of Louise's leather sausage, which, as I learnt, she had improvised for her own gratification, my mount and cunny were wonderfully developed. I was nearly nineteen, as one fine crisp morning in December we drove up to the Hall on our return from school. There stood the aunt to welcome us, but my eyes were fixed upon the youthful, yet manly figure of Bertram, who stood by her side, almost a counterpart of his sister, in features and complexion, but really a very fine young fellow, between twenty and twenty-one.

. Since hearing the story of Louise's intrigue with her friend Mr. William, I always looked at every man and boy to see what sort of a bunch they had got in their pockets, and was delighted to perceive Mr. Bertram was apparently well furnished.

Louise introduced me to her relatives, but Bertram evidently looked upon me as a little girl, and not at all yet up to the serious business of love and flirtation, so our first private consultation, between Louise and myself, was how best to open his eyes, and draw him to take a little more notice of his sister's friend.

Kate, who I now saw for the first time, slept in the little room adjoining Louise's chamber, which I shared with her young mistress. Bertram had a room on the other side of ours, so that we were next door neighbours, and could rap and give signals to each other on the wall, as well as to try to look through the keyhole of a disused door, which opened direct from one room to the other, but had long since been locked and bolted to prevent any communication between the occupants.

A little observation soon convinced us that Kate was upon most intimate terms with her young master, which Louise determined to turn to account in our favour.

She quickly convinced her *femme de chamber* that she could not enjoy and monopolize the whole of her cousin, and finding that Kate expected he would visit her room that very night, she insisted upon ringing the changes, by taking Kate to sleep with herself, and putting me in the place of Monsieur Bertram's ladylove.

I was only too willing to be a party of this arrangement, and at ten P.M., when we all retired to rest, I took the place of the *femme de chambre*, and pretended to be fast asleep in her snug little bed. The lock of the door had been oiled by Kate, so as to open quite noiselessly, but the room was purposely left in utter darkness, and secured even from the intrusion of a dim starlight by well-closed window curtains.

About eleven o'clock, as nearly as I could guess, the door silently opened, and by the light of the corridor lamp, I saw a figure, in nothing but a shirt, cautiously glide in, and approach the bed. The door closed, and all was dark, putting my heart in a dreadful flutter, at the approach of the long wished for, but dreaded ravisher of my virginity.

"Kate! Kate!! Kate!!!" he whispered, in a low voice, almost in my ear. No response, only the apparent deep breathing of a person in sound sleep.

"She hasn't thought much about me, but, I guess, something between her legs will soon wake her up," I heard him mutter; then the bedclothes were pulled open, and he slid into bed by my side. My hair was all loose, the same as Kate's generally was at night, and I felt a warm kiss on my cheek, also an arm stealing round my waist and clutching my nightdress as if to pull it up. Of course I was the fox asleep, but could not help being all atremble at the approach of my fate.

"How you shake, Kate; what's the matter? Hullo! who's this; it can't be you?" he said rapidly, as with a sigh and a murmur, "Oh! oh! Louise." I turned round just as he pulled up my chemise, clasping my arm firmly round him, but still apparently lost in sleep. "My God!" I heard him say, "It's that little devil of in Kate's bed; I won't go, I'll have a lark, she can't know me in the dark."

His hands seemed to explore every part of my body; I could feel his rampant cock pressed between our naked bellies, but although in a burning heat of excitement, I determined to let him do just as he liked, and pretend still to be asleep; his fingers explored my crack, and rubbed the little clitoris; first his leg got between mine, and then presently I could feel him gently placing the head of his instrument in the crack, and I was so excited that a sudden emission wetted it and his fingers all over with a creamy spend. "The little devil's spending in her sleep; these girls must be in the habit of frigging each other, I believe," he said to himself again. Then his lips met mine for the first time, and he was quite free from fear on that account as his face was as beardless as a girl's.

"Ah! Louise!" I murmured, "give me your sausage thing, that's it, dear, shove it in," as I pushed myself forward on his slowly progressing cock; he met me with a sudden thrust, making me almost scream with pain, yet my arms nervously clung round his body, and kept him close to the mark.

"Gently," he whispered, "Beatrice, dear, I'm Bertram, I won't hurt you much; how in heaven's name did you come in Kate's bed?" Pretending now to awaken for the first time with a little I scream, and trying to push his body away from me, I exclaimed, "Oh! Oh! How you hurt! Oh! for shame, don't. Oh, let me go, Mr. Bertram, how can you?" And then my efforts seemed exhausted, and I lay almost at his mercy as he ruthlessly pushed his advantage, and, tried to stop my mouth with kisses. I was lost. Although very painful, thanks to our frequent fingerings, &c., the way had been so cleared that he was soon in complete possession, although as I afterwards found by the stains on my chemise it was not quite a bloodless victory.

Taking every possible advantage, he continued his motions with thrilling energy, till I could not help responding to his delicious thrusts, moving my bottom a little to meet each returning insertion of his exciting weapon (we were lying on our sides), and in a few moments we both swam in a mutual flood of bliss, and after a spasmodic storm of sighs, kisses, and tender hugging pressure of each other's body, we lay in a listless state of enjoyment, when suddenly the bedclothes were thrown, or pulled off, then slap-slap-slap, came smarting smacks on our bottoms, and Louise's light, merry laugh sounded through the darkness, "Ha! Ha! Ha! Ha! Mr. Bertram, is this what you learnt at college, sir? Here, Kate, help; we must secure and punish the wretch; bring a light."

Kate appeared with a candle and locked the door inside at once, before he could have a chance of escaping, and I could see she was quite delighted at the spectacle presented by our bodies in conjunction, for as I had been previously instructed, I clung to him in apparent fright, and tried to hide my blushing face in his bosom. Bertram was in the utmost confusion, and at first was afraid we would be exposed to the master of the house, but he was a little reassured as she went on,

"What shall I do? I can't tell an old maid like aunt; only to think that my dear little Beatrice should be outraged under my very eyes, the second night of her visit. If papa and mama were at home, they would know what to do; now I must decide for myself. Now, Bertram, will you submit to a good whipping for this, or shall I write to your father, and send Beatrice home disgraced in the morning, and you will have to promise to marry her, sir? Now you've spoilt her for anyone else; who do you think would take a *cruche cassee* if they knew it, or not repudiate her when it was found out, as it must be the first night of her marriage. No, you bad boy, I'm determined both to punish you and make you offer her all the reparation in your power."

I began to cry, and begged her not to be too hard, as he had not hurt me much, and in fact had, at the finish, quite delighted my ravished senses.

"Upon my word," said Louise, assuming the airs of a woman, "the girl is as bad as the boy; this could not have happened, Beatrice, if you had not been too complaisant, and given way to his rudeness."

Bertram, disengaging himself from my embrace, and quite unmindful of his condition, started up, and clasping his Louise round her neck, kissed her most lovingly, and the impudent fellow even raised her nightdress and stroked her belly, exclaiming, as he passed his hand over her mossy mount, "What a pity, Louise, you are my cousin or I would give you the same pleasure as I have Beatrice, but I will submit to your chastisement, however hard it may be, and promise also that my little love here shall be my future wife."

LOUISE.– "You scandalous fellow, to insult my modesty so, and expose your blood-stained manhood to my sight, but I will punish you, and avenge both myself and Beatrice; you are my prisoner, so just march into the other room, I've got a tickler there that I brought home from school, as a curiosity, little thinking I should so soon have a use for it."

Arrived in Louise's own room, she and Kate first tied his hands to the bedpost, then they secured his ankles to the handle of a heavy box, which stood handy, so as to have him tolerably well stretched out.

LOUISE, getting her rod out of a drawer.– "Now, pin up his shirt to his shoulders, and I will see if I can't at least draw a few drops of his impudent blood out of his posteriors, which Beatrice may wipe off with her handkerchief as a memento of the outrage she has so easily forgiven."

The hall was a large house, and our apartments were the only ones occupied in that corridor, the rooms abutting on which were all in reserve for visitors expected to arrive in a few days, to spend Christmas with us, so that there was not much fear of being heard by any of the other inmates of the house, and Louise was under no necessity of thinking what might be the result of her blows. With a flourish she brought down the bunch of twigs with a thundering whack on his plump, white bottom; the effect was startling to the culprit, who was evidently only anticipating some playful fun. "Ah! My God! Louise, you'll cut the skin; mind what you're about; I didn't bargain for that."

LOUISE (with a smile of satisfaction).– "Ho! Ho! did you think I was going to play with you? But, you've soon found your mistake, sir. Will you? will you, again take such outrageous liberties with a young lady friend of mine?"

She cut him quite half-a-dozen times in rapid succession, as she thus lectured him, each blow leaving long red lines, to mark its visitation, and suffusing his fair bottom all over with a peach-like bloom. The victim, finding himself quite helpless, bit his lips and ground his teeth in fruitless rage. At last he burst forth: "Ah! Ah! You she-devil! Do you mean to skin my bum? Be careful, or I will take a rare revenge some day before long."

LOUISE, with great calmness and determination, but with a most excited twinkle in her eyes.– "Oh! You show temper, do you? So you mean to be revenged on me for doing a simple act of justice, sir? I will keep you there, and cut away at your impudent bottom, till you fairly beg my pardon, and promise to forgo all such wicked revengefulness."

The victim writhed in agony and rage, but her blows only increased in force, beginning to raise great fiery-looking weals all over his buttocks. "Ah! Ha!" she continued. "How do you like it, Bert? Shall I put a little more steam in my blows?"

Bertram struggles desperately to get loose, but they have secured him too well for that! The tears of shame and mortification stand in his eyes, but he is still obstinate, and I could also observe a very perceptible rising in his manly instrument, which soon stood out from his belly in a rampant state of erection.

LOUISE, with assumed fury.– "Look at the fellow, how he is insulting me, by the exhibition of his lustful weapon. I wish I could cut it off with a blow of the rod," giving him a fearful cut across his belly and on the penis.

Bertram fairly howled with pain, and big tears rolled down his cheeks, as he gasped out: "Oh! Oh! Ah! Have mercy, Louise. I know I deserve it. Oh! Pity me now, dear!"

LOUISE, without relaxing her blows.– "Oh! You are beginning to feel properly, are you? Are you sincerely penitent? Beg my pardon at once, sir, for the way you insulted me in the other room."

BERTRAM.– "Oh! Dear Louise! Stop! Stop! You don't let me get any breath. I will! I will beg your pardon. Oh! I can't help my affair sticking up as it does."

LOUISE.– "Down sir! Down sir! Your master is ashamed of you," as she playfully whisks his pego with her rod.

Bertram is in agony; his writhing and contortions seemed excruciating in the extreme, he fairly groaned out: "Oh! Oh! Louise, let me down. On my word, I will do anything you order. Oh! Oh! Ah! You make me do it," as he shuts his eyes, and we saw quite a jet of sperm shoot from his virile member.

Louise dropped her rod, and we let down the culprit who was terribly crestfallen.

"Now, sir," she said, "down on your knees, and kiss the rod."

Without a word, he dropped down, and kissed the worn-out stump, saying: "Oh! Louise; the last few moments have been so heavenly. It has blotted out all sense of pain. My dear cousin, I thank you for punishing me, and will keep my promise to Beatrice." I wiped the drops of blood from his slightly-bleeding rump, and then we gave him a couple of glasses of wine, and allowed him to sleep with Kate, in her room, for the rest of the night, where they had a most luscious time of it, whilst Louise and myself indulged in our favourite touches.

You may be sure Bertram was not long before he renewed his pleasures with me, whilst his cousin took pleasure in our happiness; but she seemed to have contracted a penchant for the use of the rod, and, once or twice a week, would have us all in her room, for a birch seance, as she called it, when Kate or myself had to submit to be victims; but the heating of our bottoms only seemed to add to our enjoyment when we were afterwards allowed to soothe our raging passions in the arms of our mutual lover.

* * * * *

Christmas came, and with it arrived several visitors, all young ladies and gentlemen of about our own ages, to spend the festive season with us; our entire party consisted of five gentlemen and seven ladies, leaving out the aunt, who was too old to enter into youthful fun and contented herself with being a faithful housekeeper, and keeping good house, so that after supper every evening we could do almost as we liked; myself and Louise soon converted our five young lady friends into tribades like ourselves, ready for anything, whilst Bertram prepared his young male friends. New Year's Day was his nineteenth birthday, and we determined to hold a regular orgy that night in our corridor, with Kate's help. Plenty of refreshments were laid in stock, ices, sandwiches, and champagne; the aunt strictly ordered us all to retire at one A.M. at latest, so we kept her commands, after spending a delicious evening in dancing and games, which only served to flush us with excitement for what all instinctively felt would be a most voluptuous entertainment upstairs.

The aunt was a heavy sleeper, and rather deaf, besides which Bertram, under the excuse of making them drink his health, plied the servants first with beer, then with wine, and afterwards with just a glass of brandy for a nightcap; so that we were assured they would also be sound enough, in fact two or three never got to bed at all.

Bertram was master of the ceremonies, with Louise as a most useful assistant. As I said before, all were flushed with excitement and ready for anything; they were all of the most aristocratic families, and our blue blood seemed fairly to course through our veins. When all had assembled in Louise's apartment they found her attired in a simple, long *chemise de nuit*. "Ladies and gentlemen," she said, "I believe we are all agreed for an out and out romp; you see my costume, how do you like it?" and a most wicked smile, "I hope it does not display the contour of my figure too much," drawing it tightly about her so as to show the outline of her beautiful buttocks, and also displaying a pair of ravishing legs in pink silk stockings.

"Bravo! Bravo! Bravo Louise! We will follow your example," burst from all sides. Each one skipped back to his or her room and reappeared in mufti; but the tails of the young gentlemen's shirts caused a deal of laughter, by being too short.

LOUISE.– "Well, I'm sure, gentlemen, I did not think your undergarments were so indecently short."

Bertram, with a laugh, caught hold of his cousin's chemise, and tore a great piece off all around, so that she was in quite a short smock, which only half-covered her fair bottom.

Louise was crimson with blushes, and half inclined to be angry, but recovering herself, she laughed, "Ah! Bert, what a shame to serve me so, but I don't mind if you make us all alike."

The girls screamed, and the gentlemen made a rush; it was a most exciting scene; the young ladies retaliated by tearing the shirts of their tormentors, and this first skirmish only ended when the whole company were reduced to a complete state of nudity; all were in blushes as they gazed upon the variety of male and female charms exposed to view.

BERTRAM, advancing with a bumper of champagne.– "We've all heard of *Nuda Veritas*, now let's drink to her health; the first time we are in her company, I'm sure she will be most charming and agreeable."

All joined in this toast, the wine inflamed our desires, there was not a male organ present but what was in a glorious state of erection.

LOUISE.– "Look, ladies, what a lot of impudent fellows, they need not think we are going to surrender anyhow to their youthful lust; they shall be all blindfolded, and then we will arm ourselves with good birch rods, then let it be everyone for themselves and Cupid's dart for us all."

"Hear, hear," responded on all sides, and handkerchiefs were soon tied over their eyes, and seven good birch rods handed round to the ladies. "Now, gentlemen, catch who you can," laughed Louise, slashing right and left into the manly group, her example being followed by the other girls; the room was quite large enough and a fine romp ensued, the girls were as lithe and active as young fawns, and for a long time sorely tried the patience of their male friends, who tumbled about in all directions, only to get an extra dose of birch on their plump posteriors before they could regain their feet.

At last the Honble. Miss Vavasour stumbled over a prostrate gentleman, who happened to be the young Marquis of Bucktown, who grasped her firmly round the waist, and clung to his prize, as a shower of cuts greeted the writhing pair.

"Hold, hold," cried Louise, "she's fairly caught and must submit to be offered as a victim on the Altar of Love."

Kate quickly wheeled a small soft couch into the centre of the room.

The gentlemen pulled off their bandages, and all laughingly assisted to place the pair in position; the lady underneath with a pillow under her buttocks, and the young marquis, on his knees, fairly planted between her thighs. Both were novices, but a more beautiful couple it would be impossible to conceive; he was a fine young fellow of eighteen, with dark hair and eyes, whilst her brunette style of complexion was almost a counterpart of his; their eyes were similar also, and his instrument, as well as her cunny, were finely ornamented with soft curly black hair; with the skin drawn back, the firey purple head of his cock looked like a large ruby, as, by Bertram's suggestion, he presented it to her luscious-looking vermilion gap, the lips of which were just slightly open as she lay with her legs apart.

The touch seemed to electrify her, the blushing face turned to a still deeper crimson as the dart of love slowly entered the outwarks of her virginity. Bert continued to act as mentor, by whispering in the young gallant's ear, who also was covered with blushes, but feeling his steed fairly in contact with the throbbing matrix of the lovely girl beneath him, he at once plunged forward to the attack, pushing, shoving, and clasping her round the body with all his strength, whilst he tried to sti- fle her cries of pain by glueing his lips to hers. It was a case of *Veni, Vidi, Vici*. His onset was too impetuous to be withstood, and she lay in such a passive favourable position that the network of her hymen was broken at the first charge, and he was soon in full possession up to the roots of his hair. He rested a moment, she opened her eyes, and with a faint smile said, "Ah! It was indeed sharp, but I can already begin to feel the pleasures of love. Go on now, dear boy, our example will soon fire the others to imitate us," heaving up her bottom as a challenge, and press- ing him fondly to her bosom. They ran a delightful course, which filled us all with voluptuous excitement, and as they died away in a mutual spend, someone put out the lights. All was laughing confusion, gentle- men trying to catch a prize, kissing and sighing.

I felt myself seized by a strong arm, a hand groped for my cunny, whilst a whisper in my ear said: "How delightful! It's you, dear little

Beatrice. I can't make a mistake, as yours is the only hairless thing in the company. Kiss me, dear, I'm bursting to be into your tight little affair." Lips met lips in a luscious kiss. We found ourselves close to Louise's bed, my companion put me back on it, and taking my legs under his arms, was soon pushing his way up my longing cunny. I nipped him as tightly as possible; he was in ecstasies and spent almost directly, but keeping his place, he put me, by his vigorous action, into a perfect frenzy of love. Spend seemed to follow spend, till we had each of us done it six times, and the last time I so forgot myself as to fairly bite his shoulder in delight. At length he withdrew, without telling his name. The room was still in darkness, and love engagements were going on all round. I had two more partners after that, but only one go with each. I shall never forget that night as long as a breath remains in my body.

Next day I found out, through Bert, that Charlie Vavasour had been my first partner, and that he himself believed he had had his cousin in the melee, which she afterwards admitted to me was a fact, although she thought he did not know it, and the temptation to enjoy her cousin was too much for her.

This orgie has been the means of establishing a kind of secret society amongst the circle of our friends. Anyone who gives a pressure of the hand and asks: "Do you remember Bert's birthday?" is free to indulge in love with those who understand it, and I have since been present at many repetitions of that birthday fun.

Helen

The merry month of May has always been famous for its propitious influence over the voluptuous senses of the fairer sex.

My uncle's is a nice country residence, standing in large grounds of its own, and surrounded by small fields of arable and pasture land, interspersed by numerous interesting copses, through which run footpaths and shady walks, where you are not likely to meet anyone in a month. I shall not trouble my readers with the name of the locality, or they may go pleasure hunting for themselves. Well, my cousin Helen, was my favourite part of my visits, first for the playing we did together and later for reasons that shall soon become clear. After dinner, the first day of my arrival, paterfamilias and mamma both indulged in a snooze in their armchair, whilst Helen and I took a stroll in the grounds. She was a finely developed blonde, with deep blue eyes, pouting red lips, and a full heaving bosom, which to me looked like a perfect volcano of smothered desires. As I had not been there for nearly three years, I requested Helen to show me the improvements in the grounds before we went in to tea.

We were now out of earshot, in a shady walk, so I went on a little more freely. "But, surely you, coz, are in love. I can tell it by your liquid eye and heaving bosom."

A scarlet flush shot over her features at my allusion to her finely moulded bosom, but it was evidently pleasing, and far from offensive, to judge by her playfully spoken, "Oh! Robert, for shame, sir!"

We were a good distance away by this time, and a convenient seat stood near, so throwing my arms around the blushing girl, I kissed her ruby lips, and drawing her with me, said, "Now, Helen, dear, I'm your cousin and old playfellow, I couldn't help kissing those beautiful lips, which I might always make free with when we were little boy and girl together; now you shall confess all before I let you go."

"But I've nothing to confess, sir."

"Do you never think of love, Helen? Look me in the face if you can say it's a stranger to your bosom," putting my hand familiarly round her neck till my right hand rested on one of the panting globes of her bosom.

She turned her face to mine, suffused as it was by a deeper blush than ever, as her dark blue eyes met mine, in a fearless search of my meaning, but instead of speaking in response to this mute appeal, I kissed her rapturously, sucking in the fragrance of her sweet breath till she fairly trembled with emotion.

It was just beginning to get dusk, my hands were caressing the white, firm flesh of her beautiful neck, slowly working their way towards the heaving bubbies a little lower down; at last I whispered, "What a fine, what a lovely bust you have developed since I saw you last, dear Helen, you won't mind your cousin, will you, when everything used to be so free to each other; besides, what harm can there be in it?"

She seemed on fire, a thrill of emotion seemed to shoot through both of us, and for several moments she lay almost motionless in my arms, with one hand resting on my thigh. Priapus was awake and ready for business, but she suddenly aroused herself, saying, "We must never stop here. Let us walk round or they will suspect something."

"When shall we be alone again, darling? We must arrange that before we go in," I said quickly.

It was impossible to keep her on the seat, but as we walked on she said, musingly, "To-morrow morning we might go for a stroll before lunch; I shall have to mind the tarts and pies next week."

I gave her another hug and a kiss, as I said, "How delightful that will be; what a dear, thoughtful girl you are, Helen."

"Mind, sir, how you behave to-morrow, not so much kissing, or I shan't take you for a second walk; here we are at the house."

Next morning was gloriously warm and fine; as soon as breakfast was over we started for our stroll, being particularly minded by papa to be back in good time for luncheon.

I gradually drew out my beautiful cousin, till our conversation got exceedingly warm, the hot blood rushing in waves of crimson over her shamefaced visage.

"What a rude boy you have grown Robert, since you were here last; I can't help blushing at the way you run on, sir!" she exclaimed at last.

"Helen, my darling," I replied, "what can be more pleasing than to talk of fun with pretty girls, the beauties of their legs and bosoms, and all about them? How I should love to see your lovely calf at this moment, especially after the glimpses I have already had of a divine ankle," saying which I threw myself under a shady tree, close by a gate in a meadow, and drew the half-resisting girl down on the grass at my side, and kissed her passionately, as I murmured, "Oh! Helen, what is there worth living for like the sweets of love?"

Her lips met mine in a fiery embrace, but suddenly disengaging herself, her eyes cast down, and looking awfully abashed, she stammered out, "What is it? What do you mean, Robert?"

"Ah, coz dear, can you be so innocent? Feel here the dart of love all impatient to enter the mossy grotto between your thighs," I whispered, placing her hand upon my prick, which I had suddenly let out of the restraining trousers. "How you sigh; grasp it in your hand, dear, is it possible that you do not understand what it is for?"

Her face was crimson to the roots of her hair, as her hand grasped my tool, and her eyes seemed to start with terror at the sudden apparition of Mr. John Thomas; so that taking advantage of her speechless confusion my own hand, slipping under her clothes, soon had possession of her mount, and in spite of the nervous contraction of her thighs, the forefinger searched out the virgin clitoris.

"Ah! oh! oh!! Robert don't; what are you about?"

"It's all love, dear, open your thighs a wee bit and see what pleasure my finger will make you experience," I again whispered, smothering her with renewed and luscious kisses, thrusting the velvet tip of my tongue between her lips.

"Oh! oh! you will hurt!" she seemed to sigh rather than speak, as her legs relaxed a little of their spasmodic contraction.

My lips continued glued to hers, our otherwise disengaged arms clasped each other closely round the waist, her hand holding my affair in a kind of convulsive grasp, whilst my fingers were busy with clitoris and cunny; the only audible sound resembling a mixture of kisses and sighs, till all in a moment I felt her crack deluged with a warm, creamy spend whilst my own juice spurted over her hand and dress in loving sympathy.

In a short while we recovered our composure a little, and I then explained to her that the melting ecstasy she had just felt was only a slight foretaste of the joy I could give her, by inserting my member in her cunny. My persuasive eloquence and the warmth of her desires soon overcame all maiden fears and scruples; then for fear of damaging her dress, or getting the green stain of the grass on the knees of my light trousers, I persuaded her to stand up by the gate and allow me to enter behind. She hid her face in her hands on the top rail of the gate, as I slowly raised her dress; what glories were unfolded to view, my prick's stiffness was renewed in an instant at the sight of her delicious buttocks, so beautifully relieved by the white of her pretty drawers; as I opened them and exposed the flesh, I could see the lips of her plump pouting cunny, deliciously feathered, with soft light down, her lovely legs, drawers, stockings, pretty boots, making a *tout ensemble*, which as I write and describe them cause Mr. Priapus to swell in my breeches; it was a most delicious sight. I knelt and kissed her bottom, slit, and everything my tongue could reach, it was all mine, I stood up and prepared to take possession of the seat of love – when, alas! a sudden shriek from Helen, her clothes dropped, all my arrangements were upset in a moment; a bull had unexpectedly appeared on the opposite side of the gate, and frightened my love by the sudden application of his cold, damp nose to her forehead. It is too much to contemplate that scene even now.

Helen was ready to faint as she screamed, "Robert! Robert! Save me from the horrid beast!" I comforted and reassured her as well as I was able, and seeing that we were on the safe side of the gate, a few loving kisses soon set her all right. We continued our walk, and soon spying out a favourable shady spot, I said: "Come, Helen dear, let us sit down and recover from the startling interruption; I am sure, dear, you must still feel very agitated, besides I must get you now to compensate me for the rude disappointment."

She seemed to know that her hour had come; the hot blushes swept in crimson waves across her lovely face, as she cast down her eyes, and permitted me to draw her down by my side on a mossy knoll, and we lay side by side, my lips glued to hers in a most ardent embrace.

"Helen! Oh! Helen!" I gasped. "Give me the tip of your tongue, love." She tipped me the velvet without the slightest hesitation, drawing, at the same time, what seemed a deep sigh of delightful anticipation as she yielded to my slightest wish. I had one arm under her head, and with the other I gently removed her hat, and threw aside my own golgotha, kissing and sucking at her delicious tongue all the while. Then I placed one of her hands on my ready cock, which was in a bursting state, saying, as I released her tongue for a moment:

"There, Helen, take the dart of love in your hand." She grasped it nervously, as she softly murmured: "Oh, Robert, I'm so afraid; and yet – oh yet, dearest, I feel, I die, I must taste the sweets of love, this forbidden fruit," her voice sinking almost to a whisper, as she pressed and passed her hand up and down my shaft. My hand was also busy finding its way under her clothes as I again glued my mouth to hers, and sucked at her tongue till I could feel her vibrate all over with the excess of her emotion. My hand, which had taken possession of the seat of bliss, being fairly deluged with her warm glutinous spendings.

"My love; my life! I must kiss you there, and taste the nectar of love," I exclaimed, as I snatched my lips from hers, and reversing my position, buried my face between her unresisting thighs. I licked up the luscious spendings with rapturous delight from the lips of her tight little cunny, then my tongue found its way further, till it tickled her sensitive clitoris, and put her into a frenzy of mad desire for still further enjoyment; she twisted her legs over my head, squeezing my head between her firm plump thighs in an ecstasy of delight.

Wetting my finger in her luscious crack, I easily inserted it in her beautifully wrinkled brown bum-hole, and keeping my tongue busy in titillating the stiff little clitoris, I worked her up into such a furious state of desire that she clutched my cock and brought it to her mouth, as I lay over her to give her the chance of doing so; she rolled her tongue round the purple head, and I could also feel the loving playful bite of her pearly teeth. It was the acme of erotic enjoyment. She came again in another luscious flood of spendings, whilst she eagerly sucked every drop of my sperm as it burst from my excited prick.

We both nearly fainted from the excess of our emotions, and lay quite exhausted for a few moments, till I felt her dear lips again pressing and sucking my engine of love. The effect was electric; I was as stiff as ever.

"Now, darling, for the real stroke of love," I exclaimed. Shifting my position, and parting her quivering thighs, so that I could kneel between them. My knees were placed upon her skirts so as to preserve them from the grass stain. She lay before me in a delightful state of anticipation, her beautiful face all blushes of shame, and the closed eyelids, fringed with their long dark lashes, her lips slightly open, and the finely developed, firm, plump globes of her bosom heaving in a state of tumultuous excitement. It was ravishing, I felt mad with lust, and could no longer put off the actual consummation. I could not contain myself. Alas; poor maidenhead! Alas! for your virginity! I brought my cock to the charge, presented the head just slightly between the lips of her vagina. A shudder of delight seemed to pass through her frame at the touch of my weapon, as her eyes opened, and she whispered, with a soft, loving smile, "I know it will hurt, but Robert, dear Robert, be both firm and kind. I must have it, if it kills me." Throwing her arms around my neck, she drew my lips to hers, as she thrust her tongue into my mouth with all the abandon of love, and shoved up her bottom to meet my charge.

I placed one hand under her buttocks, whilst, with the other, I kept my affair straight to the mark; then pushing vigorously, the head entered about an inch, till it was chock up to the opposing hymen.

She gave a start of pain, but her eyes gazed into mine with a most encouraging look.

"Throw your legs over my back, dear," I gasped, scarcely relinquishing her tongue for a moment. Her lovely thighs turned round me in a spasmodic frenzy of determination to bear the worst. I gave a ruthless push, just as her bottom heaved up to meet me, and the deed was done. King Priapus had burst through all obstacles to our enjoyment. She gave a subdued shriek of agonized pain, and I felt myself throbbing in possession of her inmost charms.

"You darling! You love me! My brave Helen, how well you stood the pain. Let us lay still for a moment or two, and then for the joys of love," I exclaimed, as I kissed her face, forehead, eyes, and mouth in a transport of delight, at feeling the victory so soon accomplished.

Presently I could feel the tight sheath of her vagina contracting on my cock in the most delicious manner. This challenge was too much for my impetuous steed. He gave a gentle thrust. I could see by the spasm of pain which passed over her beautiful face, that it was still painful to her, but, restraining my ardour, I worked very gently, although my lust was so maddening that I could not restrain a copious spend; so I sank on her bosom in love's delicious lethargy.

It was only for a few moments, I could feel her tremble beneath me with voluptuous ardour, and the sheath being now well lubricated, we commenced a delightful bout of ecstatic fucking. All her pain was forgotten, the wounded parts soothed by the flow of my semen now only revelled in the delightful friction of love; she seemed to boil over in spendings, my delighted cock revelled in it, as he thrust in and out with all my manly vigour; we spent three or four times in a delirium of voluptuousness, till I was fairly vanquished by her impetuosity, and begged her to be moderate, and not to injure herself by excessive enjoyment.

"Oh! can it be possible to hurt one's self by such a delightful pleasure?" she sighed, then seeing me withdraw my limp tool from her still longing cunt, she smiled archly, as she said with a blush,

"Pardon my rudeness, dear Robert, but I fear it is you who are most injured after all; look at your blood-stained affair."

"You lovely little simpleton," I said, kissing her rapturously, "that's your own virgin blood; let me wipe you, darling," as I gently applied my handkerchief to her pouting slit, and afterwards to my own cock.

"This, dearest Helen, I shall treasure up as the proofs of your virgin love, so delightfully surrendered to me this day," exhibiting the ensanguined *mouchoir* to her gaze.

We now arose from our soft mossy bed, and mutually assisted each other to remove all traces of our love engagement.

We returned to the house, Helen's cheeks blushing and carrying a beautiful flush of health, and her mama remarked that our walk had evidently done her very great good, little guessing that her daughter, like our first mother Eve, had that morning tasted of the forbidden fruit, and was greatly enlightened and enlivened thereby.

A Parisian Initiation

Tout le monde were in Paris when we arrived some ten days later, for it was well past Easter and the season was in full swing. To be seen in the Bois de Boulogne around noon was essential if one were to be counted among the Upper Ten Thousand of France. Before we did so, however, Pearl was insistent that we clothe ourselves a la mode, being none too pleased with the gowns and hats we had brought, for Paris fashions change so rapidly that one must ever keep up with them.

Lord Andrew's (our patron) purse suffered much depletion as a result of this, but the outcome was so much to his taste that he averred it well worth while, being thankful perhaps that we had not gone to Monsieur Worth but to a smaller salon where decolletage was accepted as a sine qua non of revealment, which Monsieur Worth evidently abhorred, having decreed with a woodenness that came, I am sure, from his English origins that he dressed only ladies. Being told this, Maude responded that we were not ladies but were enjoying ourselves. Both of course were true, but I admired her for her spirit which had so risen that she seemed to care not a jot what she did, provided it was not in public.

For my own part I was as a bird released from a cage All about us were strangers and it was indeed in this sense as if we were attending a perpetual masque. Pearl had done her work well with my parents, for neither made any remonstrance upon my going, Papa warning me only to take care of all that I did.

As to our accommodation, there could have been none finer. Maude and I possessed a suite of our own in a hotel close to the Champs d'Elysees while Lord Andrew modestly had a separate one from that of Pearl. That we would not long suffer the privations of isolation was made clear to us by our official "chaperone" upon conducting Maude and I on the first morning to the coutouriere.

"You must be seen at your finest not only fully adorned but in great part unadorned. This is to say, my pets, that your lingerie must be of the finest and the most seductive," she declared. Being of the same mind, we acceded to her every wish, the perfect undergarment—as she explained to us—being a guepiere or waist corset which constricted that part of our bodies tightly and so gave the most alluring prominence to our bottoms, hips and breasts. The latter remained uncovered, for the frilled top of the guepiere supported them beneath. At the lower extremity the glossy black corsets were cut and trimmed in a subtle upward curve so that the pubic mound was equally left revealed. So attired, and wearing naught else but stockings and shoes, Maude and I paraded ourselves with many an admiring giggle in a commodious back room of the salon before tall mirrors.

"Are we not then to wear drawers?" asked Maude of Pearl who with the proprietess of the establishment had seen to our fittings and chosen different colours for us, ranging from pink through blue to purple, and finally black.

"Why no, for how the effect would be spoiled you might well judge by trying drawers on, Maude."

Indeed, it was seen to be so, for drawers were ever large and would conceal the pretty lower portion of the corsets, so rendering the appearance bizarre rather than attractive. All colours were tried until Maude and I wore the black corsets which with matching silk stockings gave the most fetching effect that might be imagined. Pearl indeed appeared to think so, for she made no bones about standing between us before the mirrors and cupping our brazen, naked bottoms while giving praise to our charms.

The constriction of the corset first made me quite breathless, but finally pleased me.

"You must continue to wear them now in order to become accustomed to them, for all the most forward young ladies of Paris wear them," declared Pearl, turning then to the proprietess who herself was dressed most elegantly. "Is that not so, Madame?" she asked. Agreeing that it was, the lady then bade us be seated as we were in order to bring us refreshments. Being all females together, nothing was amiss in this and so we quaffed the wine she brought while warming our bare bottoms on the velour of her chairs.

Having a taste for such a good wine as came to my palate, I drank well as did Maude. It warmed me exceedingly and so much so that I began to feel drowsy. The crystal lights around the room verily danced and seemed to glitter even more brightly than I thought them to. Finding myself somewhat in a daze, and being dimly conscious that Maude had rather slumped in her chair, I heard whisperings by my side between Pearl and the proprietess.

"Comme elles sont jolies! Il va les sodomise maintenant?" I heard.

"Oui. Leurs cons ont avait deja etc lubriques. Il faut qu'elles etudient leurs lecons Grecques, Madame. Il veut bien bourrer servant pine entre leurs fesses," came Pearl's response.

Clouded as my mind was, the purport of her words came to me but dimly. I commanded little enough French, but sufficient to comprehend that our bottoms were to be put to pillage since—as Pearl had so graciously announced—our cunts had already been lubricated. Who "he" was I could only guess and my bottom cheeks fairly tightened at the anticipation of receiving Lord Andrew's considerable pestle in my derriere. My head swam. I endeavoured to glance at Maude and succeeded in only half doing so. She sat beside me, her eyes glazed, mouth open. Even then she looked remarkably attractive. It was impossible not to do so in our little corsets with our titties bulging out over the tops, our bushes well displayed, and our legs made all the more attractive in their black silk stockings which peaked to fine points where the suspenders from the corsets drew them taut.

"Alors, il faut preparer la route," declared the proprietess then.

I had noticed upon our entrance to the room two padded bars which stood supported on either side. I had thought little of them, fancying them for the odd pieces of apparatus that adorn such places and over which cloaks and other garments might be put. In an instant, however, it came clear to me that in all probability it was we who were to be put over them in order—as the lady had said—that our "routes" might be "prepared." I had not time to stir, however, before a young man entered upon some signal he had evidently been given. His years could have counted not many more than my own and he was naked. Even more noticeable than this fact, however, was his penis which stood upright, long and extremely slender, having almost the appearance of a church spire. So small was the knob that it was less in circumference than the root of his penis which was evidently strong enough and stout enough for what was intended.

Maude being less in her senses than I was then lifted up by the lady while Pearl attended to my rising and led me tottering to my fate.

"Wh...aaaaart?" I asked foolishly.

"Come, darling, you are about to be initiated in a way that will serve you well, for Phillippe will see to you both.

He has opened many a young lady's bottom to pleasure, as he will yours."

"Oh!" I cried, or at least I believe that I did, for at that Maude's voice rose above my own, but were there to have been any protests they would have arrived far too late. I being bent over by Pearl, my cousin followed suit. The bars, being made for the purpose, as I have no doubt, saw to it that our bellies were not constrained—being pressed down upon thick velvet pads—while our bottoms rose in offering.

"No! what is to do?" cried Maude, albeit in a somewhat drowsy fashion, her shoulders being well bent down by "Madame" as my own were by Pearl. So close indeed were my cousin and I that our hips touched warmly and so provided what little comfort we momentarily had. Being thought perhaps to be the most recalcitrant, Maude was taken first. Advancing upon her with solemn mien, Phillippe took her hips and thus prevented her from waggling them too much. Thereat, "Madame" with her free hand sprinkled his spire-like prick with a little oil, some of which proving surplus he proceeded to rub around Maude's most secret aperture.

At this she moaned and bumped her hip to mine, I being just able to see by virtue of inclining my head sideways.

"Hold her well, Madame," exclaimed then Phillippe to Madame, to my uttermost astonishment.

"Of course, *cheri*—do I not always? Put it to her slowly and she will take the pleasure of it. Ah, what a good boy you are to do it so nicely!"

This ludicrous remark having been made, there came a shriek from Maude at the first touch of that virile young organ to her rosette. Being patently well accomplished in the art, Phillippe made no ado about then sleeking in his knob, which accommodation, due to his slim size was— as I found for myself—by no means difficult. Maude, however, cried out again and would have risen had not Madame held her down more strongly.

"Is she tight, Phillippe?"

"Superbly, Madame. Oh, but it is not too difficult—I am almost half in."

Indeed, so he seemed to be from Maude's wild contortions. Her breath rasped from her mouth, I making then to wriggle up but being firmly constrained by Pearl from doing so. Having then my head pressed further down, I could see naught but could hear well enough from Phillippe's soft panting and Maude's cries that the dire deed was proceeding. A small, sharp screech from my cousin and he was full embedded, whereat he held her thus, her moans bubbling out the while.

"Hold well, dear, you have parted the cheeks and her bottom is filled. She will learn soon enough the delightful sustenance of it. Move now a little," abjured Madame.

"Yes, Madame," Phillippe gritted amidst ever-rising moans from Maude whose hip bumped to mine at every stroke. I could not conceive what it felt like for her, but was soon to know. Evidently very well schooled in his art, Phillippe gave her a dozen long thrusts and then, upon command, withdrew. His organ, as I felt, must have been literally steaming, though I suspect that such ideas came to me in aftermath rather than then.

"Do not tighten yourself, Bethany," Pearl murmured to me. A finger came to my rosehole that I knew was Phillippe's. Artfully he guided a thin film of warm oil all about my bottomhole and then within, by means of his fingertip, making me jerk like a young filly, as indeed I was often to be called when in my skittish moments. I tensed myself but to little avail. Phillippe was evidently hungry for this second assault or perhaps thought my bottom even more attractive than Maude's. I felt his knob. I yielded, I succumbed, knowing perhaps that resistance would but prolong the endeavour. Ah, what a sensation! It was as if a long warm cork were being impelled within me. The breath flooded out from my lungs. I made to squeal but could not. Holding my back down with one hand, Pearl stroked my hair with the other.

"Good girl—press your bottom out to him," she murmured.

Even though loathe to show myself doing so, I obeyed. The slow entry of his cock at first brought with it a strange stinging sensation that however quickly passed away with every persuasive inch. I choked, I cried out. Feeling the movement of my bottom cheeks towards him, Phillippe grew emboldened. He had some four inches to go. In one upward lunge I received all. The sensation was momentous. My head shot up—unimpeded then by Pearl's hand—and then sank again. My back rippled. I felt my nether cheeks drawn tight into his belly. I was corked. I was the recipient of that which I had surreptitiously viewed at Lord Andrew's house. I squeezed, I tried to eject him, but in vain. The constrictions of my bottomhole but served to heighten his pleasure.

"Ah, Madame, *je t'en prie!*" he exclaimed.

"Yes, Madame, let him for he has toasted the one and may now inject the other," exclaimed Pearl who, as she said afterwards, could not hold herself in at the delightful vista of seeing me so upon his prong.

"Let me hold his balls then, for he likes that—do you not, Phillippe?" the lady purred. At that Maude who had remained curiously motionless, slumped sideways, but falling upon cushions did herself no harm and no doubt had a fine view of the proceedings, looking up as she was between Phillippe's legs.

Such a scene then occurred as I only afterwards painted fully in my mind. Raising her skirt and taking hold of his balls in a light cupping gesture (which I afterwards learned from Pearl), the lady massaged her servant gently while he in turn groped her own bottom, whereat no doubt he had learned his art. Not being minded to remain spectator, Pearl then leaned sideways over me and seized Madame's lips. I, being bent over beneath all, felt only the slow shunting of Phillippe's prick which, inserting itself rhythmically back and forth—impelled by his Madame's hand—made my passage seem suddenly freer.

I confess to more pleasure in the act than I at the time allowed myself to feel. All above me were gasps and the moist sound of kisses the while that my bottom was urged back and forth. A hand groped my cunny. It was Madame's. Her fingertip cunningly sought my clitoris. I moaned the more. Her own was being assailed by Pearl's long-reaching hand, while her own bottomhole was in turn titillated by Phillippe's finger. All of this being visible to Maude who described it to me vividly afterwards. I was yet the recipient of the best. The initial stinging I had felt turned decidedly to pleasure. The gentle massaging of my clitoris assured all. My knees buckled—thus pressing my bottom ever more eagerly to Phillippe's assaults. I rendered my love juices, not once but seemingly endlessly until with fervent groans from he who was corking me, and much luscious kissing and fondling above, I received the fine spurting of his come which warmed and lubricated me deliciously until my bottom and loins all but melted.

Thus did my initiation advance, all being conducted with such ease and grace as if we were performing a gavotte. Maude for her part pretended to faint, but was soon brought around. No doubt she was surprised to find me not in tears nor writhing torturously. Phillippe then discreetly disappeared, his cock dripping not a little.

"Come, what a sport we have had—we must return now," announced Pearl gaily as if we had been at a ladylike tournament of archery or such like. I indeed had received the arrow, so may have felt that the simile was well placed. My bottom burned within, though not uncomfortably. Maude made more of it in the carriage that transported us back, declaring that she could not sit for a week, although she was doing such right then.

"That was but a prelude to your fuller pleasures. You will have larger there and in not too short a time. It is known as the Greek or Turkish method, though others more crudely call it buggery or sodomy. Your bottom has as much elasticity as your cunny and the pleasures of receiving tongues and cocks in that way are infinite," declared Pearl.

"A tongue? Would that be so pleasurable there?" I asked.

"Why indeed so, if it is done properly and the tongue neatly curled to tease your rose. It is called indeed *feuille de rose* in Paris and is a delicate act of *l'amour* much sought after. One lady does it to another before the cock is put in, for then the route is nicely moistened," said Pearl.

"Phillippe came in her—I know he did," Maude said and evidently knew not whether to laugh or not though she continued to wriggle more than I. Such an effect was to be expected at first, Pearl told us, but would not last. Our bottoms being accustomed to receiving the male plunger would soon settle. Moreover, she added, there were certain advantages to be taken of it since a young lady could not become enceinte in that way and so could absorb as much of the male sperm as she desired.

"Could you really feel it, then?" Maude asked, wrinkling her nose as though she were not certain that she liked the idea or not.

"Oh yes, it bubbled and entered deliciously in me. I felt it even more than in my cunny," I said, which remark caused me to realise the truth of it, as saying things often does.

"So then, you have both learned a little more," laughed Pearl who knew us to be greater novices than we then liked to believe.

"Ho! I do hope Lord Andrew is not to learn of this, though I cannot imagine that you could tell him," said Maude.

At this Pearl laughed, for she was as much aware as I by now of how my cousin's moments of hypocrisy came and went like grains of dust dancing in a sunbeam.

"All shall be for the best in all possible worlds, Maude, as Voltaire said, for we are in Paris now and enjoyment is not counted here a sin. Bottoms must buck to cocks and pussies must come to pricks," Pearl replied, thus unwittingly echoing the selfsame sentiments that my cousin had uttered to me when she felt safe enough out of sight of a rearing penis. I indeed nudged Maude at this and she had the grace to blush. Being more open in our talk with Pearl, more could be said and our tongues became ever bolder as we spoke of what had occurred and what might be yet to follow. It had been a signal adventure, both elegant and yet bizarre—the two elements meeting so pleasurably as to make the whole affair more piquant. To be taken by surprise, I found, was somewhat to my taste, as it was to be to Maude's. Putting up every appearance of fretting, as she often did to disguise her desires, made it the more engaging to see her put to a cock. Such moods added salt to the flavour of our adventures.

Lessons on a Train

"**T**ickets, please. Two first class to H———. Thank you, sir. Yes, I can lock the door if you like. Best train this, sir; no stoppage before arriving at C———. The next is H———."

Uncle (for that is what I called Lord Balliston, though he was really a second cousin) took me on his knee. We were off at last. We chose a Tuesday. We avoided all the weekend people—we were alone.

"How fast the train goes! I feel so happy now. I am sure this trip will do you good, Uncle. We both seemed to want air."

"It will also benefit you, dear child. London seasons are dearly bought as to their enjoyment, when you consider the wear and tear. What pretty little boots, my darling Jenny! How well they fit! What graceful outline of instep and heel! What delicate kid, and then how soft and flexible! You are so simply, yet so beautifully dressed, you would rouse an anchorite."

"If I can only succeed in pleasing my darling Uncle, I shall have arrived at the zenith of my desires. Oh, but you are roused already—wicked, naughty Uncle."

My hand was on his limb. I unbuttoned his trousers.

"Does my dear Uncle like his little Jenny to comfort this unruly thing? Does he like my soft touches? Do they give him pleasure? How stiff this is!"

He lolled back in his well-cushioned seat as the train sped along. I seized on his stiff limb and released it from its confinement. Uncle closed his eyes and enjoyed my toying. The sturdy weapon stood boldly up in the bright sunlight as it streamed in at the carriage window. I rubbed it up and down. I closed my softly gloved hand upon it. The head grew purple with excitement. A bit of fluid emerged from the tip. How I longed to lick it! I stopped my movements.

"Where are we going tonight, Uncle dear? What have you arranged?"

"We have tickets for H————. We'll sleep there. I know an old-fashioned hotel in the town with an interior garden, and plenty of fresh air. Just the place in which to repose for a couple of days."

"How delightful! This sweet thing must not be too impatient. Little Jenny will give it all the pleasure in her power tonight, but my dear Uncle must not overexert himself."

Two bedrooms adjoining—a delicious sitting room looking into a well-kept garden, in which the budding flowers already blossomed brightly. The rooms well stuffed with rich old furniture—everything polished, bright, and clean.

"My darling! My beautiful Jenny! Tonight!"

We dined well. I had the woman's weakness for sparkling wine. He liked it also. The cuisine was good. We were well served. We strolled in the garden. And by the sea. We came back to our rooms refreshed. We enjoyed our tea. We sat at the open window and inhaled the pure fresh air of the country perfumed with the sweetness of the flowers below.

I was already in bed. He came quickly from his room. I extended my arms. I opened the bedclothes. I showed him my form which only my fine lace-trimmed *chemise* served to cover. He flew into my embrace. Our bodies were in closest contact. I warmed him in my naked arms. He was radiant with lust to enjoy me.

"My Jenny! My darling! My child!"

He toyed with my breasts. He sucked the rosy little nipples. I tickled his big balls and caressed the limb already stiff and swollen with desire.

"Is my dear Uncle happy now? Does his little Jenny give him pleasure?"

His breath was agitated—his sighs, his kisses, hot and voluptuous, all denoted his condition. He rose on me. His manly body pressed my light young form. I threw my soft arms around his neck. Our tongues met. Mine slipped between his lips. I opened my thighs to him. The stiff limb pressed open my little parts. He bore in—into my belly.

"Oh, my love, my dearest Uncle! You make me suffer!"

"My beautiful darling! I must—I will!"

His large limb bore upwards. It slipped entirely into me. He was having me to his heart's content. During the act our tongues met again. He writhed on my body. He raised his head. He paused.

"My Jenny! Dearest girl! I am afraid to finish!"

"Have no fear, my dear Uncle. You are killing your little Jenny with pleasure. Let it come! Give it to me—all!"

He thrust his limb in to the balls. I felt it at my womb. He discharged violently. I felt the thrill—the spasms, with which his seed flew into me. My own sensations were celestial. He was giving me the essence of my being. I felt bathed in it. At length we slept. It was still early morning when we woke.

"Let us play a little before we get up. Be my stallion, dear Uncle, and I will be your little mare."

I rose on my hands and knees in the bed. He raised my *chemise*. He passed his palm over my plump posterior. He toyed a moment with my buttocks. He slapped them. He caressed them. Finally he kissed them.

Then he pressed down on me. I felt the stiff insertion of his parts. The knob passed in. He bore furiously up me. His balls beat against my thighs. I could hardly bear his weight. His thrusts drove me forward. My head was buried in the pillows. At last it came. He seized me round the loins. I felt the hot sperm spurting into me with each vibration of his body. He clasped me tight until he had done. We lay some time motionless in the dull torpor which succeeds gratified desire.

By degrees our spirits revived. We talked in a low voice of the subject of our secret connection. There were many things on which I wanted information. I asked many questions relating to the conjunction and the functions of the two sexes, which interested me mightily.

"You ask me what is the spasm which you experience and whether women have seed like men—I will tell you. The first is the crisis of a nervous irritation which is set up partly from outside caress and actual friction, and partly from the imagination acting on the orgasm. Both unite to set in motion the nerves which serve the glands containing the fluid. Women have no seed, properly speaking, and that secretion which they produce has no direct effect in the process of generation. These glands closely resemble those of the throat which are called salivary glands. If you observe a ripe peach, a fine pear, or experience a strong desire for any food towards which your attention is directed, these glands act instantly and sympathetically. You say your mouth "waters" for the thing. The cause and the effect are exactly similar in those glands which secrete the fluid you possess."

"But what purpose does it answer then, if it does nothing towards procreation?"

"There, you go too fast, my child. I do not say it does nothing. On the contrary it may—and probably does—do more than is supposed. What I mean is that it has no absolute necessity in the act of generation, because it is well known that conception is obtained without it. It operates, however, indirectly in preparing the way for the conjunction of the sexes. It takes exactly the part of the salivary glands which enable you to swallow, only that its influence is employed in another direction. These glands can act upon occasion abnormally and without actual contact as we know in the instance of nocturnal emission while dreaming. I have also shown you how the imagination can excite them to secretion on the part of the female. This is an obvious advantage to the performance of the act of generation. In this sense the glands of the female act in the success of the operation."

"I own I was very ignorant of all this, dear Uncle, but you explain it so nicely. When a man spends then, a woman must spend also?"

"By no means. Only too frequently the female may experience no pleasure or gratification at all. Yet conception may take place. It often does so. Professionally loose women lose the ability to enjoy from overindulgence and the prostitution of the act of generation to their everyday routine. The fluid, in such cases, ceases to secrete. Artificial means are employed to replace it. Habit brings satiety—satiety destroys pleasure. The two are inconsistent. There is no longer any yearning for the peach. The saliva ceases to flow. The functions misused are injured and the original purpose of nature rendered abortive."

"That is very interesting to your little Jenny, dear Uncle. I shall take care that all my functions are in good order whenever we are together. There is one thing more to understand. Can you tell me how it is that a woman misses conception in the act?"

"That is too wide a subject for me to explain off-hand. It is essentially a physiological one. Many causes may be at work. There is the cause I have already named. The fault may be on the part of the male, or by reason of the condition or the health of the female. The most frequent cause, however, is that already described, or that the female is barren."

"Are many women barren?"

"More probably than are suspected. The present fashionable tendency to turn girls into tomboys; the exercises, athletic and vigorous, which they now patronize is undoubtedly producing that effect, and unfitting the English woman for the softer and more natural duties of life. She is annually becoming taller, slimmer, more angular, more devoid of the marked contrasts of sex. The bust has already gone, and the dressmaker is called in with padding. False breasts occupy prominent places in London shop windows. Devices of all kinds are adopted to hide the deformity. It exists and it is on the increase. The result must be a sensible diminution of the population. Young married people now have become very alert to the conveniences of limiting the number of their offspring. You hear everywhere the society remark, "a pigeon's pair—so interesting, you know; just two and no more." Glances are exchanged—smiles exchanged. The dear creatures are perfectly au courant as to both cause and effect. There are, of course, other causes why women miss conception. Apart from artificial means purposely employed, there remains the ever increasing condition of barrenness."

"You think many women are barren then, Uncle dear?"

"No doubt many are so. Only look at the number of infructuous marriages. If you ask the cause, I have given you one. The effects of unsuitable climate for Europeans may be another, but considering the matter in a society point of view, from one cause or another, no doubt we can entertain that the habits of life nowadays contribute to this condition. The deformity of the body by tight lacing is another cause. A very slight misplacement of the mouth of the womb is sufficient to prevent impregnation. This may be natural or produced as I describe."

"I am not tight-laced, dear Uncle. You can pass your hand down inside my stays."

Soon he had undressed me and was playing with my parts. "I know, my darling. Your figure is most exceptional for an English girl. You are formed for a Venus, but for all that you may be incapable of procreating by some such impediment as that of which I speak. However, it is most unlikely. Our precautions are sufficient."

"Take me in your arms again, dear Uncle. Your little Jenny loves you. This dear thing is already stiff again. Let me kiss it. Oh, darling, what pleasure you are giving your little girl. You are sucking my button. It is the center of my sensations. Your tongue is giving me divine enjoyment. Go on! Oh, pray go on, Uncle! Shall I turn round?"

"No, my sweet, remain as you are. Take your pet between your red lips also. Suck! Suck it thus. Oh, that is lovely! It is in your mouth."

We continued mutually until nature relieved us. He discharged a shower of seed. I received all. I returned him a dose which he called the nectar of the gods.

Molly and Laura

It was in one of the big amusement parks that I first met Molly. Being alone and out for a good time, I contrived to secure the seat next to her on one of the many rides; an acquaintance was soon struck up and at the close of the festivities I was awarded the privilege of escorting her home.

She lived on the other side of the city, and upon seeing my carriage, together with George the valet, her eyes grew wide, and at first I thought she was about to refuse to go with me.

It did not, however, take much persuasion on my part to have her enter my carriage, and once she was seated on the luxurious cushions I knew the battle was won. I asked her if she wished to dine, but she informed me that she would have to arise early as she worked in the downtown district and, as it was already late, she had better hurry right home and leave it for some other time.

It is now time that I give the reader the benefit of a short description, in order that he may form in his mind the nature of the choice prize that had fallen to my lot on that evening.

Her name, as I have related, was Molly. Her nationality: typically American and an up-to-date. Her eyes were of a deep violet hue, with long silken lashes, and she had a cute pert little nose and an adorable pouting mouth.

Her age—well, that is hard to judge, in these days of modern fashion—but I judge she was not much over eighteen, although she stoutly maintained she was fully eighteen.

Her thin, almost transparent dress hardly concealed the perfect contours of her two delicately chiselled breasts, held in tight by a slender brassiere, and the sight of these two tempting mounds of girlish flesh almost made me reach forth to squeeze them, but knowing that too much advance might frighten this tender and demure morsel I restrained myself and contented myself in making a covert survey of her girlish attractions.

Her dress, as I have stated, was very short, as was common with all girls, and as she climbed into the machine, a little of her leg above the stocking top showed. At this glimpse of her bare and glistening flesh, I felt my member throb as though touched with an electric machine.

Seated beside her in the machine, I leaned close to her and felt the magnetism of her person communicate itself to me, then instructing George to take us to the address she had given, I leaned back in the seat and we slowly moved away.

George, my man, who had been in my service for years, was an observing and devoted servant (of this more hereafter) and well knew what was going on in his master's mind, and proceeded less fast than at a walk, in order, as he well surmised, to give me plenty of time to carry out whatever projects I had in mind.

I passed my arm behind her head and allowing it to fall about her waist encountered not the least resistance, so boldly drawing her close to me I snuggled her in my arms and attempted to lass her on the lips.

She laughingly repulsed me, and looking significantly at George, whose back was turned to us (although he could see us in the mirror before him), she shook a reproving finger at me.

I immediately reached forward and drew down the shade that obscured George's view, and again passing my arms about her slender waist held her closely to me in a tight embrace, now without the least resistance on her part; she allowed me to press my lips to hers and with warm kisses I held her tight to me as her arms went around my neck.

Sliding my hand round to the front of her waist, I boldly squeezed and manipulated her breasts, allowing a finger to titillate the dormant nipple to a state of erectile hardness, and then, dropping my hand down on her leg, I slipped it up under her short skirt and moulded and caressed to the full her bare and electric thighs.

At once she drew back a bit, and made as if to stop me, I pulled her back to me, and thrusting my hand right up between her thighs, I felt the bare lips of her sex and the crinkly pubic hair.

At this she lay forward on my chest, her arms about my neck, and seeing that her resistance was over, I divided the hot moist lips of her cleft, and seeking out the touchstone of her nature, by gentle and successive rubs soon had it standing and hard as if to battle an invader.

I now removed my hand for an instant, and tearing open the front of my pants, allowed my stone-hard sockaldodger to spring forth. I seized her hand and guided it to the throbbing shaft and was gratified to feel her grasp it in a firm embrace and begin to rub it slowly up and down its engorged and burning length.

The sudden magnetic touch of her tender and delicate hand on the seat of my sensations, the twining of the white, soft fingers about my shaft of love, my arrow of desire, together with the sweet, melting softness of her clinging lips, together with the soft compression of her thinly-clad body, strained tightly against my own, all conspired to send the blood leaping through my veins like molten fire, and in an access of passion I drew her roughly to me and plunged my finger, which was at the mouth of her sex, deeply up into her person almost to the second joint—which action caused her to give a little cry of pain and hurriedly draw away from me and seat herself on the far side of the car.

Her hand had dropped like a coal of fire my throbbing rod, and as I saw tears rush to her eyes, I knew that I had made a mistake, and cursing myself inwardly, quickly began apologising and begging her pardon, telling her that she had affected me too much, of my fiery nature, etc., and in a moment or two she was again snuggled to my side and my truncheon was again clasped in the soft, magnetic whiteness of her tendril-like fingers.

This time I did not do as before, but contented myself by kissing and caressing her, gently insinuating my hand again under her skirt and regaining the ground I had lost.

For some moments I contented myself with delicately moulding and squeezing her bubbies and then parting the moist lips of her little quivering slit and titillating her standing clitoris, but feeling as if the sweet compressions of her hand might cause me to spend all over her, I gently disengaged it, and pulled her astraddle my lap and pushed her dress up about her waist.

She now allowed me to do my will and, placing the head of my enlarged member against the lips of her slit, I caused her slowly to settle down upon it, and held her firmly in my arms while we began the delicious weaving dance of lust.

"Oh, oh, oh, ah-h-h!' she breathed, 'that is so, s-s-o-o-o n-i-c-e! Oh, oh, oh." She slowly wove about on my penetrating needle. Oh, how lovely; oh, oh, oh, ah, I'm going… O-h-h-h!" And she rained down upon the head of my tempestuous rod a torrent of her vital juices.

I felt myself about to melt, and wishing to pierce her deeper, I lifted her in my arms, and placing her upon her back on the cushions of the carriage, with a few deep and thrilling drives, I let go my charge and felt it bubble and boil in great soul-stirring spurts within her tender and clinging vagina!

We lay for a moment in this close embrace, enjoying the sweet aftermath of a pleasant conjunction, and then taking a handkerchief, I placed it about my rod and slowly drew out of her, causing her to clasp tightly to me as if to hold me there.

I allowed the handkerchief to remain between her thighs, and drying myself I replaced my staff and pulling down her dress gathered her again in my arms and kissed her tenderly on the lips.

She seemed all aflutter, her pulses beating like mad, and her hand nervously went to the front of my pants, and undoing the buttons she again had my limp pintle in her embrace and she rapidly waggled it to and fro impatiently, giving little cries of irritation at its softness and kissing me frantically as if, through the contact of her lips, she wished to stimulate it to renewed hardness.

I soon grew stiff, and rolling her once more back on the seat, I again plunged it within her, and with little gurgles and cries of joy she began a mad writhing of her loins, which, together with the slow jouncing of the car, served to draw forth from me a second charge of my dew, which spurted and shot from the head of my prong in tempestuous jets to be greedily swallowed by her voracious womb as though she was jealous of losing even a drop of that fluid that is so all-powerful in its effects on the feminine frame!

By this time we were almost to her house, and repairing our apparel, we sat close in each other's arms. George, bringing the carriage to a stop, awaited further orders.

"When will I see you again?" I asked her. "You are indeed a nice little girl, Molly, and I must see more of you. Will you allow me the pleasure of seeing you tomorrow night?"

"Oh, no," she answered, "tomorrow is my night out with my fellow, so I could not see you then. If you wish to make it Thursday night"—this was Tuesday—"I will be able to meet you, but we cannot stay out late as I have to be up early in the morning, so you had better pick me up around seven if you wish to."

"And indeed I do!" I answered, allowing my hand to run again under her short dress and to enclasp the lips of her slit. "I will meet you here at seven-thirty and, if you wish it, we will go somewhere where we can have some fun. Now, here"—placing my hand in my pocket and drawing forth a banknote—"here is something for yourself and if you wish you may buy yourself something to make you look pretty when I meet you."

"Oh, thanks!" she said, somewhat surprised at my liberality, as she noted the bill was a rather large one. "I will be here sure, and we will do as you say, but now"—and she held up her lips for a kiss—"I must really hurry away and get into the house as I must be up early in the morning and off to work, otherwise I may be looking for a job!" So after another long melting kiss I allowed her to depart.

You may be sure that I was anxiously on the spot agreed upon on Thursday night, and having taken the precaution of having George keep the carriage about half a block away, I was rewarded by seeing my dear little girlfriend hurrying down the street. After a hurried greeting we were soon ensconced in the car and were quickly whirled out of her neighbourhood.

'Where to?' I asked her gayly, after kissing her several times and finding for myself that she had not at all changed in a certain portion of her body, as I held her close to me in a suffocating embrace.

'Oh, I don't care,' she replied, 'I will go wherever you wish, and the only stipulation that I make is that you have me home good and early for I sure got the dickens for being out so late the last time!'

"Oh, that will be all right," I said, "you may be sure that I will be careful to have you home at an early hour, but for the present, my dear, I would like to, if you are willing, have an opportunity of enjoying you alone —all by yourself—to love, to possess you, my dear Molly, if that is all right with you."

"Well! I guess yes!" she answered. "That is just what was in my own mind, but I did not want to say so, and if you have some place that we could go to, where we might be alone ..."

"Enough," I cried. "George! You may drive at once to where I have told you!"

He immediately turned the carriage and we were soon rapidly rolling along towards an apartment that I maintained for just such incidents as this. It was situated in a rather quiet part of the town, and George, being my confidant, knew all about it and even acted as manservant in these pleasant little pleasure jousts.

In a few moments the car stopped at the door. I ushered the fair girl out, and leaving George to stable the horses, I entered the hallway and with my pass-key opened the hall-door and entered my apartments which were situated on the first landing.

Molly, of course, was all eyes, and upon me ushering her into the front parlour she gave a little gasp of astonishment at the furnishings, which, if I do say it myself, were a little out of the ordinary.

I had, as the place was designed for the purposes of pleasure only, hired the services of a capable decorator and furnisher, and he had done himself credit in the task of furnishing up the place; in the front room, instead of the usual couches, tables and spindly-legged chairs, he had placed a number of the softest and cosiest divans, all laid on the floor, and with the exception of several very fine etchings on the wall and a small table to contain cigarettes, lighter and a tray for refreshments, the room was not at all cluttered up as most are.

I closed the door behind me and slipped home the bolt knowing that George would let himself in with his key by the rear, then taking the fair girl in my arms I drew her down to me on one of the soft cushions, and gluing my lips to hers, soon had her in a perfect furor of passion and desire.

Not that this stimulation was needed for Molly to warm herself to any occasion, for by nature she was one of those naturally tempestuous creatures of lust and passion that was always ready to 'go', and needed no spur in the least to start her desirous blood shooting through her veins.

"Oh, you hurried old bear!" she panted, gently disengaging herself from my arms. "Why, Mr. Henderson!"—for such was the name that I had given her which you may be sure was a ready and fictitious one — "I am surprised indeed at your actions, that you, a gentleman as you are, would so treat a young lady when she visits you for the first time! Aren't you ashamed of yourself?" And struggling to her feet amidst gales of laughter from both of us, she made as if to leave the room, only to be caught tightly in my arms and subjected to a new torrent of the kisses, embraces and fondlings so dear to us both.

Finally, both panting for breath, we came to a halt, and I was gratified to hear a slight discreet tapping on the door; allowing my fair charge an instant to set right her short and hardly concealing frock, I opened the door and found that, as I had expected, it was George with a tray with two cocktails of a special brand that I liked very much.

"Oh," said Molly, "it's your man! Why, I did not know what was about to happen, but now that I see that he is the bearer of good news"—this with a cute grimace at the sparkling drink on the tray—"I suppose it is no more than right that we should accept it with good Laura." And taking the glass that I proffered her she gently tasted it, and voicing her approval drank almost half of it down at once.

I was glad that she seemed to like these cocktails, as they were quite aphrodisiastic in quality, and two or three given to an impressible girl of her sort would speedily make her forget whether she was on her head or her heels, so I urged her to finish it.

I drank my own, the potent liquor stealing through me and filling me with a pleasant warmth, and indicating to George that he might replenish the glasses, I again seated myself at the side of the desirable girl and engaged her in conversation, deeming it best to allow her to rest a moment from my advances, as I would have plenty of time after the liquor had taken full effect.

"Well, my dear," I said, "I see that you are all prettied up tonight, and I must indeed compliment you upon your taste in dress, as you look simply lovely and sweet, and for a girl of your age you certainly know how to clothe or unclothe yourself."

She laughed merrily at this, and then placing her hand over mine she said, "Why, really, my dear benefactor, you yourself have played a leading part in this; it was you that gave me the money to buy this pretty dress." And she lifted it up for my inspection, exposing her pretty leg almost up to her thigh, the sight of the cool, bare flesh above the rolled silk stocking-top causing my pintle to stand up and take notice. "It was you that bought me this, so you may compliment at will, but it is yourself that is the reason for what you term my prettiness upon this festive occasion!"

"Well, well!" I said laughingly, "I am sure, my dear, that now that I have seen the result of my small investment you need not be at all surprised if I repeat the experiment!" And gathering her into my arms I allowed my hands to run riot over her pretty and thinly-clad person.

"Oh, oh," she laughed, "if you are going to act that way, I will never, never in the future say a word about what I buy to you as I see you are all set on finding out for yourself just what your money has purchased. And by the way, that reminds me, this dress is not all that I have new, due to your kind generosity!"

"Oh, there is more?" I cried, pretending to be surprised. "Well, my dear, you must tell me all about this, also. What is it, the new hat?" And I gazed admiringly at the chic *chapeau* that now lay on the small table.

"Oh, no, no!' she laughed, "you are far, far away! But still!"—this with a somewhat serious look at me, which was, however, a mock one—"I am afraid, my dear, if I were to tell you about it, or them, you might want to follow the same tactics that you have done with my dress, and that, I am sure, would be perfectly terrible!" And she held up her hands in mock horror.

At this instant George returned with another of my cocktails, or to be exact, a pair of them, and handing Molly the generously-filled glass, I was gratified to see her drain it at once, as the room was rather warm, the windows being tightly closed and the shades drawn.

George discreetly left the room and again seating myself by her side, I passed my arm about her waist and drew her close to me and allowed my roving hand to take possession of one of her budding breasts, the nipple of which stood out strongly under the thin covering, and urged her to proceed. "Well," she laughed, "just as I told you, if I told you you would want to feel, and the articles that I mention are those that are not for public display, and constitute, to be frank with you, my intimate undercoverings or lingerie. So you see, I could never, never, never..." But before she could tantalise me further I had tumbled her on her back on the divan and had pulled up her dress and exposed her person to the waist and was gratified to find that her lower portion was clad in a pair of the cutest, frenchiest, laciest open-work pants that I had ever had the pleasure of looking upon!

"Cheater!" I cried. "You never told me about these!" And I passed my hand over the thin covering, allowing it to rest for an instant on the seat of her sensations, which caused her to writhe and bounce about so that I deemed it best to desist till later.

"You are a nice little girl to come here with a pair of panties like that on!" I chided her. "And they are all closed up! Are you afraid of being raped while you are in my company? Is that the reason, Molly?"

"It might be that I was afraid that I might not be!" she giggled, now showing the effects of the cocktail, as she reached to the front of my pants and tore open the buttons and allowed my throbbing charger to leap forth into the confines of her warm little palm. "May I depend upon it, my dear Mr. Henderson, that you are not at all jesting when you mention this terrible thing?"

For an answer I persuaded her completely to remove her scanty dress and retain only her very scant panties, her brassiere and her stockings and slippers, whereupon I again clasped her into my arms and covered her lips with stormy caresses.

"Off with these!" I cried, dragging at the band of the closed drawers, and they were soon dangling about her ankles, and I drew them off and laid them on the divan beside us.

"Why you rude thing!" she pouted. "Just for that, I think it no more than fair that you also be punished by being made to shed your clothes so that there will be no difference between us!" And she began to undo my waistcoat, etc., and sooner than it takes to write I was in a state as naked as Adam, and she that of Eve.

Our disrobing was no sooner completed than George's discreet knock disturbed us, and Molly, looking wildly about for something to cover her, acted a little terrified, but upon my telling her that George was an intimate of mine and had been with me for years, she made no further effort to clothe herself and lying back in my arms, all her charms exposed to view, she allowed George to enter and to tender us more refreshments.

George did not betray by the least sign that he was at all surprised at this sight, and Molly, dashing off her drink, gave a little giggle and threw herself again in my arms, one of her hands still encircling my standing and throbbing tool.

I could no longer wait, and throwing her roughly upon her back in George's presence, I guided my tool to the entrance of her slit and with one drive buried it within her to the balls, and grasping her about the cheeks of her magnificent posteriors, I plunged in and out of her sweet secret recess, her membranes clinging to my staff in a loving glove-like embrace, till she finally with great cries and sobs sucked every drop of my elixir from the head of my cock and lay back swooning and panting in my arms.

"Oh, oh, oh," she cried, "that is just delightful! Just marvelous! Oh, do it some more!" And she twisted and gyrated her loins about as though to instill renewed life in my staff which was still held tightly in the moist and burning embrace of her cleft, but alas! it was soft and limber, and as it slipped out of the clinging embrace of her sex she gave a little vexed cry of disappointment, and pressing her thighs closely together buried her face in the cushions and almost sobbed forth her unsated lust, her entire naked body quivering and tingling as though from an electric charge, and I gathered her in my arms and endeavoured to console her for my lack of 'staying power', but she angrily pulled away and refused to be at all consoled.

At this point I raised my eyes to George, who had stood by, an interested spectator to all this violent loveplay, and a plan entering my mind, I bent close to her and whispered in her ear:

"Molly dear! If you will listen a moment I am sure that I will be able to alleviate your distress in full; listen to me for an instant!" And her curiosity aroused, she allowed me to proceed.

"George," I said, "as you may well see, is quite excited at present, and a glance at the front of his pants will convince you that the sight of you, with your charms uncovered, has set him all ablaze, and I am sure that if you will allow it he will be very glad to see what he can do towards giving you a charge of what seems, at the present moment, all that you want. Look, Molly, at his pants. Do you see it?"

At this she turned a bit, and noticing the large bulge in the front of George's pants, hid her face again and said, 'Oh, it looks so big that it really might hurt me, but if you really want him to…"

I spent no further time in parley but nodded my head to George (who had followed every one of our words!); he hastily left the room and I kissed and caressed the dear girl in hopes of another rising of the senses.

"Oh," she said in a somewhat disappointed tone, raising her head and looking about, "oh, where—where did he go to? I thought—I thought that he was going to—going to…"

"He is," I laughed at her, "you need not worry at all about him! He is going to do as you wish him to do, but I thought it better that he should retire and remove his outer clothing; it might be more agreeable to both of you that way—but here he is now." At this point the door opened and George, bare to the skin, entered, his long sockaldodger standing out before him like an immense iron rod.

He certainly was a man fully gifted in these parts, his prong being fully a foot long and some inches in diameter, and being naked as he was, his huge balls dangling below this horse-like prick, it was enough to startle any girl, and Molly gave a little scream at the sight and again buried her head in the cushions.

"Come, Molly," I coaxed her, "surely you are not at all afraid of that monster! You have just been crying for more and more, and here when I provide you with a real honest-to-goodness one you immediately act as if you were scared to death. Do you want me to send him away? Say so if you do!"

There was no answer, of course, to this, and George lying down beside us, I placed the girl in his arms, and after kissing and hugging her a bit he rolled her flat on her back and climbing on top of her lifted himself up and placed the head of his prong at her slit and began to bore away at her.

Molly assisted him as much as she could, placing her arms and legs about his back, and after a few pushes and stabs he finally succeeded in entering her and the dance of love began anew.

George was an ardent cocksman, one who took a real pride in his work and who was able to satisfy the lust of almost any ordinary girl, but our dear little Molly, being no ordinary girl, indeed, stood up under two charges of his dew, and then seemed unwilling to allow him to withdraw that sweet plug of love, so effective had been his poundings, but finally it was over and the three of us lay together on the floor.

George arose and prepared fresh refreshments, this time taking one for himself, and we all talked together. Molly told us of her young man, what a fine fellow he was and how she expected to marry him, and while speaking of this I asked her if it were possible that she might bring a girl friend with her the next time that she came, and to this she immediately assented.

"I shall bring Laura," she said. "I am sure that you will like her for she is a very nice girl about my own age, and she is the girl that I go with all of the time. She is blonde, and has a wonderful shape, and likes to go out and have a good time, and I am sure that George here will find a good home for this terrible thing!" And here she seized hold of his joy-stick and gave it a wicked tweak, causing us both to laugh.

"But you must understand, Molly," I said seriously, "there are times when I have George together with us in our bouts, but you must understand that I wish you to secure this girl for me and for me alone, as George fully understands this and I wish you to, also. Is that clear to you, my dear?" And I kissed her full, pouting rosebud lips.

"Oh, yes," she laughed, "if you will have it that way, I suppose it must be. Anyway, you shall see her if you wish, and I am sure that she will prove acceptable. As far as I am concerned I would be perfectly willing to carry on all by myself…"

"That," I said emphatically, "you must let me be the judge of. As long as you are here and I remember you," here I bent a significant glance upon her, "you should be more than satisfied, and you may assure your girl friend that if she conducts herself in accord with my ideas I will treat her as liberally as I do you. Do you think that will please her?"

"Please her?" echoed Molly, her hand still encircled about George's cock and massaging it gently. "I should say it would! Laura, like myself, has ideas of getting married, and I think it will take place right soon, and as the fellow has not a lot of money, she is like a hungry little wolf for money and I think that she will do almost anything for it, so you need not worry about that part of it. When do you want her?"

"At our very next appointment," I told her, "but now, let us confine ourselves to the present. I notice that George here is in a state of appealing hardness and I myself am in no ways soft, so I judge, dear girl, that you are due for another plunging, so roll over on your back and let me see if you can reduce this to a state of shrinkability!" And I rolled her over and mounted her, and in a moment poured into her womb another charge of my balm, and arising, allowed George to fuck her, which operation lasted for fully twenty minutes till finally, with groans, twists and cries, and scratching of his back, they both drained the reservoirs of their sex, and lay panting on the floor.

I made her the usual "present" of money, which she was well versed enough to know was to reward her labour in her task of reducing my hardness of feelings, and making another appointment to meet her, I had George drive her back to her neighbourhood and dismissed her from my mind for the present at least.

At this portion of my narrative I deem it best that I acquaint the reader with some of the fads and follies of the writer, so that, later on in this sparse history of a sensual life, he may be more familiar with the traits both normal and abnormal that will at times be depicted upon the written page.

As I have stated earlier here, I am a gentleman somewhat on in years, and if I do say it myself, of somewhat pleasing appearance, especially to the opposite sex. Being left fairly well off and having a business that is practically self-operating, I devote the majority of my time to my pleasures, which, as the reader has determined by now, are mostly those of the flesh.

I am an ardent admirer of beauty in all of its manifest forms; I am a lover of flowers, paintings and the finer things of life, and like above all things the full well-developed form of the modern girl, the flapper.

Being situated financially in a manner to gratify most of my wishes I seek high and low for complaisant pretty girls, and if they are in accord with my will and desires, I treat them in a courtly fashion and repay them liberally for their time.

Not that I care to associate with the *demi-monde*, the street walkers, the prostitutes and all their ilk; much rather would I caress the clothed knee or thigh of a fair young damsel and be content with that than lie abed with a hardened old roustabout; I love youth, beauty, and the delicious freshness that is the endowment of modern feminine girlhood.

George, as the reader may well judge, is a confidential servant indeed; he has assisted me and taken an active part in many another little affair of this kind, and I trust him absolutely, and now, with this dear Molly, I was sure that I had secured another active helper.

Her promise of her girl friend, Laura, was indeed a pleasant fillip to my lustful imagination, and I carefully dressed on that evening and was on the corner long before the time set, anxious to catch a glimpse of the girl that had been so warmly described to me.

Sure enough, I saw Molly walking quietly down the street, accompanied by another girl about her size, and at a glance I saw that Molly had not misrepresented the girl's qualities in the least.

She was as Molly had told me, a truly beautiful girl with large blue eyes and a mop of golden hair which was shortly bobbed, as is the fashion.

She was perfectly formed, the shape of her youthful body being well put off by the abbreviated dress that she wore, and was without a hat, having evidently left the house on the pretext of going for a short walk.

Introductions were soon over, and I assisted both of them into the car. George started to drive slowly through a number of side streets and I discreetly drew the shades so that we would not be seen by passers-by should the car be halted at the crossings.

"Now, here you are," said the laughing Molly, "here, Mr. Henderson, I have delivered my captive, and I assure you that it was a job, indeed, for Laura is wildly in love with her Charlie, and for a while was at a loss as to whether to come at all, but I told her that I had promised you, and I am sure that once we are together a while she will forget all about her sweetheart, and will have as much fun as any of us! Isn't that right, Laura dear?" she asked, turning to the blushing girl who was seated beside me.

Laura made no answer for a moment and then allowing her head to lie over on my shoulder, passed a hand behind my back and seized that of Molly and laughed nervously and said in a low voice, "Well, you know, Molly, that this is quite—quite irregular for me to go out like this—and Charlie—that is my fellow'—(this to me)—"he is terribly jealous of me and doesn't allow me to go with anyone—if he should ever know of it, it might ruin our marriage—and I am simply crazy about him and I must watch myself. You know that, Molly."

"Oh, yes," said Molly, "I know you are crazy about your Charlie, and I am the same about Jim, but still, Laura, that is no bar on you and I having a little fun, and who, seeing there is just you and I, is ever going to know anything about it? Then besides, Mr. Henderson is such a wonderful man! I am sure after you know him better you will be just eager and waiting for the time to come to meet him! Isn't that right, Mr. Henderson?" she said, looking to me for confirmation.

I laughed at this, and passing my arms about the waists of both of the girls, I said to Laura, "I should think, my dear, that you, as you are engaged to your dear Charlie and are even getting ready right now to marry him, should be all the more accustomed to the company of men, and the fact that you go with me, and that I might—might even go as far as to treat you like Charlie does—that in itself would in no way flurry or upset you, in fact, I think—"

"Oh, Mr. Henderson," interrupted Molly, "I forgot altogether to tell you"—and here she laughed as if her heart would break—"I forget to tell you that our dear little Laura, so wild is she about her dear beloved Charlie, that she does not even stay with him or allow him to touch her—she thinks that if a girl does that then a fellow will never, never marry her. Can you imagine that?" And she laughed again.

Poor Laura blushed redly at this and I immediately set about to put things to rights by saying that in some cases that was the best plan, and was immediately set upon by Molly who evidently conducted herself in an entirely different manner with her own suitor, and a heated debate ensued between us, in which Laura took no part whatever.

By this time we had arrived before the building in which I had my rooms, and George, bringing the car to a stop, opened the door and assisted the two girls to alight.

Once within the confines of the apartment, the girls lighted cigarettes and George brought in a tray with three of the cocktails of such aphrodisiastic qualities.

To my surprise, Laura refused to drink with us and stood the guying of Molly, who taunted her unmercifully, and contented herself with looking about the room. I saw that she was ill at ease and set about to make her feel at home, and I flatter myself that I did a bit, for she sat on the cushions and was soon laughing and talking the same as her girl friend.

Knowing that we had not long to spend, I rose to my feet and taking Laura by the hand, asked her to come and see the house with me, and led her into an adjoining chamber, furnished like the one we had left, and once within I bolted the door behind me.

Molly had watched us with curious eyes, and seeing that we were to leave her alone made no remark; George entering at that instant with another drink, I knew that she would be occupied till our return, as I had instructed my servant before the rendezvous and knew that I had the fair Laura to myself for a few moments at least.

She evidently knew what was transpiring in my mind for she allowed me to draw her down gently on to the cushions beside me, and once she was in my arms, I pressed hot kisses on her lovely lips and allowed my hands to run riot all over her girlish perfection.

I found, however, that she was quite matter-of-fact in regard to terms, for drawing gently back from me, she arranged her dress, and looking about to see that we were alone she said in a low voice, "I understand, Mr. Henderson, that Molly and you have been quite close together—in fact that you know one another quite intimately—that you have possessed her—and when Molly told me that you wished to meet me and to have a party with me, you must understand, Mr. Henderson, that one of the main reasons that I accepted is that you had her understand that I was to receive something in return—that you are to pay me. This, of course, is a rather abrupt way of putting it, but you must understand that I am an engaged girl and am shortly to be married, and I do not accord these favours even to my own intended husband, and if we intend to proceed I wish that clearly understood between us. Is not that right?"

"Oh, yes," I said, relieved to find that she was so materialistic. "I told Molly exactly that, and you may be sure that I meant exactly what I said, and now that I have seen you I have no reason indeed to regret my bargain and assure you that I will do exactly as she outlined to you." And I made as if to gather the beautiful girl to me and smother her with my caresses.

She, however, held me back again, and pulling her short skirt over her knees, held up her finger at me and continued, "Molly also told me that the man that drives your carriage, that he also is to take part in the bargain, and I wish to know if that is all, because I would not, for any consideration, stand any more, not that I am not able and perhaps willing, but an engaged girl has standards to maintain, and were it not for the money involved, I would never think of starting in the first place."

"You have been stayed with?" I asked curiously, puzzled at this girl's strange conversation, so different was she from the exuberant Molly.

"Oh yes," she admitted, "I have been with men quite often, and although I deny myself to others and even to my intended, you may be sure that it is not for any dislike for the act, but the consequences attending it, such as pregnancy, etc., which fill my heart with fear. I am eager for a home and children, and in my marriage with Charlie I am sure that I would realise all of my fondest dreams. This, to me, is merely a means to an end, and I do not consider it wrong at all, but now that we have understood one another, let's get set and get going or I shall have an argument to contend with should I not return in a short space of time."

"But," I persisted, "supposing—supposing pregnancy should result from this—this occasion? Does that not enter your fears at all? Do you not fear that you would be in a delicate state in a few months should you submit to George and myself?"

"I marry in three weeks," she said simply, "and although Charlie has never possessed me, you may be sure that by that time he will be my husband, and any consequences, as you put them, will be well taken care of, so you may rest easy as to that."

At this instant I thought it best to bring this matter-of-fact discussion to a close, and pressing a bill of rather large denomination into her hand, I pressed her close to me and abandoned myself to the delightful pleasure of the contact of her fresh, youthful form.

She lay in my arms, allowing me to do my will, and pressing the front of her dress I moulded and caressed her firm young breasts, bare to my fingertips except for the thinness of her silk dress, and passing my hand over her silken-covered legs I allowed one of them to mount to the top of her stocking and revelled in the feel of her bare thighs.

My prick by this time was straining at its bonds, and tearing open the fly of my pants I allowed it to spring forth to be in an instant encompassed by her tiny hand and she submitted it to a delightful and tingling compression that made me feel as if I would shoot right into her palm and over her bare wrist and forearm.

"Oh, you are lovely," I murmured, and dividing her thighs, I allowed my hand to run up on her belly and then to slip down and play riot with her pubic curls and to squeeze and compress the lips of her sexual slit, till I was almost mad with lust and desire. I sucked her mouth into mine, and passing my arm about her neck drew her to me in a stifling embrace and sought as if to ravish her on the very spot.

"My dress, my dress!" she said, "do not get it wet, I beg you! You may go off and spot me, and I would have to…"

"Then off with it," I said, somewhat brutally, I think, and suiting the action to the word, I began to drag it over her head. She drew away and arose, and squirming out of it allowed me to see all of her form, and loosing her panties at the waist she let them fall from her and stood naked before me.

I seized her by the hand and drew her down beside me and covered all of her lovely nakedness with kisses of fire, and my cock now in a state of pulsing hardness, I pushed her flat on her back and bestrode her, almost mad with pleasurable desire.

She opened her thighs wide and allowed me to lie within them, and presenting the head of my priapus at the entrance of her slit I thrust away at her, but was agreeably surprised to find that I could not even make the head of it enter; push as I might the natural dryness of my prong, together with the tightness of her orifice, made connection impossible.

"You—will—never—never—do—it!" she gasped, the breath driven out of her tender young body at the assaults I made upon her. "I—know it—I am too tight. It is a long time—a long time since I had it before!"

I determined that she was right in her surmise, and leaping to my feet I pulled the bell cord for George and stood surveying her as she lay naked on the floor.

"What are you going to do?" she asked, looking up at me, and making as if to rise to her feet, but I again gently pushed her back on her back.

"I am ringing for George," I explained, "and will secure some cold cream to ease the situation. You need not worry at his entrance, as he is to have you, too, and it will be a pleasant introduction for him."

At this instant George discreetly knocked at the door and I admitted him and made known my wants in this particular direction. He cast a glance at the girl on the floor and she turned her face on the cushions in shame; from the opened front of his pants I knew that he had been consoling Molly; he went and fetched a jar of the desired unguent.

Placing it on the cushion beside us, I again mounted the form of the prostrate girl, and anointing the head of my staff liberally, I took her again in my arms and again essayed the ravishment of her sexual charms. This time I succeeded in wedging the head within the tightly-closed lips, and settling down full upon her, I pushed forward with my loins and soon had a full inch of my throbbing rod impaled in her vitals.

"O-o-o-o-o-h-h-h," she murmured, thrashing about on the cushions and placing her hands against my chest as though to push me from her, "you are h-u-r-t-i-n-g me! Oh, oh, oh, that is too—too big! Take it out a minute! Just a minute! It stretches me too much! You are ... wait! Wait!"

But I had gained my point and was in no mood to relinquish it, and passing my hands behind her naked and bouncing posteriors I poised myself high upon her and with one drive sheathed half of the entire length of my dart into its clinging and trembling cove, and she gave a wild scream of pain and fell back trembling and senseless in my arms.

That one cruel plunge must have hurt her, but now seeing that she was insensible I made the most of the opportunity, and with a few more drives soon was in her cove to the hilt and then lay panting upon her till nature saw fit to restore her to her senses.

I knew that the cry must have startled Molly, but depended upon George and the soothing presence of his kidney tosser to secure me from interruption, and the door being locked, waited with patience for her return to her senses.

She soon began to thrash about, and opening her eyes, moved her loins about, and the first pain of the entrance over, I began a slow weaving, rhythmic motion on her body, allowing my prong to glide in and out of the heated moistness of her glove-like membranes.

"Oh, oh, oh," she cried, "you are cruel, cruel indeed! Why could you not be easier with me?"

Then, pain giving way to more passionate sensations, she allowed her bare arms to steal tightly around my neck and her loins gave me back thrust for thrust and her lips met mine in a clinging embrace and we melted into one, a moving rhythm of lust, and our breath came in pants and bursts as I held her close to me!

"Oh, oh, o-h-h-h-h-h-h-h-h!" she sighed, thrusting upwards with all her might to meet the descending charger, "oh, oh, o-h-h-h, there... t-h-e-r-e!" as her slit opened and closed on my staff with lightning-like loving strokes. "T-h-e-r-e, that, t-h-a-t is it! Oh, ohohohohoh o-o-o-o-o, I'm coming! O-h-h-h-h, lover darling, that is s-o-o-o n-i-c-e!" And her hot flow bathed and sprayed my swelling charger.

Again and again this delightful compression of her tight slit took place, and each time she vented a shower of girlish dew upon me, and feeling that I, also, was about to spend I took her firmly in my arms and whispered in her ear, 'Here, here! Here is the child that you fear! I will spout into your womb a living, pulsing life! There, there, there,' as I exploded in her, 'that is the first fruit of your marriage! Take it and rear it as a gift from me!' And I shot and bubbled in great spurts into her womb the largest charge that I could ever recall, and driving my prong far up into her, sought the more firmly to embed it within the most secret confines of her being.

She, at the same instant, gave down another charge, and we then lay melting in each other's arms, relaxed and breathless on the cushions.

I lay on her for some time still, my throbbing prick still embedded to the balls within her, and she, as though mad with lust, began another series of wiggles beneath me; feeling life revive, I again commenced a slow weaving upon her.

This second bout was much longer than the first, and I enjoyed to the full the tight and clinging constrictions of her slit upon the heart of my sex, and after she had vented four or five times I again discharged within her and we again lay still.

I lay for a few minutes and then withdrew, the charge from her fleshy bottle spurting out on to the cushions as I removed the cork. I made my toilet. Laura pressed her thighs closely together and rolled on her side as if to hide the damage done to her pretty person, and I noticed that the wetness was stained with red and knew that her maidenhead, or at least the remnants of it, had now departed her forever, and felt a strange thrill of pride run through me as I looked at the naked girl.

"Now for George," I said gaily.

At this she turned her tear-stained face to me and held up a restraining hand and said, "Please, please, I beg of you! Wait just a few minutes at least! I will take him as I have agreed to do, but in a moment I will have regained my composure and then, if you will, I will carry out my part of the agreement."

A wave of pity overcame me, and I thought to myself that this poor girl, in order to arrange for her marriage with her lover, a man that had never known her—that is, sexually—was prostituting herself for the means of his possessing her; and here she was, about to submit to the embraces of a perfect stranger, a servant, and my seed soaking in her womb... It was too unbearable... it must not be. Suddenly it occurred to me—what if she was pregnant? With my child pulsing in her womb? Why not wait and see the outcome of it? George would be well satisfied with Molly, and should Laura, as she feared, become with child with me, how novel it would be! I made up my mind instantly that it should be as I planned.

"No," I said to her, "you will not even have to be with George. I have changed my mind, and when you have sufficiently recovered you may dress yourself and leave. Is that agreeable to you, my dear?" And I again lay at her side and covered her face with kisses.

"Oh, yes," she said, "I am glad to be let off. I am willing, as I said, to carry out my part of the bargain, but really, you have hurt me dreadfully, as I have never had one that big and it opened me up so large that I feel as if I will be unable even to walk! Will you assist me to my feet, please?"

I assisted her to arise, the spent charge of our combined balm running in pinken streams down her naked thighs, and she found to her surprise that she was not really dead. I handed her a towel and left her to repair the damage done to her person and opening the door quietly peered out to see what George and Molly were up to.

It happened that I came just in time, for they were engaged in a terrific sexual combat, tossing about with interlaced limbs: Molly, now bare of all apparel and George stripped to his shorts and drawers. I turned to Laura, and she seeing through the door the delicious act of sexual combat watched with glistening and lustful eyes as the pair melted away in a series of panting sobs and finally lay still and trembling, his dew spouting into the young girl's tender being.

At the sight of us, they grew confused and hastily scrambled to their feet and we both laughed heartily at their actions.

After this, both of the girls dressed and as I signified a desire to hear of their previous love affairs and the bestowal of their maidenheads we again arranged an early date, and conducting them to the neighbourhood of their respective homes, left them and repaired to other pleasures.

With these, the reader may not doubt that there were many channels that served to supply me, and George, in his capacity as personal servant, always had something on tap that was sure to provide me amusement, and that very night had arranged an affair that I was sure would give me pleasure. But of that more anon as it takes place.

We proceeded to another section of the city, and George parking the car, we went on foot to a somewhat disreputable hotel where George had engaged rooms earlier in the evening under assumed names, and ascending in the elevator we were soon by ourselves.

"Now, George," I said, taking a drink from a pocket flask that he had thoughtfully brought with him in the car, "what is it that you have in store this evening? I hope it is something new and uncommon, as I am pretty well tired after my bout with Laura, and promise you that you will be well taxed to provide me entertainment now, my good man."

"I thought so, sir," said George respectfully, "and in view of that I have provided for something that I am sure will meet with your approval. I am sure, in the past, that I have done my best, and I would not now think of anything that would tax your energy, and you will see that my judgement is as good as ever."

And indeed it was! And I admired him for his ingenuity and diplomacy in these matters. No doubt, many a dollar had made its way into his capacious pockets through his master's lustful desires, but that I cared naught of, so long as he provided for my pleasures, and this he really did and was ideal in this respect, and I was now all pins and needles to know what he had on tap.

"What is it, George?" I asked.

"You will see, sir," he said, and made no further revelations and I awaited with curiosity, watching his movements.

He went to the phone and, asking for a certain room, engaged in a cryptic conversation, and then with a smile replaced the receiver on the hook In a moment or two a light rap came on the door, and upon George opening it, a figure entered the room, presumably that of a girl —but what a girl!

She was scarcely three feet in height, but was perfectly formed in all particulars, indeed a miniature girl—in fact a midget! The sight of her almost floored me with astonishment, but now being somewhat accustomed to George's surprises, I hurriedly invited her to enter, and closed and fastened the door behind her.

"This," said George, somewhat proudly, "is Mademoiselle Tiny, whom you have doubtless seen at a number of the theatres about town. I have already informed her of the profound admiration that you have for her, and have at last succeeded in persuading her to come here and see you. I am sure that you will find her admirable company and now that you are together hope that you will pardon me, as I wish to step downstairs to keep an appointment that I have made."

And with this, my estimable servant bowed quite low to us and opened the door and vanished. I asked the little lady to be seated, and she looked curiously about the room and seated herself, not on the chair but on the edge of the bed, looking like a tiny little doll.

"I am certainly glad to have this opportunity of meeting you," I said, "and I must indeed compliment you upon your stage appearance" (although as far as I recollect I had never seen her on the stage, but thought to follow the suggestions so adroitly conveyed me by the invaluable George). And she smiled at this and in a low, quiet voice thanked me, and to my utmost astonishment boldly placed her tiny hands on the front of my pants and in a jiffy unbuttoned my fly and drew out my limber prick and moulded and compressed it in a manner that bespoke much previous knowledge in this delectable art!

This, of course, broke the ice, and I discarded all reserve or consideration that I might have had in regard to her, and drawing her over close to me, I sought out her tiny breasts and pulling open her little dress I soon had them out and my lips glued to one of her nipples.

She still continued to pull away at my staff, which by now was assuming a state of agreeable hardness, and allowing one of my hands to dive under her dress I found that she had her stockings rolled to the knee and I rubbed and squeezed the tiny legs and thighs and sought to get up further to her sexual parts. She had, however, a pair of bloomers on, and this in a manner put a stop to my explorations, but laughing and giggling she begged me to stop an instant, and upon my finally releasing her she detached her hands from my prick and springing lightly to the floor began to disrobe.

The sight of this tiny person, a veritable jewel of a woman, disrobing before me caused me to experience a lustful thrill, and as she quickly disrobed, unveiling to me all of her cameo-like charms, I sought to encompass her in my arms.

Her size, however, made it easy for her to avoid me, and seeing that I was only using my precious time I lay back on the bed and allowed her to continue undressing.

Finally she was stripped to her stockings, and standing proudly before me allowed me to survey all of her naked charms, even turning about slowly to allow me to see her miniature back and buttocks. I could wait no longer; I leaped to the floor and picking her up in my arms, carried her to the bed and throwing her on her back lay beside her and allowed my sensual tongue to run all over her body.

She again regained hold of my standing prick, and with both hands now held it between her tiny breasts, and I pushed back and forth as though already in the sexual embrace, and she bent her head low to it, and to my surprise engulfed the flaming head of it in her tiny mouth and with adroit tongue began to titillate and bang upon the throbbing head in quick jerks with her tongue so that I almost leaped from the bed.

I pressed the back of her head, and settled down to enjoy to the full this lustful abnormal act, and in a moment or two I felt my prick swell and throb to the bursting point in her mouth and pressing it as far as I could down the confines of her throat I let loose my seething boiling load of balm and she choked and tried to back away but all of my essence bubbled and spurted in great spurts down the back of her throat; when at last, exhausted, I fell back on the bed, she pulled away, sputtering and gasping and breathless beside me.

"Oh," she said, after she had regained her breath, "my goodness, what a load you shoot! Why, you nearly choked me! I thought sure that I was drowned!"

"Then you have done it before?" I asked, curiously, taking her again in my arms and kissing her.

"Oh, yes," she said, laughing, "my husband, who, by the way, was a much larger man than you are, always found an especial delight in that form of amusement; and I myself formed quite a liking for the 'French' act, as it is called, and there was many a charge of his that found its way down my throat. Besides, when he died—well—there were others, you understand!" And she looked at me and laughed merrily.

"Your husband was much larger than I was?" I echoed. "You mean that he was constituted physically in all ways—?"

"I know exactly what you mean," she laughed. "You are wondering whether his parts were as large as yours are, and I will tell you yes, and even more so. I am so built that it is possible for me to have regular intercourse with men of normal size, and although at first it was rather trying, after living with my husband for a few years I now not only can bear it, but take the keenest enjoyment in the act myself, provided there is mutual desire."

This was quite new to me in spite of all my experience, as I had thought that midgets and others of their ilk could and would only have intercourse with their own kind and build.

The idea that this tiny person was capable of sustaining the assaults of a fully developed man like myself was indeed intriguing to me, and in an effort to ascertain for myself the condition of these parts, I allowed my hand to slip down between her thighs, and dividing the lips of her sexual slit, I found to my surprise that it was just as she had said, and somewhat regretfully I considered the soft shrinking state of my organ and longed for hardness in order that I, too, might possess her.

She evidently was in full accord with my moods, for her tiny hand stole down to my dart and with many sweet compressions and fondlings she sought to bring it to a state of usable hardness; finally, slipping quickly down in the bed, she applied her provocative mouth to the tip of my rod and in a few instants it stood up ready to battle.

"But how?" I asked her, as she held it up for my inspection, planting a last moist kiss on the now throbbing head.

"Why, the same way," she replied, turning on her back and allowing me to mount her. She quickly guided the head of my staff to her eager and receptive slit, and I gently plunged it home, marvelling at her capacity for this giant tool, especially so in regard to her size, but the nervous clasping and unclasping of her hot, burning tissues about the sides of my torrid rod soon sent all other ideas flying from my mind and I commenced to fuck away in earnest.

The little creature pressed her cunt up close to my plunging prick as if she did not want to miss a bit of it, and I, a sadistic mood overcoming me, plunged away at her as if I wished really to split her in twain.

The previous combats that I had indulged in during the day served to prolong my pleasure and I must have bounded up and down upon her for upward of twenty or thirty minutes before nature saw fit to open the sexual flood gates and allow me to flood her womb with a bounding charge of my manly sap.

We both lay quiet, my prick being squeezed of its last spurting drops by the compressions of her tingling quim, then I gently withdrew, not without a little protest from my charming, diminutive partner who tried to hold me to her as I allowed a flood of our combined juices to flow out, down her bare buttocks on to the counterpane.

I was now quite exhausted and after allowing her to dress, I repaired the damage done to my own apparel, and awaited the return of George, who I knew was nearby watching the outcome of the affair that he had planned. I did not offer her anything for herself as I knew that George had taken care of that end of the matter. He soon entered and after enquiring if the affair had terminated to my satisfaction, he showed our visitor out.

I gave George a substantial tip for himself, as I enjoyed these affairs that he arranged for me, and we then returned to the car and I was driven homewards. I looked forward with great pleasure to a second meeting with Molly and her pretty partner Laura, and thought to myself what new methods I would plan the more thoroughly to sate my lust upon the fair bodies of the two young girls who were so willing to accept my gold in return for the divine charms bestowed upon them by nature.

Voluptuous Confessions

The chateau of my grandfather was situated outside the city in a delightful country setting. The grounds, shaded by scattered trees, mostly splendid oaks, or chestnuts, was of great extent and enclosed by walls. The grounds immediately around the house itself were laid out in splendid patterns of the finest flowers, and watered by a little river, which became lost in the country by capacious meanderings.

My old grandmother, mostly confined to the house, never went much further than the beautiful nearby lake fed by the river. As for me, my greatest happiness was to wander alone in the most uncultivated parts of the property, and indulge in the reveries of my eighteenth year. These reveries, I ought to confess, were always of the same nature. A strange feeling invaded my soul, my young imagination reveled in unknown regions and presented before my eyes images of tenderness and devotion in which a young man was always the hero. Although profoundly ignorant as to the differences between the sexes, my already awakened feelings moved the whole of my body and spirit. A secret fire circulated in my veins; often a dimness came over my eyes, my limbs trembled, and I was obliged to sit down, a prey to a weakness which combined both pleasure and pain.

It was the month of June and the weather was magnificent. My walks were mostly in the morning when I was sure to be alone.

We received a letter from Madam Terlot, The Governess, who, replying to my grandmother's invitation, announced her imminent arrival.

Madame Terlot was about twenty-six or twenty-seven and had been married at the age of twenty to an old man who had left her a widow two years since, mistress of a great fortune, and without children. She was a delightful person. She had hair black as ebony, contrasted with the whiteness of her complexion, which was lighted up by her beautiful deep blue eyes. Her mouth, small and pleasing, was set off by adorable teeth, as white as the purest ivory. She had a fine figure, perfectly formed and graceful, with medium-sized breasts and shapely hips. She dressed with taste and elegance.

I loved her very much. Her lively and playful disposition had long captivated me. Accustomed to living with my grandmother, whose age prevented her from affording me any amusement, deprived of companions, I was very happy at the arrival of a youthful relation who would be a friend to me.

A marriage arrangement had been spoken of between The Governess and Monsieur Marcel, which my grandmother immediately approved. Aunt Elise wrote at once to him, with an invitation to pass some time at the chateau, and in consequence he arrived a few days after her.

What I am going to relate now is very delicate and difficult. I have hesitated a long time! But the chances are nobody will read it; these lines are for my own perusal, after all. The pictures which I am going to draw are very lively, but they will be true. What lovers—real lovers—in each other's arms have not experienced the same? I will add that, even though now I am past kissing, I feel a veritable pleasure in recalling the soft enjoyment.

One morning very early, according to my custom, I had gone a long way in the park and sat down at the foot of a tree, plunged in my usual reveries.

I saw The Governess, whom I thought in bed, some distance off, evidently coming to the little eminence where I was. She was dressed in a fresh peignoir of white and blue. Monsieur Marcel was with her, dressed in a suit and a straw hat. They seemed to be having a lively conversation.

I do not know what secret instinct impelled me to avoid their presence. I hid behind a big tree which completely shielded me from their sight.

They soon arrived at the spot I had just vacated, and stopping for a moment, Monsieur Marcel looked all around and, convinced that at this hour no one could see them, threw his arms around The Governess. He drew her to him and pressed her to his breast, their lips so joined that I heard a long kiss, which struck to the bottom of my heart.

"My dear Elise; my angel; my sweet darling! I love you. I adore you. What a frightful time I have passed without you; but soon it will be over! Stop, that I may embrace you again! Give me your beautiful eyes, your lovely teeth, your divine neck! How I could eat them!" he exclaimed.

The Governess, far from resisting, gave herself up to him, returned kiss for kiss, caress for caress. Her color heightened; her eyes sparkled.

"My Alfred," said she, "I love only you. I am all yours."

One may judge the effect such caresses had upon me. I felt as though I had been struck by an electric spark. I seemed unable to move, and almost lost the use of my senses. I recovered myself promptly, however, and continued to be all eyes and ears. Alfred wanted something which I did not understand, and seemed to insist on it.

"No, no, my love," replied Elise. "No! Not here, I beg you. My God, I would never dare! If anyone should surprise us, I should die!"

"My dear, who can see us at this hour?"

"I don't know, but I'm afraid! I couldn't. I would have no pleasure. We will find a way of doing it; have patience."

"How can you speak of patience in the state I am in? Give me your hand; feel it yourself!"

He then took the hand of The Governess and placed it in such a curious place that it was impossible for me to understand the reason. But it was worse when I saw this hand disappear in a certain slit in his trousers which she had presently unbuttoned and she seized an object which I could not see.

"Ahh," said she, "I see very well how much you want me. How beautiful it is, and I like it so big and hard. If we had only some privacy, I would soon put you to the proof."

And her hand moved softly up and down, to the apparent pleasure of Monsieur Marcel, who stood immovably erect, his leg a little open.

"Ah!" suddenly exclaimed The Governess. "What an idea! Come, Alfred, I recollect there is near here a small pavilion, you know. It is a curious place for our love, but no one will see us, and I can be all yours. Come on."

I must explain that the pavilion of which The Governess spoke was simply a poor gazebo constructed like a thatched cottage.

Protected by some big brambles, I could approach them without fear of being seen. This I did with infinite precautions, and got to the back of the pavilion at the moment when Elise had already entered and Monsieur Marcel, after looking all around, also came in. I sought out a convenient hole and soon found one, as the planks and beams were badly joined, sufficiently large to enable me to see everything. I applied my eye and held my breath, and was witness to what I am going to relate.

Elise, hanging on the neck of her lover, devoured him with kisses.

"My darling, I was very unhappy to refuse you, but I was afraid. Here, at least, I am assured. This beautiful rod, what pleasure I am going to give him. I come already in thinking of it! But how shall we place ourselves?"

"It is all right," he said. "Let me see again your mossy valley. It is such a long time I have wanted it."

You may guess what my thoughts were at this moment. But what were they going to do? I was not left long in suspense.

Monsieur Marcel, going down on one knee, raised Elise's skirts. What charms he exposed! Under that fine cambric chemise were legs worthy of Venus, encased in silk stockings, secured above the knee by garters the color of fire. Above that were two creamy thighs, round and firm, surmounted by a fleece of black and lustrous curls. The abundance and length of them were a great surprise to me, compared to the light chestnut moss which covered my own mount.

"How I love it," said Alfred. "How beautiful and fresh your pussy is!

Open yourself a little, my angel, that I may kiss those adorable lips!"

Elise did as he demanded. Her thighs, in opening, made me see a rosy slit, upon which her lover glued his lips. Elise seemed in ecstasy! Shutting her eyes and speaking broken words, she seemed transported by this curious caress. I could see Alfred's tongue moving over her flesh, licking and darting like that of a snake.

"Ah, you kill me—go on! I—I—I'm coming! Ah, ah!"

What was she doing? Good God! I had never supposed that any pleasure pertained to that part. Yet, at that moment I began to feel myself in the same spot some particular titillations, which made me almost understand it.

Alfred got up, supporting Elise, who appeared to have lost all strength. She soon recovered herself and embraced him with passion.

"Come, let me put it in," she said. "But how are we going to do it?"

"Turn yourself, my dear, and incline against this unworthy wall."

Then, to my great surprise, Elise, by rapid and excited movements, undid the trousers of Alfred. Lifting his shirt above his navel, she exposed to my view such an extraordinary object that I was almost surprised into a scream. What could be this unknown thing, the head of which was so rosy and exalted, its length and thickness threatening to make me dizzy?

Elise evidently did not share my fears, for she took this frightful instrument in her hand, caressed it a moment, and said, "Let us begin." She pulled Alfred to her by this organ. "Come into your little companion, and be sure not to go away too soon."

She lifted up her clothes behind and exposed to the light of day two bottom globes of dazzling whiteness, separated by a crack of which I could only see a slight trace. She then inclined herself, and placing her hands against the wall, presented her adorable bottom to her lover.

Alfred just behind her took his enormous pole in hand, and wetting it with a little saliva, commenced to introduce it between the two rosy lips which I had perceived. Elise did not flinch, and opened as much as possible the part which she presented. It almost seemed to open itself, and at length absorbed this long and thick piston, which appeared monstrous to me. It penetrated so well, however, that it disappeared entirely, and the belly of its happy possessor came to be glued to the buttocks of The Governess.

There was then a conjunction of combined movements—Alfred pushing against her, Elise falling back on him—followed by broken words: "Ah! I feel it—it is getting into me," said Elise. "Push it all well into me softly—let me come first. Ah!—I feel it—I'm coming! Quicker! I come—stop—there you are! I die—I—I—Ah!"

As to Alfred, his eyes half closed, his hands holding the hips of The Governess, he seemed inexpressibly happy.

"Oh," he said, "my angel, my all, ah! How fine it is! Push well! Do you feel my prick in you? Yes! Yes! Do come! There! You're coming, aren't you? Go on—go on. I feel you're coming—push well, my darling!"

Both stopped a moment. The Governess appeared exhausted, but did not change her position. At length she lightly turned her head to give her lover a kiss, saying, "Now, both together! Let me know when you're ready."

The scene recommenced. After several minutes during which Alfred virtually slammed his belly against Elise's bottom, he in turn, cried out, "Ah, I feel it coming. Are you ready, my love? Yes, yes, there I am… I am… coming, I am yours. I… ah! What pleasure! I'm coming!"

A long silence followed. Alfred seemed to have lost his strength, and practically fell over Elise, who was obliged to put her arms straight to bear him. Alfred recovered himself, and I again saw the marvelous instrument coming out of Elise's slit, where it had been so well treated. But how changed it was. Its size diminished to half, red and damp, and I saw something like a white and viscous liquid come from it and drop to the floor.

Alfred began to put his clothes in order, during which The Governess, who had straightened up, put her arms around his neck and covered him with kisses.

What had I been doing during this time? My imagination, excited to the highest degree, made me repeat one part of the pleasures which transported the actors.

At the critical moment I lifted petticoat and chemise, and my inexperienced hand contented itself by exploring my tender slit. I thus assured myself that I was made the same as Elise, but I knew not yet what use or consolation that hand could give. This very morning was to enlighten me.

After plenty of kissing, Elise said to Monsieur Marcel, "Listen, my dear, I have been thinking. You know that my apartment is quite isolated. Since my chambermaid sleeps in the anteroom, no one would know if we rendezvous, and we could pass some adorable nights together.

"Under a pretext of wanting something for my toilette, I will send Julie to Paris tomorrow afternoon, and after dinner we can join each other. Be on the lookout; you can give me a sign during the day of the hour when you can slip away to me. I beg you to take the most minute precautions."

It was then decided that Monsieur Marcel should go first. He was to take a walk out of the park, and during that time The Governess would regain her room by the private staircase. Alfred went out, and I remained hidden in my brambles until he was sufficiently far off not to have any fear of being perceived by him. Observing that The Governess had not yet come out, I stopped and looked again. I saw Elise stoop right in front of me, so nothing could escape my view. As she did this her slit opened; it seemed to me a much more lively hue than before. The interior and the edges, even up to the fleecy mound which surrounded it, seemed inundated with the same liquor which I had seen come from Monsieur Marcel's rod.

I was going to leave my place as softly as possible when I was drawn back by what I now saw. The hand of The Governess refreshed with care all the parts which had been so well worked. All at once I saw her stop, then a finger fixed upon a little eminence which showed itself prominently. This finger rubbed lightly at first, then with a kind of fury, sometimes slipping into the same slit that had been occupied by Alfred's pole. At length Elise gave the same symptoms of pleasure which I had seen before.

I had seen enough of it! I understood it all! I retired and made haste to take a long path which brought me back to the chateau. My head was on fire, my bosom palpitated, and my steps tottered, but I was determined at once to play myself the last act I had seen, and which required no partner.

I arrived in my room in a state of near madness, threw my hat on the floor, shut and locked the door, and put myself on the bed. I turned up my clothes to the waist, and recollecting to the minutest details what Elise had done with her hand, I placed mine between my legs. My efforts were at first fruitless, but I found at length the point I searched for. The rest was easy; I had too well observed to deceive myself. I moved my fingers back and forth over the nub of flesh. By varying the speed with which I manipulated it, I could alter the intensity of the feelings that began deep in my belly. A delicious sensation seized me; I continued with fury and soon fell into such an ecstasy that I lost consciousness.

When I came to myself I was in the same position, my hand all moistened by an unknown dew.

I sat up quite confused, and it was a long time before I entirely came to myself. It was nearly time for lunch, so I made haste to dress and went down.

The Governess was already in the salon with my grandmother. I looked at her on entering; she was beautiful and fresh, her color in repose, her eyes brilliant, so that one would have sworn she had just risen from an excellent morning's sleep. Her dress, in exquisite and simple taste, set off her charming figure. As to me, I cast down my eyes and felt myself blush.

My grandmother noticed my agitation and told me so. I replied that I had overslept, and contrary to habit had not taken my morning walk.

The Governess embraced me, and as she talked of one thing and another, I recovered myself completely.

Monsieur Marcel arrived soon, telling us of an excursion to a neighboring village, and we sat down to table.

I took care, without being seen, to notice everything that passed between Alfred and The Governess. I must acknowledge I was disappointed and greatly surprised. Not a look showed there was anything whatever between them.

About the middle of the repast The Governess carelessly remarked to my grandmother, "Mother, I was so forgetful on leaving Paris that I am missing several necessaries. Have I your permission to send my chambermaid tomorrow to fetch them? I can attend to myself, and it will only be a short absence."

The day passed quietly. Monsieur Marcel took a long ride on horseback. Elise and I sat by the water, amusing ourselves by needlework. Some neighbors came to visit my grandmother, and she invited them to dinner.

In the evening we had music, and I sang a duet with The Governess. Although already a good musician, and having a fine voice, I was not equal to The Governess, who gave me some excellent lessons in taste and feeling.

Monsieur Marcel played whist with my grandmother, and was completely reserved.

I retired about eleven o'clock. I was impatient to be alone with my thoughts, so I went to bed quickly and dismissed my maid. I had no doubt that the next evening would be the time for a serious meeting between Monsieur Marcel and The Governess. I burned to assist at the delicious scenes which would be enacted. I contemplated how to be there.

Knowing all the ways of the house, I thought over the plan of Auntie's apartment. It was situated on the second floor, the same as mine, but at the opposite extremity. A corridor gave communication to all the rooms on this floor. Monsieur Marcel was also lodged on the same flight, in a turning off the principal corridor.

The Governess had at her disposition a little room in which a bed was made up for her chambermaid, a beautiful bedroom and a dressing room. I recollected that this dressing cabinet, which occupied about one-third of the side of the room, used to be contiguous to an alcove, now closed by a strong partition. I also remembered a small hole in the upper part of the alcove, only stopped up by a small and very indifferent oil painting of a pastoral scene. A door in an unoccupied room gave access to this dark closet.

It was on these recollections I arranged my plan, then went to sleep, full of resolution and hope for the following day.

Julie, the servant, started for Paris, as had been arranged. Alfred and The Governess were more reserved than ever. However, I found out what I wanted to know as the day wore on.

After dinner Monsieur Marcel leaned negligently on the mantelpiece, pretending to admire the pendulum of a superb ormolu clock. He placed his finger for a moment on the figure XI, then on the figure VI; it was easy to understand that he intended to say half-past eleven. The Governess responded by a slight movement of her eyes. I knew then all I wanted; it only remained to make my preparations.

When we were seated in the garden Alfred offered to read to us, which was accepted.

I soon slipped away under some pretext, and, sure of being unobserved on the second floor, went to the little door of the dark closet.

Everything was in the same state as I have described, but a ladder was necessary, and I knew that there was one to be found in a passage near a linen cupboard. The wooden steps were very heavy, but the burning fire of curiosity that animated my movements doubled my strength. I dragged them into the alcove, found the hole and the canvas that was stretched in front of it, and with a pair of scissors I cut a small piece out of the picture. To my satisfaction, I found I could thus have a good view of the entire room, and above all—of the bed. I came downstairs quickly, shut the door, took the key, and returned to the garden. Everything had been executed so quickly that no one had noticed the strange fact of my absence. The whole of the day and the evening seemed to me to be mortally long.

At last, about half-past ten, my grandmother retired to rest, and we all followed suit. Alfred off to his room; The Governess remained with me for an instant and saw me safely into my bed chamber. I kissed her and said, "Good evening."

I undressed without delay and dismissed the maid. Then I drew on my stockings again, put on a pair of velvet slippers and a nightgown of dark color, and waited.

At about a quarter after eleven, I slid like a shadow into the corridor, reached the little door without interruption, opened it, and locked myself in, noiselessly and without difficulty. Then I mounted the ladder, settled myself down as comfortably as possible, and looked through my peephole.

My success was complete; I could see distinctly. The clean white bed seemed like an altar decked out for a sacrifice. A lamp placed on the night table inundated the brilliant linen with an intense flood of light. Elise was in the adjoining room, where I heard her performing her ablutions.

She came back into the room at last, with nothing on but her night-gown. Going to the bed, she turned it down, arranged the pillows, and placed the lamp so as to throw a still greater light upon it. Then she took a delicate cambric chemise, trimmed with lace, and advanced towards the full-length mirror of the wardrobe. She looked in the glass for a minute or two, and by a graceful movement of her shoulders let slip the chemise she had on, which was arrested in its downward course for a second by the welling of her hips, though it soon fell twisted at her feet. She had already put off her gown and now appeared completely naked before my startled eyes.

No one could dream of anything finer! Her breasts, firm and high, stuck out boldly and were surmounted by two strawberry nipples of a bright rose-pink; the fall of her back and her backside were both admirable.

At the bottom of her white and polished belly, her luxurious ebony fleece, the thickness of which constituted a true rarity, could be plainly seen. The contrast of this enormous black spot upon a body so white gave to Elise a peculiar appearance of strange voluptuousness.

She drew her lace shift over her head, put on her nightie again, and then walked into her parlor, holding the door ajar. A moment afterwards I heard cautious footsteps. The door was shut and double locked, and Elise and Alfred appeared in the bedroom. He had slippers on his feet and was dressed in a summer smoking jacket, under which was only his shirt. Elise made him sit upon a sofa and she took her place on his left knee. Their mouths met in a lingering kiss.

"My dear angel," said he, "how I thank you for having had sufficient confidence in me so as not to have made me languish and wait for your precious favors! You lavish them on your true spouse, who will reward you by his everlasting love."

As he spoke he opened the top of Elise's dressing gown and alternately kissed the two firm globes, while The Governess, reclining backwards, shuddered beneath the caresses that seemingly caused her to shiver voluptuously in every vein. He moved to her nipples, licking, biting. Then, taking advantage of Elise's position, he once more opened the gown, but this time at the bottom. Lifting up her chemise, he toyed a moment with the lovely black hairs, of which he appeared dotingly fond. Then I noticed his finger slip upwards a little and renew the playful friction that I had seen The Governess practice herself, and the imitation of which had procured for me such great enjoyment.

As for Elise, she had seized upon and displayed the splendid pole. I could not take my eyes off it. It appeared to me to be longer and bigger than the first time I had seen it. It was fully eight or nine inches long, and as big around as my wrist.

The Governess opened her thighs and therefore stretched her slit, which did not appear longer than my little finger. How is it possible, I said to myself, that an instrument of that size can penetrate entirely into such a little place? I concluded that The Governess, by the position she was in the first time, had doubtless received that great rod not in her body, but between her thighs, and that it must have been its rubbing against her that had rendered her so happy. My error was soon rectified, as during my reflections the two lovers had continued their sweet dance in silence with Alfred's mouth still teasing the spot between her legs.

"Ah," said Elise, "my husband, my darling, go on, I am so happy! How lovely your cock is! Oh, how I shall come! I'm coming already! Do it a little longer! Ah! I die!"

There was a long and silent pause while Elise seemed quite overcome, her body arched back, her head hidden on her sweetheart's shoulder, her glorious thighs still wide apart. Monsieur Marcel gazed at her intently, ravished at the sight.

"Come, now, come!" cried Elise, rising. "Come and put it into me. I must have it all. I want it all! Come, I'm on fire. I'm burning up! Flood me with your bounteous liquor."

Elise threw off her dressing gown and stretched herself upon the bed. Alfred did the same, but before putting himself near Elise, he lifted his shirt and rolled it under his armpits. How beautiful he was, built like Hercules and Apollo; his proud pole stood up stiffly growing out of a thick bush that showed it off splendidly.

Elise was lying on her back, her legs parted and lifted a little. Alfred got between, on his knees, and lifted his darling's chemise right up to her neck, again exposing her naked form to my gaze. I expected to see her get up and turn her backside to her lover as before, as I thought that was the only way it could be done, but to my great astonishment I found it was not so. Alfred stretched himself upon her; Elise lifted her legs and crossed them on his back in such a manner that nothing escaped me. I could distinctly see Elise's hand capture the pole, and direct its head to the center of the little slit that opened to receive it. Alfred gave a vigorous stroke of the loins, to which Elise answered, and at least half of the rod penetrated into the little hole, which dilated and began to engulf it. A few more moments completed the insertion, and I saw their two growths of hair mingle together. At last I knew all about it.

Now there was nothing but movements, sighs, inarticulate words and maddening shivers. I could see that he was pushing what Elise had called his "cock" into and out of her grasping slit. When the shaft emerged, it was shiny with her juices.

"Let me have it all—Ah! How fine it is—go gently—let us come slowly—hold me tight."

"My sweet darling! Lift up your thighs so that it can get right in. There! Do you feel it? Ah! how delightful!"

"It's wonderful! Are you ready? My Alfred, I'm going to come. I—I—make haste!"

"I'm ready. It's coming. There, it comes. Come now. I'm coming! I'm coming!"

Both remained quiet for a moment, then Alfred rose and I saw the dear sausage as before, coming out little, red, and dropping a tear.

Elise remained a little longer without giving signs of life, but she got up at last, and after smothering Alfred with kisses, went for an instant into her dressing room.

I thought it was all over and began to arrange my retreat, but a secret presentiment made me stop.

Elise went to bed again, embraced by her lover in her arms, and they engaged in sweet conversation.

"I have been so happy, dear! It is so much better when we are quite at our ease, and you do it so well."

"My darling, there is not a more perfect woman than you in the whole world! I want to eat you up bodily!"

Once more pushing up Elise's chemise, Alfred covered with kisses the whole of the beautiful body that trembled beneath his caresses. When he arrived at the center of bliss, he opened it, bit it gently, and kissed it passionately.

"Stop, dear," said Elise. "Stop! You will fatigue yourself. Rest, rest!"

"No, darling, look! See? My prick once more asks permission to go into its little companion. You won't refuse me?"

"Let me see. So you've come back to your splendid state? Yes indeed. Well, well, I'll allow you in once more. There, place yourself like that, and don't move!"

"What are you going to do?"

"You know, dear, how I like a change. Remain on your back and I'll do it to you!"

So saying, The Governess straddled Alfred's hips, and taking his rod in her hand, plunged it into her up to the hilt. Then gently moving, she pushed on, stopping a little, and remained thus spitted by the enormous spindle. She teased Alfred, blew him kisses and showed him her adorable titties, smiling and pouting to him all the time.

"I have you now," she said. "You are my little wife. See how well I do it!" She bobbed up and down on his pole, raising herself so that the swollen head almost was withdrawn, then impaling herself fully once again. She thrust and ground her hips while sitting against his belly, rotating his staff within her while he lay her helpless prisoner.

After a few minutes of this dalliance, it was easy to see that the supreme moment was reached. She fell upon her lover, who received her in his arms and pressed her to him, as he took hold of the white cheeks of her bottom one in each hand. Pleasure seized them together in great spasms, then Elise left his embrace and again lazily stretched her at her lover's side.

It was late. I was crushed with fatigue, emotion, and the cramped position I occupied, yet I would not go before I knew if the amorous couple meant to arrange another appointment. I had the satisfaction to hear them fix a rendezvous for the next evening at the same hour.

I regained my room and went to bed tired out, but I slept soundly. I woke about seven o'clock perfectly refreshed. I ruminated over all I had seen and heard the day before; my imagination became inflamed, my bosom panted, an active fire coursed through my veins. Mechanically, I took up a position on my back, as I had seen The Governess do, then I drew up my chemise, as Alfred had done to her. I alternatively touched each breast, and thrilled as the nipples swelled up. Feeling my body, I reached the delicate spot and rummaged there with great curiosity. It seemed to me that a slight change had taken place. The lips of the little nook were plumper; I sought the place that in The Governess's case had greedily swallowed up the monstrous sausage, but I only found a little hole that my finger could not penetrate without pain. I pushed up my finger a little and shuddered when an indescribable sensation invaded my entire being. I rubbed softly first, then quicker, afterward slower, and again with more activity as I repeated The Governess's words: "I'm coming! I'm coming—Ah!"

At length a nervous spasm overtook me. I felt transported with immense pleasure that I could fully appreciate, as I did not faint this time. When I had gathered my scattered senses, I drew away my wet hand. I rose and dressed myself and went downstairs, fresh and happy at having enjoyed such a sweet morning's diversion.

I shall not speak of the events of the day, which was an uninteresting one, as I am in haste to come to the scene of the evening. I took the same precautions, and had safely reached my observatory when Elise and her lover met once more.

The preliminaries were much the same, but instead of going to bed afterwards, Elise said, "I have a whim, dear. Let us do it like the other morning in the closet. We are more comfortable here and it will be nicer still!"

With these words she divested herself of her gown and pulled up her shift behind. She placed a big cushion in front of the mirror of the wardrobe and knelt upon it, her head and arms much lower than her buttocks, which, thrown out and accentuated by this ravishing position, presented the path of pleasure well in view and largely open.

Alfred, far from idle, had made his preparation. He had taken off his jacket and placed the lamp on the floor, so as to light up perfectly the delicious picture that the mirror reflected in every detail. Then he placed himself behind her, and began to get into her with the pole that bobbed forth from his belly.

"Oh, you can see too much of me!" said The Governess.

"How can I see too much of such beauty? Look in the glass!" He began to thrust into her with even strokes.

"No, it's too bad! Ah! It's going into me! Stop a little. What a fine fellow you are!"

"My adored one, how lovely you are! What admirable hips. What an adorable—Arse!"

"Oh! Alfred! What is that naughty word?"

"Don't be frightened, darling; lovers can say anything. Those words, out of place in calmer moments, add fresh relish to the sweet mystery of love. You will soon say them too, and understand their charm."

While he spoke, he continued his movements. Elise, in silent enjoyment, said nothing, but devoured with eager eyes the scene in the mirror. I was stupefied to hear her say to him a minute later, "Do you love it so very much?"

"What?"

"Why—my—"

"Your what?"

"Well—my—arse!"

"Ah, Elise, how sweet you are to me. Oh, yes, I love it. Your beautiful ass I adore it!"

"Feel it then. It's yours—yours alone. My arse—arse—arse."

As she concluded her broken utterances, she let herself go until she reached complete enjoyment. Alfred, who was rapidly arriving at the height of sovereign pleasure, reached the desired goal with her and fell upon her completely overcome.

They went no further than that delicious encounter; they could not fix a fresh meeting as they feared the return of the maid. Instead, they arranged certain signals, and, if the worst should come to the worst, they made up their minds to fall back upon the pavilion in the park. I went to my room. Julie returned the next day, so that the nocturnal assignations came to an end, but I sought to discover the signs that were to have been exchanged between the lovers. Much to my disappointment, I discovered nothing.

Four days went by in like manner. I was vexed and had once again renewed my morning walks, directing my steps always to the gazebo in the grounds.

During the afternoon of the fourth day, I had gone there and I was surprised to find a garden chair that had evidently been brought from the house. I concluded therefore, and rightly too, that something would take place the next day, and I was at my post long before the arrival of the actors in the drama of love.

They approached with caution, one after the other, and shut themselves in. Elise sat upon the chair, saying, "You did well to think of this piece of furniture; my position of the other day was somewhat uncomfortable. But what are you doing on your knees?"

"You know I must greet your lovely cleft, my dear."

"Very well then, give him a kiss quickly and let us do it. It is late. You shall sit on the chair, and I'll ride upon you!"

Alfred undid his trousers after planting a lingering kiss on Elise's muff, then sat upon the chair. Elise pulled up all her petticoats and got on top of her lover. She then seized his vigorous pole and commenced the introduction by pushing down her bottom as it slowly entered. The chair was so placed that I could enjoy the sight from behind, and consequently could not miss the slightest detail. The enormous tool soon disappeared completely. Elise lifted up her legs, placed her heels on the bars of the chair, and began to rise and fall in turn.

The accustomed sighs and words rose to their lips; their souls melted in mutual enjoyment. I had intended, this time, not to rest content with the part of simple spectator. I had made arrangements in advance and chose the most comfortable position under the circumstances.

I began to do it to myself at the precise moment that Elise introduced the cock into her slit, and then, regulating my movements with theirs, operating slowly or quickly, I came at the same moment as they did, and my sighs of pleasure mingled with those of the happy couple.

When all was over, Elise left the lap of her lover, and during her movement I saw Alfred's cock drop out of its retreat. A large quantity of the milky liquid, the cause of which I as yet ignored, trickled along her thighs and fell to the ground. The lovers readjusted their dress.

Monsieur Marcel communicated to Elise that in three days' time he would make the official demand for her hand, and should then leave to make all requisite preparation. They further arranged to meet at the pavilion for the last time two days later, in the morning. I went away, sadly, to the house. I was to fall back once more into the dead calm of my life, but still, the hope of being soon married and tasting in my turn the divine pleasures I had witnessed sustained my spirits.

On the third day I was in my hiding place; Alfred came first, and Elise a minute later. There seemed a slight cloud on her beautiful countenance, yet she threw herself into her lover's arms, and he, after a few caresses, tried to put his hand up her clothes. This time she prevented him.

"No, dear. Today is impossible! I am sorry, I assure you, but there are womanly obstacles in the way. We must put it off till you return."

"How unlucky for me."

"And how about me?"

"Take hold of it. Look how it throbs for your touch!"

Alfred drew his splendid instrument out of his trousers. Elise fondled it, saying, "No, no, not without me!"

"But I beg you."

"You insist? Well, I suppose I must not be selfish. But I assure you that I am grieved to see such good cock wasted. And you must not get into the habit of doing it without your companion."

With these words, Elise had turned up the sleeve of her dressing gown. Alfred had dropped his trousers and lifted the tail of his shirt as he stood up.

"No!" said Elise. "Take your trousers right off. Since I am to have nothing, I will at least enjoy a good view."

Alfred did as she desired and gave himself up to her. She placed herself a little behind him, put her left arm around her lover's waist, and with the right began a soft movement of the wrist that seemed to procure extraordinary pleasure to Monsieur Marcel. She pumped up and down, uncovering and covering by turn the head of Alfred's tool.

"Ah! How finely you do it!" said he. "Gently, my angel. Uncover it well. Now, quicker—stop—go on again! Ah! I feel it coming! Quicker—I'm going to come!"

He gave two or three strokes of the loins, and Elise, who had carefully followed his instructions, pressed the instrument higher in her hand. Suddenly, to my great stupefaction, I saw a stream of white liquid spring out in jets and fall full three paces off, the emission seeming to drive Alfred mad with joy.

After a few moments Elise wiped the rod herself with her embroidered handkerchief. Then she thrust the diminishing organ away, saying, "You are a naughty boy to have spent without me. You owe me one for this, and you shall pay for it at the first opportunity."

I let them both depart, and when they were far off, I entered the pavilion and closely examined the fresh traces of the ejaculation I had witnessed. The sight inflamed my imagination. I pulled up my clothes and got astride the chair, placing my hand on the seat, my middle finger upraised. I pressed myself down upon it, found the little orifice, and imitating Elise's movements stretched myself as widely apart as possible. Working my bottom up and down, I imagined I was taking in the coveted instrument.

A lively sense of pain did not stop me; I redoubled my efforts and got in nearly half of my finger.

Then I repeated Elise's words: "I'm coming—I come—my arse!" until suddenly the spasm seized me and I twisted my body about in an agony of pleasure.

My hand and the chair bore the marks of my enjoyment. I hastily wiped them away and returned to the house.

In the course of the day Alfred had an interview with my grandmother and formally asked for The Governess's hand. All was arranged and he left for Paris to press on with the preliminaries. It was decided that Elise should remain with us for a few days. I was to assist at her marriage as bridesmaid, so she took me away with her.

The ceremony was celebrated with pomp, and, for the first time in my life, I attended a grand ball, where I may say without vanity that I attracted a pleasing degree of attention. I should have liked to have been present when the bride and bridegroom were put to bed, but my observatory was far away and I had to put up with solitary pleasures.

Three days afterwards, Monsieur Marcel took me back to my grand-mother's, and went off to Italy with his wife.

I was returned once more to the monotony and dullness of my early life, only with my senses now quickened and the knowledge, that my temperament required perhaps much more than many women. I dreamed of nothing but marriage, and Monsieur Marcel remained my ideal of a husband.

I often made visits to the pavilion in the park and became engulfed in the recollections that hovered thickly there. I had left there the chair used by Elise and Alfred, which often became my throne of solitary pleasure.

This means of relief was not only necessary, but I may say indispensable, as raging fits of love would sometimes come over me. My eyes would grow dim, there would be a ringing in my ears, my legs would totter beneath me, and simply by pressing my thighs together I would feel that charming part that makes women get wet and palpitating.

In those moments no resistance was possible; I was obliged to give way! My finger was my master; when I came fully once, I experienced a wholesome calm, and a delicious languor overwhelmed me. I am convinced that without this practice I would have fallen dangerously ill, though I did not do it too often.

Thus I attained my twentieth year. I was truly beautiful, and I will here trace my portrait. It shall be an exact resemblance, without false shame or ridiculous self-praise. My stature was a little above medium height; my hair was abundant and of a fine, dark-chestnut color. My eyes, with long lashes, were hazel, brilliant, and swimming with voluptuous moisture. My mouth, rather large and very sensual, was furnished with fine teeth; a black mole, on the right side of my upper lip, gave piquancy to my physiognomy. I had an admirable bust, the breasts apart, firm and well-placed; my figure was neat and supple with shapely buttocks that were perfectly handsome; and my mount of Venus, very much pronounced, protected a nook that it appears was a rare and pure pattern, both in form and exceptional voluptuous quality. While not possessing the rare bush of The Governess, I was well provided in that way with a pretty pelt of silky fur.

How often, dear Will, you have placed me so as to enjoy the view of that mossy growth! What caresses! What kisses! But let me not get ahead of myself.

My grandmother felt her end approaching, and fearing for my future, tried to get me a husband without letting me know. An old friend of hers made her a proposition one day that seemed to suit her hopes and my dearest wishes.

Monsieur de Cocteau was introduced to us. He was twenty-eight years old, of medium stature, very genteel in manner, with a graceful bearing and regular features. His family was a good one, and his fortune satisfactory. He did not present such a manly appearance as Monsieur Marcel, but as he was, he pleased me and I secretly gave him my heart from the first moment.

As for his heart, he was dazzled by my beauty and his mind was made up as soon as he saw me, so that we were all agreed. The marriage being decided, we were to be united two months afterwards. We resolved to pass a short time with my grandmother, and then depart for Nice, where my husband was employed.

Elise came to assist at my wedding with her husband. She was as pretty as ever, and quite as happy. I told her my little secrets, and how I felt inclined to love my husband with all my heart and soul. A single thing vexed me, however, and that was that I found him rather cold and reserved, although always affectionate and gallant. Elise burst out laughing and assured me that all would soon change.

The important day arrived; she acted as A Lady and dressed me herself. I felt the day get shorter and shorter with unspeakable desire and fear. The act that I was about to accomplish, although well-known to me in theory, filled me with terrible apprehension.

The ceremony proceeded without mishap, and when the evening

came to an end at last, Elise led me to the nuptial chamber. It was her room, and on the bed where I had seen her so bountifully treated I was to be made a woman.

Elise put me to bed and sat by my side to instruct me with what in her idea I was profoundly ignorant of. She went through her lesson with tact, but left nothing unexplained, kissed me, recommended obedience, and went away.

A minute afterwards my new husband came in clothed only in a dressing gown. He drew near to me, kissed me heartily, said some very affectionate things, took off his garment, and got into bed. I barely had a glimpse of his manhood, so quickly did he jump beneath the covers.

Charles, for that was his name, pressed me in his arms; the contact of his naked flesh against mine made me jump! He kissed me softly, telling me to fear not, and drew still closer. I trembled all over; I didn't dare speak, and yet I desired to. He whispered: "Would you like to have a little baby?" and at the same time his right knee insinuated itself between my thighs, so as to separate them. I resisted at first, then little by little I gave way. Soon Charles was on top of me, and I felt the head of the much-coveted object.

This first contact acted upon me like a spark upon gun-powder. All the warmth of my being was concentrated in the besieged nook—I almost came! Charles was awkward, either too high or too low. I couldn't move; I couldn't help him! I was panting and on fire! At last I felt him in the right place. He pushed on vigorously; I felt a sharp pain, started violently and drew back, on the point of shrieking.

Charles, bewildered, asked my pardon, supplicated me to have a little courage, and took up his post once more. I remained still and was artful enough to creep into a better position. He pushed again and the pain came back. I resisted it, and shoved my body up to meet the blows, so as to finish quicker. It seemed to me that Charles did not act very vigorously, and that there was a great difference in size between the instrument that perforated me and that of Monsieur Marcel. Moreover,

Charles did not speak, he did not utter one of the words I had heard, which I believed were part and parcel of the operation.

Charles, at last, seemed to gather a little strength. He gave a solid stroke of the loins and I did the same, stiffening my body. The pain was so great that I cried out, but I had the satisfaction to feel myself penetrated, for the whole instrument—thin as it was—was sheathed within me! My husband continued his backward and forward movement a moment, then shivered, sighed several times, and stopped short. I felt a hot liquid inundate me and diminish the smarting to a slight degree.

Charles got off and lay down by my side, visibly fatigued.

In spite of my desires and my imagination, I had felt no pleasure. That did not astonish me, as I had been taught so by Elise. Charles kissed me, and wishing me good night, turned his back and fell asleep.

I was very much surprised and quite embarrassed. I fully expected we should begin again, and in spite of the pain was quite ready to do so. At last I resigned myself to the inevitable, and slumbered too.

I awoke the next morning very late—I was alone. On hearing the sudden movement I made in sitting up, Charles came out of the neighboring room and approached me. He was completely dressed already, and he kissed me on the forehead, uttered a few kind words, and asked me if I had slept well. But all this was cold and distant. My heart, ready to spring towards him, stopped in its flight. It seemed to me that he should have waited until I awoke, to take me in his arms and speak of love and happiness, and then recommence the caresses of the night. A doubt for my future flashed across me; this was not what I had dreamed! Charles went out, saying that he left me to dress, but I had no thought of doing so. I busied myself in sad thoughts. The next moment, a well-known voice called me, and Elise ran to embrace me.

I put my arms around her neck, held her tightly, and began to cry.

"Gracious me! What is the matter, dear child?" she said.

I didn't know how to answer her, as I had no complaint to make. I only felt that I was not loved as I had hoped to be and that my ardent furnace would never be able to burn freely.

Elise thought that I was simply hysterical, and calmed me by gentle joking.

My natural gaiety soon got the upper hand; I rose and took a bath that my maid had already prepared.

The day passed slowly. Everybody was happy around me; my husband seemed enchanted, acting as tender and gallant as his nature would permit. I was pleased with him and timidly responded to his distant caresses. Night came; he led me away at an early hour and we went to bed. Less timid than the night before, he took me in his arms, said that he loved me, and kissed me tenderly. I was bold enough to tell him that I also loved him, and gave him a kiss that electrified him. Already I felt on my naked thigh something hard that promised much.

As on the preceding evening, he placed his lips to my ear and said, "Shall we do like last night?"

I could not answer, but I also could not help opening my thighs and lifting my nightgown in secret. He got over me and I held him fast in my embrace, waiting and impatiently desiring the supreme moment.

I soon felt the head of his cock. A shivering fit seized me, during which I took care to introduce it as far in as possible. I still felt a tolerably severe pain, but that did not stop me; the happy fire that circulated through my veins made me support all. Already I felt the advance symptoms of enjoyment. I could not to speak; I wanted to cry out and tell all I felt. I now perfectly understood The Governess's words, but the silence of Charles, who seemed wrapped up in himself, prevented me from giving vent to my feelings.

He continued his movements and kissed me, but he did not seem overwhelmed with passion, as I would have wished. I could not resist the impulse to push up my bottom and cry out! Then I remained perfectly still. I was coming, so intensely that I almost lost my senses.

Charles stopped for a second, and seemed astonished at my response. I curbed myself, and he resumed his pleasures.

He was a long while performing his sweet duty, though machine-like, and I poured out the sweet dew four times! At last I felt him shudder and sigh, and a fiery, flaming jet inundated my entrails.

We both remained quiet. I was exalted, in a fever, but ready to begin again; he was broken down, and only required rest. So we fell asleep.

The next morning, on awakening, I found myself once more alone. I was not sorry, and my brain replayed the scene of the night till I felt a curiosity that impelled me to examine my body. I sat up on the pillows, my legs well apart, and with my hands opened the lips of my crack. I found a great change—the interior was much more rosy, the opening was wider, and my entire finger easily plunged within it. This examination amused me, and would have produced certain consequences, but a discreet rap at my door made me cover myself up hastily and take a natural position in bed.

It was Elise, who found me fresh and gay, and when I smiled she kissed me. We gossiped like sisters as I dressed. I was a real woman now, and my pretty aunt treated me as one. She gently drew certain secrets from me that seemed to interest her. I told her what took place. She seemed much surprised when I said that I had felt great pleasure four times, while Charles had only done it to me once. Evidently the slight amount of my husband's virile strength, compared to the vigor of hers, surprised her greatly.

The day passed away, and, as my husband was a great sportsman, he went out shooting. I took a walk with Elise. We all met at dinner and passed the evening with a little music.

Night arrived, but how different from the two preceding ones. Charles popped an ugly silk handkerchief on his head, chatted about our early departure, about our new house, and so on, but never mentioned a word about love. He simply embraced me coldly and slept.

I awoke on the morrow before he did, and a terrible longing seized me to look at the instrument that I had only felt twice, and which did not much resemble Monsieur Marcel's in size or strength. I was favored by circumstances. It was warm, and Charles had thrown off the sheet that only just hid the particular part. Luckily, his shirt had been pulled up; I had only to draw down the sheet a little, with infinite prudence, before I caught sight of the sad tool which was to be my only consolation.

What a difference, indeed, to that of Alfred! Small, wrinkled, and in a shriveled skin, one could hardly guess at the presence of its limp head. Henceforward, I believe, my destiny was fixed.

Charles stirred. I made haste to turn around and pretended to sleep, and he left the bed first, as was his habit.

The limit fixed for our sojourn at my granny's house drew near. I was far from being unhappy, as my husband was good to me and loved me as heartily as his cold nature allowed him. He was proud of my beauty and refused me nothing, but all this did not suffice. It was not what I had so much desired—namely, a voluptuous, lascivious, ardent love, for which I would have sacrificed everything, for which I was capable of real devotion! I could see laid out before me a monotonous life, probably without the birth of a child, but too difficult to support for a temperament like mine.

Charles did it to me once or twice a week, and always in the same despairingly reserved style. He only kissed my cheeks or my forehead—my firm young breasts received no caresses. His hand seemed to flee those charming places that would have so gladly welcomed its touch. In turn I felt that I dare not try to feel him, as instinctively I knew he would have repulsed me.

After two years of marriage, my temperament was in full blast and had increased in passion, instead of growing calmer! My husband did it less and less, and as I feared, I had no child. A baby would have changed my one fixed idea.

My grandmother had been dead a year. We had a lovely home in Nice, where Charles occupied an exalted position that obliged him to be frequently absent. These little journeys suited his taste for hunting and shooting. Therefore I was often alone, and in spite of music, which I continued to love and successfully cultivate, my brain was always at work picturing scenes of delirious love. What fearful nights I used to pass alone, writhing between the sheets in lascivious positions that I instinctively invented!

My finger was powerless to satisfy me now. I would take my pillow and embrace it with twisted legs and twining arms, as if it could realize my desires. I would rub against it and reach a degree of comparative enjoyment that drove me still madder. I would change my position and get astride it, rubbing myself, till the sluices of pleasure, swollen to the utmost by this stimulant, burst open and procured me some relief.

These nervous fits brought on hallucinations that manifested themselves by an inconceivable state of hysteria. My calm and gay temper became unequal and capricious. I resisted as well as I could, but at last I avowed myself vanquished. Was I very, very guilty?

I was very friendly with Madame Dumond, wife of the principal magistrate, a slight blonde who may have been pretty once, but who was already beginning to fade. I thought that she must have had many intrigues when young.

One day, when visiting her, she informed me that Monsieur Fanon had come to take command of the garrison. He was a young officer who had been much talked about. He had fought with rare courage on the battlefield, and had rapidly earned the rank of lieutenant-colonel. He was about thirty-six and unmarried.

Madame Dumond told me that she had invited him to dinner and that my husband and I were to meet him. Was it a presentiment? I knew not, but I returned home quite pensive and slightly jealous of Madame Dumond.

I must confess, I prepared what I thought was a most ravishing dress, and three days afterwards the dinner came off. When we entered the drawing room, Monsieur Fanon was already there. In a moment, I had examined him. He was tall, vigorous, and well-built, his countenance frank and open, and his manner well-bred. He was introduced and his sweet persuasive voice charmed me. My heart grew cold, and then all the blood in my veins rushed to my face. Oh! I was a captive caught in the toils at last, and I did not even seek to combat the influence that invaded my soul.

The dinner was served and it turned out a very gay affair. Monsieur

Fanon was able to show his brilliant and cultivated wit. He sat at Madame Dumond's right hand. I could have killed her!

After dinner, he approached me, asking if he might be allowed to pay me a visit, and talked to my husband, whom he pleased vastly. Madame Dumond sat down at the piano and played a lively waltz; Monsieur Dumond said that I was a good partner and asked me to take a turn with him, but he was old and soon fatigued, so Monsieur Fanon offered to take his place.

As I felt his arm encircle my waist I was taken with a nervous tremor that evidently did not escape him.

I gave myself up to the charm of the hour. Monsieur Fanon boldly profited by the embrace in which he held me, in spite of the spectators. As he turned a corner of the drawing room, he was able to press me so tightly to him that I felt for a second against my belly a certain object so hard and stiff that I nearly fainted.

That waltz was the signal of my defeat!

The happy evening was too soon over. Once more at home, I undressed quickly, and pretending fatigue said goodnight to my husband and jumped into bed, not to sleep, but to dream.

I was placed on my left side, my bottom turned to Charles. A caprice seized him; I felt him softly lift my linen, and then pressing against me, he tried to get into me from behind. I was vexed at first, but, my temperament overpowering me, I gave way to his designs. Unfortunately, he could not manage it, and he did not get in.

I lost all patience and rapidly threw off the sheet by a sudden movement. I passed my hand behind me, seized the tool, which was useless without a guide, and stuffed it into my slit to the last inch. I was thinking of Monsieur Fanon the whole time. I imagined that he was behind me, and that he was doing it to me. Under my breath I addressed to him all that I was burning to say at such a moment. I pushed back against Charles, pretending it was another belly that slapped my buttocks. I rolled my hips passionately, imagining it was a different pole stretching my crack.

Three times the dew of love gushed out for him, for him alone! My husband, profiting unwittingly by the result of my thoughts, did his duty a little better than usual, and refreshed me with a copious ejaculation.

When he had finished, I feared that, with his habitual ridiculous reserve, he was going to make a fuss about the spontaneous movement that made me seize and imprison his cock myself. But he seemed, on the contrary, grateful to me. I made a note thereof for the future.

The next day, Monsieur Fanon came to pay us a visit, but we were out and I was really grieved when I found his card. He returned on the third day, and his persistence pleased me greatly. My husband was at home; we received him as cordially as possible and pressed him to come often.

I fancied that he treated me with particular warmth of feeling, and I was happy at the thought!

A gentle intimacy quickly sprang up between us, my love grew greater each day, and I already saw that my adored Will reciprocated the feeling. Although he had said nothing as yet, I was sure of it—what woman ever makes such a mistake?

We had, as yet, never been alone together. I ardently desired and yet feared that moment. I did not wish to abandon myself entirely at the first opportunity, though I felt that it would be impossible for me to resist one single instance! I resolved to know more of him, to try him, but all my strength of will melted away as soon as I saw him. In such a state of mind, how could I resist his attack?

That was quickly proved! One day he came at three o'clock. My husband was away, but I had a visitor—a wearisome female who had no idea of getting up and going. I could see my dear Will waiting and suffering, but at least, not being decently able to remain any longer, he took his leave, giving me a supplicating look that I was powerless to resist.

I said to him, "Has not my husband promised you a certain book?"

"Yes, madam, and I had hoped to be able to take it with me today."

"I will give it you. Pardon me, madam," I said to my eternal bore, "and permit me to leave you for an instant."

We were in a small reception room that served as my boudoir. Will, who understood me, went out and waited for me in the big drawing room where I rejoined him with an odd volume in my hand.

In an instant he declared his passion. What he said, what I answered, I do not know. I remember nothing.

I led him towards the hall for fear we should be overheard. There was a double door between the drawing room and a little vestibule where I would be able to hear an approaching servant. As we reached there, Monsieur Fanon, beside himself, seized me in his arms. A lingering kiss, a kiss of fire, a kiss that penetrated to my soul, arrested a shriek that I would not have been able to stifle.

At the same time, his prompt hand had lifted my petticoats and was caressing my burning slit that quick as lightning poured out upon his fingers palpable traces of the love potion that filled it to overflowing.

"Begone—begone—away," I said, with stifled breath. "Go—tomorrow—three o'clock." Then I fled in a state I cannot describe.

Happily, the lady who was waiting was not very clever and did not notice my disordered state.

I shall not undertake to narrate my feelings till the next day. All that I can remember is that I firmly resolved to satisfy my erotic longings.

My husband intended to absent himself for two or three days on business matters, and I arranged so as to send my servants on different errands. I dressed myself carefully and waited.

My dear Will arrived. I opened the door to him myself and led him to my boudoir.

We sat down, much embarrassed. He was very respectful and asked my pardon for what he had done the day before, saying that he was unable to master the delirious rage that had seized him, and that his love for me was such that he would die if he was unable to enjoy me.

I knew not how to answer. Both our hearts were too full. He took my hand and kissed it. Shuddering, I rose. Our mouths met. I confess I made no more attempts at resistance. I had not the strength to do so.

I fully enjoyed this intense happiness. I felt that he was carrying me along—but to where? What were we to do? In my boudoir there were only a very narrow low sofa, some armchairs, and ordinary seats without arms.

Will, still holding me in his arms, sat on a chair, so that I found myself in front of him, leaning over his head and face. I felt one of his arms at my waist; soon my clothes were all up in front and Will tried to pass his knees between my legs.

"Oh, no," I said, between two sobs. "No, please, have pity. I am a married woman."

Will made efforts to pull me down, so as to straddle across him; but on instinctive feeling, although I longed for it, I still resisted, and stiffened myself against him. We soon became exhausted. At last, having dropped my eyes a little, I saw something that put an end to the struggle.

He had taken out his prick for the fray. Its ruby, haughty head stood up proudly. In length and thickness it was truly uncommon; it vied even with that of Monsieur Marcel. I had no strength to resist such a sight; my thighs opened by themselves. I slid down, hiding my face on my lover's shoulder, and I gave myself up to him, opening myself as much as possible, desiring, and yet fearing, the entrance of such an imposing guest.

I soon felt the head between the lips of my grotto, which the thin tool of my husband had not accustomed to such a bountiful measure. I made a movement to help him, and had hardly introduced the head when I felt myself flooded by a flaming jet of loving liquor that covered my thighs and belly.

The prolonged wait, and his own passion, had made the precious dew pump up too quickly, and I had not been able to enjoy it as I should.

I could not help showing a little disappointment, but my lover, covering me with kisses, told me that I need wait but a brief period of repose, and that I should soon be more satisfied with him.

We sat on the sofa, entwined in each other's arms, telling one another of our love and happiness. We had fallen in love at first sight, and both had given way to irresistible passion.

In a few moments I saw that my lover was ready to begin again, and I asked myself how we were going to do it. I did not wish to try again that posture that had turned out so badly for me, and I could see Will also looking about him.

An idea struck me. I rose, smiling, teasing him. When he rose too, I retreated, and he eagerly pursued me till at last I went and leaned with nonchalance upon the mantelpiece, presenting my bottom, that I wriggled like a cat, and at the same time turning my head and throwing him a provocative glance.

Ah, how he understood me. Will rushed upon me and kissed me, saying, "Thank you."

Then he got behind me and threw my petticoats over my back. When he saw the beautiful shape of my bottom, he gave a loud cry of admiration. I expected as much, but did not dream of the homage he paid to it.

He threw himself onto his knees, and after having covered my backside with kisses, he drew the globes apart, just at the top of the thighs, and I could feel his lips, even his tongue. I shrieked and was overcome.

Will rose up and began to put it in. His enormous instrument could not easily penetrate, in spite of our mutual efforts, so he drew it out, put a little saliva on the head and shaft, and soon stabbed me to the very vitals. I was filled and plugged up, and in a state of unspeakable ecstasy.

My lover, leaning over me, glued his lips to mine, that I offered to him by turning my head; his tongue dallied with mine. I was beside myself. I felt myself going mad. He plunged his tool into me again and again, drawing it out nearly to the tip before driving it in to the balls. I felt those twin plums slap my buttocks with each stroke and so great became my excitement that I reached down and began to massage the throbbing nub of my clit. I could feel my juices running down my thighs as that great prick continued to ravage me. The supreme moment arrived. I writhed about, uttering inarticulate sounds.

Will, who was reserving himself, was delighted at my joy; he let me calm down, and then I felt his sweet movement again.

Ah, how he knew to distill pleasure, and double it by a thousand delicate, subtle shades. That first lesson; I can feel it, as I write, between my thighs.

"Dear angel," he said, "tell me what you feel. It's so nice to enjoy each other's soft confidence when we form but one body, as at this moment."

Oh, how his speech made me happy. I, who had always wished to hear and say those words that had almost driven me wild when The Governess was at work! I did not hesitate an instant longer.

"I must do it again," I said, "It's coming—push in—again—right in—finish me—ah! I'm coming!"

"My adored one, I'm coming too—it's bubbling up—Oh! Oh! I'm going to explode!"

Will gave a final push and fell against me. I felt his ejaculation and nearly fainted under the force of the jet.

How was it that I did not die during that embrace? Nothing that I had imagined at the sight of The Governess's sweet struggles could approach this reality! I remained overwhelmed, my head in my arms, my bosom heaving, incapable of movement.

Will drew out. I still spent. I kept on spending. I stood as I was, without sense of shame, naked below the waist, trembling, mechanically continuing the movement of my bottom and causing the overflow of liquid to fall to the ground.

Will took pity on me. After rapidly adjusting himself, he pulled down my petticoats and, taking me in his arms, sat by my side on the sofa. I was delirious for a second. He calmed me; his sweet voice was a song. I begged him to leave me to myself, and he went away.

I at last regained full consciousness, though my heart still pounded and threatened to burst. I was in an extraordinary state of disorder and was obliged to change my linen. My chemise and stockings were not only stained by loving liquid, but by numerous spots of blood. My womanhood could not accept such a full-sized cock with impunity.

When I had set in order my toilette and my ideas, I went to bed and slept soundly, my husband not intending to return till late in the evening. I awoke about seven, happy, fresh as a lark, and stronger than I had felt for many a day.

I will not restate all the thoughts that crowded in upon my brain, as I have already said that I had been drawn on by my irresistible feelings, and above all by a natural absolute craving for the sexual act. It was as necessary for my life as simple food.

Yet, I was far from depraved! I loved my husband as a sure friend, as the companion of my existence, and if he had possessed the manly vigor that was necessary for me, or if even he had known how to answer my clever caresses, I should never have dreamt of being unfaithful to him! I resolved to spare him all sorrow, and I have fully succeeded, as he has never had the least suspicion!

This torrid affair demanded much care, trouble, and discretion. The community was much inclined to scandal, and it was very difficult for me to hide my connection, so I had to take endless precautions.

I warned my lover, who, wishing above all to save my reputation, promised to do all in his power not to excite suspicion. I knew I could rely on his honor.

A few days went by without our meeting; I suffered greatly, and he as much as I! A sign, a look during our walks was our only consolation for eight long days!

At last, Will could bear it no longer and came to pay us a visit. We chatted in an ordinary way. A business associate arrived and Will decided to leave; my husband showed him out and returned to the room. I don't know what instinct warned me that Will had not left the house! I got up, with some excuse that seemed all the more reasonable as the visitor was keeping up a technical conversation with my husband, and went into the vestibule. I was not mistaken. Will, seeing no servants about, was waiting by the side door.

As soon as he saw me, he threw himself upon me, clasped me in his arms and with violent passion exclaimed, "Darling angel, how I suffer!"

"No less than I."

We were once again between the double doors. Before I knew where I was, our mouths were glued together, my petticoats were up to my navel, and his finger pushed itself into my burning slit that opened beneath its pressure. My hand had seized the darling object between his thighs.

What more can I say? In a second or two—after a few movements of our hands took place—I nearly swooned with joy. I drew away my own hand, bathed now with an abundance of Will's warm liquid.

Yet a few more days went by without our being able to meet, till at last a happy moment of liberty was granted to us. A whole hour was ours.

Ah, how we profited by it! My lover came into my boudoir. I rushed to receive him and I devoured him with caresses.

"Let us do it quickly," we both exclaimed together. "Let us enjoy to the utmost our secret happiness."

I tore myself from him, removed my clothes, and getting onto the sofa on my knees, presented my bottom.

He put his throbbing cock in at once. There was little in the way of reservation or prolongation. We had been apart so long our passion would permit no delay. Will simply rammed his wonderful cock into me and pistoned it in and out until I thought it must emerge from my belly. His balls slapped my bottom and his hands reached around to crush my trembling breasts as he continued his shattering strokes. I very soon swooned beneath his copious discharge. We then sat down, but my lover was not satisfied. Despite my fears, I could not refuse. He went on his knees between my legs, then made me stretch wide apart. I took his vigorous firebrand in my hand; it was already as hard as ever. I stroked it a second, then pushed it gradually into my slit while I savored slowly the delightful pleasure.

When the arrow had completely disappeared in its quiver, Will leaned over me and, lifting my two legs over his arms, threw me backwards. He went to work so lustily, ramming and pumping, that soon a second ejaculation became added to the first, with which I seemed to be already filled.

I do not intend to retrace day by day all our delicious meetings. I will limit myself to a description of the most striking facts of this adorable liaison that I wished would last out my life! My lover knew how to vary our pleasures without ever reaching satiety, he felt a singular pleasure in teaching the art of enjoyment, and he found in me a most docile and willing pupil.

He taught me the names of everything, sometimes making me say them, but only in the whirl of passion; he used them himself in supreme moments of bliss, proclaiming that such spice should never be too overused or it would lose its flavor!

What cunning caresses! What lascivious postures he taught me! What whims, infantile play, and even prolonging on both sides! What refinements of pleasure we realized as soon as we'd thought of them! I made such progress, under such a good master, that often I surpassed him.

I used to vastly like to change the way of doing it. For instance, sometimes when plugged from behind, one of my favorite positions, I would unhorse my rider, turn around quickly, give a kiss to my still-erect conqueror, wet with my passion cream, and escape to the other end of the room. I would place myself in an easy chair, my legs upraised and my pussy quite open, while I gave it a provoking twitching movement. My lover would be hardly in me again when by a fresh whim I would draw it out, make him sit on a chair, get on his knees, my back turned towards him, and taking his tool, plunge it in my body to the very hilt.

His cock, the splendid instrument of my joy, became my passion, the object of real worship. I never tired of admiring its thickness, its stiffness, and its length, all equally marvelous. I would dandle it, suck it, pump it, caress it in a thousand different ways, rub it between my titties, holding it there by pressing them with both my hands. Often when captive in this voluptuous passage it would throw out its thick offering of sperm.

My lover returned all my caresses with interest. My pussy was his goddess, his idol. He assure me that no woman had ever possessed a more perfect one. He would open it and frig it in every conceivable way. His greatest delight was to apply his lips thereto, and extract, so to speak, the quintessence of voluptuousness by titillations of his tongue. It almost drove me mad.

I got so fond of this delicious method of procuring orgasm that hardly one of our meetings took place without Will making me enjoy it.

I had adopted for this joy a favorite position. I would recline in a large easy chair that I had purposely placed in my boudoir. I would sit on it with my thighs open and thrown over the arms of the piece of furniture; my lover, on his knees before me, would lick and suck and tease my pleasure bud with his teeth. When I wriggled and twisted in the paroxysm of pleasure, pressing his head to my belly, gently pulling his hair and ears, and slapping his cheeks, he would drag himself from my grasp, plunge his cock into my cunny, and, enlaced together as one, we would come till we almost lost our reason.

Other times, I would kneel on the sofa and receive his tongue from behind, my lover clamping his face between the cheeks of my bottom and finding the delicate spot that received him with joy.

One day, after a rather long separation, my dear Will was able to find me alone. Alas! my monthly obstacle rendered our usual pleasure impossible. I could see he was suffering and looking at my hand in a supplicating way. I was quite disposed to accord him this means of relief, when a mad idea crossed my brain! I remembered the last scene between The Governess and Monsieur Marcel in the pavilion in the park. The situation was identical. I wished to reproduce it in every detail and easily induced Will to humor me. I made him get up, placed him in the same position as Alfred had been, and proceeded to do exactly the same as Elise. I fisted him tightly, drawing the skin of his tool up and down and running my palm over the engorged head. With my other hand I dandled his balls where they hung pendulous and full. I jerked him faster and faster until I could see the color rise in his chest and face. He spurted out his dew afar, and I gathered the last few pearls in my handkerchief.

When he had done, I could not help laughing.

He asked me the cause of my merriment.

"Nothing," I answered thoughtlessly, "it reminded me of something."

I saw his face change, and quickly guessed the mistake I had just made and what suspicions were gathering in the mind of my lover. Not wishing to cause him the least shade of vexation, I made him sit close to me and, sure of his discretion, I told him all that had happened to me before marriage. The story amused him greatly; he made me enter into the most minute details. When I told him how I was led on to procure sweet pleasure for myself, he exclaimed, "Ah, darling! What I would have given to see you frig your delicious little cunt!"

He asked me more questions about my solitary habits, and I went so far as to tell him that on the day of our meeting at Madame Dumond's, I was so full of thought of him that I had done it that very evening.

"Why," he answered, "this is truly curious! Confidence in return for confidence, dear angel. Know that the same night and probably at the same hour, we were exchanging our souls in mutual spending!"

"What do you mean?"

"Listen. I went home, madly in love with you. I wanted you as soon as I had seen you. I could not yet believe that I would be lucky enough to possess you, but all my efforts tended to that desired end. I went to bed and thought only of you! I was in a fearful state. I put out my light and, conjuring up your image, covered your face with imaginary kisses. Then I did what you were doing, and the pleasure was so great that I am sure we came at one and the same time."

"What? Can men frig themselves as we do?"

"Certainly. Why should this natural means of relief be denied to them? What your pretty hand has just done for me, my ugly paw provides for my solitary gratification."

"Really? Well, I should like to see that!"

"Nonsense! You don't want me to!"

"Yes. You must show me how you do it!"

"But you know very well how. I do it like you!"

"Oh, please! Grant me this little pleasure!"

So saying, I gathered up his meatpole, which, excited by our conversation, had once more shot up to its most splendid proportions. I took his hand and placed it upon it.

"No, really, this is rank folly!"

"No, sir!"

"But I would sooner have your fingers, or your beautiful tits, if you will only use them instead."

"But me no buts! I command you to make haste and do it to the very end, or I will no longer love you."

My dear lover could refuse me nothing, and after a little more hesitation he said, "I consent, but on condition that you in your turn shall give me as soon as feasible a representation of your own pleasures."

"To that I consent, but do what I want at once!"

He began, and leaning over him, I followed his convulsive shaking with a singular feeling of pleasurable curiosity. I was fascinated by the way he manipulated his own tool. He used his thumb and three fingers on the shaft, rather than his entire fist. He moved the skin up and down slowly, maintaining a steady rhythm. His breathing was increasing in tempo as his pole twitched in his gentle grip. It hardened still more and was now enormous. I soon took pity on him, however, and unlacing my stays, I knelt down before him and made him finish between my breasts.

Shortly after this caprice of mine, my dear Will had his revenge upon me. He reminded me of the promise I had made, and despite a certain amount of shame, I stretched myself on the sofa and prepared to satisfy him.

"No, not like that," he said. "You placed me as you liked; let me do the same."

"What do you mean?"

"You shall soon see. Get astride of that chair!"

I obeyed.

"Yes, that will do nicely. Now show me your little cunt, and frig yourself with your left hand."

Again I obeyed, wondering greatly.

During this exercise Will unhooked my dress and stripped me to the waist. I now wanted to spend fearfully. My lascivious instincts began to blaze. The operation that I had begun jokingly to perform, only to please him, had become serious in the extreme. Suddenly I felt that Will was behind me, with his trousers down, and pressing the upper part of my nude body to him. He had insinuated his organ under my right arm. The originality of this fantastical idea inflamed my imagination more than ever. I bent my head and avidly contemplated the beautiful tool, the head of which appeared and disappeared at each stroke of my dear lover, who kept his eyes fixed on my left hand that was massaging my dripping cunt.

Soon we warned each other that the end was near and our double discharge took place simultaneously!

A few delicious months went by in like manner!

Our love increased daily, instead of becoming feeble or worn out by the frequency, the subtlety and the complete liberty of our connection! The precautions we so carefully took assured us perfect secrecy, and once only were we almost caught in the act.

We thought that we were certain not to be interrupted, as my husband was away from home and all the servants out.

That time, after a chat and a few caresses, I had, by a well-known sign, made my lover aware of what I wanted. He placed me as he desired, my body reclining in the large chair, my legs stretched asunder, and he had begun his adorable, lecherous licking.

I was about to come in his mouth! My eyes were closed and I was wrapped up in my enjoyment, tasting every one of the thousand delicious sensations that his tongue conjured up, when suddenly we heard footsteps and voices in the adjoining room. Quick as lightning, we were on our feet, our clothes arranged, and seated at proper distance.

My maid, who had returned without my knowledge, opened the door and announced the visit of a lady of our town.

I felt terribly giddy, but the cool presence of my lover, who knew the lady, gave me time to collect my scattered senses.

We were saved!

It was summer. It had been planned that I would vacation at a seaside village a little distant from my residence. I was not looking forward to it, for it would momentarily separate me from Will.

My lover was in despair, but this journey was arranged, and Charles wished me to go. He could not accompany me, as business kept him at Nice, but he was to visit me frequently and come to me as soon as possible. It would have been too imprudent to receive Will when alone there.

I went off very downcast and passed the first moments at my new dwelling in absolute privacy.

My husband came to see me at the end of a week, and told me that he would bring with him next time Will and two other friends to spend a day. That hope sustained me; I awaited the blessed moment with feverish anxiety.

At last, ten days later, I received a letter announcing that the journey was arranged.

The gentlemen arrived at four o'clock in the morning, and my husband came at once and got into bed with me.

I soon saw that absence had awakened a rare longing in Charles, and although I expected to be bountifully feasted by my adored Will, I must here confess that I willingly lent myself to these desires.

I clasped Charles to my arms, slipped my hand under his nightshirt, and taking hold of his member, gently pumped it for a few minutes. When I had encouraged it into a most glorious state of erection, I popped it into my slit.

Charles did it better than usual, fucking me with unusual energy, and confessed that the caresses of my hand had afforded him the most vivacious sensations of pleasure. I have often used the manual exercise with him since and whenever he asked me.

We slept till eight o'clock.

We breakfasted at a restaurant in the town with the gentlemen; the meal was good and we were all very happy, my dear Will brimming over with wit and good spirits. Our eyes only spoke, but how we understood their language! His seemed to say, "When can we meet?"

My husband, involuntarily, fixed our assignation.

He proposed a picnic in the woods when the heat of the day should abate, and said that after having seen me home he would go to sleep and so work off the fatigue of the preceding night's journey.

Will said that during that time he would make a few visits to some old friends, and the other gentlemen went off to bathe in the sea.

A glance at my lover and all was understood.

At one o'clock in the afternoon my husband was snoring downstairs and Will had slipped into my room. Knowing his taste, my hair was carefully arranged; I had put on pink silk stockings and high-heeled shoes. I only had a slight dressing gown thrown over my shoulders, and I awaited his coming with delirious impatience. As soon as he appeared I hung myself around his neck and kissed and bit him.

"At last, I've got you, my angel, my love! How I wanted you! Let me devour you!" I said, as I locked the door and drew him towards me.

"Come to my arms! Fifteen days without you. I shall die, I'm sure. How I've suffered!"

"And I've been just as badly off, darling. We have but little time to spare, so let us make the most of it. Suppose we are interrupted?"

"He will sleep for hours. I am yours. Do with me as you will."

As I finished speaking, my gown was already on the ground. My lover, undressed, sat me on the edge of the bed and put two pillows behind me. He uncovered my titties, felt and sucked them for some time, then pulled up my chemise. He went on his knees and applied his burning lips to the fiery nook that welcomed the caress with a spasm of happiness.

"Ah, darling," I said. "I'm coming already! I'm coming—again! Oh, what delight—enough—you'll kill me—give me your beautiful cock now! I want to feel your prick inside me. Come into my cunt. Come and fuck me!"

Will then rose, lifting my legs over his arms, and brought the head of his cock to my slit. Softly, reposing, I looked down at the sweet introduction with languishing eyes. He pushed his enormous tool in and began shuttling in and out, varying the motion by rotating his hips and alternating short strokes with long ones.

"Do it slowly," I said. "Make it last. Ah, it is so nice! I can feel it penetrating me. It fills me. I'm dying—stop a little—I'm coming! I'm coming!"

"And so do I! Ah! I can't keep up—my darling—my fucktress—I spend—take it all—take all my sperm!"

I almost fainted as he shot off into my cavern, but I was not yet satisfied. My love had sunk down upon me. I encircled his head with my arms and glued my mouth to his.

"Ah," said I in a whisper, "you spent too quickly."

"I could not help it; but don't move now!"

"What are you going to do?"

"You see, I'm still inside."

"But I'm all wet!"

"No matter, I mean to fuck you again without withdrawing."

"That isn't possible!"

"You'll see. What adorable tits you've got, darling. Give me your tongue. That's right. Move your dear ass up and down gently. I'm waking up again. Do you feel it?"

"Yes. It's getting stiff again. Ah! I can't bear it; I just have to come again. Push on once more. Quicker. Ah. I'm going mad. I'm so giddy. I'm coming again. I'm fucking. I'm still spending. Are you ready?"

"Yes. It's coming—there! Oh, God!"

A second discharge mingled itself with the first flood. For some time we both remained helpless, and at last Will, dropping his hold of my legs, drew out. A veritable deluge of the extract of love came pattering down on the floor.

I rose and took my lover to my heart.

"My adored one," I said, "what a splendid fuck! How happy you make me! I've never come so much in my life! I was coming all the time without a second of interruption."

We were obliged to remove all trace of our prodigious struggles. My thighs and belly were literally covered with gobs of sperm. I had no dressing room, but dared not remain in such a state. I got my wash basin, and making Will turn his back, began my ablutions.

My love, far from obeying, did not miss a movement. He took hold of me, with my petticoats still pulled up, and kissed me as he said, "I must fuck you again."

"Oh, no, please. You'll be ill!"

"But see, it's up again."

The sight completed my madness. I fell on my knees, seized the beautiful head between my lips, engulfed it in my mouth and sucked it with raging delirium. I took it down my throat, pulling and attempting to draw the juice from it. I licked around the head and down the shaft, even taking his balls one at a time into my mouth.

Suddenly, I heard a noise in the passage. I rose with a bound, rushed to the door, and looked through the keyhole. If it was my husband, we were lost. Happily, I was mistaken. It was just the house cat.

I sighed to Will that there was nothing to fear. In this position, with my eye fixed to the door lock, my buttocks were exposed, and my shift was all tucked up. In a twinkling, my lover was behind me, and before I had time to collect myself I was penetrated again, filled up by that adorable instrument that seemed to know no rest. Ah! How I helped him by opening and shutting the cheeks of my backside. I writhed, twisted, and swooned with joy.

Our time had passed quickly. In haste, I sent Will away, made the bed afresh and arranged a neat toilette for the promenade. I was scarcely ready when the carriage drove up and Charles came to fetch me. He found me flushed and lively. I told him that overcome by the heat, I had fallen asleep.

We went downstairs and I was joyfully saluted by the gentlemen, who complimented me on the good taste of my dress. On the sly, I looked at Will, but nothing betrayed that anything extraordinary had taken place. We started off.

The forest we were exploring was deliciously cool and picturesque. We went to the lodge of a gamekeeper where a rustic repast had been prepared. Our picnic was merrily enjoyed; I was forced to drink several glasses of champagne, although I did not require that to stimulate me.

After the meal we set out walking again, my husband gossiping with Will. I was with them. The two other guests had strolled onto another path when we arrived at a wild spot, studded with rocks and shaded with large trees.

At this moment one of the gentlemen, who were now far off, called out to my husband, "Come, quick, come and see!"

Charles waved his acknowledgement and left us. No sooner had he disappeared from view than Will glued his mouth to mine.

"Angel," he said, "let us profit by this moment!"

"You are mad!"

"No, I love you! Let me do as I will."

"My God, we shall be discovered! I am lost!"

"Not if you hurry. Stoop!"

"I did so immediately, lifting my skirts. Are you in?"

"Here I am. It's going in!"

"Ah! Make haste."

He thrust furiously, driving his rock in and out so fast that little pleasure could truly be gained in this fashion.

"There, darling—spend—spend again!"

"Ah! I've come! There! Now go away."

Only just in time. My petticoats, all up behind, were barely readjusted when I heard the rest of the party returning.

I went to meet them and we found they had fetched us to see a swarm of bees at the top of a tree.

We got into our carriages and returned to the town. We danced the night away and then said farewell to the gentlemen, who went away early the next morning.

It is easy to guess my thoughts when at home once more, as I began to undress for the night. I was brushing my hair in front of my mirror when Charles, delighted with the day's outing, came up behind me.

I was in my shift, which clung tightly to my figure and showed the seductive shape of my backside. I could see in the glass that Charles was looking at it, and that his eyes sparkled.

Aha! I thought. Can it be possible that for once he will be able to do it to me twice in the same day?

I wanted him to fuck me, and coquettishly struck an attitude that threw out into still greater relief what I knew was one of my greatest beauties. Then, negligently putting one foot on a chair, I took care that my chemise would be more raised than was absolutely necessary. I undid my garter.

This rue succeeded. Charles, also in his shirt, got up, and coming near me, kissed me on the neck, then put his hand between the cheeks of my bottom.

"Oh! Oh!" I said, turning round and returning his kiss. "Whatever ails you tonight?"

"My dear wife, I find that you are extremely beautiful!"

"Am I not the same every day?"

"Oh, yes, but this evening still more so!"

"Well, what are you driving at? Come on!"

So saying, I put my hand on his cock. It stood a little, although it was far from being in a proper state of erection.

"You see that you can't do anything!"

"Yes, I can! Caress it a little bit!"

"What makes you excited?"

"Why?"

"Well now—what?"

"Your beautiful bottom!"

"Indeed, sir. Well, you shan't see any more of it unless you respond quickly!"

As supple as a kitten, I trussed up my linen with one hand, so that my buttocks were naked, while my front parts were reflected in the mirror. At the same time my other hand had not loosened its grasp, and cleverly excited what it held. I soon had the satisfaction of feeling it get hard. Wishing to profit by his momentary desire, I made Charles sit and got over him, but I soon found that such a position stretched me too much and, widening my slit, was quite unsuited for his thin tool.

I got up and had to begin all over again. I was too excited to be daunted now, and once more started the caress of my agile hand. I resolved to do my best, and he helped, so that soon I was pleased to see it once more in its most splendid state! Then I drew a chair to the glass, placed one foot upon it and the other on the ground, and put his prick in from behind.

Charles, led on by me till he was almost beside himself, did it in such a manner that I spent three times. He thrust up into me feverishly, poking and stroking, using the entire length of his thin rod. He was a long while in coming, but nevertheless finished by discharging, thanks to the clever movements of my buttocks and the talent I had acquired in pressing and pinching his wretched little tool.

Both very much fatigued, we retired to rest. Thus, in this memorable day, I had been fucked six times! I do not exaggerate in saying that I had come more than twenty times!

But such was the force of my temperament and my aptitude for amorous encounters that I rose the next day from my couch as fresh and as well as if nothing had occurred.

I went back to Nice, and Will and I relapsed into our sweet habits once more, which, though frequently interrupted, grew more ardent after each successive deprivation.

My husband now rarely went away for more than one day at a time, so that our pleasures only lasted during the short instants snatched during an occasional afternoon. Nevertheless, a few exciting encounters took place, and we profited by them.

One evening, happy in a few hours of security, we determined to completely enjoy our happiness. My love proposed that we should undress and get on my bed. I accepted with avidity. He was soon stripped and laid on his back, while I unlaced my stays. I joined him clad in nothing save that with which I had been born. He seized me in his arms and we were clasped together in an instant!

He contemplated my nakedness with ecstasy, then covered my entire body with burning kisses without omitting one single spot!

I was mad, delirious! In turn I wished to reproduce for him the pleasure I had felt. I kissed with ardor every part of that body, so manly and so handsome. When I arrived between his legs and found that darling jewel that proudly, stiffly stood, I stopped and kissed it, I sucked it, I would have liked to have eaten it!

In this position my buttocks were turned towards my lover's face. I could feel that he had seized my left thigh and was trying to pass it over him.

"What do you want?" I said, turning my head a little.

"Put your legs over me."

"But how? Why?"

"I'll soon tell you. There, that will do!"

I found myself astride his breast, my head still in the same place!

"Now," he said, "bend down, push out your lovely ass—there—now place your cunt on my mouth."

"Here I am!"

"Good. Now let us both use our tongues. Tell me in time, and we'll come together!"

Although rather puzzled at this new method, I gracefully gave way to him, and soon I felt his clever and delicate tongue travel over my cleft. I went off into a mad rage. I once more took hold of his instrument that I had let go for a moment, got the entire head into my mouth, and pumped at it with frenzy! An electric current seemed to envelope my entire frame. Each stroke of Will's tongue was answered by my mouth!

What delirious joy! I had already spent thrice, and when feeling that the fourth time was near, and that my lover, shuddering and palpitating, was also nearing the supreme moment, I exclaimed, "I'm ready! Come, darling, come in my mouth!"

What happened then? I don't know! I lost consciousness as Will's flood of passion exploded down my throat.

* * * * *

My lover's adorable lessons had rendered me very knowledgeable, and I thought I had no more to learn. I was mistaken; there was one supreme lesson left for me to learn.

I have often repeated that my buttocks, or rather my ass, was of rare beauty. The furrow that divided the oval had already received thousands and thousands of my lover's kisses, whose greatest delight was to place me so as to enjoy this spectacle thoroughly. He would then open the lips of the gap of love, caress it, kiss it, and worship it in every manner. Sometimes his finger would wander higher up, and I could feel a strange titillation at the opening of the dark orifice above! Sometimes, even when plugged up to the roots by his magnificent tool, fainting beneath the divine dew that was spouted into me, I felt the finger penetrate far up the narrow path!

That singular caress caused me quite a peculiar erotic joy that I had not sought to analyze.

On one of the rare evenings when we were able to get between the sheets, after having felt each other all over for some time, my lover took off my chemise and looked lovingly at my nakedness.

Knowing his passionate love for my ass, I presented it to him, stretching myself as wide open as I could. Will got up behind me, but instead of getting into my cunt as usual, he contented himself with rubbing the head of his prick against my bottom.

"Put it in!" I cried, "You are teasing me dreadfully!"

"Wait a bit!"

"What are you doing? You hurt me. Not there!"

And indeed, I felt the head trying to penetrate the singular aperture I have just mentioned.

"Let me do as I please, my adored one! I entreat you. A delicious woman is cunt all over; no single part of her beautiful body must remain virgin."

"But it's impossible! It can never go in!"

"I can get it entirely in if you will let me."

"But you'll kill me. I'll suffer. I'll scream. I won't come at all."

"Yes you will, and afterwards you'll say how nice it was. I'll wager that you will often ask me to do it."

"No, it's impossible. Come, darling, put it in lower down, it's just as nice for you!"

"But I supplicate you to let me do it. It's the greatest proof of love that a woman can give. I demand that proof."

"Oh, heaven! I can't refuse you. Go along then and do it. How funny all the same." Of course I didn't know what to expect.

I said no more and remained passive, presenting as well as I could what was required of me. My lover went to the toilet-table and lubricated his tool with a stick of cosmetic, then, taking up his position again, he once more knocked at the narrow gate. His first attempts did not succeed; I suffered horribly and felt no pleasure at all. Still I loved him so much that I would have suffered greater agonies. And, besides, my curiosity and a desire for the unknown sustained me. My lover ceased his efforts for an instant, and, passing his hand between my thighs, began to massage my cunt. Symptoms of pleasure now arose and I myself begged for a second trial, but my lover's leaning posture was too uncomfortable. He took my hand and placed it where his had stroked me. I understood him and rubbed away myself. Again I felt the terrible point, though the pleasure in front helped to neutralize the agony that my poor bottom still felt.

At last, I felt as if an enormous ring was dilated within me, and suddenly the monstrous cylinder slipped in entirely. I quickened the movement of my hand. An immense, twofold, sharp, extraordinary spasm overpowered me. I almost fainted and fell forward in an indescribable fit.

My lover, luckily, had not been unseated. He followed my movement and laid his full length upon me. He gave a few more strokes in the snug passage and filled his strange shelter with a hot ejaculation that he spurted forth with many groans and sighs.

We remained some time in this position without speaking. I felt a certain shame that I could not explain, and was almost vexed at having spent so well by the ravishing of that unusual nook. On the other hand, I could not prevent myself being delighted by the opening of this new source of pleasure.

Will kissed me and whispered, "Well, what do you think of it?"

"I hardly know."

"Did you come?"

"Well, yes!"

"Are you vexed at having submitted to my whim?"

"No."

"Will you ever ask me to do it again?"

"I think I shall, but not often. It is too exciting, too awfully good, and too painful!"

During our chat, the position remained unchanged; my lover's peg was still planted in my tiny hole. I felt it diminishing as he tried to withdraw. I pinched in my buttocks, so that I kept him trapped at his post.

"You wanted to get in," I said, "and there you shall stay!"

I relied on his well-tried strength, and while I waited for it to return to its former state I teased him, using all the words he had taught me.

"What do you call this style of fucking?" I asked. "You haven't touched the poor little cunt that has had nothing this time."

"It's called—well—butt-fucking."

"Well, darling, butt-fuck me again, I begin to like it. Ah! I can feel your nice prick reviving. Treat kindly this ass you love so much. Don't go away yet, I beg of you. I want your sperm once more."

As I rattled out all these little bawdy words that I knew electrified my lover, I loosened the tightness of my buttocks gradually, so as to leave him full liberty of action.

I began to feel again the advance symptoms of that double pleasure I had just felt. Will was not yet quite ready. In fact, I seemed to feel him get weak, so I told him not to leave me as we rose again with infinite care to our first posture.

"Now, my darling," I said, "don't move. I'll do it all myself!"

I began to wriggle my rump carefully backwards and forwards. My lover, on his knees, as still as a statue, was passionately contemplating this libidinous sight. He could see, as he told me afterwards, his cock, held as though in a vice, appear almost entirely, and then be completely lost to view in its narrow sheath.

After a few minutes of this delicious fun, my lover had recovered his pristine vigor. I could tell that by the growing thickness and stiffness of the member that bound our bodies together. I soon felt him shiver; broken utterances issued from his lips. I let him know that I was ready, and a fresh jet of passion potion caused us both to swoon away with joy.

* * * * *

My well-beloved Will was right. I grew to like it indeed! How many times since has he not said with his soft voice, as he leans over me, "Where will you have it?"

And how often I have pointed to my bottom, with my finger, and answered, "THERE!"

The Spell of the Rod

When Lucy's fine rump was first bared to the twigs,
She was finely cut up and her flesh torn in shreds;
She cried out for mercy in her dire distress,
Promising amendment as we lowered her dress.
She had been most naughty, and a bad rude girl,
Who presumed the hair on her fanny to curl;
But the birch reached her quim as well as her bum,
The height of her agony was glorious fun.
Her frightened looks, and deep blushes of shame,
Set our hearts pit-a-pit, and our senses in flame;
The old cockolorums our cunnies would grope.
Then tossed us on sofas and had a fine stroke.
So all those slow coaches, who a rise scarce can get;
Come, pay your respect to Our Lady St. Bridget;
She'll warm up your blood till it boils in your veins,
And your penis all his pristine vigour regains.
Let the birch be your love, St. Bridget your saint,
Never flinch from the rod, nor think of a faint;
Swish – swish – let it fall, till the glow of desire.
Will run thro' your senses, and set them on fire.
Ah! then you can fuck! and fuck, ah! so well!
That my Muse quite fails your joys to foretell;
But with oceans of spending, the fuck never ending,
Your ecstasy goes on, for a long time extending.

Elizabeth in the Linen Closet

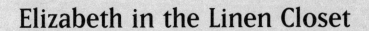

During the summer I spent as a guest at Lord Robert's country house, I had noticed Lord Robert's eyes upon me more than once. Whenever this happened, I looked down demurely and walked away, but never failed to be disappointed when he failed to follow me. For I knew he was considering proffering an invitation to one of his notorious country soirees. Once I asked him when he would do more than look and the matter appeared to have played upon his mind for that selfsame day he succeeded in cornering me in a passageway upstairs close to my room, saying that he would have converse with me. A nearby linen closet being unattended I allowed myself to be escorted within, my Lord Robert closing the door with solemn mien.

On either side of us were shelves upon which sheets and towels and other necessities were stored. The space between was such that we were brought to stand close together, I making no demur when he passed his arms about my waist and drew me against him.

"My dear Elizabeth, my sweet girl, there is a matter of some import I must convey to you."

"Yes, of course, Lord Robert, what frets you? Oh, what a pretty kiss! Have you brought me in here only for this?"

"No, my pet, but you are truly irresistible and therein lies the crux of the affair."

"Pray do tell me, then, for naught shall pass my lips of what is said here," I replied with great solemnity while he, passing his hand down from my waist, made bold to caress the *rondeur* of my bottom.

"There are country pleasures of which you know not, Elizabeth. The guests on such occasions are given to great frivolity. I hesitate to say to what extent. Suffice perhaps to tell you in all confidence—and such of course must never reach the ears of my dear wife—that the ladies are given to doffing much of their attire, as also are the gentlemen. There follows much amorous play, of course, for in select and well-chosen company such is accepted as a pleasurable pastime and no ill is thought of it. You see my dilemma?"

I feared at first to speak, not so much out of modesty but because in speaking he had slowly gathered up my skirt at the back and—first fondling my bared thighs and the sleek silk of my stockings—succeeded in cupping my bottom cheeks which protruded boldly upon his hand. Appearing much confused I pressed myself as if protectively against him and hid my face. My drawers being of fine batiste permitted the warmth of my derriere to exude over his hand which searched the hillocks somewhat feverishly. It was an amusing situation, for I swear that the poor man was struggling twixt desire and the need to advise me of my future fate.

"Shall we then need to take our drawers off?" I asked while not permitting him a view of my expression.

The question being so put caused his penis—which had already thickened—to rise measurably against my belly through our garments. The proud rod strained. I felt its anguish.

"Those and much else," he replied thickly, whereat his febrile fingers loosed the ties of my drawers and caused them to slither slowly down my legs. "It will be so, you see," he went on, raising my chin with his free hand and passing his lips across mine. I quivered and strained, for the seeking of his hand beneath my bottom cheeks caused me to rise up on tiptoe. A sweet, sickly sensation invaded me. By passing his forefinger under my derriere he was able to touch the soft warm lips of my quim which moistened instantly. The impress of his mouth upon my own grew stronger. My lips parted. I received his tongue. Roaming his hand all about, he then brought it to the front between our bodies and fondly cupped my pulsing nest. "It will be so, my love, while you in turn will be required to grasp your partner's cock and frig him. Feel my own for it has grown mightily for you."

Thereupon he rapidly unfastened the flap of his breeches and passed the monstrous organ into my hand. So lusty in girth was it that my fingers could not hold fully around it. It throbbed like an engine. I felt the veins outstanding against my flesh. My belly swirled. I could not help but widen my thighs as much as my fallen drawers would permit to allow his finger to seek up between the lips of my lovenest. I know not what words passed between us in those brief moments save that on his part they were lewd and on mine excited. I moved my hand gently up and down his shaft. My senses reeled. Second by second I could feel my cunny moistening the more. Our tongues flashed together in such utter yearning that the moment clearly could no longer be delayed.

"You must know how it will be, Elizabeth, must you not?"

"Yes!" I assented, though I scarce recognised my voice as my own. I felt myself being borne back. We fell together upon the floor, he taking care that I would not harm myself in doing so. Without more ado my drawers were ripped from my ankles. With a certain roughness that thrilled me exceedingly, he thrust my legs apart, raising himself a little above me on one hand while with the other he fumbled his enormous cock against my slit.

"You will be put so upon the floor, or upon a couch, and fucked, Elizabeth."

"Oh!" I moaned. His knob was at the portals. I felt the huge bulb of it press into my wetness. For a second or two our hot eyes locked together and then with an ineffable groan he inserted two inches of his meaty shaft and was full upon me. Our lips meshed. I was in such an ague that I wriggled my bottom to obtain more of his prick, though to my Lord Robert the movement must have appeared evasive in intent for he seized me strongly about the waist and embedded his throbbing peg the more so that in some magical wise my cunny expanded to receive it.

"You will be thoroughly fucked, Elizabeth—do you wish to be?"

"HAAAAAR!"

I could not speak. I was filled with him. His huge balls hung beneath the lower bulge of my bottom. His lips savaged my own. With a passionate jolt of his loins the peg was fully inserted and then all but withdrawn so that I near cried out for its return. His face appeared haggard and flushed. I saw the ugliness of male lust and desire that soon enough melts into fiery passion as two bottoms begin to work in unison.

"You wish to be—you wish to be!" he exulted.

"Oh, Lord Robert—oh!"

Some inner wisdom in me told me not to respond directly, though I would have fain have cried out that I wanted his prick to work me strongly. Some measure of modesty must be present at all times in the first moments of erotic bliss. Such draws the male on to excite one the more. They would have us all be whores in bed.

"You do, you do—confess it! What a luscious little cunt you have— how tightly it enclasps and sucks upon my prick. I shall come in you ere I mean to. Ah my god, yes, work your bottom!"

In my fever, I was doing so without knowing it. It mattered not. We were lost in that world wherein fulfilment is all. The selfsame cock that I had seen pistoning back and forth in Helen's bottom was now in my own enamoured possession. I gloried in each powerful stroke of it. My spendings sprinkled his balls. I implored his tongue the more by twirling my own in his mouth. I was as one who drowns in passion and seeks to do so. Cupped now upon his broad palms, the tight cheeks of my bottom rotated savagely, though it was then to my gain that he thought me endeavouring to fight free from under him by so doing and hence his tool rammed in and out the more lustily.

His questions poured upon me. It was my first lesson in discovering how a man will try to draw the lewdest words and phrases from his mount, seeking to find beneath her apparent innocence the hottest pits of desire. I answered not except by chokes and sobs. Advised by instinct that he would think me otherwise a schemer, I held back the lascivious responses that would fain have come to my lips. It is no folly to use them when one knows one's stallion, though all should be spoken haltingly and not in too great an efflorescence of words, for such would render the female common. The lure must always be that all is not said which it is wished to be said by one's partner. Thus is he kept in thrall, ever convinced that he will finally succeed in drawing one out to confess all one's innermost desires and—indeed—prior adventures. One is not so foolish, however, as to disrobe one's mind fully in front of, or indeed underneath, others.

My legs lay limp, my knees slightly bent. He was near-ing the end of his course, as I sensed by the roughness of his panting. His praise for the tight sleekness of my cunny was ever expressed. I continued to moan. I evaded his mouth from moment to moment as though in inner conflict at what I was permitting. His kisses rained upon my cheeks and neck. I felt the throbbing of his cock increase.

"It will be so, if you come," he croaked.

I am coming, I thought—but told him not. I bucked, I clung, my soft cries grew ever wilder. All that had been promised to me by Elaine was true. With a last rattling cry he flooded me. His effusion pumped into me—a veritable leaping of thick gruelly sperm that I received with joy. Our mouths fastened together again, for I could refuse him not in that moment. With every inward thrust a fresh jet spattered me. The strokes of his cock grew shorter. Panting, he thrust it in to the full and lay all too heavily upon me for a long moment until he stirred. I felt the slow withdrawal of his weapon with infinite regret. Had another taken his place upon me then, I would have welcomed it. Drawing me up, his eyes searched mine. I hid my face and affected great confusion. Thick and limp, the big worm of his prick dangled against my thigh.

"You will not tell anyone about it, will you?" he demanded hoarsely while caressing my long brown hair with a certain tenderness. I quivered and pressed in. My skirt being caught up still, the warmth of my belly stirred his doughty weapon.

"No," I comforted him softly, "yet what of the reception? Oh, pray say that only you will do it to me if I have to take my drawers off."

The apparent naivety of my words—tinged as they were with eroti-cism—struck exactly the right note, as I had intended they should. He laughed and mussed my hair, awarding my yielding lips a long kiss.

"Only I, my pet."

I giggled. I pressed my cheek to his. "I believe so. If you do it to me again at the reception, I shall know better and tell you. But haste, we must not stay here or a servant may discover us. Pray go first and then I will follow."

"You minx, I truly believe there is more to you than anyone could imagine," he chuckled and thereupon—fastening his breeches with evident regret—made his way out. I followed not long after.

As might be imagined, I dreamed much that night of what had passed and became restless for more. My cream puff had been well filled, but sought extra dosages. I was not to be lacking in them, as will be seen. That which I immediately ventured upon was wicked in the extreme and I doubt not that had I demurred in the linen room and been of lesser daring, my Lord Robert would have sought some excuse not to take me, for it was apparent to me that he saw in me a mischievous but innocent girl who knew as little as I had seemed to him to do about the ways of the world.

A Royal Affair

I entered the bridal bed a virgin. When the bridesmaids left me I trembled with apprehension and covered up my head under the bedclothes. It was because I had heard so many stories of the trials and hardships of a virgin on her marriage night and not because I had any antipathy towards my husband; On the contrary, I liked him.

His courtship had been short, for he was a busy man in the diplomatic service of the Greek government. He was no longer young, but he was good-looking and manly, and I was proud that he had selected me from all the other Athenian girls. My heart beat still more violently when he entered. He came to the side of the bed and, turning down the clothes from my head, he saw how I was agitated. He simply kissed my hand, and then went to the other side of the room to undress. This conduct somewhat reassured me.

When he got into bed and took me in his arms my back was turned towards him. He took no liberties with any part of my person but began to converse with me about the incidents of the wedding. I was soon so calm that I suffered him to turn me with my face towards him, and he kissed me first on the forehead and then on the lips.

After a while he begged me to return his kisses, saying that if I did not it would prove that I disliked him; thus encouraged I returned his kisses. When I had so long lain in his arms that I began to feel at home, he turned me upon my back and unfastened the bosom of my chemise and kissed and fondled my breasts. This set my heart beating wildly again, but we kept exchanging kisses till he suddenly lifted the skirt of my chemise and lay between my thighs.

Then I covered my face with my hands for shame, but he was so kind and gentle that I soon got so accustomed to the situation that I suffered him to remove my hands and fasten his mouth to mine in a passionate kiss. As he did so I felt something pushing between my thighs. It entered my curls there and touched the naked lips beneath. I felt my face grow hot with shame and lay perfectly passive.

He must have been in bed with me two hours before he ventured so far. He had his reward, for a soft desire began to grow in my brain, the blood centred on my loins and I longed for the connection which was so imminent. I returned him a kiss as passionate as he gave; it was the signal for which he had been waiting. I felt a pressure on the virgin membrane, not hard enough, however, to be painful. The pressure slackened and then pushed again and again.

By this time I was wanton with desire and not only returned the passionate kisses, but I wound my arms around him. Then came the fateful thrust, tearing away the obstruction and reaching to the very depths of my loins. I gave a cry of mingled bliss and agony, which I could not help repeating at each of the three deep thrusts that followed. Then all was still and an effusion like balm filled my sheath in the place of the organ that had so disturbed it. A delightful languor stole over my frame and I went to sleep in my husband's arms.

In less than six months circumstances compelled me to deceive him. After we had been married awhile our position required us to go a great deal in company. Card playing was very fashionable and the stakes got higher and higher. One night the luck ran terribly against me; I proposed for the party to double.

My husband had gone on a journey a few days before and had left a large sum of money in my charge. It was nearly all his fortune. A portion of this money I now staked, thinking that the luck could not possibly go against me again, but it did. I was rendered desperate. Again I proposed to double it would take all I had left if I lost.

The ladies who were playing withdrew; the gentlemen were too polite to do so. The cards went against me. I felt myself turn dreadfully pale. The French ambassador, Duke Henri, who was sitting beside me, was disposed to conceal my terrible embarrassment. He was a handsome man, but, unlike my husband, he was very stalwart. His manners were very engaging. He kept up a stream of small talk till the others had dispersed to other parts of the room, then he offered to bring me on the morrow the amount I had lost.

I turned as crimson as I had before been pale. I knew the price of such assistance. I made him no reply, my look dropped to the floor and I begged him to leave me, which he politely did. All next day I was nearly distracted; I hoped Duke Henri would not come. My cheeks would burn as on the evening before and the blood all rush back to my heart.

At three o'clock he came; the, valet showed him into the parlour, closed the door and retired. Duke Henri must have known he was expected, for I was elegantly dressed in blue silk and my shoulders were set off with heavy lace. I was so weak from agitation that I could not rise from the sofa to greet him.

'May I have the happiness,' he said, 'of being your confidant?' as he seated himself beside me, holding in one hand a well-filled purse and dropping the other around my waist. I could not reject the purse. If I kept the purse I could not ask him to remove his arm. I was giddy with contending emotions.

'For God's sake, spare me,' I murmured. My head dropped, he caught it to his heart I had fainted away.

When I again became conscious I was lying on my back upon the sofa in the arms of the Duke, the lace on my bosom was parted, my heavy skirts were all turned up from my naked thighs and he was in the very ecstasy of filling my sheath with sperm.

It was this exquisite sensation which had restored me to consciousness, but I was too late to join in the ecstasy. His shaft became limber and small and I was left hopelessly in the lurch. Then I beseeched him to go as it was no time or place for this.

'Will you receive me in your bedroom tonight?' asked the Duke, kissing my bare bosoms.

He had so excited my passions that I no longer hesitated. 'The front door will be unfastened all night,' I replied, 'and my room is directly over this.'

Then he allowed me to rise. I adjusted my disordered dress as quickly as possible, but I was not quick enough. The valet opened the door to bring in the card of a visitor. He saw enough to put me in his power.

After the Duke had gone I found the purse in my bosom; it contained more than I had lost, but my thoughts were not of money. My lips had tasted the forbidden fruit; I was no longer the same woman; my excitement had culminated in lascivious desire. I could hardly wait for night to come.

When finally the house was still I unfastened the front door, retired to my room, undressed and was standing in my chemise with my nightgown in my hand ready to put on when the door of my room opened and Alex, the valet, stood before me with his finger on his lips. He was a fine looking youth of eighteen, a Hungarian of a reduced family, who acted half in the capacity of secretary and half in that of valet for my husband. I could not help giving a faint scream, while I concealed my person as well as possible with the nightgown I held in my hands.

'My lady,' said he, 'I know all, but I shall be discreet. I only ask you to give me the sweetest proof of your confidence.'

There was no help for it. With a murmured 'For shame,' I sprang into bed and hid under the bedclothes. He quickly undressed and followed me. My object was to dismiss him before the Duke came; I therefore suffered him to make rapid progress. He took me in his arms and kissed my lips and breasts and, as he raised my chemise, our naked thighs met. He was much more agitated than myself. I had been anticipating a paramour all the afternoon and he could not have known what reception would be accorded him. He could hardly guide his shaft to the lips that welcomed it.

As for myself, I began where I had left off with the Duke. My sheath with wanton greediness devoured every inch that entered it and at the very first thrust I melted with an adulterous rapture never felt in my husband's embrace. Just at that moment I heard the front door softly open and shut. I pushed Alex away with force that drew his stiff shaft completely out of me.

'Gather up your clothes quickly and get into the closet,' I said. Madly eager as he must have been to finish, he hurried with his clothes into the closet as the Duke entered.

The Duke came up and kissed me. I pretended to be asleep. He undressed hastily, and, getting into bed, took me in his arms. But I delayed his progress as much as possible. I made him tell me everything that had been said about my losses at cards. I used every artifice to keep him at bay until his efforts should arouse my passions.

Then he mounted me and his stalwart shaft distended and penetrated me so much deeper than that of young Alex that it was more exquisite than before. Again the wild, adulterous thrill penetrated every part of my body. I fairly groaned with ecstasy. At that moment the front door loudly opened. It must be my husband unexpectedly returning.

'Good heavens, Duke!' I cried, 'under the bed with you.' He pulled his great stiff shaft out of me with a curse of disappointment that he could not finish and scrambled under the bed, dragging his clothes after him.

My husband came in all beaming with delight that he had been able to return so soon. I received him with much demonstration. 'How it flushes your cheeks to see me,' he said.

When he had undressed and come to bed I returned his caresses with so much ardour that he soon entered where Alex and the Duke had so hastily withdrawn. I felt pleasant, but feigned much more rapture than I felt.

To console the Duke I dropped one of my hands down alongside the bed, which he was so polite as to kiss, and, as my husband's face was buried in my neck, while he was making rapid thrusts I kissed my other hand to Alex, who was peeping through the closet door. Then I gave a motion to my loins which sent my husband spending and repeated it till I had extracted from him the most copious gushes. It was too soon for me to melt with another thrill; my object was to fix him for a sound sleep, but the balmy sperm was so grateful to my hot sheath that I felt rewarded for my troubles.

He soon fell sound asleep. Then I motioned for the Duke to go. With his clothes in one hand and his stiff shaft in the other he glided out. Soon after, we heard the front door shut and the disconsolate Alex cautiously came forth. With his clothes under his arm and both hands holding his rigid shaft, he too disappeared.

The Female Syringe

O nce more the train to Calais, once more the dreadful sea sickness. I am free. No more school; no more *pensionnat* for Susan! I was meeting my Papa. He had returned from India. His term of service had expired. He had received his C.B. He was now retiring as a Major General. His breast was covered with the medals he had won, yet except some mere scratches, he had never received a wound. He was still a young and vigorous man in the prime of life. He was also the lineal descendant of an ancient family, and a Baronet.

I was considered to have arrived at an age when I might bid adieu to educational routine. I was to spend a few months at home in Mayfair, to improve the occasion in the reception of music and singing lessons from the first professors. Not that A Lady desired my return; she had her own reasons for her unwilling assent. Lady L——had never overcome her antipathy for her only daughter. Sir James, however, had a distinct desire to have me at home. It was to him I owed my emancipation. My sympathy was all for him. I shared his desire to meet again after so long an absence.

Sir James was absent shooting in the North when I arrived. A Lady was suffering, so she informed me, from rheumatism. She kept to her room. My time did not hang too heavily on my hands for all that. I had plenty of liberty. The carriage was at my disposal. We were rich. The house was commodious. The servants were numerous and well paid. They were evidently overjoyed to welcome me to my home, and have someone to break the monotony of their existence.

I very soon began to discriminate among them. There was the senior footman, Henry Parker, who was particularly polite and attentive to me. A Lady preferred to take her meals in her own room upstairs. I dined all alone, save when I invited a young friend of my own age to share my meal. On the occasions when I was quite by myself, Henry would venture to suggest various choice portions from the dishes set before me. He cut and arranged them on my plate. He interested me. He was a man of some eight and thirty, not very tall for a footman, but stout and broad. I thought in my ignorance he was magnificent in his handsome livery, with his gold garters, black silk stockings and his crimson plush breeches. He made a great impression on me. I suppose I showed my interest in him too plainly. He soon became more attentive, more subservient—more familiar.

"How long have you been here, Henry?"

From the first I could never bring myself to call him Parker.

"Three years, miss, come Christmas."

"You must find it very dull now that Sir James is away and Mr. Percy is in Canada. I expect you have gay times downstairs, when your work is over in here."

"Well, miss, not so much. The others are not a very gay lot and the cook goes out when the work is done. The girls both sit upstairs with my lady's own maid. Now you're here, miss, if I may be allowed to say so, the house is not at all the same. It seems quite lively—at least to me, miss."

"Where is my maid, Henry? She has not brought my shoes. I cannot bear these boots any longer, I am tired."

"Mary is upstairs, miss, shall I call her?"

"No, Henry, if you will be so good as to undo these laces, I can sit more comfortably at the table."

I pushed out my foot. I placed it on a stool. Henry stooped over it. He began to fumble at the knot. His hand trembled.

"I am afraid, Henry, you are not quite a lady's maid, but I think you are very nice all the same."

Henry chuckled. I gave a little kick out with my foot. It touched his plush breeches.

"Oh, you hurt me, Henry—no—not your knuckles—it's the lace at the back of the instep—see here—

He took my foot in his hand. He touched my ankle.

"It's just there, Henry, please rub it a little."

Henry set to work to rub the ankle. As he rubbed, I swayed my foot backwards and forwards upon his plush breeches. Something hard seemed to grow up under my foot.

"What have you got in your pocket, Henry? Is it a flute?"

"No, miss, I am not musical. I don't play any instrument."

The man blushed scarlet as his breeches, and seemed quite confused.

"It feels exactly like one, Henry, and it gets bigger and bigger."

I pushed my little kid boot into closer contact with the thing. Henry's hand was now resting on my calf, and my black silk stocking evidently delighted him, for he made any and all pretenses in order to linger where he was.

I put on my most innocent and childish air.

"Do all men have those things there, Henry? The girls at school told me lots about them."

"I don't know, miss. I suppose so. I—really! Miss! I'm afraid someone may come."

"Don't be alarmed, Henry, no one will come. I want to feel it."

"Good Lord! Miss—if they should know—if I am found out I shall lose my place."

"But you won't tell, Henry, will you?"

"Oh dear, no miss! But you might let it out unawares-like."

I sprang forward. I seized the object in his red plush breeches with my hand. Henry stood quite still and breathed hard.

"Good Lord, miss! If they come, if we're found out!"

"They are all upstairs—we are alone. I must feel it. I know what it is, Henry. My goodness! How it throbs—how big it is getting now—let me feel it."

The footman submitted with a good grace. It was clear he was by no means unwilling. He evidently enjoyed my fingering. I slyly undid the corner button of his flap. I audaciously slipped my hand in. I ran it quickly down his belly. I encountered his nice clean shirt all warm. Then my hand fastened on his limb. I pulled away his shirt. I grasped his naked member. It felt very fat and thick. It was still stiffening. I gave it a sudden twist. It stood up now against his belly.

"Is that nice, Henry?"

"Good Lord! Yes, miss, it's heavenly, but I'm afraid we may be caught at it."

He appeared to have an enormous limb, not so long as the horrid *concierge*, but very thick and strong. I managed to pull back the skin. I felt a big soft, beautiful knob on the end. He turned towards me. He favored my toying by thrusting and grinding at my palm, but the space was too confined to enable me to stroke it as I liked.

Just then the front door bell rang.

I withdrew my hand. Henry buttoned up. The next minute he was opening the door with the grand air of a butler who could crush the comer with a glance.

I set to work to scheme a way to arrive at the sum of my desires. There are some things one must do for oneself. I nerved myself for the occasion. I went to a quiet street in Soho. I had noted a second-rate shop which was fitted up as an apothecary's—as we say in London, chemist and druggist. I entered. I had chosen the quiet time in the early afternoon. No one was in the shop. A good-looking, fair-haired young man advanced from the back room.

"Good morning. I want a syringe—a female syringe; show me some of your best."

"Certainly, miss, please to step this way."

He led me to the further end of the counter. He produced from a drawer a number of the articles in question.

"These are all good, but this pattern is the one we specially recommend. It is of vulcanite. It cannot break, or do any mischief."

I looked them over with a professional air.

"Yes, you are right. I will take the one you recommend."

Probably he saw I was a little awkward in handling the thing. I looked him in the face with a smile. His eyes sparkled.

"Do you understand how it should be applied, miss?"

"Well not properly, perhaps."

He smiled this time. I laughed softly.

"How do you fill it, and with what?"

"We have a detergent always made up, miss. If you will wait a moment, I will get some water and explain the action."

I nodded gently. He went into the back room. In a few moments he returned.

"Please come in here, I can show you how it works."

I followed the good-looking, fair young man. He filled the syringe with water, and squirted it out again into a basin.

"You should always wipe it after use and return it nicely to its case—thus."

I laughed again softly.

The young man laughed also. I was wicked enough to encourage his hilarity. He evidently took me for a representative member of a class to which I had not the honor to belong. I determined to humor him. He grew more familiar.

"After all, it is not at all equal to the real thing. Would you like me to try it for you? I shall be delighted to serve you, miss."

"Thank you, but I should prefer the real thing, it if it acts at all like the imitation. Probably you have none in stock?"

He laughed outright this time. He glanced around. We understood one another in a moment. He caught me round the waist.

"You beautiful devil! Where do you come from?"

"Are we quite sure to be alone? Suppose someone enters the shop?"

"They must wait. I can shut the door. See, there is a muslin curtain. We can see out. They cannot see in."

"Then try the real thing—if you have one?"

He was very good-looking and had roused my lust. He locked the door and pushed me towards a sofa.

"You really mean you will let me do the job for you, eh? You are awfully pretty, you know. I never saw such a beautiful girl. You are so beautifully dressed. I am not rich, you know; you will not want to bother me afterwards?"

"I ask nothing. I should not like to disappoint you."

"Oh, my God! What fun! I never had such a chance. How sweet your kisses are! Let me feel."

"Where is your syringe? Oh, my goodness! What a beauty! It is much larger, though, than the imitation. Kiss me?"

"Yes, much larger and almost as stiff. It holds nearly as much also, as you will soon find. Oh, your kisses are sweet."

I held his limb in my gloved hand. His fingers were in the moisture of my slit. He was beautifully made—not nearly so large as the concierge. I was dreadfully excited. I longed for him to "do the job," as he called it. He was stiffly erect.

I had not long to wait. I was utterly devoid of modesty. I fancied I knew how best to please him. I played my part.

"Be quick—I want it! Come!"

I pulled up all my clothes. He saw all my nudity. I felt the air on my exposed parts. The coolness of it was in such great contrast to my own heat that my slit grew all the slicker. The handsome young chemist eyed me with a lasciviousness I had come to appreciate. I wagged my tongue across my teeth. I undulated my lower body. But rather than inspire an assault, this moved him to express his admiration vocally.

"My God, what lovely legs! What fine stockings! What exquisite little boots! My God! Oh—what a chance!"

"You tarry so. I said I wanted it. Must I repeat myself? Do not make me beg further or I shall deny you. Can you not tell I want it now?"

The young man mounted quickly upon me. In an instant I felt him penetrating my orbit. My slit was all on fire with longing.

"My God, how tight you are—keep still—it's going in now. Oh, my God, how nice! I'm right into you now!"

It was true. I tasted the pleasure of coition for the first time with a full-grown man. I could not speak—I could only sob and moan in the ecstasy of that encounter. I clutched him by the shoulders. I felt the light hair of his belly rub on my flesh. He thrust vigorously. His limb grew stiffer and harder. It seemed to push to the extremity of my capacity. The pleasure was divine.

"Oh, Christ! I'm coming! I'm—coming! Ugh! Ugh! Ugh!"

"The syringe! The syringe! Give it all to me!"

The young man discharged—gush after gush. He had spoken the truth. His syringe was ample. His sperm squirted into me in a flood.

"You beautiful little devil! How deliciously nice you are. Now you must make use of the imitation. I will get you some water."

"Thanks. Remember to wipe your syringe and return it carefully to its box."

I walked home. I was no longer afraid of Henry now.

Before My Wedding

W e lived in Seville. When I attained the age of eighteen my parents promised me in marriage to a wealthy gentleman, whom I had seen but twice and did not admire. My love was already given to Juan, a handsome young officer who had just been promoted to a lieutenant for bravery. He was elegantly formed, his hair and eyes were as dark as night and he could dance to perfection. But it was for his gentle, winning smile that I loved him.

On the evening of the day that my parents had announced their determination to me, I had gone to be alone in the orange grove in the farthest part of our garden, there to sorrow over my hard fate. In the midst of my grief I heard the voice of Juan calling me. Could it be he who had been banished from the house and whom I never expected to see again?

He sprang down from the garden wall, folded me in his embrace and covered my hair with kisses for I had hidden my blushing face on my bosom. Then we talked of our sad lot. Juan was poor and it would be impossible to marry without the consent of my parents; we could only mingle our tears and regrets.

He led me to a grassy bank concealed by the orange trees and rose bushes, then he drew me on his lap and kissed my lips and cheeks and eyes. I did not chide him, for it must be our last meeting, but I did not return his kisses with passion. I had never felt a wanton desire in my life, much less not when I was so sad.

His passionate kisses were no longer confined to my face but were showered on my neck, and at length my dress was parted and revealed my little breasts to his ardent lips. I felt startled and made an attempt to stop him in what considered an impropriety, but he did not stop there. I felt my skirts being raised with a mingled sensation of alarm and shame which caused me to try to prevent it, but it was impossible I loved him too much to struggle against him and he was soon lying between my naked thighs.

"Inez," he said, "if you love me, be my wife for these few moments before we part."

I could not resist the appeal. I offered my lips to kisses without any feeling save innocent love, and lay passive while I felt him guide a stiff, warm object between my thighs. It entered where nothing had ever entered before and no sooner was it entered than he gave a fierce thrust which seemed to tear my vitals with a cruel pain. Then he gave deep sigh and sank heavily upon my bosom.

I kissed him repeatedly, for I supposed it must have hurt him as much as it did me, little thinking that his pleasure had been as exquisite as my suffering had been. Just at that moment the harsh voice of my duenna resounded through the garden, calling, "Inez! Inez!"

Exchanging with my seducer a lingering, hearty kiss, I extracted myself from his embrace and answered the call. My duenna eyed me sharply as I approached her.

"Why do you straddle your legs so far apart when you walk," said she, and when I came closer, "Why is the bosom of your dress so disordered and why are your cheeks so flushed?"

I made some excuse about climbing to get an orange and hurried past her to my room. I locked the door and prepared to go to bed that I might think uninterruptedly of Juan, whom I now loved more than ever. When I took off my petticoat I found it all stained with blood. I folded it and treasured it beneath my pillow to dream upon, under the fond illusion that Juan's blood was mingled there with my own.

For weeks afterwards I was so closely watched that I could not see Juan. The evening preceding my marriage I went to vespers with my duenna. While we were kneeling in the cathedral a large woman, closely veiled, came and knelt close beside me. She attracted my attention by plucking my dress, and, as I turned, she momentarily lifted the corner of her mantle and I saw it was Juan in disguise. I was now all alert and a small package was slipped into my hand. I had just time to secure it in my bosom when my duenna arose and we left the church.

As soon as I regained the privacy of my own room I tore open the package and found it contained a silken rope ladder and letter from Juan requesting me to suspend it from the window that night after the family was at rest.

The note was full of love. There was much more to tell, it said, if I would grant the interview by means of the ladder. Of course, I determined to see him. I was very ignorant of what most girls learn from each other, for I had no companion. I supposed when a woman was embraced as I had been she necessarily got with child, and that such embraces therefore occurred at intervals of a year or so. I expected, consequently, nothing of the kind at the coming interview. I wanted to learn of Juan if the child, which I supposed to be in my womb, would be born so soon as to betray our secret to my husband.

When the family retired I went to my room and dressed myself elaborately, braiding my hair and putting on all of my jewelry. Then I fastened one end of the rope ladder to the bedpost and lowered the other end out of the window; it was at once strained by the ascending step of Juan. My eyes were soon feasted with the sight of my handsome lover, and we were soon locked in each other's arms.

Again and again we alternately devoured each other with our eyes and pressed each other to our hearts. Words did not seem to be of any use; our kisses and caresses became more passionate, and for the first time in my life I felt a wanton emotion. The lips between my thighs became moistened and torrid with coursing blood; I could feel my cheeks burn under the ardent gaze of my lover; I could no longer meet his eyes my own dropped in shame.

He began to undress me rapidly, his hand trembling with eagerness. Could it be that he wanted to pierce my loins so soon again, as he had done in the orange garden? An hour ago I would have dreaded it; now the thought caused a throb of welcome just where the pain had been sharpest.

Stripped to my chemise, and even that unbuttoned by the eager hand of my lover, I darted from his arms and concealed my confusion beneath the bedcover. He soon undressed and followed me then, bestowing one kiss on my neck and one on each of my naked breasts, he opened my thighs and parted the little curls between. Again I felt the stiff, warm object entering. It entered slowly on account of the tightness, but every inch of its progress inward became more and more pleasant.

When it was fully entered I was in a rapture of delight, yet something was wanting. I wrapped my arms around my lover and responded passionately to his kisses. I was almost tempted to respond to his thrusts by a wanton motion of my loins. My maidenhead was gone and the tender virgin wound completely healed, but I had still some remains of maiden shame.

For a moment he lay still and then he gave me half a dozen deep thrusts, each succeeding one giving me more and more pleasure. It culminated at last in a thrill so exquisite that my frame seemed to melt. Nothing more was wanting. I gave a sigh of deep gratification and my arms fell nerveless to my sides, but I received with passionate pleasure two or three more thrusts which Juan gave me, at each of which my sheath was penetrated by a copious gush which soothed and bathed its membranes.

For a long time we lay perfectly still; the stiff shaft which had completely filled me had diminished in size until it slipped completely out. Juan at last relieved me of his weight by lying at my side, but our legs were still entwined.

We had now time to converse. My lover explained to me all the sexual mysteries which remained for me to know, then we formed plans which would enable us after my marriage to meet often alone. These explanations and plans were mingled so freely with caresses that before my lover left me we had melted five times in each other's arms. I had barely strength to drag up the rope ladder after he departed.

The day had now begun to dawn. I fell into a dreamless sleep and was awakened by my duenna pounding on the door and calling that it was nearly ten o'clock and that I was to be married at eleven. I was in no hurry but they got me to church in time. During the whole ceremony I felt my lover's sperm trickling down my thighs.

Ode to Orifices

When cunt first triumphed (as the learned suppose)
O'er failing pricks, Immortal Dildo rose,
From fucks unnumbered, still erect he drew,
Exhausted cunts, and then demanded new;
Dame Nature saw him spurn her bounded reign,
And panting pricks toiled after him in vain;
The laxest folds, the deepest depths he filled;
The juiciest drained; the toughest hymens drilled.
The fair lay gasping with distended limbs,
And unremitting cockstands stormed their quims.
Then Frigging came, instructed from the school,
And scorned the aid of India-rubber tool.
With restless finger, fired the dormant blood,
Till Clitoris rose, sly, peeping thro' her hood.
Gently was worked this titillating art,
It broke no hymen, and scarce stretched the part;
Yet lured its votaries to a sudden doom,
And stamped Consumption's flush on Beauty's bloom.
Sweet Gamahuche found softer ways to fame,
It asked not Dildo's art, nor Frigging's flame.
Tongue, not prick, now probes the central hole,
And mouth, not cunt, becomes prick's destined goal.
It always found a sympathetic friend;
And pleased limp pricks, and those who could not spend,
No tedious wait, for laboured stand, delays
The hot and pouting cunt, which tongue allays.
The taste was luscious, tho' the smell was strong;
The fuck was easy, and would last so long;
Til wearied tongues found gamahuching cloy,
And pricks, and cunts, grew callous to the joy.
Then dulled by frigging, by mock pricks enlarged,
Her noble duties Cunt but ill discharged.
Her nymphae drooped, her devil's bite grew weak,

And twice two pricks might flounder in her creek;
Till all the edge was taken off the bliss,
And Cunt's sole occupation was to piss.
Forced from her former joys, with scoff and brunt,
She saw great Arsehole lay the ghost Cunt.
Exulting buggers hailed the joyful day,
And piles and hoemerrids confirmed his sway.
But who lust's future fancies can explore,
And mark the whimsies that remain in store?
Perhaps it shall be deemed a lover's treat,
To suck the flowering quims of mares in heat;
Perhaps, where beauty held unequalled sway,
A Cochin fowl shall rival Mabel Grey;
Nobles be ruined by the Hyaena's smile,
And Seals get short engagements from th' Argyle.
Hard is her lot, that here by Fortune placed,
Must watch the wild vicissitudes of taste;
Catch every whim, learn every bawdy trick,
And chase the new born bubbles of the prick;
Ah, let not Censure term our fate, our choice,
The Bawd but echoes back the public voice;
The Brothel's laws, the Brothel's patrons give,
And those that live to please, must please to live;
Then purge these growing follies from your hearts,
And turn to female arms, and female arts;
'Tis yours this night, to bid the reign begin,
Of all the good old-fashioned ways to sin;
Clean, wholesome girls, with lip, tongue, cunt, and hand,
Shall raise, keep up, put in, take down a stand;
Your bottoms shall by lily hands be bled,
And birches blossom under every bed.

Emma and Thomas

I had been spending a wonderful afternoon in the most lustful fantasies, when I was informed that Thomas had arrived. As if on cue with my daydreaming, Thomas made his appearance. I was at once struck by the young fellow's really distinguished appearance. His apparent awkwardness of manner was evidently only due to so unusual an introduction, but his bearing, his personality were conspicuous. They were more: they were most uncommon.

He was rather fair than dark. His height could not have been less than six feet two inches. His hair, of a rich auburn, was naturally curly and glossy. His complexion was clear and bright; his eyes remarkably fine and expressive. Poor fellow! It was sad to think he could neither hear a human voice nor express his ideas in speech. His individuality, however, compensated in some measure for these defects.

He came straight up to me with a rather weak smile on his face, as if he was shy. So, in truth, I found him. I motioned him to sit down by me. I made room for him on the sofa. I noticed how he watched furtively all my movements and seemed to be impressed by my personal appearance.

I remembered my mistake. I wrote my remark on the slate. He broke into an intelligent smile at once. His whole being seemed to wake in response to my sentence. He was evidently vain, your fellow. He commenced writing rapidly. I followed his pencil.

"Nature has not been wholly unkind to me. I am strong. I am young. I rejoice in life. I have the means to enjoy it."

I smiled and, putting my left hand on his shoulder, I wrote: "Can you make love?"

"It would not be difficult for anyone to love you. I could die for a girl like you. I have never seen a more beautiful woman."

"Are you in earnest? Would you really like to make love to me?"

In an instant his arms were round me; his lips pressed mine. His breath was sweet as an angel's; his eyes shone into mine with the awakening of uncontrollable passion. He wrote rapidly: "I love you already—you are so sweet! I want you! You will let me, will you not?"

I took up the crayon: "We are here to make love together!"

Again there was no use for the slate. He pressed my form to his. He thrust his trembling hands towards my bosom. I denied him nothing. He panted; he breathed in heavy jerks. It was plain he was becoming more and more excited. He covered my face, my neck, my hands with burning kisses. Love and desire have no need of words. It is a language understood without sound, communicated without speech. He felt its influence. Its intensity brought with it an insupportable necessity for relief.

He wrote rapidly on his slate: "Do I make myself clear? I possess unusual advantages with which to please a beautiful and voluptuous girl like you."

I read. I believe I blushed. I playfully pulled his ear. He kissed me on the mouth in mock revenge. He became enterprising. He essayed familiarities which were hardly decent. I feigned sufficient resistance to fan his rising flame. Suddenly he released me again to write:

"I conclude there need not be too much modesty between us to interfere with our mutual pleasure?"

"No. I am here for your pleasure. You are here for mine. We should enjoy together. Let us make love in earnest."

His eyes shouted flames of lust. He took the slate.

"You are no less sensual than beautiful. We will drown ourselves in pleasure. I love pleasure. With you it will be divine."

He threw off his coat. He assisted me to remove my bodice. Soon I stood in my corset of pale blue satin and a short skirt of the same color and material. He rapidly divested himself of his outer things. He caught my hand. He carried it under his shirt.

"Oh, good heavens! What a monster!"

His instrument was as long as Jim's. It was even thicker. It was stiff as buckram. It throbbed under my wanton touches.

He pressed my hand upon it and laughed a strange silent laugh. Then he wrote on the slate:

"What do you call that?"

This was evidently intended as a challenge. Not bashful, I took it up.

"I call it an instrument—a weapon of offense—a limb."

"I call it a cock."

"Well, he certainly has a very fine crest. He carries himself very proudly—his head is as red as a turkey-cock—he is a real beauty."

The slate was thrown on one side. Thomas drew me on his knee. He tucked up my short, lace-trimmed chemise. I made only just sufficient remonstrance to whet his appetite. He lifted me in his strong arms like a little child. He bore me to the bed. He deposited me gently upon it. He was by my side in an instant minus all save shirt, which stuck up in front of him as if it was suspended on a peg—as indeed it was. Thomas laid his handsome head on my breast. He toyed with my most secret charms, my round and plump posteriors seemed specially to delight him. I grasped his enormous member in my hand. I ventured to examine also the heavy purse which depended below. His testicles were in proportion to his splendid limb. I separated them from each other. There seemed to be something I did not understand. I felt them over again. Surely—yes, I was correct—he had three! He led me eagerly to the soft couch. Once on the bed he recommenced his amorous caresses.

I seized him once more by his truncheon. It was so nice to feel the warm length of flesh—the broad red nut—the long white shaft, and the triangle of testicles which were drawn up tight below it. It was so strange, too, that this fine young fellow could neither hear nor speak! The spirit of mischief took possession of me. The demon of lust vied with him in stimulating my passion. I slipped off the bed. Thomas followed me. I raised my chemise up to my middle and laughingly challenged him to follow. The view of my naked charms was evidently appetizing. He tried to seize me again. I avoided his grasp. He ran after me round the table which stood at one end of the room. His expression was all frolic and fun, but with a strong tinge of sensuous desire in his humid eyes and moist lips. I let him catch me. He held me tight this time. I turned my back to him. I felt him pressing the brown curls of his hairy parts upon my plump buttocks. He pushed me before him towards the bed. His huge member inserted itself between my thighs. I saw its red-capped head appear in front of me. I put my hand down to it. To my surprise, he had placed an ivory napkin ring over it. It reduced the available length. It certainly left me less to fear from its unusually large proportions. I had already taken the precaution to anoint my parts with cold cream. I adjusted the head as I leaned forward, belly down, on the soft bed. The young fellow pushed. He entered. I thought he would split me up. He held me by the hips. He thrust it into me. It passed up. I groaned with a mingled feeling of pain and pleasure. He was too excited to pause now. He bore forward, sitting himself solidly to work to do the job. I passed my hand down to feel his cock as he called it, as it emerged from time to time from the pliable sheath. Although I knew he could not hear, yet it delighted me to utter my sensations—woman must talk—they can't help it. I was every bit a woman at that moment! Besides, I could express my ideas in any language I liked, as crudely as I chose—there was no one to hear me—no one to offend—no one to chide. I jerked forward.

"Oh! Take it out! Don't spend yet! I want to change—it's so delicious! How sweetly you poke me—you dear fellow!"

The huge instrument extricated itself with a plop! Thomas divined my intention. He aided me to place myself upon the side of the bed. I took his cock again in my little hands. I examined it voraciously. It was lovely now—all shining and glistening, distended and rigid in its luxury.

"I want it all—all—all!"

He evidently understood. He slipped off the napkin ring. He presented it again to my eager slit. It went up me slowly.

"Oh, my God! It is too long now. Oh! Oh! Never mind—give it me all—all—oh! Ah! Oh! Go slowly! You brute—you are splitting me! Do you hear? Poke! oh! Push—push now! I'm coming, do you hear? You cruel brute! Coming—oh, God! Oh!"

He perceived my condition; he bore up close to me as long as my emitting spasms lasted. My swollen clitoris was in closest contact with the back of his weapon which tickled ecstatically.

I clung to him with both thighs. I raised my belly to meet his stabbing thrusts. I seized the pillow. I covered my face. I bit the pillowcase through and through. When I had finished, he stopped a little to let me breathe.

"You have not come yet, but you will soon. I know it. I can feel it by the strong throbbing of your cock. I want it—oh! I want it! I must hold your balls while you spend. I want your sperm!"

He became more and more urgent. He was having me with all his tremendous vigor. His strokes were shorter—quicker—my thighs worked in unison. His features writhed in his ecstasy of increasing enjoyment. He was nearing the end. I felt every throb of his huge instrument.

I draw the veil over the termination of the scene. I cannot even use ordinary terms to describe it. My whole nervous system vibrated with voluptuous excitement. My senses deserted me.

When I recovered consciousness, to my astonishment, my companion had disappeared. Papa was standing over my prostrate form. How he had been occupied I did not then know. His face was turgid with satisfied lust. His hands trembled. His dress was disordered. He held in his hands a towel with which he was bathing my aching parts.

Before he departed, he assisted me at my toilette.

Edmund and I

After luncheon I asked Edmund to smoke a cigarette in my room, which he at once complied with.

As soon as I had closed the door, I said, "Old fellow, did you ever see *Fanny Hill*, a beautiful book of love and pleasure?"

"What, a smutty book, I suppose you mean? No, Stephen, but if you have got it I should wonderfully like to look at it," he said, his eyes sparkling with animation.

"Here it is, my boy, only I hope it won't excite you too much; you can look it over by yourself, as I read the Times," said I, taking it out of my dressing-case, and handing it to his eager grasp.

He sat close to me in an easy lounging chair, and I watched him narrowly as he turned over the pages and gloated over the beautiful plates; his prick hardened in his breeches till it was quite stiff and rampant.

"Ha! Ha!! Ha!!! old fellow, I thought it would fetch you out!" I said, laying my hand upon his cock. "By Jove, Edmund! what a tosser yours has grown since we used to play in bed together a long time ago. I'll lock the door, we must compare our parts, I think mine is nearly as big as yours."

He made no remark, but I could see he was greatly excited by the book. Having locked the door, I leant over his shoulder and made my remarks upon the plates as he turned them over. At length the book dropped from his hands, and his excited gaze was rivetted on my bursting breeches. "Why, Stephen, you are as bad as I am," he said, with a laugh, "let's see which is the biggest," pulling out his hard, stiff prick, and then laying his hands on me pulled my affair out to look at.

We handled each other in an ecstasy of delight, which ended in out throwing off all our clothes, and having a mutual fuck between our thighs on the bed; we spent in rapture, and after a long dalliance he entered into my plans, and we determined to have a lark with the girls as soon as we could get a chance.

In the course of the evening, Edmund and myself were delighted by the arrival of a beautiful young lady of eighteen, on a visit to his sisters, in fact, a school fellow of Anna and Molly, come to stop a week at the house.

Miss Rose Redquim was indeed a sprightly beauty of the Venus height, well proportioned in leg and limb, full swelling bosom, with a graceful Grecian type of face, rosy cheeks, large grey eyes, and golden auburn hair, lips as red as cherries, and teeth like pearls, frequently exhibited by a succession of winning smiles, which never seemed to leave her face. Such was the acquisition to the feminine department of the house, and we congratulated ourselves on the increased prospect of sport, as Edmund had expressed to me considerable compunctions as to taking liberties with one's own cousins.

The next morning being gloriously fine and warm, myself and friend strolled in the grounds, smoking our cigarettes, for about an hour, till near the time when we guessed the girls would be coming for a bath in the small lake in the park, which we at once proceeded to; then we secreted ourselves secure from observation, and awaited, in deep silence, the arrival of cousins and friend.

This lake, as I call it, was a pond of about four or five acres in extent, every side thickly wooded to the very margin, so that even anglers could not get access to the bank, except at the little sloping green sward, of about twenty or thirty square yards in extent, which had a large hut, or summer-house, under the trees, where the bathers could undress, and then trip across the lawn to the water. The bottom of the pond being gradually shelving, and covered with fine sand at this spot, and a circular space, enclosed with rails, to prevent them getting out of their depth.

The back door of this hut opened upon a very narrow foot-path, leading to the house through the dense thicket, so that any party would feel quite secure from observation. The interior was comfortably furnished with seats and lounges, besides a buffet, generally holding a stock of wine, biscuits, and cakes, during the bathing season. Edmund, having a key to the hut, took me through onto the lawn, and then climbing up into a thick sycamore, we re-lighted our cigarettes, awaiting the adventure with some justifiable impatience.

Some ten minutes of suspense, and then we were rewarded by hearing the ringing laughter of the approaching girls. We heard the key turned in the lock, then the sounds of their bolting themselves in, and Rebecca's voice, saying: "Ah! Wouldn't the boys like the fun of seeing us undress and bathing, this lovely warm day"; to which we heard Rose laughingly reply: "I don't mind if they do see me, if I don't know it, dears. There's something delightful in the thought of the excitement it would put the dear fellows in. I know I should like Edmund to take a fancy to me; I'm nearly in love with him already, and have read that the best way a girl can madly excite the man she wishes to win is to let him see all her charms, when he thinks she is unconscious of his being near."

"Well, there's no fear of our being seen here, so I am one for a good romp. Off with your clothes, quick; it will be delicious in the water," exclaimed Anna.

The undressing was soon accomplished, excepting chemises, boots, and stockings, as they were evidently in no hurry to enter the water.

"Now," said Anna, with a gay laugh, "we must make Rose a free woman, and examine all she's got. Come on, girls, lay her down, and turn up her smock."

The beautiful girl only made a slight feint of resisting, as she playfully pulled up their chemises, exclaiming: "You shan't look at my fanny for nothing. La! Molly has got no hair on her fly trap. Does she shave it? What a pretty pouting slit yours is, Rebecca. I think you have been using the finger of a glove made into a little cock for Anna, and told her to bring home from school for you."

She was soon stretched on her back on the soft mossy grass, her face covered with burning blushes, as her pretty cunt was exposed to view, ornamented with its *chevelure* of soft red hair; her beautiful white belly and thighs shining like marble in the bright sunlight. The three sisters were blushing as well as their friend, and delighted at the sight of so much loveliness.

One after another, they kissed the vermilion lips of their friend's delightful slit, and then turning her on her face, proceeded to smack the lily white bottom of their laughing, screaming victim, with their open hands.

Smacks and laughter echoed through the grove, and we almost fancied ourselves witnesses to the games of real nymphs. At last she was allowed to rise on her knees, and then the three sisters in turn presented their cunts to their friend to kiss. Molly was the last, and Rose, clasping her arms firmly round my youngest cousin's buttocks, exclaimed: "Ah! Ah! You have made me feel so rude, I must suck this little hairless jewel," as she glued her lips to it, and hid her face almost from sight, as if she would devour Molly's charms there and then. The young girl, flushed with excitement, placed her hands on Rose's head, as if to keep her there, whilst both Rebecca and Anna, kneeling down by the side of their friend, began to caress her cunt, bosom, and every charm they could tickle or handle.

This exciting scene lasted for five or six minutes, till at last they all sank down in a confused heap on the grass, kissing and fingering in mad excitement.

Now was our time. We had each provided ourselves with little switches of twigs, and thus aimed we seemed to drop from the clouds upon the surprised girls, who screamed in fright and hid their blushing faces in their hands.

They were too astonished and alarmed to jump up, but we soon commenced to bring them to their senses, and convince them of the reality of the situation.

"What rude! what lascivious ideas! slash away Edmund!" I cried, making my swish leave its marks on their bottoms at every cut.

"Who would have thought of it, Stephen? We must whip such indecent ideas out of their tails!" he answered, seconding my assault with his sharp, rapid strokes.

They screamed both from pain and shame, and springing to their feet, chased round the lawn; there was no escape. We caught them by the tails of their chemises, which we lifted up to enable us to cut at their bums with more effect. At last we were getting quite out of breath, and beginning fairly to pant from exhaustion, when Rebecca suddenly turned upon me, saying, "Come, come, girls, let's tear their clothes off, so they shall be quite as ashamed as we are, and agree to keep our secret!" The others helped her, and we made such a feeble resistance that we were soon reduced to the same state in which we had surprised them, making them blush and look very shamefaced at the sight of our rampant engines of love.

Edmund seized Miss Redquim round the waist, and led the way into the summer-house, myself and his cousins following. The gentlemen then producing the wine, &c., from the buffet, sat down with a young lady on each knee, my friend having Rose and Molly, whilst Rebecca and Anna sat with me; we plied the girls with several glasses of champagne each, which they seemed to swallow in order to drown their sense of shame. We could feel their bodies quiver with emotion as they reclined upon our necks, their hands and ours groping under shirts and chemises in every forbidden spot; each of us had two delicate hands caressing our cocks, two delicious arms around our necks, two faces laid cheek to cheek on either side, two sets of lips to kiss, two pairs of bright and humid eyes to return our ardent glances; what wonder then that we flooded their hands with our spurting seed and felt their delicious spendings trickle over our busy fingers.

Excited by the wine, and madly lustful to enjoy the dear girls to the utmost, I stretched Anna's legs wide apart, and sinking on my knees, gamahuched her virgin cunt, till she spent again in ecstasy, whilst dear Rebecca was doing the same to me, sucking the last drop of spend from my gushing prick; meanwhile Edmund was following my example, Rose surrendered to his lascivious tongue all the recesses of her virginity as she screamed with delight and pressed his head towards her mount when the frenzy of love brought her to the spending point; Molly all the while kissing her brother's belly, and frigging him to a delicious emission.

When we recovered a little from this exciting *pas de trois*, all bashfulness was vanished between us, we promised to renew our pleasures on the morrow, and for the present contented ourselves by bathing all together, and then returned to the house for fear the girls might be suspected of something wrong for staying out too long.

After luncheon Edmund smoked his cigarette in my room; the events of the morning had left both of us in a most unsettled and excited state. "I say, old fellow," he exclaimed, "by Jove! it's quite impossible for me to wait till to-morrow for the chance of enjoying that delicious Rose; besides, when there are so many of us together there is just the chance of being disappointed; no, no, it must be this very night if I die for it; her room is only the other side of my cousins'."

I tried to persuade him from doing anything rashly, as we could not yet be certain that even excited and ready as she had shown herself, that she was prepared to surrender her virginity so quickly. However, arguments and reasonings were in vain. "See," he exclaimed, "the very thoughts of her make my prick ready to burst," opening his trousers and letting out his beautiful red-headed cock, as it stood in all its manly glory, stiff and hard as marble, with the hot blood looking ready to burst from his distended veins; the sight was too exciting for me to restrain myself, the cigarette dropped from my lips, and going upon my knees in front of him, I kissed, sucked, frigged, and played with his delicious prick till he spent in my mouth with an exclamation of rapture, as I eagerly swallowed every drop of his copious emission. When we had a little recovered our serenity, we discussed the best plans for the night, as I was determined to have my share of the amusement, which Edmund most willingly agreed to, provided he was to go first to Rose's room, and prevail upon her to consent to his ardent suit; then when all seemed to be en regle, I was to surprise them in the midst of their fun, and join in the erotic frolic.

After dinner we adjourned to the drawing-room, where a most pleasant evening was enlivened by music and singing, leaving Edmund turning over the leaves for Rose and Molly, as they sang "What Are the Wild Waves Saying." Rebecca and Anna whispered to me that they should like a short stroll in the garden by moonlight, so opening the window, a few steps brought us on to the soft gravel path, where we could walk with an almost noiseless tread. Papa and Mama were in the library playing cribbage, and we felt sure that Edmund and Rose would not run after us, so passing rapidly down a shady walk, with one arm round each of the dear girl's waists, and alternately kissing one and the other of them, we soon arrived at a very convenient spot, and the instinct of love allowed me to guide the willing girls into a rather dark arbour without the least demur on their part.

"How lovely the honeysuckle smells!" sighed Anna, as I drew them both down by my side in the corner, and began a most delicious kissing and groping in the dim obscurity.

"Not so sweet as your dear little pussey," said I, playfully twisting my fingers in the soft down around the tight little grotto of love which I had taken possession of.

"Oh! Oh! Mind, Stephen dear!" she sighed softly, as she clung round my neck.

"Will you let me kiss it, my little pet, it will give you such pleasure; there's nothing to be bashful or shamefaced about here in the dark; ask your sister if it wasn't delicious."

REBECCA. – "Oh! let him, Anna dear, you will experience the most heavenly sensations."

Thus urged she allowed me to raise her clothes, and recline her backwards in the corner, but this would not admit of Rebecca having her fair share of the game, but as she was now all aflame with excited expectation, there was no difficulty in persuading her to kneel over my face as I reclined on my back at full length on the seat; lovely hands at once let my eager prick out of his confined position in my trousers, and as I commenced to suck and gamahuche Anna, I felt that the dear Rebecca had taken possession of my cock for her own special benefit.

"Oh! let me kiss you, Anna dear, put your tongue in my mouth," said

Rebecca, straddling over me, and putting away my excited engine of love up her own longing crack, and beginning a delightful St. George; I clasped the younger girl firmly round the buttocks with one arm, Whilst with my right hand I found and rubbed her stiff little clitoris to increase the excitement from the lascivious motions of my tongue in her virgin cunny.

Rebecca was in a frenzy of voluptuous enjoyment, she bounced up and down on my prick, and now and then rested for a moment to indulge in the exquisite pleasure of the devil's bite, which she seemed to possess to a most precocious extent, the folds of her cunt contracting and throbbing upon my swelling prick in the most delicious manner.

Anna was all of a tremble, she wriggled herself most excitedly over my mouth, and I licked up her virgin spendings as they came down in a thick creamy emission.

"Oh! Oh! Oh!" she sighed, hugging and kissing Rebecca in fondest abandon. "What is it, dear? I shall choke, Stephen. There's something running from me; it's so delicious. Oh! What shall I do?"

Rebecca and myself met at this moment in a joint spend, which left us in an ecstatic lethargy of love, and the two sisters almost fainted upon my prostrate body.

When we had recovered a little, I sat up between the loving sisters. Anna, throwing her arms round my neck, quite smothered one with her burning kisses, as she whispered in my ear: "It was indeed pleasure, dear Stephen. Is that one of the delights of love, and what was Rebecca doing, for she was as excited as I was?"

"Can't you guess, darling?" I replied, taking her hand and placing it upon my still rampant cock. "That is what she played with."

"But how?" whispered the innocent girl. "She was kissing and sucking my tongue deliciously all the while, but seemed as if she could not keep still a moment."

"She had that plaything of mine up her cunny, my dear, and was riding up and down upon it till we all fainted with the pleasure at the same time. You shall have a real lesson in love next time, and Rebecca won't be jealous, will you, dearest?"

"No, no," Rebecca protested, "We must all be free to enjoy all the games of love without jealousy. I wonder how Edmund is getting on with Rose by this time. We must now make haste back to the house."

Anna was anxious for more explanations as to the arts of love, but was put off till another time; and all being now in a cooler state of mind, we returned to the house, where we found Edmund repeating the game of the morning, by gamahuching Rose, whilst Molly was gone out of the room.

The red-haired beauty was covered with blushes, as she suddenly dropped her clothes on our entrance, and only recovered from her crimson shamefacedness when Rebecca laughingly assured her that we had been enjoying ourselves in the same manner.

"Oh! How rude and indecent of us all," exclaimed Rose, "but who can resist the burning touches of a handsome young fellow like your cousin; he was so impudent, and it sends such a thrill of voluptuousness through the whole frame," commencing to sing, "It's naughty, but it's nice."

The supper bell rang, and, after a light repast, we all separated to our rooms. Edmund came into my chamber to join in a cigarette and glass of grog before finally retiring.

"It's all right for to-night, old fellow," he exclaimed, as soon as we were seated for our smoke. "I begged Rose to let me kiss all her charms, in her own room without the inconvenience of clothes. She made some objections at first, but finally consented not to lock the door, if I promised not to go beyond kissing, on my honour as a gentleman."

He was too impatient to stop long, and, after only one smoke, cut off to his room. Undressing myself as quickly as possible, I went to him, and escorted him to the door of his lady-love; it was unlocked, and he glided noiselessly into the darkened chamber. She was evidently awake and expecting his visit, for I could hear their rapturous kissing and his exclamation of delight as he ran his hands over her beautiful figure. "My love, I must light the candles to feast my eyes upon your extraordinary beauties. Why did you put out the lights?" She made some faint remonstrances, but the room was soon a blaze of light from half-a-dozen candles.

I was looking through the keyhole, and eagerly listening to every word.

"My love, let us lay side by side and enjoy feeling our bodies in naked contact before we begin the kissing each other's charms."

I could see that his shirt and her *chemise de nuit* were both turned up as high as possible, and his prick was throbbing against her belly. He made her grasp it in her hand, and pulling one of her legs over his thighs, was trying to place the head of his eager cock to the mark between her legs.

"Ah! No! No! Never! You promised on your honour, sir!" she almost screamed in alarm, and struggling to disengage herself from his strong embrace. "No! No! Oh! No! I won't, indeed!"

His previous soft manner seemed in a moment to have changed to a mad fury, as he suddenly rolled her over on her back, keeping his own legs well between her thighs.

"Honour! Honour!" he laughed. "How can I have honour when you tempt me so, Rose? You have driven me mad by the liberties I have been allowed. Resistance is useless. I would rather die than not have you now, you dear girl."

She struggled in desperate silence for a few moments, but her strength was unequal to his; he gradually got into position, and then taking advantage of her exhaustion, rapidly and ruthlessly completed her ravishment.

She seemed insensible at first, and I took advantage of her short unconsciousness to steal into the room, and kneel at the foot of the bed, where I had a fine view of his blood-stained weapon, thrusting in and out of her shattered virginity. After a little she seemed to begin to enjoy his movements, especially after the first lubricating injection of his love juice. Her buttocks heaved up to meet his thrusts, and her arms clung convulsively round his body, and seemed reluctant to let him withdraw, until both seemed to come together in a luscious spend.

As they lay exhausted after this bout, I advanced and kissed the dear girl, and as she opened her eyes, I placed my hand across her mouth to stop any inconvenient scream of surprise, and congratulated her on having so nicely got rid of her troublesome virginity, and claimed my share of the fun, drawing her attention to the rampant condition of my cock in contrast to Edmund's limp affair. I could see she was now eager for a repetition of the pleasure she had only just begun to taste. Her eyes were full of languishing desire as I placed her hand upon my prick.

She was persuaded to ride a St. George upon me, my cock was inserted in her still tender cunt, with great care, and allowed slowly to get his position, but the excitement was too great for me, with an exclamation of delight I shot a stream of sperm up into her very entrails, this set her off, she began slowly to move upon me, her cunt gripping and throbbing upon the shaft most deliciously, and we were soon running another delightful course; this was too much for Edmund, his cock was again as hard as iron, and eager to get in somewhere, so kneeling up behind her he tried to insert his prick in her cunt alongside of mine, but found it too difficult to achieve, then the charming wrinkled orifice of her pink bottom-hole caught his attention, the tip of his affair was wet with our spendings, and his vigorous shoves soon gained an entrance, as I was holding her fast and she was too excited to resist anything, only giving a slight scream as she found him slip inside of the part she thought was only made for another purpose. I asked them to rest a few moments and enjoy the sensation of feeling where we were, our pricks throbbing against each other in a most delicious manner, with only the thin membrane of the anal canal between them; it made us spend immediately to the great delight of Rose, who at once urged us to go on.

This was the most delightful bout of fucking I had ever had; she made us do it over and over again and, when we were exhausted, sucked our pricks up to renewed cockstands. This lasted till the dawn of day warned us of the necessity of precaution, and we retired to our respective rooms.

Charlie and Maude,
or Instruction Libertine

Foreword

Charlie, twenty-eight years of age, brilliantly healthy, enjoying a moderate income, which he derived from the honest labor of his father in business, had as his mistress, Maud, over whose pretty head twenty-four summers had passed. She was the wife of a worthy fellow, whose icy temperament formed too great a contrast with that of his better half, so that it was no wonder that she should seek elsewhere that which she had no chance of finding in her husband's arms.

Charlie, free to do as he liked, was fond of the ladies, but in a tranquil fashion and brooking no delays, had met Maud at social gatherings, and she seemed fitted for his simple, albeit lecherous, tastes. She, too, had remarked Charlie, who by his discreet, polite, and ardent manner, seemed well fitted to compensate her, without fear of scandal for the insufficiency of her husband, resulting from his frigidity in the pleasures of love.

When two people are suited to each other, it is not long before they come to an arrangement, so a "liaison" was quickly established between the couple. Charlie possessed a neat little room, in a different neighborhood from that of his residence, where could be found a bed, cozy armchairs, sofa, divan, chairs, cushions, rugs, and all furniture and necessary linen for the pursuits for which the nook was destined. All was arranged without useless luxury, but with care and cleanliness, and commodities of all kinds. Two little keys, of which Charlie and Maud each possessed one, allowed them to repair thither separately at the day and hour fixed by Maud, either by a sly "billet-doux" communicated at parties where the lovers often met, or by a note that she carried herself to the little room, for it was understood that Charlie should go there every morning, between ten and eleven, except when they had met overnight.

This state of things had lasted for eighteen months, the lovers having exhausted without lassitude every resource of free and happy passion.

They agreed perfectly, in spite of time and satisfied enjoyment, that they were well suited. They had confidence in each other. Maud found that Charlie was not only a discreet and indefatigable lover, but also a man of firm mind, just and sensible, free of all prejudices, but respecting them for the sake of the world's opinion.

Charlie recognized in Maud a good-hearted woman, not very capricious, but leaning towards the pleasures of passion in consequence of her fiery temperament, held in check, however, by a sensible brain; farseeing too, but desirous of learning. Their two souls were destined to agree.

One day, Charlie found in his boudoir a word from Maud, telling him that the same day she would come to pass the night, all the next and the following night, having obtained from her husband the permission to spend two or three days with a female friend a few miles out of London. She intended to go there on the third day and only stop twenty-four hours, so as to devote an entire day and two nights to love.

The two lovers had long desired to be able to sleep together at least one night and this had been impossible up to the present.

Charlie was delighted; it seemed to him as if he was now only for the first time about to really enjoy his mistress, although he had oftentimes passed many hours in bed in her arms, both of them in a state of nature, in the happy little lodging.

He awaited her coming therefore with impatient felicity, almost as if it was the first "rendezvous" with Maud, who took care not to break her word, as she experienced in a like manner this tender feeling of her lover, so she arrived at seven o'clock in the evening.

Charlie had caused a light repast to be prepared, prettily laid out, but substantial withal. The table was near the bed; they gaily supped and retired between the sheets very early, so as to have more time for the amorous struggles, to which they gave themselves up with all the ardor of true, young, and vigorous lovers.

After having taken a large amount of voluptuous exercise, our two turtledoves rested awhile and began to chat about the sweet pleasure they had had. They were both full of their subject. Curious little Maud began to speak first.

ENTRANCE TO THE TEMPLE
DIALOGUE I. On the Physical Conformation of Man and Woman

Maud. —You must confess, my dear boy, that you are a great libertine. I don't say that to reproach you, as frankly, I get all the benefit, and not being a hypocrite I state the plain truth, but you seemed imbued with the science of Venus to your fingers-ends, and I believe that there is not a single branch unknown to you.

Charlie. —I think you are right. I cannot help myself. From my most tender youth, it seemed to me that there were no other real pleasures than those given by the goddess of love, especially when a man had enough empire over himself not to abuse them. By this I mean that each one should know his own strength, otherwise definitive debility steps in, or premature old age, and impotency worse than death. I soon lost all scruples regarding the ways and means to arrive at enjoyment, and I tried to inculcate my ideas to all the women who succumbed to me, gently and warily, having due respect for their feelings of coyness and shame. I could never understand that one style of enjoyment should be more to be blamed than another, therefore I lent myself freely to all the capricious imaginations of my sweethearts. For they had various caprices, and all women who are loving and voluptuous and practice love's games have them too. In the same way, I persuaded them to give way to my salacious will, however extravagant the realization of my dreams might be. Add to this that I had read everything, or nearly everything, that had ever been written in Latin, French, English or Italian on the art of voluptuous passion, and you are therefore correct in saying as you did, that there is very little, if there is anything at all, that I do not know in theory or in practice of this vast subject. The only thing that I have really never yet put into active experiment is sodomy, or any kind of debauchery with my fellow men. I have always felt unconquerable repulsion for the carnal approach of a male, and that feeling has not yet left me. I wish all those who have masculine tastes plenty of fun and pleasure and blame them not, because I believe that every desire is natural, that they become good and bad desires in merely a relative manner, and that each one should be free to amuse himself as he thinks best, as long as he does so without noise, scandal, or violence and harming no one. But for my own self, I do not understand the pleasures of man with man, while there is nothing which I am not ready to taste with any woman who pleases me.

Maud. —After what has passed between us, I can speak without circumlocution. You know that all women are full of curiosity? I am no exception to the rule. I should like —you will laugh at me perchance, but I care not —to be treated like an innocent girl desiring to learn all that you know so well of love and love's diversions, as if you were the professor of a maiden ignorant of everything, even of the difference of sex. My husband has taught me very little about all this, scarcely a few word, so that it has happened that when out of doors I sometimes cannot understand certain words whispered in worldly conversation. I hear the sounds, without knowing their meaning. This vexes me, I look foolish, and no one likes to appear silly. When I talk of this to my husband, either I make mistakes, or he pretends I do, or what is more probable still, he knows very little more than me. Anyhow, he puts me off and there I am with my questions and no satisfactory answers. You are my first, my only lover; it is your duty to enlighten me.

Charlie (laughing). —I will willingly believe you, because you tell me so, that I am at this present moment your only lover, but as for being the first... Never mind, I am not your father confessor, I never trouble about the past life of a woman who pleases me, especially when her reputation is a good one. But that is not the question. You desire me to treat you like a perfectly innocent pupil, wishing to become learned in the science of Venus? Good, I can refuse naught that is in my power and that can be agreeable to you. But remember that first of all I must use technical terms without screen or veil, or double meanings, and I fear for your delicate ears.

Maud. —I know, sir, that, in the pleasures of science, the beginning is not all roses, but as I wish to learn, so as to be as wise as my master, I must perforce submit to walk at first mid thorns and briars. Fear not to wound my ears, any more than you have hitherto feared to wound other parts of my body, which it suited occasionally to handle as you chose without thought of what I might suffer in consequence.

Charlie (laughing still). —As you are blessed with such sweet resignation, fair lady, I will try all I can to satisfy you.

Therefore I begin:

The Sexual Parts of Man

Man and woman, though meant for each other, are constructed in a totally different manner, especially as regards the genital organs, which particularly distinguish one sex from the other and which are placed at the bottom of the belly between the thighs. These are called the "genitals," because they serve to engender the human race. The etymology is a Latin one and for that reason I need not tell it you.

The parts of the male are composed of a canal covered with flesh and muscles, forming by their mass a member which is more or less long and thick, springing from a kind of bag of skin containing two reservoirs shaped like beans, also more or less voluminous. This canal is called the urethra, and the entire organ is known as yard, prick, cock, virile member and a thousand other suggestive titles, such as: thing, lance, dagger, spear, dart, perforator, pego, tool, John Thomas, piercer, etc. It grows out of the lower part of the belly, surmounting and between the man's thighs at a spot called the "pubis," which becomes covered with hair at the age of puberty. It terminates with the nut or glans, which is a kind of acorn split at the exterior extremity, covered with a move-able skin that folds back at will, and during copulation, so as to leave this head naked and render the tickling of the sexual parts of the woman more enjoyable when it is introduced therein. This skin is fixed to the lower part of the nut, by a kind of membrane called the "frenum" or fiber, which gets partly ruptured at the first venereal act of the man to permit the backward movements of this delicate covering, yclept prepuce, or "foreskin." This fiber, which it shelters when at rest, is very tender, and to rub it or stretch it by pulling the foreskin strongly backwards gives the man great pleasure. The seat of pleasure in the male is undoubtedly the sensitive top of his manly staff and by caressing and tickling it, you are sure at last to bring about the emission of his seed or spunk, by the orifice which is at the extremity of the glans. This seed is a whitish, viscous, salty liquid that, spirited by the virile member into the sexual parts of the woman, operates the miracle of generation and fecundates the female. By this aperture of the head of the glans the man also pisses.

The brown purse or bag is nothing more than a prolongation of the skin of the inner parts of the thighs, of that near the bum-hole and the cock, which also gets hairy at the age of puberty, and contains the reservoirs I just told you about. They are two glandular organs secreting the seed, spunk or sperm, made by the kidneys. This apparatus, the bag and its contents, in their entirety, are called the testicles, or the bollox, and there are other figurative names for it such as balls, etc., etc. Always on account of the two little round reservoirs. Beneath this bag is the continuation of the canal of the urethra, which extends from the neck of the bladder to the extremity of the penis. This configuration, resembling a raised stitch, and on which is a sort of seam, is called the "perineum." It divides the testicle bag into two parts and extends from the front edge of the arse-hole to the end of the prick. The whole length of the canal, or rather the flesh and muscles of which it is composed, swell up and stand out when the man has carnal desires, or when he feels the wish to discharge the superfluity of seed that he possesses. That is called "getting the horn," "getting stiff," having a "cockstand," or an "erection," etc.

The Sexual Parts of Woman

Woman's sexual parts are composed of a slit which is called the "vulva," from a Latin word signifying a doorway, of which the two outer lips appear to be the folding doors.

This opening begins at the bottom of the belly, where there is the "os pubis," or pubis bone, as in the male, and terminates at the perineum, near the hole in the bottom, or anus. This space comprises two large lips on the exterior of which, as well as on the pubis, is a growth of hair more or less abundant and of different shades, following generally the color of the woman's tresses at the age of puberty, as with men in the same part of their bodies. Lifting open these large outer lips, we find within two little tongues, called small lips or nymphae, on the summit of which, at the point where they meet, is a kind of little button or growth of flesh, resembling the top of the fiber of the head of a man's prick. It is called clitoris, button, etc., and is the seat of enjoyment for the woman, exactly as for the man the top of the prick and the fiber, which it resembles.

Beneath the clitoris, and close to the nymphae, is a round hole with elastic ridges which forms a passage into the woman's body. This is the entrance of the vagina or neck of the womb, which is the name given to the interior parts of woman, where she conceives and where the child is nourished during gestation or pregnancy, generally lasting nine months.

This opening is partly stopped up when the woman is a virgin by a membrane called the hymen, unless they have broken it by pushing in a finger or any other rounded object.

Above the hole, under the clitoris, is another little aperture forming the opening of the canal which serves to void her urine. It is called "meatus urinarius," or female urinary organ. Between the external orifice of the vagina and the meeting of the large lips below, near the arsehole, is a little sunken space called "fossa navicularis." The pair of small lips or nymphae form above a triangular space called the vestibule. At the base of this triangle of which the clitoris forms the opposite angle and beneath it, the "meatus urinarius" is to be found.

The point of junction of the big lips near the os pubis and the mount of Venus (name given to the little swelling formed by the flesh covering the os pubis) is called commissure of the vulva above. The junction of these same large lips beneath the "fossa navicularis" is called the fourchette or fork, or commissure of the vulva below.

The slit of the woman and all its organs together, as detailed above, is vulgarly called the "cunt." It has, like the man's member, a number of facetious and figurative appellations such as sheath, furrow, in opposition to the cock, known as the spear, dagger, ploughshare. The cunt is also known as the cunny, pussy, cockleshell, buttonhole, etc.

Sometimes the name of the mount of Venus is also given to the same part found between the man's prick and the bottom of his belly.

We call seed, spunk, sperm, or seminal fluid, the liquid that is secreted by both men and women, which springs out of their reservoirs by the rubbing of their sexual parts together, and this discharge procures for both indescribable enjoyment. Some learned men pretend that woman has no real seed but only a moisture without prolific value.

Besides these parts which form the female sex, women have usually on their breast two half globes which develop themselves about the age of puberty and become more or less large with age, filling with milk when the woman is a mother. These demi-globes vary in size and shape; they are sometimes close together, sometimes wide apart. Each of them is adorned in the middle by a pink button, whence issues milk which is given up to the eager sucking lips of the newborn babe. These buttons are called nipples and the globes are known as titties, teats, bubbles, dairies, bust, maternal hemispheres, breasts, bosom, or "charms." This last word applies to all the other beauties of the female form and some-times to those of the male. Man is generally fascinated by the view of the feminine breast. He can scarcely ever view the naked titties, or even a small part of them, and still less kiss them, without feeling at once the desire to be carnally joined to the woman thus exposed, and he has an erection more or less strong according to his constitution.

The carnal union takes place by the intromission of the manly prick in the feminine cunt. The action of the introduction and the move-ments made by both sexes, or by only one of them, to hasten the dis-charge or emission of the seminal liquor, inevitable result and the desired end of this action, when continued long enough, is called fuck-ing, poking connection, getting up or into a woman, Philiping, coition, copulation, having a go, etc.

The buttocks of a woman also excite the imagination of the man immensely. They are generally worshiped and caressed just before fuck-ing. These parts, very handsome when the female is well-built, with their rounded contours, their whiteness, and softness of the skin, are effectively often very attractive, and some men prefer them even to the cunt as an object of adoration.

For my part, I must tell you that I think woman is cunt all over and the contact of any part of her body pleases me, excites me and gives me desires, terminating by the act of enjoyment, which I willingly effect all over a woman, that is to say in or on any part of her person, so much do I love all and everything that is a part of this enchanting sex. On the other hand, my opinion is that a woman should have no repugnance in receiving all over her body the homage of the man to whom she consents to abandon herself. She should be unreserved with him, refuse him nothing and let him burn his incense on whichever of her altars that most excites his desire. He too, naturally, in grateful exchange of good will should renounce all individuality to the caprices of his mistress' imagination. This exchange should be complete and reciprocal.

Maud. —My dear friend, these are excellent principles and I frankly declare that they are mine. I think I have proved to you that indeed I do believe that there is no single part of my frame where you have not placed your lips, or caressed with your hands, and where you have not also, as you say, burnt incense to the god Cupid. All of my body, inside; and outside, where it is impossible for you to penetrate, has received the liquid and burning proofs of your lechery. You have not had my maidenhead in front, the bird had flown when you discovered the nest, but you have had the virginity of all the other parts of my body. As for me, I have felt you all over with my hands, caressed every bit of you with my lips and tongue and by the contact of my own entire self. My pussy has clung to you and rubbed against you in every direction, and so has my bosom and my bottom on every part of your person. You have readily lent yourself to all my whims and, I believe, I have satisfied all your lustful fancies.

Charlie. —Truly spoken, my angel. But I remarked that when talking of these things you seem to fear to use technical terms. That is a ridiculous weakness between us two, assured as we are of being perfectly alone and safe from all surprise or spies. As we have no secrets from each other, why not call things by their proper names, which makes them more intelligible than those worldly roundabout phrases of pardonable use, perhaps necessary out of respect for conventionality? In society, it is quite essential to be more chaste in words than in action, but such conduct is useless in a "tete-a-tete" of lovers such as we are, when confiding abandon and loving frankness should reign supreme.

Say then innocently that my prick has touched upon every part of your person in every possible way, as your cunt, your bubbles, and your arse. Your hands have touched every bit of my body, and we have both emitted reciprocally in every part of ourselves that excited our desires of our caprices. Chastity of words is meaningless at the point we have both reached. If such is good and fitting in society, it is out of place and without motive during our meetings. I warn you therefore that you will be punished, if wishing, as you declare, to completely master the science of Venus, you do not start at once to speak the true language of the voluptuous goddess. In a word, you must call by their legitimate names the instruments used in love's temple and the true titles of all the rest. I shall slap your bottom as hard as I can and condemn you to caress and name three times, to get you used to it, any object that you do not in future call simply by its true designation.

Maud (laughing). —That will not be a very severe punishment, for you kiss more violently than you beat my bottom which you so cruelly threaten, but which you love too much to ill-treat too greatly.

Nevertheless all you tell me seems right, but you must not be surprised that the habit of using very reserved language remains unwittingly, although it's become useless or even ridiculous between us. Therefore, please excuse me and I will truthfully say that your cock, your hand, and your rake's mouth have touched every part of my body a thousand times; that you have inundated my cunt, my mouth, my bubbles, my hands, my arse, my buttocks, my thighs, my armpits, my feet, my back, my loins with your burning spunk; that I have received it spurting in my eyes, my hair, and my ears; that I have even swallowed some of it in many a moment of delicious delirium. That you yourself have pumped and sucked my spermatic liquor with your mouth; that I have moistened your tongue, all your face, your hands and even your randy feet which have also frigged me. To sum up: that we have reciprocally covered each other with our mutual discharges.—And now are you happy? If you like, I will add that I take my solemn oath to the truth of this statement, and that I have experienced as much pleasure as you in all these wild bypaths of voluptuous passion, even to wishing often that you had a hundred pricks so that I might feel them simultaneously digging into me and ramming me all over, drowning me entirely with your seed both inside and out!

Charlie. —And I should like, my angel, to realize your desire, would it were possible for me to crush my whole being into your sweet body; in your velvet mouth; your pretty rose-pink cunt; your delicious chocolate bum-hole and to caress all your frame with my hands and my burning tongue, while at the same time I would squirt therein countless jets of thick, rich seed which you would return with usurious interest as is your divine habit.

Here occurs a pause in the dialogue. Our dramatis personae, worked up to fever heat, have suited the action to the word and have given themselves unreservedly up to the most delicious fucking. Our lovers exhaust themselves by repeated discharges in arse-hole, cunt, bubbies and mouth. They enjoy delicious feeling, and countless tickling bouts on every part of their bodies, finishing up by a game of Sixty-Nine (No. 3, and Section II, Dialogue IV, page one hundred twenty-nine), during which Charlie's staff disappears almost entirely in Maud's mouth, in whose throat he sends a last lightning discharge, eagerly swallowed to the very last drop in the excess of momentary lust, while Charlie sucks the divine essence of Maud till he well-nigh draws blood, as the lecherous lover presses almost all his face into her cunt, carrying therein his stiffly held and lengthy tongue. At last, these two real lovers, overwhelmed by their delightful spendings, calm down a little, and refresh and restore themselves with some port wine and sandwiches; and then, languidly stretched out in repose, without strength to entwine their bodies, slumber peacefully, waking but four hours later, at about five in the morning.

After a yawn and a good stretch, the couple exchange kisses, but do not yet feel inclined to start on their merry games again. Besides, they wish to husband their resources for the next night. Maud nestles her shapely head on Charlie's robust shoulder and begs him to continue his lecture. Willingly he consents, and Maud opens the debate, reminding her professor where he left off and telling him what impression he has made upon his pupil so far.

DIALOGUE II. On the Various Ways of Varying the Pleasures of Love between Man and Woman

Maud. —The different and vivid pictures that you so graphically described this morning have enlightened me on many subjects completely new to me, as I am quite a novice with regard to all voluptuous pleasures except those that a lover can enjoy with a mistress who reciprocates his tender feelings. Those joys are the only ones that appeal strongly to me, so I must ask you to describe them fully and without restraint as they interest me more than anything else. You must, my dear boy, tell me all you know and explain every possible way that exists under the sun for an ardent woman and a vigorous lover to enjoy each other fully, even if you have to recapitulate the different tricks that we have tried together. You understand, I want a complete lecture on this, to me, most important topic.

Charlie. —It will take me some little time, my pet. Up to the present, in all the books I have read, I have never heard spoken of more than twenty different ways. That is no niggardly figure, you must admit, but there are a lot more, although the conclusion is naturally always alike, while many resemble each other very much, at least to all appearances, but there are important differences when once put into action. Anyhow, I have promised to satisfy as fully as I can your curiosity and your wish for instruction. I shall therefore give you all details, sketching each method separately under a different and special name to help your memory and distinguish one from another. I confess that I speak from experience, as I have practiced nearly all these delightful dodges myself, either because they pleased me or in order to satisfy the tastes of the various ladies with whom I have had loving connection. Between you and me, some of these sweet charmers were uncommonly lewd and naughty, and the frenzy of their lascivious brain was far from displeasing. So I begin without further preamble.

I shall divide this important subject into three chapters. The first will treat of the different postures that two lovers, mutually helping each other, can put in action to procure complete reciprocal enjoyment. This chapter will be divided into two sections, of which the first is again subdivided into two paragraphs.

The second chapter will explain the various attitudes by which a man obtains the pleasurable discharge alone, by the caresses of a woman.

The third chapter will instruct you concerning everything relating to the diversity of means that allow a woman to obtain entire spending satisfaction by herself, but with the aid of the caresses of a man.

A general rule applies to these three important chapters, which is, that to fully appreciate the joys of fucking, the actors must be quiet and undisturbed, in a cosy, secret nook where there is no fear of surprise or prying eyes, and where they can find besides every possible commodity; a soft carpet; a good spring-bed, not too soft; divans, sofa, armchairs; ordinary chairs; footstools; cushions, and pillows. Plenty of water; two bidets; some perfumes; sponges, towels, and something nice and substantial to eat; wines, spirits and liqueurs.

Lastly, the principal thing to be done by the actors is to strip absolutely naked, both in a state of pure nature. Such is the only costume that is suitable for all true priests and priestesses of Venus.

CHAPTER I. Postures Giving Complete Enjoyment to Two Lovers

SECTION I. Postures with Introduction of the Member

I. Introduction of the Cock In the Cunt

1. The Ordinary

The woman lies on her back, on a bed or anywhere else. She opens her outstretched legs and thighs, and receives between them her lover who at first kneels near the knees of his mistress, then he leans over her, his legs and thighs united, upon her, supporting himself by one hand near the woman's shoulder. They are thus belly to belly, their faces close together. With the other hand the man gently opens the outer large lips of the cunt and directs between them his stiffly-standing prick, introducing it just far enough to prevent it slipping out. He then withdraws the guiding hand, lets the upper part of his body fall on his mistress' breast and, his lips glued to hers supporting himself on one elbow, so as not to crush her by the weight of his body, his hands should wander all over her frame caressing every charm he can reach to, his tongue all the time working in and out of her mouth, meeting her velvet rosy tip as well. The active fucker now pushes up and down as sturdily as he can until the complete spending discharge of both the players, together if possible, but if not, the woman first, and last of all the lord of the creation.

2. The Inseparables

This posture is almost the same as the preceding one, in theory, but when the woman is duly plugged she embraces the man by putting both arms round his neck (they were immobile and lying by her side in the foregoing) and crossing her legs and thighs over his loins, which was also omitted. This makes an immense difference in practice, especially for the degree of pleasure experienced, as the prick goes in much better in this second posture. The first one is generally used by cold couples and frigid fuckers, who do not like a woman to move during copulation, while the second is suitable for ardent combatants who, on the contrary, are only satisfied when the woman they are stroking answers every thrust with an upheaval of her arse and returns a hug for a squeeze, navel bumping against navel, until a mutual discharge ends the round.

3. The Ordinary with Legs Up

If the woman, instead of throwing her legs over the man's loins (as in the preceding attitude), will stick them straight up against his ribs, the feet pointing to the ceiling, forming thus by her legs and thighs two complete right angles with her body and that of her fucker placed one upon the other—as shown by a perpendicular line upon a horizontal one—the couple will demonstrate the "Ordinary, with Legs Up." The rest as before, terminating with a double libation to the goddess of love.

4. The Bucker

The woman lies across the bed, her bottom on the edge, with outstretched legs, one hanging outside and the other supported at the calf by one of the hands of the man, who stands upright between her thighs. With the other hand he directs his magic wand into the center of delight, and then caresses the bubbies, the belly, the "mons veneris," and the clitoris of his lady fair, and any other beauties he may manage to reach, vigorously pushing his prick all the time in the little oven, until the loaves are baked and he has spent freely, while his partner shows her gratitude by spending with him.

5. The Saint-George

The man lies on his back on the bed and the woman straddles across him, on her knees. She covers with her cunt the uncapped prick of the male in erection, and gradually lowers herself upon it till their hairs mingle. Then she moves up and down, as if she were Saint-George himself on horseback galloping away to fight the dragon. The man seconds her in the furious dance by jerking his loins backwards and forwards, not forgetting to stroke with rakish hands every bit of her body. He feels her thighs, hips, her buttocks, and the lower part of the belly. He pats and caresses and their combined movements cause them to let fly a mutual gush of lovers' balsam.

6. The Ordinary Reversed

The couple first place themselves as for "The Saint-George," and when the woman is fixed on the cock, she bends forward and stretches her legs out on those of the man, knee to knee. Her breasts press on the manly chest beneath her, and she encircles his neck or shoulders with her arms, according to her size. His arms in return are crossed over her back and he caresses as he chooses her loins and her buttocks. His fingers play about the crack of her arse and the little hole itself, which he should gently excite with a moistened digit. The result is inevitable, and the lovers die in each other's arms, in the midst of a burning double inundation of fiery sperm. This is truly called the "Ordinary Reversed," as it is nothing more than the first position in contrary order: the woman above and the man below.

7. The Back-View

The man is on his back, the woman turns her back and rides over him, on her knees, near his. She settles down on his tool and mutually they dance up and down. Taking advantage of her position the woman plays with the man's balls, and he having both hands free can feel her back, loins and buttocks, of which latter charms he has a superb view, as the title of this pretty posture denotes. The lovers thus pleasantly occupied, and pushing properly, soon each of them furnishes an ample discharge, the proof of the pleasure they both experience.

8. The View of the Low-Countries

This resembles "The Back-View" (No. 7). Here the woman is riding the man in the same way, but instead of remaining straight up on her knees, she leans forward her face towards the man's feet, her bosom touching his knees and he therefore can see the entire ass stretched open, the hole of mystery, and the distended cunt, with his own prick moving in and out. He is quite at his ease to feel all these charms and tickle all round the genital laboratory, sharpening the work by prodding a finger in the anus that seems to him to be the eye of a Cyclops staring him out of countenance. To reward him for his caresses the lady tickles his bare feet with her velvet tongue. Now you know what is meant by "The View of the Low-Countries," and this enchanting prospect, combined with the couple's cunning caresses, leads the fuckers on to furious movements, of which a copious and mutual discharge promptly becomes a natural consequence.

9. A Woman's Resignation

The woman lies on her back, her arms crossed below the breasts, the loins on the edge of the bed, the legs and the bottom free. The man stands up between the woman's legs, tucking one under each arm. He opens the cunt-lips, plants his prick therein and pushes forward without the woman making the least movement. When he is well on the citadel, his hands and forearms are at liberty to excite by all kinds of sly touches the arse and the rest of the beautiful, indolent, resigned charmer. She cannot resist this play very long and soon her discharge mingles with that which her lover bedews her secret charms, rendered full of lewd feelings by this sweet unction.

10. The Elastic Cunt

The woman sits on the edge of the bed, leaning backwards a little, resting on her hands. The man stands between her thighs, lifts her legs off the ground, takes one of her feet in each hand and holds them straight so that her heels touch her own buttocks. In this position he puts his prick in her cunt and while he shoves backwards and forwards, he lifts up, kisses, holds apart and brings together alternately the feet he holds, one after the other, or with a contrary movement, or both together. This creates delicious movement inside the cunt, rendering also the friction of the tool much more delightful, making up for the deprivation of all the other habitual caresses from which the lovers are momentarily debarred, their hands being occupied and their faces far from each other. But the exciting titillations are doubly exquisite inside the temple of love, on the altar where the sacrifice is made and the libation soon flows from the spermatic canals of the two worshipers.

11. Impalement Backwards

This is the foregoing posture reversed. It resembles a "Back View," (No. 7), without being exactly the same. In No. 7, the woman is on her knees. Here she is on her feet, crouching over the man's prick, her back towards him, so that the cunt is forced out in a much more satisfactory manner. Her legs and thighs are forced up left and right of her belly instead of dropping down as when she was on her knees on the bed. The lovers gain at least an inch of prick. The man need not fear that his fuckstress will fall backwards, and if she did, she would fall upon him and not hurt herself. He supports her with one hand and the other serves to press and feel all her charms within his reach, in front or behind. She can enjoy the backward and forward movement of the prick and can frig herself and even play with the root of the cock, and the balls of her lover. This posture is a delicious example and procures extraordinary delights for the actors by the reciprocal discharges it cannot fail to bring about.

12. Impalement in Front

This posture is very much like "The Trot." Here the man, instead of being seated, is lying down and the woman rides across him crouching down, her feet on the bed, her face turned towards that of the man. Instead of holding on to his shoulders, she clasps one of his hands. Thus they have each one hand free, and they can indulge in mutual caresses. She, turning a little to one side, can seize the root of the man's prick and his balls by passing her hand underneath her thighs. He can enjoy all the charms of the front of her body: her breasts, thighs, belly, and her mossy cleft, without hindering their natural fucking movements. On the contrary, they quickly lose their strength and their essence at this sweet game, in the midst of the most intense and delightful sensations.

13. The Herculean Feat

The man stands up, his cock ready, so stiff that it looks if it was trying to fuck the navel above it. The woman, undismayed, is in front of her lover, impatient with desire. She throws her arms around his neck, bends down and then springs up, legs and thighs wide open, throwing them around his body near the hips, joining them behind his loins, her heels on his arse with one hand, guiding his tool with the other and plunging it within her, till their hairs are mingled together. He then presses her towards him by the cheeks of her arse, and supports her loins to keep her fixed to his clutch. Thus upstanding, he swivels her manfully and she returns each shove of his arse till the abundant double libation is poured out, proving the battle to be a drawn one. It can be well understood why this posture is called "The Herculean Feat," as there are few men sufficiently adroit and athletic to put it in action with a stoutly built female.

14. The Crossed Scissors

The woman lies on her side, half across the bed, her elbows leaning thereon on the same side, crossing her forearms on the pillows. The man, standing near her feet, takes her right leg in his left hand, lifting it off the bed and passing between the bed and this same right thigh of hers, which comes thus against his belly. His right hand is directed beneath her loins, between her and the bed, lifting her a little and causing her right thigh to fall outside the bed, and it is drawn away from the other which he supports. The right leg naturally passes between his calves. Then, with the left hand, which just now supported her left thigh, he directs the arrow to the target, and by force of the position he fucks her sideways in dog-fashion. Once therein he treats her like a hungry lover. The lady turns a laughing, provoking visage towards him. She is hugely excited by this position which leaves her well-nigh powerless to assist him, but nevertheless the merit of the conclusion is proved to them by a copious emission. The title of this posture comes from the crossing of the lovers' legs, resembling two pairs of scissors, the blades opened and crossed.

15. The Sharpshooter

When executed this posture is akin to the preceding one if reversed a little on the man from left to right.

The man lies outstretched upon the bed, the right knee uplifted. The woman mounts over him crossways. She puts her right knee on the bed, passing her folded leg underneath his lifted knee, her foot towards the other edge of the bed. By this maneuver her cunt is just above the prick half dog-fashion. He passes his left hand under her thighs, guides his member into the proper place, lifts up her loins to force his way, and pushes up and down, feeling her beautiful arse with the right, tickling the arse-hole a little, while his left can be busy with her bubbles and the disengaged parts of her cunt. She supports herself with the right hand behind the uplifted knee of her lover, stroking his face with her left. All soon terminates as usual with a double volley. It is the position of the knee of the woman on the bed that causes the appellation: "The Sharpshooter," recalling the command: "Front row, Kneeling!" Recommended to military men.

16. Lazy Style

The woman lies up on the bed, her arms crossed over her head on the top of the pillow, her arse and loins are turned away from the side where her lover reclines, crossways, but his face towards his mistress. He gets between her thighs, lifting one up and passing it over his hip. He brings his prick to the mark, by passing his body above the thigh of the woman, so lazy that she does not move. He then places one arm on her shoulders and with the other strokes her bosom, neck and face, and gives her a fair rousting, which obliges her to finish by discharging, as she feels her lover inundate her with burning essence of manhood, an excellent medicine to cure laziness in the female.

17. Lazy Style Reversed or in Dog-Fashion

This is the exact opposite of the foregoing, i.e. it is now done dog-fashion.

The woman lies half across the bed, turning her back, head and shoulders on the pillow which is placed rather high up. The man appears at her feet, drops on the ground her leg which is nearest to the edge of the bed, seizing the other at the knee and, passing behind, places it on his hip, the point of the foot resting on a convenient stool. He passes one arm under her shoulders, and she has her arms nonchalantly thrown to the right and to the left. Passing his other hand in front, he guides the peacemaker under shelter, introducing it from back to front, and afterwards this same hand caresses her bubbles or the environs of the grotto and the clitoris. He kisses her mouth, her half-shut eyes, and all her face. She lets him work his sweet will without making the least movement, but in spite of this immobility all ends by her discharge, showing her pleasure by the thrill of her arse and the nipping of her cunt sucking up the spunk which bursts from her fucker's ruby nozzle.

18. Double Lazy Style

The woman lies on her side, passing her arms round the neck of the man who lies on his side too, facing her. He passes his legs and thighs between those of his companion, clasping her round the body under the arms, after having, of course, introduced his stiff visitor into the nook of joy, which opens all alone by the way the male has installed himself between her ivory columns. The actors go to work mutually but without undue bustle or hurry, joining their mouths greedily, but soon are warmed up by the soft reciprocal heat of the magnetic attraction that draws the sexes together. After having tasted a few moments the happiness of feeling their frames thus joined together without any painful effort, their movements quicken in spite of themselves and the torrent that rushes from both sources obliges them to embrace with a fury which is quite a contrast of the indolent commencement of the struggle.

19. Double Lazy Style Reversed

This is the same system as in the preceding directions, but the woman, lying on her side, turns her back to her lover who, also on his side and with his belly to her arse, lifts up her thigh —the one that does not rest on the bed—and places himself between the sturdy pillars thus separated, advancing his legs and knees forward beyond the woman's body in front of her. Her uplifted thigh now rests upon her lover's hip; her bottom is in front of his prick, which he directs dog-fashion from behind into her cunt, plunging it to the hilt and now fucks grandly in this commodious and far from tiring position. His hands are at liberty to press and pat all the surrounding beauties, especially the redundant cheeks of her arse which rub against his pubis and which he can caress and slap at will. His partner soon feels the effect produced and experiences herself the discharging delights, when the neck of her womb palpitates and is sprinkled by her lover's elixir.

20. The Game of Touch

The man sits on the bed or on the ground, his back and loins supported by pillows or cushions, his legs apart, and his dagger, like a Freemason's, threatening the sky. The woman squats between his thighs, straddling her white pillars over the brawny limbs of the man. She crams his tidbit into her orifice, leaning against him. The two lovers entwine their arms and advance their lips to fence with their tongues; the woman leaning her arms on her champion's shoulders. With the aid of her frisky backside, she makes the backward and forward movements in the style of those made by children as a preliminary to their games of "hide and seek," or "touch," when it is necessary to find out who is to go and hide or to run and try and place a hand on one of the other players. The man is not ungrateful and returns blow for blow, so that this simultaneous action soon starts the couple's pumps, to put out the fire that devours them, making it impossible for them to decide who "touched last."

21. Dog-Fashion Sideways

The woman lies full-length on her side, on the edge of the bed, horizontally, her bottom outside, the legs and thighs folded half perpendicularly to the couch, so as to give full prominence to the arse. The man stands upright behind the tempting buttocks, lifting the uppermost thigh, by seizing her foot by the heel and dragging it backwards. The other hand is passed in front to direct his prick from behind into the cunt, and when placed therein, he is at liberty to pinch and stroke all the rosy flesh within his reach. He frigs the reclining beauty and she holds his head with one hand, her other arm being on the pillow. He feels her belly, her bubbies, her backside, her loins, etc., at the same time driving home his piston. Its vigorous in and out action produces the usual effect, bringing into play the double fountains of burning spunk, with their attendant ecstasies.

22. Dog-Fashion Kneeling

The woman is "all fours," upon her knees and elbows, on the bed or on the floor. The man kneels behind, adjusting his prick between the lips of his charmer's cunt, which he opens. He can see the rosy retreat well, because her head is lower than her arse. When installed, he can, by putting a hand in front, frig the button of the cunt while he fucks, and tickle her hairy mount, while with the other hand, by leaning forward a little over her back, he is able to take hold of her globes, and tickle the strawberry nipples, kissing and licking her shoulders and spine. The woman, not to be behindhand, can support herself on one elbow only, and pass the free hand between her thighs to gently daddle the balls belonging to the prick within her. She must lean forward also just a little more, as the more the woman is bent double, the more the entrance of her cunt is facilitated, enabling the lovers to gain one or two inches more of length of prick, especially if her fair forehead entirely touches the floor or mattress. By this position it must not be forgotten that not one drop of the divine elixir of their reciprocal gush is lost; all remains in the thirsty cunt, to their great and mutual delight.

23. Dog-Fashion Straight

Now the man kneels and the woman approaches him backwards, presenting her backside to his face. She opens her legs and thighs, passing her hand between them to seize his swollen prick, which she directs herself, introducing it into her cunt from back to front. Then the man clutches her hips and helps to claw her on to his cock. She pushes quickly forward and backward, up and down, and leaning in front, passes her hand between her thighs to play with the stones and the lower end of the reeking dagger. Soon both overflow voluptuously. This posture is so called, because the woman is nearly, upright.

24. The Spikey Chair

The man sits on a chair, almost on the edge. The woman turns her back to him and comes and sits down on his lap, but she bends forward a little at first, to allow her workman to adjust his tool in her cunt, from behind her arse to the front. When it is quite sucked in, the woman lets herself fall back seated on his thighs, turning her face towards him so as to suck his lips and tongue. You now see why this posture is dubbed: "The Spikey Chair." The man's hands at liberty serve to feel all the lady's charms. He can press her breasts, tickle her nipples, caress her whole body and exciting her and himself by these lewd touches, added to the joint action of their loins, they are soon forced to open their sluices together with voluptuous abundance.

Here the dialogue, which has been more or less a monologue, was interrupted by the entrance of the punctual charwoman, heralded by a timid honeymoon knock at the door. It was six o'clock and she brought the dinner, and laid the cloth. During the repast, the conversation became uninteresting on account of the presence of the faithful "slavery," whom it was unnecessary to scandalize, although she knew perfectly well the extent of the understanding that reigned between Charlie and Maud. When appetite was satisfied, the old woman cleared everything away, but did not forget to leave on the table another clean service, some cold viands, wine, spirits and mineral waters, for fear the lovers should feel inclined to pick a little before retiring for the night, and she disappeared with strict orders not to trouble unless she heard the bell. The door bolted, Maud reclined upon the sofa and, summoning her lover, begged him, to continue the subject he had let drop when dinner was served. Charlie, as usual, wanted but very little asking and started again to finish the lecture that so excited his mistress.

DIALOGUE IV. Introduction of the Cock Into the Cunt (continuation)

25. The Donkey Ride

This is a very amusing manner, but it is not everybody who can carry it out successfully. You must first get a donkey, not too obstinate, and the lovers must have some idea of how to ride these capricious beasts without being frightened, and the woman must mount like a man. In these bicycling days there should be no difficulty about so small a matter. The woman cocks her leg over the donkey's back, where there is no saddle, only a rug, and a pair of shortened stirrups. If the spot chosen for this randy ride is not secluded enough for the cavalier and his lady to be completely naked, the female must lift up her petticoats back and front, lean forward encircling the donkey's neck with both her arms, throwing up her arse by rising in the stirrups. The man mounts behind her, leans back, holding on the donkey's tail with one hand, while with the other he slips his cock into the loving cunt, dog-fashion, which by the position she is now in, is easy enough. When all is ready, the woman, impaled, drops down between her fucker's thighs, and her lover catches hold of the animal's tail with both his hands behind him. Now they dig their knees into the donkey's sides, which starts him off and at the same time holds them fast in the postures they have chosen. The donkey trots and shakes their backsides well right and left. That movement increases their pleasure and, when they are about to spend, the lover pulls the ass's tail, which finally causes him to kick out behind, or jib, however patient by nature he may be, forcing the man's prick to penetrate still further, to the great and certain voluptuous satisfaction of both parties. But they must not lose their head when they lose their cream, as it sometimes happens, for then the jibbing beast gets rid of his double burden and the lovers find themselves on the ground with all their spendings knocked out of them.

26. The Gunner and the Cannon

The woman lies on her back and loins; arse, thighs and legs outside the bed and across it. The man stands in front of her, taking one of her feet in each hand just above the ankle and holds them up as high as possible, a trifle forward, but straight up and slightly open. He can thus take a proper view of the breech and point his rammer to clean the cannon.

He pushes his prick forward and by his position it should slip in by itself. Once within, he shoves on with might and main, at the same time thrusting up and down one or the other of the legs he holds, or both together, which causes all sorts of varied motions to be felt inside the cunt, not forgetting nippings and rubbings which voluptuously excite the thrice happy prick, making it stiffer than ever, and communicating to the two working partners indescribable pleasure, which finishes — alas! but too soon —by a double reciprocal ejaculation.

27. How to Get a Girl

The man tucks under his right arm the left thigh of the female. Then with his left hand he lifts the woman's right leg straight up, so that her right side is higher than the left. The rest as in the preceding position, where I have explained the idea of the learned authorities.

It results from these two postures, and from the reasons given, that we might attain the same result in many different ways of fucking ("The Ordinary," "The Inseparables," or any other where the woman lies on her back: her arse uplifted by cushions or a pillow), as long as we do not forget that, where the birth of a boy is desired, the woman should have her left side higher than the right and "vice versa," if she yearns to bring yet another cunt into the world, to delight the butterfly Philiper who flits from flower to flower, tasting the honey of each. There can never be too many cunts on this earth!

28. The Living Mattress

The man lies on his back stretched out at full length on the bed, his prick stiff standing like Nelson's monument. The woman mounts upon him and takes her place as in the "Encampment Backwards," (No. 20). When she has herself lodged the column in its nook, she stretches out her thighs on those of her companion and leans backwards, reclining with her shoulders upon his chest, and she turns her face towards him a little to give and receive lascivious kisses. Thus she rests as upon a mattress, and the man, his tongue between her lips, presses her titties, her belly, the bushy mount and the clitoris, passing his hands from behind over her sweet body. They move gently and cautiously, as with heavy strokes the prick might slip from its prison, as in this posture it does not advance very far into the cunt, where the woman can, however, keep it in its place with her hand. To perform properly thus a long prick is needful.

29. The Toad

The woman lies on her back at full length on the bed, a large pillow or even two under her arse to force the cunt well up in front; her head and shoulders are also supported by cushions. (In Scotland, I believe, the heavy family bible is often made use of in this posture —a favorite one across the border).

The man gets over her in ordinary fashion. When he is in, the woman lifts up her legs and thighs as high as she can, keeping them well open, so that her heels touch her buttocks above the line of her thighs. Her knees press against her lover, near his armpits. They are pressed together in each other's arms, and the man profits by the position of the woman, who in this way presents her cunt as open as possible, to shove in his tool till their bushes mingle. With many a groan and sigh of lust, with repeated strokes of loins and arse they enjoy transports of erotic joy which do not last forever and shortly a double emission brings down the essence of love.

Charlie (stopping). —I think now that I have finished my task for the day. The longest and most difficult is done, but it is now ten o'clock; I am a little tired through talking so long, so let us to bed, so that I may rest in your arms. I suppose that you are not visiting me with the sole idea of listening to my talk. Your letter promised me a day and two nights of love and passion. You must keep your word. My lecture on the diverse moves of sacrificing to Venus must not cause my darling to perjure herself.

Maud. —Wicked man! I expect you want to try and realize a few living pictures with me, copied from some of the lewd canvases you have unrolled just now. I consent, but promise me that, after a few hours of pleasure, you will continue your enchanting dissertations, which interest me so much that I don't intend to sleep a wink until after you have thoroughly exhausted the subject, even though I sat up listening to you the whole night long.

Charlie. —You know well that your will is law for me. But first to bed!

The lovers retire between the sheets and they try a few experiments, realizing a respectable number of the foregoing postures, and then Charlie, faithful to his word, continues his sermon on the mount... (of Venus), as if he had not sustained the delightful interruption.

DIALOGUE V.
II. Sodomy With Women

Charlie. —I have finished the description of the various methods used to fuck a woman in the natural orifice, and I now come to a few other ways.

An old song says:

"The distance between a girl's cunt and arse-hole,

Is but a foul crab's jump without vaulting pole."

Thus being mathematically incontestable, we must conclude therefore that all the postures I have already described can serve nearly all just as well for sodomizing a woman as for Philiping her.

But although a woman is cunt all over for a true fucker, the act of sodomy or buggering even with the feminine sex, should only be a momentary caprice for him and not a leading habitual vice. The sodomite in general is right up to a certain point when he maintains that all tastes exist in nature and the best of all is our particular one, whichever it may be. But it is none the less logical to say that, if all men had this exclusive propensity for spending in the woman's arse, the world would come to an end. This motive alone shows the dangerous trap into which we should fall if we allowed such principles to be indefinitely applied. They are true at bottom, if you will, as this limitless extension would soon bring about a radical solution of the problem of depopulation. But happily there are a very small number of exclusive sodomites, in proportion to the considerably stronger army of old-fashioned cunt-fuckers, so that there is very little harm done and we need not trouble about the question. Let everyone do as he or she likes, as long as strict secrecy is kept, without scandal, or moral and physical violence. I frankly confess that it has always seemed pitiful to me to draw arguments from religious law against pederastic pleasure. I go further and declare that religion has nothing to do with fucking in any shape or form whatsoever, if quietly carried out as I said just now. I am at liberty to speak freely as I am a perfectly disinterested party, this peculiar taste never having been mine. I have perforated a few blushing backsides, I confess, out of pure, or rather impure, wayward fancy, and curiosity, with women only. Some of the sweet innocents have even begged me to distend their wrinkled sepia factory, either because they wanted to try the experiment, or as they told me, for fear of getting that swelling behind the navel that rarely goes down under nine months. But I have always preferred the true road to paradise and I think it is rank blasphemy to mix up our babies and rayers in all these fucking follies. When will common anserous herd, as credulous as they are silly and addle-headed, clear their muddy brains and cease to listen as if they were oracles, to certain individuals of different religious denominations, who are not such fools as they look and who mix up, or more truly "feign" to mix up, so-called sacred decrees with sociable-laws and sentiments of true morality, the only ones that nature inspires man with at his birth, with the repugnancies that the prejudices of conventional education alone bestow on simple and timid minds! These gentry who preach from acting as they talk and, when together with their colleagues, they do not fail to unmask and agree that everything is generally permissible when no one is hurt. They do not stop even there when it comes to the application, as they admit without restriction that nothing is forbidden if it is hidden. But enough of such serious argument, I am getting too serious and my theme is a gay one. Let me return to my bottoms.

Nearly all the postures for cunt-fucking can be used for buggering a woman, by reason of the neighborhood of the two apertures. To my knowledege there exists no way of bottom-piercing that cannot also be used for copulation in front and, as I believe I have described every possible way of plugging a cunt, it would be going over the same ground again to explain them all once more as applied to sodomy with your enchanting sex. Let it suffice for me to tell you that in all the postures described as for the cunt, it is only necessary to place the man's cock a few inches higher or lower according to the position of the woman for her to be fucked in the arse, as the two holes are so near to each other that the realization of the attitudes is just as easy and the change of lodging is indifferent for the action in itself.

It must also not be forgotten that in all cases and in all ways of sodomizing the female, it is the man's duty to take up his position in such a manner that one of his hands can frig her cunt, although his prick neglects it, tickling the clitoris, the nipples, etc. The entrance, too, should never be effected with brutality or violence and, until the little known hole is sufficiently dilated to admit the prick easily, a little grease should always be applied and the masculine acorn will be all the more comfortable if anointed also before the Socratic act. A very pretty preparation before inserting the battering ram in the back precincts is a simple kiss or warm caress of a moist tongue, when the saliva takes the place of cold-cream. Indeed, this voluptuous kiss is generally well received by both sexes, even when no pederastic violence is intended.

To sum up, men should never be selfish or ungrateful; we ought to try to give as much pleasure as we can while we are receiving voluptuous joy from the woman, and the feeling that we are doing our duty to our companion will double our lubricity.

CONCLUSION. Love and Security; or, How to Fuck Without Danger of Fecundation

Maud.—My darling, I have yet one more thing to ask you and that is some information and explanation concerning so called secret methods by which a woman can give herself up to the pleasure of the caresses and embraces of the man she loves without danger of getting in the family way.

Charlie.—Frankly, the best and surest way would be to prove mutual love by caresses, without introduction of the prick in the cunt, for if it goes in ever such a little way, or even if the discharge takes place only just within the outer lips, with some women the greedy orifice has such avidity for spunk, that it can suck up enough to effect the dreaded result of conception. A man, if he really loves the woman he fucks and does not wish to risk getting a child, must feel very sure of the moral control he exercises over himself to get into her with the firm intention to withdraw in time to discharge completely outside. He must be away before the fountain starts playing and not return until the prick is carefully washed and pressed, so that not a drop of seed remains at the end, nor in the canal, which is needless to say the man cleans at once by the simple act of pissing. The least drop falling into the vagina suffices to cause pregnancy. The same remark applies to the second introduction, where after having once gone away, discharging outside, the prick goes back without having been cleansed and wiped, with something remaining of the preceding discharge either at the orifice of the glans or in the canal that can penetrate into the sexual organs of the woman by the friction of a fresh venereal act, even before causing a fresh spurt of semen. Therefore we must be out "too soon" so as not to leave "too late." To finish, the man can use his hands, or his lady's, or migrate to any other part of her frame as may suit, as I have pointed out in all my descriptions of postures without real intromission. Better be outside "too soon" than to run the risk of dropping the little liquid parcel in the dangerous greedy hole and causing an illness of nine months' duration. To conclude my remarks, I can only say that too much prudence can never do any harm, especially as the doctors with all their learning have not yet been able to tell precisely how the female is fecundated. So I shall be excused if I make mistakes in the delicate subject I am now treating, as what I know is from experience only, having no real scientific knowledge to boast of.

1. No Bottom-Fucking Allowed

One of the secrets of not getting the woman with child is, to begin with, not to put the prick in the cunt, and I note a vulgar error which bars even the arse-hole as being too near the genuine aperture! It has also been said that after a first discharge one may fuck as one will, second and later copulation being unable to cause pregnancy. I need hardly stop to point out the insanity of this belief.

2. Snuffing the Candle

Another way which is as good as any with a man who can be reasonable, even while fucking, is to go ahead and enjoy oneself and content our companion in every way possible, as long as we dislodge our tool before the discharge begins, and slip it up to her navel, or jerk it on one side so that the woman can finish us off with her hand far from the cunt and receive in her soft palm the spunk of which she fears the prolific power.

This is called "Snuffing the Candle."

3. No Mutual Spending Permitted

Another vulgar error consists simply in not "coming" together, that is to say that the woman takes care not to open her sluice-gates until either before or after the man's dew has moistened her rose. The persons who consider this method as infallible declare that conception only takes place when the lovers spend together, their seed mixing at the moment of the mutual ejaculation, and that the least interval between the two jets deprives the mixture of all its virtue and stops fecundation. I do not believe in this system, although admitting that the pleasure in fucking is doubtless greater when the lovers spend together and that the genital organs in such a case are better disposed to receive the germ. But it does not follow that there will be no conception without simultaneous discharge, as proved by the fact of many wives of icy temperament bearing large families without ever having really "spent," "come," or "enjoyed" in the whole course of their conjugal career. Women violated while under the influence of narcotics, or victims of rape without the slightest feeling of pleasure have also been known to bear children.

4. The French Letter

A well-known check is the use of the French letter, a name given to a kind of elongated bag or case made of a very thin skin or fine india-rubber. This is slipped over the prick and being made for the purpose, has the proper shape and length to fit the member, just as the umbrella case fits an umbrella, with the exception that naturally the French letter is only open at the end where the cock goes in. They are blown out before using to see that they are sound and being wetted stick tightly round the shaft and head of the virile organ.

With ease the man starts fucking as soon as his cock is thus covered. His seed, instead of spurting into the woman's vagina, is forced to remain inside the sheath, which is so thin that neither the man nor the woman can scarcely perceive its presence during the action, which can be consequently carried to a natural end with the same voluptuous pleasure as if there was nothing at all to separate the sexual parts of lover and mistress.

This protecting skin is also worn to prevent contagion and to guard against venereal disease when fucking doubtful women, but being so thin there is always a doubt that it may burst in the thick of the battle, or the friction of cunt and cock may cause a leak, and then the subtle liquid escaping renders its aid a delusion and a snare. Such accidents may happen, but rarely, especially if a good article is bought of a respectable chemist. I have used them often with ladies who feared pregnancy and never found one split. But their use, becomes fastidious and troublesome by the care and bother necessary before going into action, and afterwards as they should be renewed at each fresh fuck.

We have seen some lately which are only little round bags fitting over the nut of the prick, fastening under the ridge of the acorn, and I must not forget to tell you that the late Doctor Ricord, the great French venereal specialist, declared that the French letter was "a cobweb against contagion and a shield against pleasure."

5. *The Sponge*

Another precaution against pregnancy that I know of is founded on a scientific truth, which is that to produce conception the seed should be pure and without the least foreign admixture. A drop of any fluid, a little atmospheric air or anything else you can think of, added to the seed immediately deprives it of all prolific virtue. If we combine the formula with this other necessity for generation—that the man's seminal fluid must penetrate into the woman's womb to fecundate her—we may make her use a little round fine sponge, about the size of a small nut, fastened to a thin silken string about ten or twelve inches long. This sponge, if moistened with weak vinegar and water, or any other acid may be used, if sufficiently diluted, and it is then plunged into the cunt, leaving the end of the riband outside, so as to be able to withdraw after coition, in order to rinse it, moisten it again and replace it for a fresh fuck.

It can be easily understood that, by means of the presence of this moistened sponge in the vagina, not only does the man's discharge find an obstacle to prevent it reaching the womb, but even if some drops do manage to get past the sponge, they are mixed with the acidulated water with which the latter is wetted and this admixture is calculated to rob the liquor of its wonderful procreating power.

Instead of the sponge a small india-rubber pessary can also be used. They are sold at all chemists and bandage shops, and sometimes soluble pessaries can be purchased for the same use.

6. *The Injection*

The last and most convenient check to stop large and small families is that the woman should jump up immediately the man has spent freely within and pump a sufficient quantity of weak vinegar and water into her cunt. I think that this means is certainly as good as any others, but how can the woman tell if the boiling virile essence has not already reached her womb? She may inject as long as she likes and clean out her vagina and the neck of the womb with oceans of liquid from her enema, but if the tiniest drop of dangerous seed is already within, there is no hope for her.

But all said and done this is a very uncertain and risky matter, as once the seed is sown it is well-nigh impossible to prevent the child being born, unless criminal practices are resorted to, to the imminent danger of the mother's life.

How many poor girls suffer, if they are a few days behind with their monthly derangement and what relief when the crimson flow appears!

And even that means nothing sometimes, as pregnant women often have regular or irregular courses.

I have now told you the little I know to prevent conception. Now let lovers choose and invent fresh means if possible, if they have no confidence in the saying that in love and war many blows are given in vain and the biggest cowards are the soonest captured. Having put on one side, as I told you, all religious scruples when treating of these matters, I have great indulgence for the weaknesses of women who wish for pleasure without running the risk of getting with child. But this indulgence I no longer grant when I have a proposition to destroy the result of their voluptuousness, as in that case a sin is committed against society at large. The act which was the original cause can no longer be excused and becomes nothing more than the first step in the path of crime. When checks are employed to prevent conception, no harm is done; we are no more guilty than when we fornicate each other, but if you seek to destroy the generative result you murder a being who belongs to the community of which you yourself are a member, and you trample under foot all human and social laws.

So I shall tell nothing concerning the methods in vogue to procure abortion, which means, as you know, the destruction of a child already conceived and breathing.

Maud.—And you are right, this last topic is so horrible to my mind that it does not inspire me with the least curiosity. I cannot thank you enough for all your teaching, being now fully satisfied on all the obscure points that I wished cleared up, and I am ready to prove my gratitude in any way you like for the trouble you have taken and the patience and amiability you have shown.

Here the dialogue ceases. The lovers give themselves up to lewd and libidinous voluptuous enjoyment more enjoyable than any talk, and sleep overcomes them in each other's arms, until the moment arrives for separation and Maud starts off to the country to effect her alibi.

FINIS

Adventures and Amours
of a Barmaid

Molly Pennington was the daughter of an innkeeper in a small market town. From the earliest infancy she was not less remarkable for the vivacity of her temper than the beauty of her person. Her father contemplated with the greatest delight the growing charms of his youthful daughter, which, with a proper education, he thought would be a most captivating ornament for the decoration of his bar when she arrived at maturity.

Accordingly, at the age of twelve, Miss Molly was sent to a boarding school a short distance from her native home for the purpose of learning a few fashionable embellishments. After staying at this seminary a competent time, the lovely girl was returned to the longing eyes of her fond father, replete with every accomplishment that is in the power of those elegant receptacles of female education to bestow.

For a few months after Molly's arrival at her home, her father gratified every wish of her heart. He soon began to perceive, however, with inexpressible regret, the taste his fair daughter had acquired for expensive dress, and every other extravagance which young ladies who have had the benefit of a boarding school education generally learn. He then lamented with the greatest concern the sums which he had lavished in the vain hope of making his beloved child a perfect mistress of the business of keeping an inn. Molly now had an utter contempt for everything that was low and vulgar. Even the admiration of the country squires could not but be disgusting to her.

During the time of our heroine's being barmaid, a company of strolling players arrived in the town in order to exhibit their talents for the amusement of the country folks. Miss Molly was greatly pleased at this, for she had been once or twice indulged with a play while at school, and had a taste for theatrical performances. The King's Head being the principal inn in the town, it cannot be supposed but the merry performers made it a house of constant resort; nor is it surprising that in their frequent visits the greatest notice should be taken of the captivating Molly. Indeed, the manager, who was a very polite man, soon made himself intimate with her, and all the hours that he appropriated to the drowning of care were spent in the company of our heroine. There was little they left undone. She learned to take his raging tool in her mouth once she overcame her initial reluctance. Swallowing the passion cream of her lover soon became her most ardent pursuit. She surrendered her virginity to him as well, losing it in the throes of passion during a dark and stormy night when their entwined bodies were lit by the streaks of lightning that crossed the sky. Molly's screams of pain and ecstasy went unheard as the manager's long pole pierced her to the core and stretched the taut lips that had never before endured the harsh passage of a man's pride. She had been long a stranger to adulation, and it is not to be wondered at if the insinuating eloquence of the leader of the acting tribe had not great influence over the heart of this lively and beautiful girl. In short, he prevailed upon Molly when the company was about to quit the town to accompany him. She was delighted with the thought of exhibiting her person on the stage before a country audience, so the manager had not much difficulty in gaining her consent, especially upon promising that her first appearance would be in the character of Desdemona.

Mr. Pennington, being as tired of his daughter's extravagance as she was of the business of retailing, did not give himself any sort of trouble on her being supposed to have gone off with the player folks. On the contrary, to use his own words, he "was very glad she had taken herself off."

The personal charms of our heroine, which were universally acclaimed to be inexpressibly beautiful, attracted the merited admiration of every lover of female excellence. Her manifest deficiency in every acting part she undertook, however, could not escape observation.

Indeed, the manager well knew this, but it was the desire of enjoying the person of the fair Molly that prompted him to decoy the unsuspecting maid from her father's house. Yet, now that she had effected her escape from her home and what she took to be her drab existence, she was not quite as willing to give of herself. The manager tried every art in vain to once again sample her charms; and when he was fairly convinced the port was impregnable, he sincerely began to hate the poor girl as much as he had formerly loved her.

Our heroine could not but perceive this. This, together with the thought of owing a considerable sum to her landlady for board and lodging, and for which she had been more than once solicited, gave her some unpleasant moments which even the natural liveliness of her temper could not at all times dissipate.

As she sat one morning ruminating upon these matters, a note was brought to her in the following words: "Colonel Hardeson's compliments to Miss Pennington. He would be exceedingly happy if she will grant him an hour's conversation this evening, after the play is over." Our heroine, seeing a servant in fine dress waiting for an answer, imagined this note could come from no person of mean circumstances. As she was now really destitute of money, and her landlady had become very troublesome, she began to think that the best way to solve her financial difficulties would be to market that commodity which had been so much wished for by more than one. Of course, no price, in her own estimation, offered any way equal to the value of the purchase. With these thoughts in her head she answered that she should be happy to see the colonel at the time appointed.

During the whole time of that evening's performance our heroine's eyes were cast round the whole theatre in hopes of seeing her admirer. Her lovely bosom heaved with thoughts of a different kind from what she had ever before experienced, but yet could not fix upon any particular person in the house to whom she might ascribe the note sent her in the morning. Her curiosity was wound up to the highest pitch; in short, she never spent so disagreeable an evening.

At last the time came. The fair one hurried home, threw off her theatrical dress and attired herself in the most engaging nightgown. Her lovely blue eyes languishing with desire, and her snowy bosom half exposed to view so that the nipples were just hidden from sight, could not, she thought, fail to captivate any beholder. Anticipating the arrival of a charming, youthful lover, she planned to set herself off to the best advantage.

At length the wished-for hour arrived. A knock at the door was heard and she ran herself to open it. How great was her disappointment when, instead of an amorous, impatient, lovely youth ready to spring into her arms—the fond idea she had cherished—she beheld coming into the room a decrepit old man, who, as soon as he was seated, began to open his business in the following manner: "Your condescension, madam, in permitting me the honor of this visit, has made me infinitely happy!"

Molly was not sufficiently recovered from her astonishment to make him any answer. The antiquated lover pursued his discourse: "From the first moment I saw you, loveliest of women, I found I passionately loved." It would tire the reader to repeat the conversation that ensued.

The colonel said that he knew of her situation and very gallantly offered to extract her, on the simple condition that she would reside at Hardeson Hall where she would be her own mistress. To avoid the insinuations of a malicious world, she would pass for the housekeeper's niece. At the same time he frankly confessed that he was not physically able to pay his tribute to her properly at the altar of Venus, therefore he hoped the lovely maid would have no objection to his proposal if it were accompanied with a weighty purse. This last argument had more effect on the mind of our heroine than anything Hardeson had hitherto said.

After juggling in her mind the difference between starving as an actress and living in a house, though with a debilitated old lover, and under the character of his mistress, though he rarely would be able to stir the pot, so to speak, she determined to choose the last. She therefore consented to his urgent entreaties, and it was agreed that the colonel's coach would come for her the following day.

We will pass over in silence the consternation of the actors and actresses when they heard of the departure of their lovely and beautiful companion. In a short time Molly was an inmate of Hardeson Hall, in which situation she was mightily contented for a little while. It might be here thought necessary to inform the reader why the colonel, who so readily confessed to our fair one that it was not for the sake of sacrificing at the altar of love that he wished to persuade her to go to his home. It was more on this account—the colonel was ambitious that the world should think he was not so debilitated as was generally supposed, and that it should be said he had one of the finest girls in the kingdom then in keeping and whom he was pleasing on a regular basis.

In a few months after her arrival at Hardeson Hall, Molly began to wish for a change in situation. She had been glad that the old fellow had not touched her. Yet, her young blood required more than the simple adulation paid by the colonel. She had heard much praise of London, and imagined, with a great deal of truth, that her lovely person would not long remain in that gay metropolis unnoticed. Being naturally of a warm constitution, Miss Molly, in reality, sighed to taste of those joys of which she had sampled only once before with the manager.

The colonel had not been at all stingy with his mistress, but what he had bestowed upon her was chiefly for the decoration of her lovely person. The money, the first present he had made her, was now almost exhausted. This made our heroine determine that at the first opportunity every possible means should be taken to fill her purse again, or to get more from someone else, and then to set out for London.

One night when the dessert was taken away after supper, the colonel and Molly began to talk as they usually did at such time. She thought it a splendid moment to begin her maneuvers, as she well knew her old lover had that day received a great quantity of money, some of which she hoped to obtain.

"My dear one, you seem a little fatigued; your tenants were so troublesome to you this morning!"

"Indeed, my love, I am; but I have not forgotten you. That parcel on the table is yours, my charming girl; so are these stockings. Do, my dear, permit me to draw a pair on those charming limbs. Come, put your pretty foot upon my knee."

Molly did as she was directed. The colonel placed the candle on the floor so that his tired eyes might be more capable of seeing his way. He could not help placing his withered hand above her knee and working his way up. The touch was ecstatic—the stocking was forgotten. His pulse beat quick and his whole frame shook. His withered claw slowly advanced along her thigh, trembling, sweating, then dared to brush the mossy patch between her legs. While his rude hand dawdled there Molly grasped the purse, which the colonel in his agitation had left upon the table.

"Put it in your pocket, angelic woman!" were now the only words the trembling colonel could articulate.

As Molly removed her foot from the colonel's knee, one of her snowy breasts came in contact with his face. She had bent over so that its fullness was apparent and one nipple had sprung loose from its confines. "Oh, heaven!" He said no more and absolutely fainted. Molly was frightened, but her fears were soon dissipated when she saw her lover open his eyes.

"My charmer, I feel new vigor; suffer me to come to your chamber tonight."

At a reasonable time the impatient lover approached to what he hoped would be the chamber of bliss. Molly was a most irresistible figure, shrouded only in her chemise. The curves of her delectable body showed through the filmy material. The colonel had used the most stimulating provocatives, and it must be confessed that he had acquired a greater share of vigor than he had possessed for many years before, and was, with a little assistance, able to wage war with a willing victim. But our heroine was fully determined that her body should not be given to so feeble a lover; having determined very shortly to bestow it on some more worthy example of male flesh.

So did our old hero in one moment find himself robbed of all that store of manhood which had been accumulating for years. Molly simply removed her garment while the old fellow stood watching, his body shaking as with the ague as she slowly removed the cloth from her shoulders and let it drop to the floor. She was sure he was going to collapse at the sight of her firm young breasts and their dusky nipples; and if that was sufficient to make him flee consciousness, then he surely was on the verge of death as he absorbed the spectacle of her strong limbs and lightly mossed pussy. The spittle fairly flew from his lips as she lifted his shirt and laid her hand on the half-erect cock that wasn't quite so unattractive as she might have expected. She was not to see how vigorous his tool could become, however, for no sooner did she touch it and give it one or two gentle tugs than a sadly diminished stream of sperm dribbled from the tip and spattered onto the floor. Often since did this charming girl, when her spirits were enlivened with the juice of the exhilarating grape, relate to her enraptured lovers the particulars of this entertaining scene.

Our heroine had now, by the recent bounty of the colonel, sufficient money to defray her expenses to town, as well as something to subsist on while there. She therefore determined to engage a place in the coach that passed by Hardeson Hall every day. This being done, and having conveyed as many of her clothes as she conveniently could to a cottage bordering on the high road, she fixed a time for her departure. We will not relate the means taken to get away from the colonel unobserved, or the consternation that ensued when it was discovered that the housekeeper's niece had eloped. Suffice it to say that by the time her absence was noted she was with a gay young barrister, the only other passenger in the coach, on the direct road to the great metropolis.

It cannot be supposed that this limb of the law could coolly observe the exquisite loveliness of his companion. He soon entered into conversation with her, and if he before admired the beauties of her person, he was now not less charmed with the brilliancy of her wit. Finding she was not averse to love, he plied her with the kind of language that a man who is long acquainted with the world knows how to use with success.

Our heroine was quite captivated with him, and as the night wore on suffered him to take a few liberties, which might have alarmed the delicacy of a more modest woman, but Miss Molly thought no harm in granting. In no time at all his hand rested on her bosom, and then it insinuated itself within her garment and found one of the warm, ripe mounds of flesh, which seemed to melt beneath his hand. His other hand worked its way up along her thigh while Molly gazed out the window. She continued to take no notice while he kneaded her nipple and at the same time found the moist boundary of her cleft. His fingers explored the delicious slit and were encouraged when Molly subtly moved her thighs apart just enough to allow them greater freedom of access. When he brushed against the engorged nub of flesh that promised pleasures to come, she shuddered and thrust her hips forward. The young barrister immediately buried a finger in her crevice and worked it around until Molly began to writhe against him. The natural warmth of our heroine's constitution could not long resist the ecstatic dalliance that ensued without discovering those palpitations which to the feelings of a lover and a seducer are so delightful. Her watchful companion soon perceived that the wished-for moment had arrived, and without any further ceremony daringly advanced to the center of joy. Modesty, or rather mock modesty, caused Molly to gently resist.

It is well-known that in love resistance, instead of allaying, inflames the passions to a greater degree. This was the case with our successful pleader. All that had gone before encouraged him to drop his breeches without further delay. Molly looked over casually as he withdrew a long, thick cock with a purpling head that was destined to be submerged in her muff. She looked away just as casually as he pried her legs apart and moved between them, stretching her out on the carriage bench. Taking his cock in hand he brought the head to the entrance and nudged it inside. Then, while Molly groaned as if he were taking unpermitted liberties with her, he thrust his length in and began to shuttle in and out as best he could in the cramped quarters. He began to become comfortable as he increased the pace of his fucking and the pussy in which he was entrenched became well oiled. His presumption had no sooner thrown his fellow-traveler wholly in his power than a large stone in the road upset his most devout intentions. Had he been on horseback, it might have been said that he was fairly tossed out of the saddle.

This sad discomfiture induced the barrister to make a speech on the inconveniences of coaches, which led him to move that the ultimate trial should be put off until their arrival in London.

London was not speedily reached in those days, and singularly fortunate were the individuals who could gain the metropolis without some little adventure. It was not the lucky fate of our heroine to miss a little affair which served at least to break the monotony of the journey.

Soon after the incident with the barrister, a party of Gypsies were encountered, who encamped by the roadside and presented a most picturesque appearance. Over sparkling fires pots were hung, and anyone near enough could sniff the fragrant odor which rose from them, none the less pleasing to the olfactory organ because the chickens which were cooking were stolen.

"Of all things in the world," said Molly, "I have dearly longed to spend a night in a Gypsy camp."

"Don't talk of spending," said her companion. "It brings to my mind too keenly my disappointment. But it is a strange whim of yours, and stranger still that I have for years entertained the same notion. It shall be done! Gypsies are strange people; there may be some fun to be had with them. I don't know about stopping the entire night. We will at least make their acquaintance."

It has already been stated that our fair heroine and the barrister were the only occupants of the coach—no other passengers then could be inconvenienced by delay. A present to the coachman soon overcame his scruples; his ready wit could easily invent some lie to account for the delay to their masters, and so the matter was quickly arranged. The coach was stopped, and young Capias (for so the barrister was called) and Molly approached the Gypsies.

For a moment the natural timidity of her sex made Molly shrink from the swarthy figures they were approaching. The next moment she was reassured, for a young girl, with eyes black as night, hair dark and glossy as a raven's wing, and a scarlet shawl showing off her lithe figure, approached her.

"Tell your fortune, fair lady?" said she. "The Gypsy girl will tell truly what the stars foretell."

"You have just hit it, my girl," said Capias. "Tell the lady her fortune. Show us into one of your tents, and as bright a guinea as ever carried King George's head shall be yours."

Thrusting aside the curtain of a tent, Mildred, the dark-eyed girl, led them into the interior. A great fire smoldered in the center, the air of the tent was warmed and even perfumed by its smoke. A bed of soft moss was in one corner of the tent, and being spread over with a rich scarlet shawl it looked a couch which a Gypsy queen would not disdain to employ as the scene of a sacrifice to love.

It is needless to repeat the pretty phrases which Mildred poured into Molly's willing ears. She promised her all sorts of good things in the future, and then, with a meaningful look at Capias, slipped out of the tent, so taking care that Molly should have good things in the present.

Before many minutes had elapsed, the coy lady was spread upon the mossy couch and Capias was duly "entering an appearance" in a court in which he had not practiced before. But as there was no "bar" to his "pleading," he contrived to make a very sensible impression. His few "motions" were rewarded with a verdict of approval; his "attachment" was pronounced a valid one. In short, his argument was "penetrating" and "drove home" the points he wished to make. All of which is to say he fucked her well. This time he was not thrown from his steed as he had been in the carriage. His cock, once buried deeply in Molly's quim, remained there, though in varying lengths depending on the stroke of the moment. He lay atop her, belly to belly, her thighs close together, his lance working in and out of her excruciatingly tight sheath. While he worked thus he kneaded her breasts and rolled her nipples between his fingers, reveling in the way they swelled to his touch. His strokes were long and steady and seemed to extend deep into her dripping grotto. They reached the supreme moment at the same time and began to writhe upon their bed of moss—Molly wrapping her legs around Capias's back and he driving into her as the great shuddering spasms overtook him.

It did not take long to remove from their flushed cheeks and disordered dress the evidence of the encounter, and Molly and Capias issued into the open air to meet Mildred and reward her for her considerate attention.

The sounds of singing and revelry from a large tent well lit next attracted our lawyer's attention, and thereto he went. Around a large fire was seated a group which might well have tempted the brush of Murillo or Rembrandt. The luscious leer on the faces of the men and women showed how keenly they were enjoying a highly spiced song of one of the company. The right hands of most of the men, being hid in the folds of the drapery of the women, gave evidence of a desire to realize some of the stanzas.

A bold-looking, bronze-faced youth was singing, and the following verses give a fair example of his song:

Oh merry it is when the moon is high
To chase the red, red, deer;
And merry it is when no keeper's nigh
To trap and to snare without fear.
But better I ween is a night with my queen,
To lie in the arms of my love;
And to spend my sighs on those breasts I prize,
For a joy all others above.
Then here's to the things that each woman doth wear,
Though we cover it up with our hand;
Its forest is hair, but still I swear,
'Tis better than acres of land.
I've sipped red wine from the golden cup,

I've handled the guineas bright,
But a sweeter draught from my Chloe I'll sup,
Her eyes give such a bright light.
I'd sooner taste the nectar sweet,
That flows from her ripe red quim,
Then I'd put to my lip that beaker's tip,
Though with Burgundy filled to the brim.
Then while I've a soul I'll go for that hole,
It gives me the greatest joy;
My pulses beat with a fevered heat
Whilst I my cock employ.
And when I'm dead lay under my head
A tuft of her fragrant hair,
In the silent land it will make me stand
As if my true love were there.
Then shout and sing for that glorious thing,
That each one loves so well;
Keep me out of my meat, then heaven's no treat,
I'd rather have Chloe in hell.

Capias listened, so did Molly, with mixed feelings to this very irreverent song, but the night was wearing on and they had some thought of the long journey before them.

Mildred approached Capias with a smile, and said, "The gentleman will not stop long in the Gypsies tent. Only let the gentleman be generous, and Mildred will show him and the lady a rare sight."

Capias was generous indeed, and Mildred quietly led the way to a tent some little distance off.

"Step lightly," said she. "These are two of our people; they have eaten bread and salt today—they are now man and wife. Would you like to see the joys of their wedding night?"

Of course an affirmative answer was soon given, and Capias and Molly were led to a hole in the canvas wall.

At first only the dim outlines of two figures could be discerned in the interior of the tent.

"Wait a moment," Mildred whispered to Molly. "Gypsies always have a good light; no one would have his bride in the dark on his wedding night."

The peepers kept very still, and presently Mildred whispered again, "Timothy is going to light up; you'll see him look Miriam all over before he really has her for better or worse, as your marriage service says."

The obscure figures now released themselves for a long embrace, the female giving an audible sigh, which seemed to give expression both to her amorous desires and timidity as to what was coming. Striking a match, the swarthy bridegroom lit three candles stuck in a common tin triangle suspended from the center of the tent, which was a rather large one set apart for the use of various members of the tribe on such special occasions.

"Now strip thee, lass, and gie us a sight of thy juicy koont afore I fook thee!" said Timothy imperatively. "Thou's now all mine or now't, as I find thee."

Setting her a good example, he threw off jacket, vest, and breeks till he stood a dingy-looking Hercules in shirt and stockings, the former of which seemed anything but a clean wedding garment, looking a fair match in its unwashed tints to his olive-colored skin. She, too, was too dark for it to be seen if her blushes betrayed the shock to her modesty from the sight of his tremendous prick, the purple head of which jutted out beneath the dingy shirt.

"Tak't in thee hond, gal, and feel how randy 'tis!" he said, lifting up her smock the moment she stepped out of her skirts. The pair could then be seen standing side by side in the full light of the candles, their lips glued together in a sucking kiss, whilst each one's hands were busy caressing the other's privates. She was a fine young woman of about eighteen, with a mass of black hair falling loose over her shoulders. Her lovely eyes were hidden by the closing lids, as if she were afraid to look in her husband's face, or see her fate in any way.

"Oh! you hurt me, Timothy; did you think I'd lost my maidenhead?" she said, flinching from the insertion of his big middle finger.

"Thou'll do; thou's right, my gal. Now kiss my cock and swear to be true to it, and never take another as long as you have me," he said.

She knelt down before him and almost reverently imprinted two or three ardent kisses on the object of her desires, swearing the required oath in a peculiar kind of lingo quite impossible for Capias and Molly to understand. They could see he was tremendously excited. Suddenly she took him in her mouth. The entire massive length disappeared with such speed Molly could scarcely believe her eyes, yet the girl surely had the thick pole down her throat. She began to bob her head up and down; the shaft glistened as it emerged into the light on the upstroke. Her mouth and throat were filled with the monstrous prick, yet she continued her ministrations without difficulty and seemed to take great pleasure in it. For just a moment she let it slip free so that she could lick around the swollen head and flick at the slit with the tip of her tongue. Then she again consumed the entire thing like a choice morsel and seriously began to pump it with the muscles in her throat until the man put a sudden halt to the activity. Lifting the fine girl in his brawny arms, he carried her to a heap of blankets laid over a soft bed of ferns and heather, and falling upon it with her by his side, his hands opened her willing thighs, giving a delicious view of a black bushy mount with just a discernible vermillion slit at the bottom of the swarthy belly. He was between those plump thighs quicker than it takes to say so, and throwing his body over her, began to kiss her face and neck in the most passionate manner, being too long in the body to do so to her heaving bosom, which he caressed and kneaded with one hand. The girl seemed instinctively to open her thighs yet wider as he put the head of his tremendous cock to the small-looking slit, opening the lips with his fingers until the head got in about an inch. Her hands pressed his buttocks down with all her force and his shaft was jammed into her. Both seemed to quiver with emotion and spend at this moment, as they then lay motionless for a few seconds. She gave his bottom a rare slap with one hand, and loudly whispered, "Try again, Timothy, my love. You did make me feel nice and I shan't be so tight now! Go on—go on—Oh! Oh! Oh, oh, oh!" He gave a hard push, sending his rammer in three or four inches, and then, before she could recover from the agonizing pain, thrust again and again. He clasped her fainting body with his muscular arms, grinding his teeth in erotic rage and behaving like an anaconda enfolding its victim, until his prick was sheathed to the roots of its hair and dripping with her virgin blood at every withdrawal.

Molly and Capias were deliciously groping each other as they looked through the peepholes. At this moment a loud burst of tambourines and rough music arose from the campfire, followed by a jolly chorus—

Hurrah, hurrah, for the bloody strife,
That ends by making man and wife;
Hurray, hurray, she's a maid no more,
But a fucking wife forevermore!

This startled Molly and Capias from their total distraction.

"Ha! Is it like that with you two?" whispered Mildred. "I thought it would stir your blood!" as she glided off into the gloom and left them to peep and enjoy themselves all alone.

The noise and Timothy's throbbing instrument in her tight sheath had now roused Miriam to life, as well as action. In response to his movements, she heaved up her rump and writhed in a perfect state of erotic frenzy, calling him to fuck her well, to shove all, all—balls and all—into her cunt, even biting his shoulder as she used all the bawdy expressions possible to think of. She was a demon at the game now, once thoroughly aroused, and to judge by her sighs and screams of delight, was spending almost every few seconds. For his part, Timothy continued to plunge his rod into her dripping crevice, drawing it out almost to the tip before driving it in again to its full length. Miriam demanded more and more of it as he filled her with his creamy flood, till she fairly exhausted her husband, who rolled off her body in spite of all endeavors to keep him on the go. He lay fairly vanquished beneath his rampant bride, who at once in triumph, straddled over him and transfixed his still-stiff cock in her insatiable chink, riding him with all her might, till with an oath at her randiness, he threw her off and declined any more of it for a while.

Thus ended the episode of the Gypsy camp, and our heroine with her friend returned to their coach and continued the journey to town, while he related to her a tale of the seduction of two sisters, which by the assistance of a reading lamp he read from a piece of paper taken out of his jacket pocket.

"In a retired part of Devon lived Mr. Firman, a widower, a man of a calm and settled disposition, fond of study, and, having experienced much of adversity, rather at discord than union with the world. He had been a Bristol merchant, and was growing rich when it happened that his slave ships, together with most of their several living cargoes, were all destroyed within twelve months. Their owner in consequence declared a bankrupt.

"One ship was burned by a cask of spirits taking fire; another was wrecked; a third foundered; and a fourth fell a sacrifice to no less than three hundred slaves, who in a frantic effort for freedom set fire to the magazine, and blew themselves and the whole crew up. What became of the other two was never rightly understood. We mention the reason of Mr. Firman's failure merely because he used afterwards to confess his misfortune as just punishment for being concerned in such infamous traffic.

"As companions of his retirement, as consolation to his solitude, Mr. Firman had two daughters, Sophia and Eliza, and a son, Frederick. The former were twins, about eighteen years of age and very beautiful. Though young, their bodies were those of mature, well-endowed women. Frederick, who had been left a small fortune by a maiden aunt, was also a very amiable youth, and intended for the profession of the law. He was about nineteen and studied under the classical care of a clergyman at Exeter.

"Mr. Firman, though fond of his girls, was determined to send them to some respectable seminary of industry. Seeing an advertisement in a London newspaper that two young ladies were wanted by a milliner at the west end of the town, he immediately wrote to a friend, desiring him to make inquires as to the terms, situation, and character of the advertisement. The friend, without much attention to duty, made the business as easy as possible. He saw a large house in a grand neighborhood and was received by an attractive woman; to his shallow capacity that appeared sufficient.

"Mr. Firman received a satisfactory answer. The terms being reasonable, and the report being thus satisfactory, Mr. Firman immediately wrote to his friend, desiring him to conclude the business. His hopes were that his daughters would not only be companions to each other during their apprenticeship, but they would commence business together. And that as they had some very near relations in the fashion world, he hoped they would make a flourishing fortune in a short time.

"As it would be tedious and melancholy to relate the preparations, and the separation of a fond father and his darling children, we shall pass over those events and set the sisters down in Jermyn Street, at the house of Mrs. Tiffany, where one hundred and twenty guineas were paid as apprentice fees.

"The correspondence between Mr. Firman and his two daughters was for some time regular and reciprocally affectionate; but by degrees both punctuality and tenderness upon the part of the latter declined. They were hurried with business, they were indisposed, they were in the dull season of the year, or they were upon visits to Mrs. Tiffany's friends in the country. In short, filial duty soon fell off entirely, and the poor old man at length wrote until he was tired to no purpose. They never corresponded except for when they drew upon him for money to purchase fine clothes, and that they did oftener than his circumstances conveniently admitted of.

"It now became the time when the son was to leave Devonshire in pursuit of his professional studies. He was made apprentice to a very eminent attorney in Gray's Inn, and had letters of recommendation to several persons highly respected in the law.

"Being settled, his first business was a visit to his sisters. The good lady of the house received him with much kindness, but the Miss Firmans being a little way out of town, and not expected for some days, he was invited to call again. He particularly noticed three young ladies in the house, highly dressed out and made up more like toy-shop dolls than females connected with the humble and respectable occupation of business.

"Frederick, though but nineteen years of age, and only just come from the most retired part of Devonshire, then formed conclusions not very favorable to these girls. And from the appearance of the place he entertained as well very strong forebodings of his sisters' safety.

"Young Firman took his leave very much dissatisfied, but, concealing his suspicions, promised to return in a few days, expressing a hope that by that time his sisters would be arrived from the country.

"Among other letters it happened that young Firman had one recommending him strongly to the son of a west country baronet, who, to qualify him for the bar, or perhaps the bench at Westminster Hall, was studying Paphian theology in Lincoln's Inn. Frederick lost no time in delivering his packet, and as he was a very comely youth, and had a fashionable—though innocent—appearance, young Mr. Thornback, the student, concluded Frederick would not disgrace him. He also thought Frederick's ignorance would afford him and, in short, condescended to ask him on the next day, which was Sunday, to accompany him in his carriage to Windsor.

"On the road they became more intimate, and young Thornback opened to Frederick the intention of his journey, which was to see a damned fine girl that he had in keeping in the neighborhood, who unluckily he had got with child. Young Firman was too much of a greenhorn to relish this sort of visit, and Thornback tried to cheer him by assuring him that his favorite had a sister, another damned fine girl, with whom he could sleep if he pleased that night, as she was then upon a visit at his lodgings.

"This did not, however, dispel the gloom of young Firman. A thousand thoughts of home, and of the new scenes into which he was entering made him appear more and more embarrassed. They stopped at the gateway of a very handsome house in the outskirts of Windsor before he could recover sufficiently to make any coherent reply.

"They had no sooner alighted than a female servant, with a melancholy face, informed the Squire that her mistress was brought to bed with a fine boy, but added, with a flood of tears, that its mother was no more! Thornback, though an aristocratic snob of little feeling, was greatly shocked at the information, and a tear was seen to steal down his cheek. On entering the parlor he threw himself in a fit of grief on the sofa. At that moment the ears of the young Firman were assailed and his soul rent by the loud lamentations proceeding from a female voice to which he had been somewhat accustomed. "Where is he? Where is he?" repeated the now well-known tongue. The door burst open, and the only surviving daughter of the unhappy Firman, with hands extended, disheveled hair, and distracted features, threw herself upon the neck of young Thornback.

"Surprise, shame, grief, and distraction, all united in the soul of the wretched brother. His emotions became too strong for his nature and he sank senseless on the carpet. The servants, who were the only persons in possession of themselves, assisted to raise him up and seat him in a chair. The noise and confusion occasioned by his situation in a few moments roused the sister—her transition was from grief to agony— from agony to despair—especially upon beholding in the person of a supposed stranger, whom she had not before noticed, that of a beloved brother!

"From that moment she became insensible to everything around her—she became positively mad—and nothing less than the strength of three servants prevented her from putting an end to her existence.

"A few words regarding Mrs. Tiffany. She had been seduced at an early age by the assistance of a French milliner. After several changes she was kept by a West India merchant from whom she obtained sufficient monies to take the house in Jermyn Street. She affected the business of a milliner that she might the more unsuspectedly carry on that of bawd and seducer.

"The two lovely Firmans were but six months in her house and just eighteen years old when they were prostituted—one to a gambler for two hundred pounds, and the other for five hundred pounds to an old debilitated viscount. From that point on they were much in demand and were fucked from morning to night."

As Mr. Capias finished the account of the seduction of the milliner's girls, they were already entering London, and were soon set down at the noted La Belle Sauvage Inn, Ludgate Hill. A hackney coach was called and Capias easily persuaded Molly to go with him to his chambers. It was yet early in the day, so after a good breakfast provided by the housekeeper, they lay down to rest on his bed until the evening, when he expected a friend to supper.

"Now darling," exclaimed the young barrister, throwing aside his clothes, "undress yourself, and let us enjoy without restraint those delicious pleasures which the accident in the coach interrupted, and of which afterwards in the gypsy tent we had only a rough taste." He eyed her breasts with undisguised lust. "What exciting charms; let me caress those swelling orbs of snowy flesh, which I see peeping from your loosened dress. What a difference there is in titties. Some girls have next to nothing, others are so full they hang down like the udder of a cow; and then again some of the finest barely have nipples to set them off. Yours my love, are perfection. Let me kiss them, suck them, knead them in my hands!"

This attack upon her bosom almost drove Molly wild with desire. Her blood tingled to the tips of the toes as she heaved with emotion. "Oh! Oh! Oh!"

He gradually pushed her towards the bed, and presently, when her back rested on its edge, one of his hands found its way under her clothes to the very seat of bliss.

"What a lovely notch. I had scarcely time to feel what a beautiful fanny you had when I was so hot from watching the bliss in the gypsy tent. Now, darling, we can enjoy everything in perfection, and increase the delights of fucking by such preliminary caresses as these, which will warm our blood, until you beg me to let you have it at once and my excited prick revels in your juicy gap."

She was nearly spending just at the touch of his hands, and begged with sighs of delight for him to satisfy her irresistible longings.

"Not with your things on, dear. Off with them, quick—see what a glorious erection I have got. There, caress it, press it in your hand."

He had taken off everything and helped her to do the same. Then he tossed her on the bed and was between her opens legs as they stretched wide to receive him. But he toyed with her yet for a minute or two, letting the head of his prick just touch between the warm juicy lips so anxious to take him in.

"Ah, you tease! Do let me have it!" she almost screamed, heaving up her bottom to try and get him further in. "Oh, do; don't tease me so. I'm coming again! Oh! Oh!"

He awfully enjoyed this dalliance, but at length took pity on her languishing looks and slowly drove in up to the hilt, until his balls flapped against the velvet cheeks of her rump.

"I like to begin slowly," he whispered, "and draw out the pleasure till we both get positively wild with lustful frenzy. That is the only way to get the very acme of real enjoyment. A young fellow who rams in like a stallion or a rabbit, and spends in a moment, scarcely makes the girl feel any pleasure before he finishes and is off.

"Many married women have stupid husbands of that sort, who never fuck them properly. Is it to be wondered that women get awfully taken with a man who introduces them to the real delight of love?"

"Yes—yes—you darling—but push it in faster now. Ah, I feel its head poking the entrance to my womb at every thrust; that's so delicious. Are you coming? I'm simply swimming in my juices. Oh, there it is, it's like warm lightning shooting into me. Oh, oh; don't stop—go on a few more strokes. I'm coming again. Ah, you darling. Ah—more! Oh!"

To comply with Molly's wishes, he drove into her long and hard, banging against her pelvis from the force of the strokes. He raised himself on his knees and took her legs in his hands, lifting them so that her pussy was more widely opened. His prick was still lodged inside her, only now he could better see it as it slid in and out on its mission of pleasure. He jiggled his hips and thrust forward, enjoying the way Molly's breasts bounced in response. He did this more and more, alternating short thrusts with long until she was squirming and screaming from the unrelenting pleasure of it.

Capias smiled grimly and continued, relishing the way his prick felt rock-hard and indestructible as it plumbed her depths. He liked to see her this way, pinned beneath him, spread open, a slave to every movement of his cock. When she began to beg him to fuck her harder he did so until it seemed she would swoon from the continuing spendings she was experiencing. At much the same time he began to spurt his thick sperm into her in bubbling gouts that left him trembling and exhausted.

After this they had a sound sleep till seven o'clock, when the housekeeper knocked to say Mr. Verney had come. Thus awakened, Molly was delighted to find the young barrister's prick still tightly encased in her tightly contracted sheath.

She wanted another stirring up, but Capias declined the invitation, and promised to make up for it at night.

"You're so lucky, my boy!" said Verney, as his friend Capias introduced him to Molly. "No other fellow ever has such luck as you have in love."

"Her action is better than her looks," replied Capias, making Molly blush up to her eyes while he threw off the covers and exposed her glorious nakedness to Verney's hungry gaze. "Nothing to be ashamed of, my darling. I always tell Verney all about my love affairs. He's a devil for the girls himself, and one to please them, too. Now for supper; she's taken all the strength out of me, and I want refreshing."

"Nothing like a refresher after a good fuck, is there, Capias? Ah! I wish I was you; the very sight of Miss Molly will make me uncomfortable all night, unless my landlady's daughter takes pity on me and slips into my bed when I get home!"

At supper and during the evening Verney scarcely took his eyes off our heroine, who could easily see how she had influenced him. Capias seemed anything but jealous, and paid far more attention to the bottle than to his new love, which rather chagrined her. Verney was a brilliant pianist, playing and singing with great feeling, and casting his eye on Molly when there was any suggestive point in the song.

It was a dreadful night out of doors, so the housekeeper was asked to make up a bed for Verney on the sofa. He gave Molly a significant glance as this arrangement was made, and also looked at the liquor stand, to give her a hint of his plans. Capias when in convivial company was too much given to whiskey and water, which he drank like a fish, giving no heed to the pleasures Molly would expect from him when they retired to bed. At length she said she felt tired, and bidding Verney good night asked Capias not to sit up too long, then went into the bedroom. Verney mixed his friend an awfully stiff glass for the last, and as Capias swallowed it, wished him pleasant dreams and plenty of fucking, adding, "I shall have a hard-on all night myself thinking of you."

The sot scrambled into bed to be received in Molly's longing embrace.

"Now, sir, you're almost drunk and sleepy. Keep awake till I'm satisfied, or my name's not Molly if I don't leave you and ask your friend to do your duty for you. You haven't taken a bit of notice of me all evening. Ah! You can't even get hard," as she groped with her hand and found only a limp noodle for her trouble.

He was not so stupid, but he knew his deficiency. Taking one of her nipples in his mouth he tried to raise the requisite desire. Her fingers did their best to second the feeble effort while his fingers on her clitoris aroused her amorous flame in all its intensity. At last he dropped into a sound drunkard's sleep, just as she was becoming fanatic with baffled desire.

"You brute, you sot!" she angrily exclaimed, pushing him away from her. "You're sodden with Irish whiskey. See if I don't keep my threat. Verney is a fine fellow who only wants a chance to have his way."

Springing from the bed, with nothing but her chemise on, she rushed into the other room and threw herself into a chair, sobbing as if her heart would break as she covered her face with her hands.

"By Jove, damn it, what's the matter?" exclaimed Verney as he awoke from a real sleep. He could just make her out by the light of the fire, so, throwing off the bedclothes, he got off the sofa and knelt at her feet on the hearthrug.

"What's he done, to turn you out of the room, my dear? Do tell me; I'd kick him into the street for your sake, Molly!"

"It's what he hasn't done!" she replied, sobbing. He continued to ask the cause, and had put his arm round her waist, till her head rested on his manly shoulder.

"Oh, oh, I couldn't bear to lie all night in bed with a drunken man. I'll get my clothes and leave this place!"

His hand was now up between her thighs, and his lips imprinted hot kisses on her burning cheeks. Higher and higher crept that insinuating hand, till he got fair possession of her slit, all moistened as it was with warm creamy emissions. She still sobbed on his shoulder as her legs slightly parted, while a perceptible shudder of suppressed emotion told him too surely that his success would soon be complete. Withdrawing his hand for a moment from that burning spot, he shifted her naked foot till it rested on his rampant tool, as still and hard as iron, and it throbbed under that caressing foot which his hand directed.

From her face his lips found their way to her bosom, and her sighs too plainly spoke her feelings. Taking her boldly in his arms, he carried Molly to the sofa. Stretching himself by her side, with his tremendous truncheon stiff against her belly, he placed her hand upon it. Opening her legs she directed it herself to her cunt. The head of his cock sank into her pussy as he pushed against her. They commenced a delightful side fuck, their lips glued together. This made him come in a moment, but rolling her over on her back, he kept up the stroke, until she also spent in an agony of delight. Resting for a few moments, he went on again, her legs entwined over his loins as she heaved and writhed in all the voluptuous ecstasy of her lascivious nature. She spent every few minutes a perfect flood of warm joy juice, to the intense delight of his prick, which fairly reveled in the delicious moisture, exciting him more and more every moment.

Their bounding strokes made the sofa fairly creak, and anyone not in such a drunken sleep as Capias must have been awakened.

"Ah!" sighed Molly, scarcely able to catch her breath. "You beat him fairly, and I thought no man could possibly have given me more pleasure than he did. Drive on, push it in, balls and all—oh, fuck, fuck me. Oh! I'm coming again. How you shoot it into me, you dear fellow."

After this he promised to take care of her, and gave her an address where she could get two nice rooms. Then he persuaded her to lie down by the side of Capias again, saying, "And when he wakes in the morning, dearest, don't let him touch you—say 'no! You couldn't fuck me last night, and now you shan't again!' That will be a good excuse to leave him."

She followed this advice and got clear of Capias in a few hours, without the barrister suspecting his friend Verney had had a finger in the pie.

Molly drove to the address, where Mrs. Swipes, the landlady, said she was always glad to welcome any friend of Mr. Verney's, who was such a very kind gentleman.

Her new lover called in the evening to renew his fucking, much to the ever-randy Molly's delight, and left her several bawdy books to read, including large and especially interesting volumes full of colored plates. These, of course, were for her later perusal and pleasure, for he wished to occupy their time together with passionate fucking. This they did with increasing frenzy. Varney seemed insatiable as he took her in every position they were capable of assuming. He particularly liked placing Molly on her belly and entering her from behind. He said there was little to match the pressure that was put upon the cock in this position as it worked in and out of the pussy. He also enjoyed the sensations as he drove into Molly's receptive quim and his belly slapped her soft buttocks with each stroke.

When he'd finished in this fashion, he turned her on her side and lifted one of her legs, again entering from behind. Only this time he was able to shift her onto his lap when the moment was right so that the pace of the fuck was regulated by her. Molly happily complied and impaled herself again and again on his upstanding rod, raising and lowering herself so that she could feel every inch of his meat penetrating her. In this way they spent the night, eventually losing count of the number of times they each came.

On taking leave after breakfast next morning, Verney particularly advised her to be guided by Mrs. Swipe's advice in everything. "And you can easily be the best of friends with the old woman by indulging her love of gin every day; half a pint doesn't cost much and I'll pay all your expenses. Be agreeable to the other girls in the house and you'll be as happy as a queen. I'm not a jealous sort and I guarantee you'll get plenty of the staff of life!"

By this Molly guessed she was in a bawdy house, but felt pretty confident of taking care of herself. She picked up a purse of gold he left for her on the table.

"My dear," said Mrs. Swipes shortly thereafter as she lapped her Old Tom, "gin gives one such an appetite. I can always eat well, but it's too depressing for men, takes all the starch out of their pricks you know. So never offer anything so vulgar to gentlemen friends; let them send out for champagne or brandy or whiskey, even, is not bad. You know the saying, 'Whiskey makes the love hot, and brandy makes it long.' For my part, dear, give me a man who can keep his place well and go on with his fucking, getting stiffer and bigger inside my cunt, till he stirs my blood and raises all my passions to a fever pitch. When at length both come together, it is really the melting of two souls into one, and leaves you to fall into that blissful ecstasy which only true and experienced lovers really understand."

Wetting her mouth with the gin, she again went on. "Fellows who are so hot that they no sooner get into a girl than it is all over don't give a bit of pleasure. Even some old men are so warm that they only require the sight of a naked tit to make them come in their breeches. My dear, you can't imagine what a nasty lot of fellows there are in London, both old and young, who go about in crowds, or ride in coaches, where they can feel girls' bottoms, or tread on their toes, which is all they need to bring on a spend, instead of having a straightforward honest fuck. Never notice such fellows; always slap their faces. Now, my dear, if you would like to meet a real nice gentleman, a handsome fellow, a real lord, lots of money, plenty of fizz, and everything jolly—why, my love, he likes to fuck me, old as I am. Sometimes, as he says, plenty of good soup can be made in an old pot. Iris Jones is awfully crazy about him, and he is coming to supper with us tonight if you'd like to be one of the party. What do you say, dear?"

"But how will Iris like it if you introduce me?" asked Molly.

"Do you think I'd have a jealous fool in my house? Why, his lordship always expects me to introduce him to every new lady who comes into my house. Iris and you will be the best of friends."

Here there was a tap at the door of Molly's apartment.

"Come in," exclaimed Mrs. Swipes. "Oh, it's you, Iris. Let me introduce you to your new lady, Miss Molly—ahem, what's your name, my dear?"

"Never mind that. What will Miss Iris take to cement the introduction?" said Molly.

"I know what I should like to give her, and that's a good birch rod on her fat bum, for disturbing our quiet little confab," said Mrs. Swipes.

"Would you indeed, you dear old girl," said Iris. "You do like to see a rosy bottom getting redder under your strokes till the blood fairly trickles down at last. Let us have a bottle and I won't even mind lending you my ass for a few minutes; it leads up to such pleasant sensations and may be a novelty for our new friend Miss Molly. I must apologize for my intrusion; the fact is I heard your voice in the room as I was going downstairs to ask if Lord Rodney is coming to supper this evening."

"Fudge!" exclaimed Mrs. Swipes. "Why don't you honestly say you guessed we'd got a drop of drink. I'll soon fetch the liquor and take the price out of your arse, my impudent, cheeky beauty, although I know you enjoy the touch of the twigs as much as I do using them. The sight will give Miss Molly here a new sensation, or I'm not a judge of character. She looks ready enough for anything!"

"Thank you for the compliment," replied our heroine. "I admit I'm not a lump of ice, and I'm curious to see the birching."

The landlady went to the cellar in person and soon reappeared with a bottle of true Widow Cliquot, in which the three ladies pledged each other "long life and plenty of fucking."

Mrs. Swipes had also brought with her, from the lower regions of the house, a long brown paper parcel, from which she unrolled a beautiful little tickle-tail, composed of a few fine strips of birch handsomely tied up with blue velvet and red silk ribbons at the handle end. The tips of the twigs were so arranged as to spread out and cover a considerable area of any devoted bum they might be applied to.

"Lay me over the end of the sofa, and Miss Molly must hold my hands," said Iris, slipping off her dressing gown. This at once revealed that she had only her corset, chemise, and drawers to hide her person, which was set off to the best advantage by pink silk stockings, pretty gold garters, and elegant high-heeled French slippers.

"As hard as you like, Swipes, dear, but you know I expect your tongue for a wind-up at the finish."

"I'll be there when the tingling cuts make you spend, my darling. I wouldn't miss sucking up every drop for the world," replied Mrs. Swipes, taking up the switch. Iris kneeled over the sofa and gave Molly her hands to hold.

The landlady now quickly unbuttoned the band of Iris's drawers, pulling them down to her knees. She tucked the tail of the thin cambric chemise out of the way under her corset, both before and behind, so as to give a full view of a truly magnificent white rump, and as much of a handsome and pretty young whore as one could wish to see.

"No use delaying," said Mrs. Swipes, giving a very spiteful swish across Iris's buttocks to commence with. "I'll just lay them on heartily and we'll see what pleasure Iris derives from it. "How do they feel, dear?" She followed up with a succession of sharp cuts, which fairly reddened the flesh of Iris's posteriors and made her writhe under the stinging sensation.

Molly could see as she held the victim's hands how her face flushed at the first smart of the rod, then how Iris squirmed at each cut, getting ever more and more flushed as she bit her lips to prevent crying out.

Molly could also very well see the reddening surface and rising weals as they appeared under the ruthless and stinging switches of the landlady, whose face flushed with delight as the flagellation proceeded.

This made the blood tingle in the veins of our heroine, who quite shivered with emotion and was nearly overcome by an indescribable feeling of voluptuous desire.

In about five minutes Miss Jones gave most evident signs of the approaching climax of her passions. She closed her eyes and hung her head over the end of the sofa. Her bottom and thighs fairly quivered with the excess of her emotions till Mrs. Swipes, throwing aside the now useless birch rod, rushed on her victim with all the energy of an excited lesbian. She turned the girl over on her back and buried her face between Iris's thighs. She licked and sucked up every drop of moisture from her victim's quivering quim, to the great delight and excitement of Miss Molly, who sat down, shoved her fingers into the waistband of her drawers and began massaging her aching pussy. While Iris continued to have her slit lathered, Molly leaned back and kneaded her folds of sensitive flesh. She watched as Mrs. Swipes kept her mouth glued to Iris's pussy; Molly could occasionally see her tongue darting past the threshold into the membrane-lined interior. The voluptuous sight set her blood on fire and she slipped a finger into her own quim in an effort to find release. She worked it around and in and out, then added another digit. With her thumb she found her engorged love button and teased it gently until she began to shudder from the feelings that coalesced inside her. She thrust her fingers harder and faster, burying them to the second knuckle and watching as they emerged wet with the juice of her passion. She neared her orgasm as Mrs. Swipes finished off Iris with several slashes of her tongue; both girls came in a rush that left them faint and gasping at the intensity of the emotions that washed over them.

About ten o'clock, Lord Rodney was announced and shown into the drawing room where Molly, Iris, and their landlady awaited his arrival.

"Strangers first," said his lordship, kissing Molly in the most amorous fashion, tipping the velvet tip of his lascivious tongue into her mouth as he did so.

"Look at the man! What a whoremonger he is. I can't have a modest girl in my house but he takes the most impudent liberties with her," exclaimed Mrs. Swipes. "How dare you, sir, thrust your wicked tongue into Miss Molly's mouth like that?"

"Mind your own business, you old bitch," retorted his lordship, a handsome young fellow of about twenty-eight, "or I won't lend Iris my dildo to fuck you with presently."

Supper was pleasant but soon over, and his lordship, who had sat beside Molly all the while, encouraging her to caress his prick under the table, arose from his seat with a yawn.

"So who'll take the care of this hard-on for me?" he exclaimed. "Will you give way to Miss Molly?" he asked Iris.

"With the greatest of pleasure," she answered, "only I mean to prepare you for it with the rod, so as to make you truly excited and not tease her with one of your lazy fucks."

All three helped to disrobe Molly, who was soon as naked as Eve when first presented to Adam. They opened the folding doors into a bedroom, where she was laid down on a quilt, blushing and quivering with excitement as Lord Rodney, equally reduced to a state of nudity, got between her legs and lay over her with his stiff cock throbbing against her belly. It was long and thick and capped with an engorged helmet that darkened as they watched.

"Look at his laziness," said Iris. "He isn't even going to get into her when he knows she is dying for a good fucking. Wait a moment till I get my things off."

This was quickly done, and taking up a good thick bunch of birch twigs, she let him have it hard on his brawny rump. It took a good many cuts before he would begin to do his duty, but the effects were plainly visible on his cock, which stiffened still more and swelled immensely. Molly, impatient for him to begin, took hold of it herself, and directing the fiery head to her burning slit, began to slip it in.

Miss Jones handled her bum-tickler with vigor, carefully applying the twigs so that they not only cut well into Lord Rodney's buttocks, but every now and then caught him well in between the tender inner surface of his thighs, licking the back part of his balls and even inflicting little stinging touches on the lips of Molly's fanny. This made the two of them writhe and fuck away with perfect abandon until the sheets were saturated by the profusion of mingled love juice that oozed from Molly's cunt at every thrust of the rampaging prick buried inside her.

Iris dropped the birch and, taking a huge dildo from a drawer in the dressing table, fitted it onto herself and proceeded to fuck Mrs. Swipes. That lady threw up her clothes and took in the big rubber instrument with the greatest of pleasure as she reclined backwards on a sofa.

"Look, Rodney," exclaimed Iris, "you can fuck me dog fashion as I give the old bitch the pleasure she is so fond of!"

Rodney immediately withdrew his throbbing prick from Molly's quim, and told her to pay his backside for the insult. Then, getting behind Iris, he clasped his arms around her loins, until he could frig her in front by getting his fingers under the straps of the dildo, his well-oiled cock slipping into her longing cunt from behind.

As for Molly, her unsatisfied desires made her so randy, that she clasped his ass in the same way he had Iris, rubbing her dripping cunt on his backside and stroking his prick in front with her hands as it poked in and out of Iris.

The chain of throbbing human flesh moved together as each member sought release from the mounting passions that threatened to overwhelm them. Iris continued to pump Mrs. Swipes with the enormous dildo—ramming it in and out of her unmercifully—while Rodney fucked her from the rear. He slammed against her bottom with a jarring crack, so forceful were his strokes, which only served to increase the force with which the rubber cock invaded Mrs. Swipes. Molly, meanwhile, continued to thrust her mound against his bottom while she pumped his tool on the upstrokes.

All this lasciviousness had its effect on the participants, for within a very few moments all of them began to shudder and shake and release such a torrent of honey and sperm as had rarely been seen in that house.

After this bout, his lordship confessed himself quite used up, but fortunately for Molly, whom the scene had left in a state of raging unsatisfied desire, a late visitor to the house—a real prince from the west coast of Africa—was prepared to have her for the night. He was indeed a real prince, and a champion of love between the sheets. Molly accepted him willingly, though she blanched when she first saw the black enormity of his tool. She thought he would never be able to get it into her without splitting her apart. Never had she seen its like. It was fully a foot long and as thick around as her fist. The head was a massive helmet that leered at her darkly as the prince greeted her in the shadows of her room. He, however, thought nothing of the difficulties that his size might impose and immediately moved between her legs.

Molly shrugged and spread her thighs as wide as possible. It was possible that she would get to enjoy a cock of this size only once in this world, so she resolved to accept whatever came. The prince brought the head to her slit and slowly worked it past the folds. Molly grimaced as the first needles of pain assailed her. The enormous helmet wormed its way past her entry. It wasn't quite as uncomfortable as she'd thought; her pussy had stretched seemingly beyond itself to accommodate the intruder. Reassured by Molly's moans of pleasure, the prince reared back and began to thrust into her. Suddenly her eyes started from her head and she was racked with pain. Apparently she'd spoken too soon.

Yet she grimaced and indicated to her lover that he should continue. He withdrew a bit and then pushed forward again, burying nearly half his length in Molly's cunt. She groaned in combined pain and ecstasy; never before had she felt so stuffed with cock. She could feel every inch of this enormous tool scraping her pussy walls. The prince began an abbreviated pumping motion, attempting to oil the passage so that more of his rod could fit within. As Molly's juices began to flow, he worked more and more of his meat into the receptacle. Finally he simply lunged forward and buried the remainder to the balls.

Molly squirmed and writhed on the mattress; she felt like a butterfly pinned to a board. She was impaled on this enormous black hook that was starting to stir the most lascivious and intense feelings in her. As the thick pole shuttled in and out of her, she began to thrust her hips to meet the strokes, never allowing too much of the lance to leave her pussy.

The prince rammed into her two or three more times, then stiffened as he began to pour a massive quantity of boiling sperm into her cunt. Molly had long since come a multiplicity of times and was almost relieved when the prince's spasms ended.

"Well," he said, smiling down at her, "now that you are accustomed to the size of my weapon, are you ready to go again?"

Molly simply rolled her eyes and nodded. It was going to be a long night.

His tremendous tool was so untiring in its exertions that next morning at breakfast where they all met again, the landlady asked Molly, who looked a little blasé, "if she still wanted more fucking."

"Good God, no!" ejaculated poor Molly. "His monster of a salami hasn't left a drop of lovejuice in me. He came again and again throughout the night, and even just now would have done it again, had I let him, to give him an appetite for breakfast."

Mrs. Swipes, expressing her desire to just for once feel such a champion cock in her, begged Prince Motumbo to jam it in her as soon as possible. He was only too glad to oblige her, and Iris afterwards, when he saw how her eyes glistened at the sight of his coal-black battering ram.

Lord Rodney and the recently arrived Verney very much enjoyed the scene as the ladies removed their garments. They handled the prince's enormous prick, putting it up against one moist slit, and then the other. His lordship made some very learned remarks on the capability of the female organ to accommodate itself to the biggest pricks, as he saw how easily the women managed to take in all Motumbo could give, notwithstanding its enormous size.

The fucking proceeded apace, with Molly watching from a safe distance. Prince Motumbo had both women lie side by side, their legs well spread, and then proceeded to screw himself into first one, then the other. He would drive into Mrs. Swipes, give her two or three vigorous strokes, then pull and jam his meat into Iris's eager cunt. This continued for a surprising length of time. Prince Motumbo's endurance was unbelievable and the subject of commendation among the men. He fucked and fucked while the women moaned and screamed and begged him to return to them immediately upon his withdrawal. He also had more than enough sperm for them both, as he filled those pussies equally when his volcano finally erupted.

Mr. Verney did not appear a bit jealous after finding that Molly had been the eager recipient of that same meatpole. Realizing that Molly was so well supplied with gallants, his visits gradually became more and more rare, until at length, finding she was quite capable of taking care of herself, he kept away altogether.

She was such a favorite that in a few months she saved enough money to furnish a house for herself. She became so clever in her profession, as well as select in her circle, that she became one of the most fashionable and expensive bits about town. Noted for the extraordinary versatility of her sexual ideas, every visitor to her cosmopolitan boudoir went away delighted.

An incident in the experience of the one-time barmaid will fitly conclude this tale of her amorous adventures.

Taking a walk early one summer's morning she entered Kensington

Gardens and sat down by herself on a chair in a rather secluded spot. She closed her eyes as various pleasant reveries overcame her.

"What a lovely leg! Alas! Get thee hence, Satan!" she heard ejaculated in low trembling tones. Opening her eyes, she fixed them on an elderly gentleman, whom she at once recognized as a particularly pious earl of great repute.

"Excuse me, young lady, I really thought you were asleep. May I present you with a little tract? It will show what dangerous temptations we men are subject to from the attitudes or coquettish dress of the pretty girls of the present day. Please do read it!"

She held out her hand and glanced over its contents. It read as follows:

Young women, your dress is often the creator of your thoughts and feelings. When modesty has presided at your toilette, the looks of men have neither the boldness nor the fire of desire. Kept within the limits of discretion and respect, they do not offer to your imagination the always-tempting image of pleasure— and your sensibility remains favorable to your virtue. A dress calculated to inflame the passions of men produces a contrary effect. Their countenances tell you soon what you ought not to be told. Why do you blush if you do not understand their language? How could you blush if that language did not force in your heart a sentiment it is not decent for you to indulge? When you are in a dishabille that half conceals and half reveals your charms, you generally avoid the company of men. Is it virtue or fear that makes you so cautious? It is fear! You are conscious that, in those circumstances, men have over your virtue an advantage, of which all your prudence might not deprive them. Should Nature happen to be silent, vanity would speak, and bring the same rapturous confusion into your heads. The transports of a lover are so flattering—his admiration is so eloquent a praise of your charms—there is such a life in his looks and actions—we are, in our hearts, so inclined to let him praise and admire. Young women, I say it again, sip not in the intoxicating cup, turn your sight from it, in flight only can you find your safety.

Her face flushed with indignation.

"Now, sir, where's one of the park officers? I intend to lodge a complaint for an indecent assault, you whore-mongering, religious hypocrite. Now, which will you do, be locked up, or come with me to my house, where for a £20 note you shall have such pleasure as you seem quite unacquainted with?"

His face turned white and red, and his knees fairly shook under him as he stammered, "The sight of your leg quite upset me. I am so sorry if that tract has offended you. You must excuse me, I mustn't be seen in your company; my reputation would be blasted forever."

He turned to go, but Molly seized him by the arm and hissed in his ear, "Where you go, I go! Is it to be the police station or my house? Expect no pity or respect for a hypocrite's reputation! I care nothing for that after your gratuitous insult!"

The poor old man was lost, and making the best of a bad situation, elected, as a sensible man would do, to go along with the beautiful whore.

So finding him submissive, she told him he could hold his handkerchief to his face if he was ashamed to be seen walking with her.

They walked out of the park. Hailing a cab they were soon driven to her pretty little house, but not before the pressure of her electric fingers had already raised an erection for the mortified old man, who sighed and protested in vain against such wickedness.

Earl Goodman sensibly recovered himself as soon as the retreat of love was reached and he felt safe from observation in Molly's elegant and luxurious boudoir. It was amusing to her to watch the variations of his face as, picking up a decidedly naughty book, he eagerly scanned its contents. At first his withered face flushed a little, then his eyes fairly started from his head, and she could actually see his old cock stiffening in his trousers.

"That is the kind of book to warm up your blood," said Molly. "You relish that kind of literature, my lord?"

"Humph! Awfully disgusting! How such ideas could be evoked from the human brain I can't understand. It's ruin to body and soul to read such suggestive filth!"

"You know as well as I do, bawdy books don't drive religious people mad, or out of their minds in any way," Molly sniffed. "Used properly they act as a stimulant to the natural pleasures of love!"

She tugged twice on the bell cord by the bed, and presently a young lady entered, perhaps eighteen years of age, as naked as the day she was born, carrying a bottle of alcohol and glasses on a tray. Her full-nippled breasts jiggled with each step, and her lithe buttocks quivered as she set down the tray. Earl Goodman couldn't tear his eyes from her luscious mounds, or from the mossing of golden hair on her mount.

"Oh! Satan! God help me! I must not see this! And not a drop. Let me get out of this den of temptation. I'll write a check for the £20—do let me go!" he pleaded as he noticed a stern smile on Molly's face.

"Another insult, my lord! Call Saunders and Ruth," said Molly, turning to the girl, "they will know what is wanted."

Earl Goodman trembled with fright as the cook and housemaid, entering their mistress's apartment, seized him like a child, and tearing down his trousers, fairly spread-eagled him on a sofa.

"What are you going to do? Oh, heavens, she's going to birch me."

"That I am, and two paying gentlemen will see it all from behind a screen. When your impudent backside has smarted enough I will accept your apologies and the check—but not for a paltry twenty pounds, mind you—I don't birch such as you for less than half-a-hundred."

He whined and begged for mercy as the blows began to fall across his buttocks, fairly screaming every now and then as the twigs cut into his tough flesh. Molly enjoyed her profitable joke so much that she fairly wealed his rump, till the small drops of blood stood like beads on the broken skin. She even varied her strokes by birching up along the crack between his bony hemispheres, or administering whistling undercuts that nipped at his sensitive sac and made him howl. Meanwhile, one of the girls was frigging him all the time until he came under the extraordinary excitements he was so unused to.

At length Molly made him kneel in front of her, kiss the frayed rod, and promise never to offend a lady again by offering objectionable tracts, and also to call and see her now and then on the quiet.

"My balance is awfully low; the late May meetings at Exeter Hall have quite drained my resources," he groaned as Molly made him write her a check.

"Thanks," said Molly, "I'll take a cab and cash it as soon as you're gone."

"Please don't go for it yourself! You might be known. Send in some friend to the bank while you wait outside."

"Well," said Molly, with a smile, "you are a dear old man in your way, and I will humor you about that. But I must say you have made miserable use of a long life with good health never to have enjoyed as you ought to have done the pleasures of love. You shall have such a taste of it now as I am sure will bring you back here before long.

"Since your other 'resources' were already drained, my girl shall see what she can do for you. He's in his second childhood, Sissey, so give him some titty, while Ruth sucks him until he's hard."

His lordship had arranged his clothes before writing the check, but made no resistance as Ruth and Sissey drew off his trousers again until he was left in nothing but his shirt and stockings.

Sissey was still naked, so she reclined on the sofa and, taking his head in her arms, presented to his eager mouth one of her lovely round boobies, the firm strawberry nipple of which was indeed a morsel to tempt a hermit. She made him raise his shirt so that her warm belly pressed against his hairy chest as he lay between her legs, which were amorously entwined around his body.

This position left her bottom a little above his cock, which Ruth, kneeling down by the side of the sofa, took in her mouth and titillated with the tip of her lascivious tongue.

This attack on his virtue overcame him at once, so yielding himself up to the excitement he could not avoid, he clasped and pressed the young, firm, warm flesh of Sissey's bum, or groped a finger into her lightly mossed slit, while the other pressed and stroked the head of pretty Ruth as she was giving him such exquisite pleasure with her tongue. He sucked frantically at Sissey's tits, his mouth watering, his teeth raking the engorged buds of her nipples. His cock gradually swelled till in a few minutes it rose proudly and Ruth showed it in triumph to her mistress. She continued to softly pump it with her hand, while her tongue continued to tease the slit in the swollen head. She lapped at it back and forth, then swirled around and over the entire cap.

"Don't you think his cock too big for Sissey? Shall I let him have me?" asked Ruth of Molly, evidently longing to enjoy the fruits of her labors.

"No," said her mistress, "she'll manage it. Instead, take my ivory dildo out of the warm water and fuck yourself with it as you sit in front of his face."

No sooner did Ruth lead Goodman's tool to Sissey's box than the lecherous little whore slipped herself down upon it. Assisted by his eager fingers she succeeded in wriggling it all into herself as she managed to slip under him and get him fairly on top in the orthodox position.

He began to pump into her, assisted by her upthrustings that were designed to drive his cock more deeply into her tight quim. The excitement of being buried in such a young, grasping, willing cunt drove him near to ecstasy even before he'd made more than two or three strokes. Sissey, however, was skilled in keeping a man's tool hard inside her and worked him cleverly so as not to get him too worked up before she'd derived some measure of enjoyment from the episode. She thrust up at him with alternating slow and fast spasms of her hips, the slow ones allowing the tide of rising liquid in his shaft to subside before being churned to a state of overflow again.

The old man was fairly carried away by his lustful feelings. Aided by the sight of Ruth working the ivory dildo in front of him, and Molly's hands behind, as they handled his buttocks and fondled his balls—he groaned with ecstatic anguish. He had never been in such a tight little cunt before, or felt such warm nippings on his prick, which seemed to grow larger and larger every moment.

It was too much for the old man when the final crisis came on him once more, and he spurted his flood into Sissey's pussy in three great gouts. He fainted from the excess of his enjoyment, and it almost took them all they knew to bring him around.

As a finish to this tale of Miss Molly's amours, it may be said that Earl Goodman, although very careful to preserve his reputation, often called to give her a check for the "Midnight Mission," and she actually got a little taken with his grand old prick, which she said was a delightful fuck once it was put in working order.

More from Magic Carpet Books

THE COLLECTOR'S EDITION OF VICTORIAN EROTICA

Edited by Major LaCaritilie

Fiction/Erotica • ISBN 0-9755331-0-X
Trade Paperback • 5-3/16"x 8" • 608 Pages • $15.95 ($18.95 Canada)

No lone soul can possibly read the thousands of erotic books, pamphlets and broadsides the English reading public were offered in the 19th century. It can only be hoped that this Anthology may stimulate the reader into further adventures in erotica and its manifest reading pleasure. In this anthology, 'erotica' is a comprehensive term for bawdy, obscene, salacious, pornographic and ribald works including, indeed featuring, humour and satire that employ sexual elements. Flagellation and sadomasochism are recurring themes. They are activities whose effect can be shocking, but whose occurrence pervades our selections, most often in the context of love and affection.

THE COLLECTOR'S EDITION OF VICTORIAN LESBIAN EROTICA

Edited By Major LaCaritilie

Fiction/Erotica • ISBN 0-9755331-9-3
Trade Paperback • 5 3/16 x 8 • 608 Pages • $17.95 ($24.95Canada)

The Victorian era offers an untapped wellspring of lesbian erotica. Indeed, Victorian erotica writers treated lesbians and bisexual women with voracious curiosity and tender affection. As far as written treasuries of vice and perversion go, the Victorian era has no equal. These stories delve into the world of the aristocrat and the streetwalker, the seasoned seductress and the innocent naïf. Represented in this anthology are a variety of genres, from romantic fiction to faux journalism and travelogue, as well as styles and tones resembling everything from steamy page-turners to scholarly exposition. What all these works share, however, is the sense of fun, mischief and sexiness that characterized Victorian lesbian erotica. The lesbian erotica of the Victorian era defies stereotype and offers rich portraits of a sexuality driven underground by repressive mores. As Oscar Wilde claimed, the only way to get rid of temptation is to yield to it.

THE COLLECTOR'S EDITION OF THE LOST EROTIC NOVELS

Edited by Major LaCaritilie

Fiction/Erotica • ISBN 0-97553317-7 • Trade Paperback • 5-3/16"x 8"
608 Pages • $16.95 ($20.95 Canada)

MISFORTUNES OF MARY – Anonymous, 1860's: An innocent young woman who still believes in the kindness of strangers unwittingly signs her life away to a gentleman who makes demands upon her she never would have dreamed possible.

WHITE STAINS – Anaïs Nin & Friends, 1940's: Sensual stories penned by Anaïs and some of her friends that were commissioned by a wealthy buyer for $1.00 a page. These classics of pornography are not included in her two famous collections, Delta of Venus and Little Birds.

INNOCENCE – Harriet Daimler, 1950's: A lovely young bed-ridden woman would appear to be helpless and at the mercy of all around her, and indeed, they all take advantage of her in shocking ways, but who's to say she isn't the one secretly dominating them?

THE INSTRUMENTS OF THE PASSION – Anonymous, 1960's: A beautiful young woman discovers that there is much more to life in a monastery than anyone imagines as she endures increasingly intense rituals of flagellation devotedly visited upon her by the sadistic brothers

THE COLLECTOR'S EDITION OF VICTORIAN EROTIC DISCIPLINE
Edited by Brooke Stern

Fiction/Erotica • ISBN 0-9766510-9-2
Trade Paperback • 5 3/16 x 8 • 608 Pages • $17.95 ($24.95 Canada)

Lest there be any doubt, this collection is submitted as exhibit A in the case for the legitimacy of theVictorian era's dominion over all discipline erotica. In this collection, all manner of discipline is represented. Men and women are both dominant and submissive. There are school punishments, judicial punishments, punishments between lovers, well-deserved punishments, punishments for a fee, and cross-cultural punishments. These stories are set around the world and at all levels of society. The authority figures in these stories include schoolmasters, gamekeepers, colonial administrators, captains of ships, third-world potentates, tutors, governesses, priests, nuns, judges and policemen.

Victorian erotica is replete with all manner of discipline. Indeed, it would be hard to find an erotic act as connected with a historical era as discipline is with the reign of Queen Victoria. The language of erotic discipline, with its sir's and madam's, its stilted syntax and its ritualized roles, sounds Victorian even when it's used in contemporary pop culture. The essence of Victorian discipline is the shock of the naughty, the righteous indignation of the punisher and the shame of the punished. Today's literature of erotic discipline can only play at Victorian dynamics, and all subsequent writings will only be pretenders to a crown of the era whose reign will never end.

Send check or money order to:

Magic Carpet Books
PO Box 473
New Milford, CT 06776

Postage free in the United States add $2.50 for
packages outside the United States

MagicCarpetBooks@aol.com